# DARKEST
# DAY

# DARKEST DAY

## Christopher Fowler

LITTLE, BROWN AND COMPANY

A *Little, Brown* Book

First published in Great Britain by Little, Brown and Company 1993

A CIP catalogue record for this book
is available from the British Library.

ISBN 0 316 90534 8

Typeset by Leaper & Gard Ltd, Bristol
Printed in England by Clays Ltd, St Ives plc

Little, Brown and Company (UK) Limited
165 Great Dover Street
London SE1 4YA

Each culture produces the delinquency proper to it.

*Kellow Chesney*


Not one, nor thousands must they slay,
But one and all if they would dusk the day.

*Death Song for Alfred Linnell*

For Richard Woolf

*Si fractus illabatur orbis,*
*Impavidum ferient ruinae.*
Horace

# Acknowledgements

Writing a book isn't really like having a baby. You can reschedule your delivery and you have contracts rather than contractions, but I'd still like to thank the gallant team who made me push harder before allowing this one into the world. Chief Nurse Nann du Sautoy and Sister Ann Hebden remained on duty night and day, armed with sound advice, charm, wit, gin and whips. Staff Nurse Helen Goodwin made me take my medicine, Dr Andrew Wille shook his head and told me bits would have to come off, Jane Warren announced the birth and my ever-present specialist Serafina Clarke kept everything running smoothly. I consulted many friends during my confinement at the computer, and I'd like to thank Jim Sturgeon, Mike Devery, Sarah Fforde, Dave Hughes, Bal Croce and the lovely Di, Alan Moore, Alison Hatfield, John and Liliana Bolton, Clive Barker, Pete Crowther, Susan Schulman, Steve Jones, Michele Slung, Christina Crosse, Bob Wyatt, Jennifer Luithlen, Nicholas Royle, Kim Newman, Martin Butterworth and Graham Humphries.

Special thanks also to the hardworking staff of the Savoy Hotel, the first of London's truly modern hotels and perhaps the last of the great ones.

# Prologue

'Damn it, man, you said you would take me.'

Although the sun had set with its usual lurid flourish more than an hour ago, James Makepeace Whitstable could feel the sweat dripping from his chin to the starched high collar of his shirt.

'I brought you to this place, but I will not go inside.' The warehouse keeper shook his head and stared down at the dusty, pot-holed road. The lamp he had set at his feet was smothered in enormous brown moths, and threw a mottled, moving light.

'Then you must wait for me here, you understand?'

The night-noise in the forest around them threatened to drown his command. James Whitstable pushed past the little man and approached the darkened entrance to the building. Raising his silver-topped cane, he slowly shoved open the peeling wooden door.

The men had been alerted to his arrival. Five of them were sitting or standing around a refectory table, upon which some large object lay covered with a muslin cloth. The oldest of them turned and rose. He wore a dhoti, his

1

nakedness mitigated by a shoulder-length fringe of grey hair.

'Welcome, Mr Whitstable,' he said, gesturing to a chair set beside the table. 'We had expected you earlier.'

Whitstable checked the gold pocket watch in its shagreen casing. 'The road from Calcutta is not an easy one to pass along,' he replied. 'There were wild dogs.'

'The dholes will not harm you in this area,' said the old man. 'They bark because they are afraid.'

'Do they have good reason to be?'

'You are the best judge of that.' He pointed to the chair once more. Whitstable refused the seat and remained standing. Although his legs ached from the walk, he was determined not to show the discomfort. They were studying him carefully, the fine Western gentleman, searching for some sign of weakness.

'Then show me what I have come to see.'

'You will drink with us.' One of the men passed him a tumbler half filled with arrack. He had been told to expect this. The coca liquid was blood warm, and numbed his tongue as he swallowed. He watched as the old man raised up an oil lamp held by one of his sons, fixing it on a hook above the table. In swaying yellow light the folds of the muslin cloth were gently pushed back, revealing the upper half of the body that had been laid out before them. It was a boy of no more than sixteen years, but it was impossible to tell if he was dead or merely asleep. The face was slick and unmarked, the eyes closed, at peace.

The old man was rubbing a pungent grey ointment across the boy's forehead and throat. A needle flashed in his hand.

'What are you doing?' Whitstable demanded to know. 'How can I tell that he is really dead? I shall not pay for this unless I see everything that occurs.'

The old man turned to him. 'We must have our secrets, the same as you,' he said.

'I demand to see.' He stepped nearer the body, but as he did so, the old man's sons drew sharply closer. 'My company ...' he began.

'Your company is not the first to come here.' The voice was harsher now. The old man's bony features were bitten away by shadows. 'Surely I need not remind you of the East India Company's fate in Calcutta, Mr Whitstable. How many survived the horrors of the Black Hole on that most terrible of nights?'

'But that was nearly a hundred and thirty years ago. Now we have an empire.'

'Indeed.' He sounded unimpressed. 'There are things here in India that remain beyond the reach of your Queen Victoria, I think.' He opened his hand to reveal two long steel needles, and raised them to the light, slowly passing them through the flame until they glowed at the tips. 'Lest you imagine I am cruel, the heat is to remove the impurities,' he explained.

Turning to the prostrate figure, he moved to the head of the table and leaned over, gently pricking the shiny brown lid of the boy's right eye and inserting the first needle through the skin, then the eyeball, all the way to the back of the socket.

One faint hiss followed another as he inserted the second needle into the left eye, pushing it hard with his thumb until it was buried up to the engraved silver stud set in its hilt.

James Whitstable bent forward to gain a clearer view, and was astonished to see the boy's eyelids fluttering as the orbs beneath them sought to regain their vision. Moments later, the corpse's eyes had opened as far as the pins would allow.

'He would speak if the same procedure had not been performed elsewhere.' The old Indian depressed the cadaver's jaw and indicated that his guest should approach. Whitstable hunched down, looking on in wonderment. A pair of thick wooden splinters had been driven through the boy's tongue into the roof of his mouth. The tongue was squirming and contracting like an impaled pink fish.

'What happens if you remove the pins now?' cried the fine Western gentleman, unable to disguise the growing excitement in his voice. He fingered the roll of damp banknotes in his pocket, vindicated by his decision to travel here.

'You shall see for yourself very shortly,' replied the old man, advancing upon the table with fresh steel glinting between his fingers.

# I
# THE DYING OF THE LIGHT

'Let there be light!' said God, and there was light.
'Let there be blood!' says man, and there's a sea!

*Lord Byron*

# CHAPTER

## 1

She recognised the symptoms immediately.

The sudden stipple of sweat in the small of her back. Ice-heat prickling across her cheeks and wet forehead. A sense of panic spreading outwards from the pit of her stomach. As she began to walk faster she forced herself to rational thought. *This is absurd, it can't harm me. Remember what Wayland said.* But beneath the loud voice in her mind ran another, soft and urgent. *It's not the night itself that harms you, but what waits in it.*

She wouldn't listen to the whispering, refused to think of what could be out there. The sun had barely set, but the road ahead was already becoming indistinct in the fading light. *The Prince of Darkness is a gentleman,* hissed the voice, a phrase recalled from her school studies. Well, she sure as hell had no intention of meeting the prince this evening. She quickened her pace, not daring to look back. Night was falling fast behind her. The cyanosis of the sky ran overhead like ink blossoming in water, threatening to overtake her. Blackbirds skirted the trees, taking measure of the rising wind.

For as long as she could remember, Jerry Gates had been terrified of the dark. The cause of this nyctophobia was beyond the reach of her memory. Some early trauma in her pram, perhaps. Wayland often accused her of having an overactive imagination; the good doctor made it sound like a harmful thing. In her case he was right, of course. Others would have only discerned the gloomy road ahead, the misted fields on either side, bare elm trees blurring in the dusk. She could see demons swarming.

She tried to read her watch, but it was too dark to interpret the face. Screw Nicholas and his country weekend. If only he'd shown some warning sign of his intentions, she would never have come here in the first place. The man should be made to wear a red toggle, *Pull To Inflate Ego*, like a lifejacket. His personality had changed in a moment — the moment he'd found out she wasn't going to sleep with him.

Now it was growing darker by the second, and she was stuck in the middle of the deserted Kent countryside on a Sunday night, without a car, in the freezing cold, with an irrational dread nipping at her, goading her into a trotting pace. She was a town girl, used to city lights and cars and noise and people. It was so quiet around here you could hear a goose fart five miles away.

To keep her fears at bay she thought back over the weekend. What a mistake it had been to accept his invitation! On Saturday morning they had 'motored down to the lodge' — his words, as if they were living in the roaring twenties — in the red MG that kept breaking down, its roof folded back to admit the freezing country air.

The 'lodge', a damp Victorian monstrosity situated on

the far side of Dettling, seemed to have been designed in such a way that the light and warmth of the winter sun were excluded from it through every phase of the earth's rotation. The ground floor was surrounded by tall wet nettles, the brickwork obscured by fifty types of fungus. The rooms were virtually devoid of furniture. There was no central heating. Nicholas's family might have breeding, but they obviously had no money. The upkeep of such a property, he'd explained, was staggering, and his parents preferred to stay in their Knightsbridge flat.

It didn't take her long to realise that Nicholas used the empty house primarily for fucking. One look at the way the bedrooms were decorated told her all she needed to know. Adult magazines, wine bottles, mirrors and candles lay everywhere. The blinds were drawn tight in all the upper rooms, and no doubt remained so throughout the year.

Her partner's conversation over dinner had consisted of college tales laden with sexual innuendo. He was a different person on his home ground, all smirks and swaggers, and she hated it. It was as if she had ceased to be his friend, and had become his quarry. The second time he fondled her breast while reaching for the brandy decanter, Jerry had announced that she was retiring early to bed. No amount of persuasion could keep her from the stairs.

She'd spent a sleepless night barricaded in her room, wearily listening to him through the door, wheedling and begging to be admitted.

She had never looked forward to dawn so much in her life. Rising at the earliest opportunity, she had breakfasted alone, listening to the farming forecasts of incoming rain while she fried herself bacon and eggs. Shortly after ten Nicholas had appeared in his dressing gown. The blackness of his mood barely allowed him to acknowledge her presence. The rest of the morning passed in chilly silence. Denied his twenty minutes of sweaty pumping, Nicholas had regressed to a sullen schoolboy.

The uppermost thought in her mind had been the problem of getting home. Trouble with the car — beneath which he passed most of the afternoon — prevented Nicholas from running her to the station. Typically, there was no Sunday cab service operating in the area. Jerry found herself left alone to wander the rooms of the musty old house. As she examined the discoloured paperbacks that had been bought to bulk out the shelves, she grew more bored and more upset.

Finally she had told him exactly what she thought of his behaviour and, throwing her overnight bag across her shoulder, had struck out across the field in the direction of the nearest main road.

She would have added that she wished never to see him again, except that she knew he would be there the next morning, at work. They even shared the same damned desk. Christ, what a fool she had been.

She pushed the black fringe from her eyes and looked up at the road, hoping to see a light of some kind, but there was nothing. The darkness was becoming complete. So far as she could tell there was no rising moon, so she would not be able to see a foot in front of her. The thought forced the breath from her chest in an asthmatic gasp, and her fever sweat returned.

She began to run along the narrowing lane just as the downpour started. The rain reduced her vision further, adding to her deepening sense of terror. Bare branches entwined above her like the spiny legs of insects. The trees and hedgerows were filled with scampering black imps that dropped with the rain and tried to catch her, but she ran on, following the barely discernible curve in the road.

The darkness was drawing forth the stalking men. They lay in wait for her, pressing back into the wet leaves, ready with their scythes and razors. They could not survive in London, where there was always a glimmer of light even in the darkest hour, but here in the black woods and meadows they could pursue their obscene pleasures without restraint ...

And then, just as her mind was rendered incoherent with panic, she saw the light of the telephone box. It was set back from the road, an old red one with rectangular windows and directories and a butter yellow lightbulb that glowed through the torrent. She raced toward it blocking all else from her sight, thinking not of the eyeless crawling things that clutched at her but only of the sanctuary ahead. It was only when she had wrenched back the door of the booth on its leather straps and thrown herself inside that she realised she was crying.

The relief afforded by the warming light washed through her like the purifying strength of God, and she sank to her knees, filling the booth with angry sobs, furious with her own weakness. Everything had gone wrong. She had intended to use the weekend as an opportunity to protest. Instead of attending some God-awful charity dinner at the Grosvenor with her parents, instead of keeping her Harley Street appointment with Dr Wayland, she had taken off for the weekend with a man she hardly knew just for the hell of it. She might even have had sex with Nicholas if he'd proven to be a halfway-decent human being. She'd only wanted to show everyone that she had a mind of her own, but even carrying out this simple task had proven beyond her. It was as Dr Wayland always said, she just wasn't ready. It was beginning to look as if she never would be.

As the rain pounded against the roof, she drew her bare

knees up into a foetal position and cried, crouching low in the ammonia-stinking booth, protected from surrounding blackness as hostile as the surface of an alien planet.

She remained trapped in the haven of light, not daring to move until a passing motorist found her, almost three hours later.

# CHAPTER

2

*Daily Telegraph, 6 December*

## MONDAY'S WEATHER OUTLOOK

The fine sunny spells of the last few days are set to end as we bid farewell to the capital's unseasonally fine weather this afternoon. Tumbling temperatures and strong northerly winds are on their way, bringing with them moderate to heavy rains. This will affect all parts of the Greater London area by nightfall.

It looks as if winter is finally arriving in the city — with a vengeance.

The elderly lawyer dropped the newspaper on to the marble surface of the counter. Nothing in the business section about the Japanese bid. At least that was something to be thankful for. Besides, he had another pressing matter on his mind.

He was still annoyed about his hotel room. There was no way he could pursue the matter further. He'd already complained as much as he dared; to say any more now would risk drawing attention to himself.

He filled the washroom sink with hot water and splashed some on his face. What a business. Never in all his years of dealing with the family had he heard of such a thing. His mirror image stared back from tired, red-rimmed eyes. He needed a good night's sleep. He could do with being ten years younger, too.

He unplugged the sink and dried his hands on a soft cotton towel. A reflected movement in one of the stalls made him turn from the washbasins. Only one of the cubicles was occupied. As he watched, the toilet door swung half open. The frame behind it remained in shadow, silently watching.

'Look here, what do you think you're up to?' He took a step forward, trying to see the face. The door swung slowly back until it was against the wall.

When he saw the sore, scarred eyes and mouth of the figure inside he stumbled back against the sink, his heart punching against his ribs. He tried to cry out but the wretched creature ran forward and reached up his damaged hands to press them over his face ...

Then he remembered nothing.

Nothing at all.

It was a second, a minute, an hour later.

He had no idea how much time had passed. He was still in the gentleman's toilet, still standing at the basins, swaying slightly. He slowly raised his hand to his forehead. He suddenly seemed to have a terrible headache. His neck hurt. The washroom was empty now. The cubicles stood with their doors wide open. The silence was broken only by a dripping tap. He needed to sit down, to take a short nap. Unable to puzzle out what the hell had happened to him, Max Jacob picked up his newspaper and returned to the lobby of the Savoy Hotel. Then he found himself an armchair in a quiet corner, where he could rest without being disturbed.

Jerry checked her watch again and frowned. 5.55 p.m. Another five minutes until the evening receptionist was due to take over. Through the foyer doors she watched the turning taxi headlights, their beams fragmenting through needles of rain. It still hurt to think about last night, but she was determined not to let it show. It was past midnight when she had finally reached home. She'd never seen her parents so angry before. Thankfully, Nicholas had ignored her for most of the day, except to comment that she looked tired.

The hotel was unusually quiet for a Monday afternoon, but the lull would not last long. Many of the three hundred rooms above their heads were being readied for delegates from all over the Commonwealth. They were arriving to attend an international conference scheduled to start in Downing Street a week from today, on 13 December.

For the moment, the lobby was a haven of peace. A disoriented American family stood with maps folded under their arms like weapons, patiently waiting for the rain to stop before venturing out in their brand-new matching Burberry raincoats. Someone was dozing beneath a newspaper in one of the armchairs near the entrance to the American Bar. A small girl was wired into a Game Boy unit, and sat rhythmically tapping the controls while she waited for her mother.

Nicholas was dealing with a pair of regular patrons, two querulous Spanish women who had been visiting the hotel together for the past thirty years. For many guests the Savoy was a second home rather than a hotel, idiosyncratic and personalised in its handling of their requests, famed for its worldliness and its attention to detail.

Although she had joined the hotel just a few weeks ago, Jerry had been made to feel like a long-standing member of an exclusive family. The work was proving to be more interesting than she had expected, owing to the distinctive demands of the guests. Her mother had blown a fuse when she announced her intention of taking the job. Gwen and Jack had long expected her to apply for a position in the family business. For their only daughter to have chosen her own employment — and as a *menial* — was simply unthinkable.

She scowled at the thought as she gathered up her belongings. Let them think whatever the hell they liked. She enjoyed the anonymity of her work.

'You're in a rush,' observed Nicholas. 'Going on a date?' There was no hint of sarcasm in his voice, but she knew better than to trust him now.

'Chance would be a fine thing.' She threw a paperback into her case and closed the lid. 'I'm going to my figure drawing class.'

Nicholas flicked a strand of blond hair from his eyes and studied her as if seeing her for the first time today. 'It's none of my business,' he said, 'but if you're really interested in studying art, what on earth are you doing working here?'

'You're right,' Jerry agreed. 'It's none of your business.' Nicholas had thin hairy wrists and ankles, a bony throat and sprouting nostrils. He was a dim snob who used his public school accent to ward off undesirables like a vampire hunter with a crucifix. What could she ever have seen in him? A means of escape perhaps, certainly nothing else. She realised now that his habit of sniggering whenever women were mentioned should have tipped her off to some kind of sexual inadequacy. Thank God she hadn't unlocked the bedroom door. Presumably their weekend encounter would never be mentioned again. People like Nicholas were very concerned about saving face.

'Wait a minute.'

Nicholas pointed at the revolving door. The porter was carrying through several extremely battered pieces of luggage. 'There's someone checking in. You may as well make it your last job tonight.'

'Thanks a lot.' She dropped her case on to a chair and returned to the counter. The man walking across the carpet toward her was tall, slim and as white as neon. He was dressed entirely in black, so that his skin contrasted in stark monochrome. His battered leather jacket was studded with his name at the shoulders. Dyed blond hair stuck out beneath a black baseball cap set back on a high forehead. Knotted in complex patterns and tied with multicoloured lengths of coloured rope, blond extensions fell in tightly woven strands between his shoulderblades, like the mane of a lion. Standing amid a jumble of ancient, scuffed bags he looked like a particularly confrontational piece of modern sculpture.

'Hello, I think I'm staying here. My name is Joseph Herrick.' The voice was dark, softly seasoned with a Scottish accent.

As she confirmed the new guest's reservation and checked him into one of the larger suites she found herself averting her eyes, so as to perform a prime Savoy hospitality function of not expressing surprise at a guest's appearance. The elderly Spanish women stared at the young guest's leggings and black motorcycle boots in distaste, lowering their heads to the floor and up again as if expecting someone to come and remove him. Jerry felt like coming to Mr Herrick's defence. He had as much right to be here as they, didn't he?

After accepting his credit card and registration form she found herself speaking with rather more volume than necessary. 'Here is your suite key, sir. If I can do anything at all to make your stay more comfortable, please don't hesitate to call me.'

'The personal touch, I like that,' he replied with a grin. 'Good evening, ladies.' He smiled politely at the scandalised old couple and strode across the lobby, just in time to pull the first of his cases back from the porter.

'I hate to take your job, but you'd better let me have those,' he said, loud and friendly as he began hefting the bag straps on to his arms. 'There's stuff in here I never trust to anyone else. Don't worry, you'll still get a tip.'

His cheerful attitude made her smile. The English crept into smart hotels as if entering cathedrals. They queried their bills in whispers, slinking to their rooms like criminals. People like Mr Herrick hardly ever stayed at the Savoy. If they were young and wealthy, they stayed in the fashionable Kensington hotels. The less well off stayed in Earl's Court, or — God help them — King's Cross.

Nicholas looked over at her, surprised and disapproving. 'You'd better check the validity of that credit card,' he said. 'It might be stolen.'

She picked up her case, disgusted. 'Do you have to be such a snob all the time?'

'My dear girl, this is the Savoy. There are certain standards to be upheld. Codes to be adhered to. The other guests don't want to see —' he searched for the right phrase '— *street people* — hanging around the lobby.'

'I don't see how you can judge someone so easily.'

'Clothes maketh the man,' said Nicholas. 'He's probably in the pay of some awful media company. All that swaggering about just shows a lack of breeding. It's like those gold-covered Knightsbridge women who get checked in by their executive boyfriends. They're little more than prostitutes. They don't belong here.'

To reply would probably encourage an airing of his disturbing views on the need for the class system. Funny how Nicholas had kept this side of himself hidden before the weekend. She decided that it was safer to leave quickly.

'I'm running late. I'll see you tomorrow.'

She was returning from the staff room in her overcoat when she noticed the sleeping man again. He'd been sitting there in a corner of the lobby with a crumpled *Daily Telegraph* over his face for quite a while now. As she passed Nicholas at the desk, she pointed at the recumbent figure. 'You'd better wake him up.'

'You're standing over there, lovey. You do it.'

'I already told you I'm late.'

'You're nearer than I am.'

Sighing, she walked across to the chair and gently removed the newspaper from their guest. The unveiled face was florid and middle-aged. A flap of grey hair was leaning back from the man's head like a half-open trap door. She recognised the sleeper as a guest who had checked into the hotel on Friday evening. She tapped him gently on the shoulder. Overhead, the lights in the central chandelier flickered, momentarily dimming the room.

'Mr Jacob, time to wake up ...'

Jacob's lips rattled out a furious blast of air and he sat sharply upright.

'What the devil—?' His eyes stood out, his throat distending as he lurched forward in his seat, clutching at the arms. For a moment Jerry thought she had startled the guest in the middle of a dream. Now she saw that he was choking. Before she could take any action, the terrified man's body flexed taut and he released a mouthful of blood, spraying a dark crimson mist before him.

She saw Nicholas reaching for a telephone as she tried to hold the agitated guest down in his seat.

'Nicholas, come and give me a hand, he's having some kind of fit!'

The body beneath her was bucking in the grip of violent convulsions. Jacob's left foot shot out and cracked her painfully on the shin. Together they fell to the floor, landing hard on their knees just as Nicholas reluctantly arrived at their side.

'What's wrong with him?' he asked, gingerly attempting to grab an arm.

'How the fuck should I know? He could be an epileptic. Did you get through?'

'The house doctor's on his way down.'

Jacob's eyes had rolled up in their sockets so that only the whites showed. A shining band of blood hung from his chin, spattering as he kicked and thrashed. Jerry wasn't sure of the procedure in such a situation. With her knees planted on the twisting shoulders of the choreating victim, she grabbed his tie and wadded it into his mouth in an attempt to prevent him from biting through his tongue. She felt inside his jacket and pulled out a wallet, flicking it open, but could find no card warning of an unusual medical condition.

Jacob's limbs suddenly fell limp and he became heavy, dropping flat on to the floor, taking Jerry down with him. There followed a moment of absolute stillness, as if the man's spirit was wrenching free from his body. With a final barking cough he emptied the contents of his stomach, blood and bile flooding out on to the intricately patterned carpet. Moments later he lay dead in the young recep-tionist's arms.

Jerry looked from the warm, fleshy corpse in her embrace to the ornately carved ceiling above, where cherubs smiled benignly down from their corner clusters. She had physically felt the man die. As the full realisation hit her, a wind began to rush in her ears and the room distanced itself, telescoping away as her consciousness faded gratefully into the dark.

# CHAPTER

**3**

London hides its secrets well.

Beneath the damp grey veil of a winter's afternoon, the city's interior life unwinds as brightly as ever, and the rituals interred within the heavy stone buildings remain as immovable as the bricks themselves. Much of London still bears the stamp of a vanished empire; its grandeur, its obduracy — and, sometimes, its violence.

Having survived another day of rummaging through handbags without discovering a single gun, knife or bomb, the security guards at the entrance to the National Gallery were about to console themselves with a strong cup of tea.

Mr George Stokes checked his engraved silver pocket watch, a gift of thirty years' loyal service, and turned to his colleague. 'Twenty to six,' he said. 'In another ten minutes you can nip up and ring the bells. There won't be anyone else coming in now.'

'Are you sure, George?' asked the other guard. 'I make it nearly a quarter to.'

Outside, freezing December rain had begun to bluster around an almost deserted Trafalgar Square. Flumes from the great fountains spattered over the base of the towering Norwegian pine that had been erected in the centre of the piazza. The tree stood unlit, its uppermost branches twisting in the wind.

An ominous black sky distended over the gallery, absorbing all reflected light. The building was emptying out, its patrons glancing up through the doors with their umbrellas unfurled, preparing to brave the deepening night.

As the two guards compared timepieces, the entrance door was pushed inwards and a figure appeared, carrying in a billow of rain.

'Fair pelting down out there,' said Mr Stokes, addressing the dripping figure. 'I'm afraid we'll be closing in a few minutes, sir.'

'Time enough for what I have in mind.'

The guard shrugged. Office workers sometimes stopped by on their way home to seek solace in a single favourite painting. He took a good look at the man standing before him, and his brow furrowed in suspicion. 'Do you mind if I check inside your bag?' he asked.

There is a mosaic set in the floor of the National Gallery which highlights many emotional concepts; COMPASSION — WONDER — CURIOSITY — COMPROMISE — DEFIANCE — HUMOUR — LUCIDITY — and FOLLY stand amongst them. Bill Wentworth was beginning to realise that these states only existed on the walls. He tugged down the peak of his cap, and stepped back to allow a party of Japanese school-children to pass him by. That was where the excitement of the job lay, in the paintings themselves, certainly not in the enquiries of the general public. His fingertips brushed the maroon linen wall of the gallery as he walked. He had entered Room 3, (Paintings of Germany and the Netherlands). Rain drifted darkly against the angled skylights in the corridor beyond.

It was Wentworth's first day as a gallery warder, and he had been looking forward to answering visitors' questions. He'd seen the job as a chance to finally use his art history training.

'You can forget that,' his superior, Mr Stokes, had warned during their morning tea break together. 'Times have changed. Few people ask about the Raphael or the Titian or the Rembrandt any more. They just want pointing at the toilet, the snack bar or the French Impressionists. Especially the young. They're not interested in the older stuff because it takes more understanding.'

Stokes was a fan of the old Italian schools. He preferred a Tintoretto to a Turner any day of the week, and was happy to tell you so.

The new warder walked slowly about the room, waiting for the last few members of the public to depart. The only sound was the squeak of his shoes on polished wood and the drumming of the torrent on the glass above. He paused before an arrangement of Vermeers, marvelling at the way in which the painter had captured these small, still moments in the lives of ordinary people, peaceful figures of light and shade, opening letters, sweeping their houses, cool and calm and timeless.

'The public are no problem,' Stokes had informed him. 'Soon you won't even notice them. But the paintings, they'll take on a life of their own.' He had gestured at the priceless walls surrounding them. 'You'll quickly start noticing things you never saw before. Little details in the pictures, always something new to catch the eye. They'll bother and intrigue you, and the subjects will make you care for them. Just as well, because there's bugger all else to do around here.'

'Surely it can't be that dull,' Wentworth had asked, growing despondent.

Stokes had thoughtfully sucked his moustache. 'I know how to say "Don't touch It, Sonny" in seventeen languages. Do you find that exciting?'

Wentworth was still considering their conversation when Stokes himself came puffing in from the main entrance to the gallery, flushed and flustered.

'Mr Wentworth, have you seen him?'

'Who's that, Mr Stokes?'

'The old gentleman!'

'Nobody's been through here, as you can see.' Wentworth gestured about him. There was only one exit to the exhibition room, and that led back to the main stairwell.

'But he must have passed this way!'

'What did he look like?'

Stokes paused to regain his breath. He waved his fingers over his shoulders. 'Tall fellow, broad, with mutton chop whiskers. Heavy tweed cape and a funny hat — stove-pipe, like an Edwardian gentleman. Carrying a carpet bag.'

For a moment Wentworth wondered if his boss was suffering a side effect of spending so much time surrounded by the past. 'What's he supposed to have done?' he asked.

'I tried to search his bag and he shoved past me,' explained Stokes. 'He ran up the steps and disappeared before I could make after him.'

'I'll help you look.'

The guards marched from the room and headed for the circular stone stairs that led to the Lower Floor Galleries. They had just reached Room 14 (French Painting Before 1800) when a breathless young warder slid to a stop beside them.

'We've just seen him on the far side of the Sunley Room,' he shouted.

'Going in which direction?'

'Away from us.'

'Then he's heading for the British Rooms,' replied Stokes. 'We can cut him off by going through 44 and 45.'

Once more aware of the fragile safety of their treasure house, the three warders now galloped through the empty halls in pursuit. As they raced across a side corridor they mistook an elderly member of the public for their quarry and grabbed his arms from either side, causing him to slide over on to the floor. The old man rose indignantly and hauled his trailing scarf about him as his attackers apologised, set him on a bench and thundered on. At the corner of the next room the guards were met by a startled fourth.

'He's heading for ...'

'The new exhibition,' called Stokes. 'We know.'

The British artists' section was housed in a series of chambers leading from a central octagonal space. Here the high walls were filled with imposing commissioned portraits of forgotten English landowners. Tilted to the public eye and ornately framed in gold, they were topped with a splendid glass dome through which rain glittered in a shower of dark diamonds. At the moment, however, Wentworth had no time to appreciate this pleasing theatrical effect. He had just spotted their suspect standing in the room ahead.

The four guards collided to a halt at the entrance to Room 37.

The Edwardian gentleman was standing by the far wall with the carpet bag at his feet, and a cane tucked beneath his arm, looking for all the world as if he had just stepped down from one of the paintings at his back. He ignored them, bobbing his head from side to side as he searched the room. Finally he seemed to find what he was looking for and reached down into his bag.

'Stop right there!' called Wentworth, throwing up an arm. The other guards crowded in behind him.

For a moment, nobody moved.

The Edwardian gentleman slowly raised his head and turned his attention to his pursuers, as if noticing them for the first time. His eyes glowered beneath the brim of his tall hat.

'Leave me be and none of you shall suffer,' he said, low menace sharpening his voice. 'I must warn you that I am armed.'

'Did you press the alarm?' whispered Stokes to one of the others.

'Yes, sir,' the boy whispered back, 'soon as he started running.'

'Then we must keep him from harming anything until the police get here.'

Wentworth could hardly see how. The most lethal item he had on him was a plastic comb. He knew none of the others were likely to be packing a pistol. For want of a better course of action, they stood by watching as the old man stooped and reached inside his carpet bag. As soon as Wentworth realised what he was about to do, he started out across the floor toward the far side of the chamber, but even as he ran he saw that he had not given himself enough time to prevent the disaster.

For now the gentleman's arms were free of the bag and rising fast with a jar held firmly in his right hand, the broad rubber stopper being deftly removed by the fingers of the left, and the clear contents of the glass were flying through the air, the liquid splashing across one of the canvasses, searing the paint and filling the air with the stinging smell of acid. As Wentworth dived on to the floor and slid hard into a wall, the vandal hurled the emptied jar at him. The glass splashed and shattered noisily at his side.

Now the other warders were running past his head, and there were further footsteps coming from one of the distant halls. He heard a shout and then a shot, both small and sharp. Stokes fell heavily beside him, blood gushing from his nose. Acid was pooling along the base of the skirting board, crackling with acridity, the fumes burning Wentworth's eyes. He realised that it was no longer safe to lie still, and rose to his feet.

The warders were in disarray. Stokes was unconscious. Another appeared to have been shot. One of the paintings was completely destroyed. The police had arrived and were all shouting into their handsets. Of the Edwardian gentleman there was no sign at all.

'Excuse me, please.'

Now the elderly man they had accidentally assaulted in the side corridor was tapping a policeman on the shoulder.

'I said Excuse Me.'

The constable turned around and began to push him back toward the entrance of the chamber. 'No members of the public allowed in here,' he said, holding his arms wide.

'I am most certainly not a member of the public,' said the old man, hiking the endless scarf about his neck like the coils of a particularly drab snake. 'I'm Detective Inspector Arthur Bryant, and I think you've just allowed your criminal to escape.'

*

George Stokes stared unhappily from the tall windows like a man preparing to face the scaffold. He was obviously concerned for the future security of his position. Arthur Bryant crossed the floor of the gloomy staff room and stood beside him.

'How's the nose?' he asked.

'It's a bit bruised,' said Stokes, gingerly touching his tissue-filled nostril. 'The poor lad, though. Fancy being shot at.'

'He'll be fine. It was a small-calibre bullet, just nicked the top of his arm. Went on to make a nasty little hole in a still life by Peter De Wint.'

'You don't understand, Mr Bryant,' said Stokes, watching the rain sweep across the deserted square below. 'We are the custodians of the treasures of the Empire. The paintings housed here form part of the very fabric of our heritage. They are entrusted to us, and we have failed to maintain that trust.'

'Human beings are fallible creatures, Mr Stokes. We never attain the perfection of those exquisite likenesses in the gallery. This sort of vandalism has occurred before, hasn't it?' Bryant unwound his scarf and draped it over a chair. He turned back to the steaming mugs on the table and withdrew a silver hipflask from his overcoat, pouring a little brandy into each. The police were clearing away the mess downstairs, and several agitated members of the board were already waiting to speak to their head warder. Bryant wanted to interview Stokes while his memory was fresh, before the recollection of the event had hardened into a much-repeated statement.

'Yes, it has happened before. The da Vinci *Madonna* was damaged with a knife a few years ago. There have been other small acts of violence toward the paintings.' Stokes shook his head in bewilderment. 'The people who do these things must be deranged.'

'And do you think this gentleman was deranged?'

Stokes thought for a moment, turning from the window. 'No, actually I don't.'

'Why not? You say he had an odd manner of speaking.'

'His speech was archaic. He looked and sounded like a proper old gentleman. Turn of the century. Victorian perhaps, or Edwardian. Funny sort of an affectation to have in this day and age. I was suspicious the moment I laid eyes on him.'

Bryant pulled out a chair and they sat at the table. The detective made unobtrusive notes while the warder sipped his tea.

'There must have been something else apart from his speech that made you think of him as Victorian.'

'You must have glimpsed him yourself, sir. His clothes were a full hundred years out of date. When he first came in, he reminded me of someone.'

'Who?'

Stokes waved the idea away. 'Oh, nobody still alive. He looked like the painter, John Ruskin. Because of the whiskers, you see.'

'Did he seem to know his way around the gallery?'

'He must have been familiar with the floor layout, because there's only one exit from that side of the gallery and he ran towards it immediately after the attack. You just have to go through two rooms, 34 and 41, before reaching the stairs that lead down to one of the exits.'

'You don't think his act was one of arbitrary vandalism? He couldn't have been equally happy say, knocking the head from a statue?'

'Oh no, certainly not. I had the feeling he knew exactly where he was heading.'

'Which was where?'

'Toward the new Pre-Raphaelite exhibition in the British Rooms.'

'And you think he was aiming for a specific painting in the exhibition?'

'Well, yes. That's where the acid went, all over one picture. *The Favourites of the Emperor Honorius* by John William Waterhouse. It's quite a large canvas, but he covered the whole thing.'

'I don't know much about restoring,' said Bryant. 'Do you think they'll be able to save it?'

'It depends on the strength and type of acid used, I imagine. From an international point of view, this is very embarrassing for us, Mr Bryant,' said the warder. 'Many of the paintings in the show are on loan from the Commonwealth.'

'Including the one that was attacked?'

Stokes nodded.

'Where had it come from?'

'A gallery in South Australia. Adelaide, I believe.'

'The painting is insured, though.'

'That's not the point.' Stokes drained his mug and set it down. 'It's not a particularly important picture, but even so it's quite irreplaceable. If it can't be saved, then a piece of history has been eradicated forever.'

# CHAPTER

*Now the stalking man suddenly stops dead in his tracks, and I rush up behind him at such a terrible speed that I can't stop, and the figure turns, and the vile beast is at once both familiar and strange, horrific and inevitable. My mouth stretches wide to scream, but he reaches out and fills the betraying cavity with his hand, and I cannot breathe. His fingers reach into my throat, nails tearing the roof of my mouth, reaching deeper and deeper to rip out my soul, and I know that I will die in a matter of seconds . . .*

Her scream was muffled by the bedclothes which had knotted themselves around her sheened face. Jerry fought her way free and hurled herself from the sweat-soaked bed. She fell to the floor and lay naked on the carpet, waiting for her heartbeat and breathing to return to normal.

She had never seen anyone die before. Was it any surprise that she was having nightmares? He was supposed to have suffered a heart attack. But why had there been so much blood? The man was old enough to die, perhaps his time had come — and yet — to be confronted with the sheer, overpowering finality of death. Her childhood had passed in the quiet frustration of being seen and not heard, in the patient wait for a chance to show the world what she could do — and to be confronted with mortality now, to be gripped by a man in the very act of leaving the world, what could be a more terrible omen for the future?

The dream was an old one in a new guise. As she angrily thumped the pillows and threw back her head, determined to blot out her vision of darkness, she knew that something had been awoken inside her, something that would not allow untroubled sleep again.

Wayland would want to know why she had missed her last session; he'd sense that something was troubling her. He'd be waiting to report her latest imagined ailment back to Gwen.

At least lying to him gave her something to look forward to.

*Daily Telegraph, 7 December*

# VANDALISED PAINTING SPARKS SECURITY ROW

The National Gallery is at the centre of an escalating international row following an incident yesterday afternoon when a valuable artwork was vandalised beyond repair. The painting *The Favourites of the Emperor Honorius,* by the Victorian British artist John William Waterhouse, was one of several on loan from the Australian government for the largest exhibition of Pre-Raphaelite art assembled in Britain this century.

The Australian minister for the arts, David Carreras, has lambasted the National Gallery for its 'shoddy and inadequate' security arrangements, and is said to be considering legal action against the British government.

As this year's Commonwealth Congress is expected to examine the EC's new rulings on the movement of national treasures between member countries, Mr Carreras's rebuke could prove to be an ill-timed embarrassment for the government. In the light of the vandalism, the Greek government is expected to renew its campaign for the return of the Elgin marbles.

Leslie Faraday, the newly appointed junior arts minister, is now likely to head an enquiry into the gallery's security arrangements. Faraday's appointment is a controversial one. It is only two weeks since he allowed New York's Museum of Modern Art to purchase Andy Warhol's *Coca-Cola Bottle* from the Tate Gallery, describing the sale as 'good riddance to bad rubbish'.

John May's office in the North London Serious Crimes Division was directly above the red tiled arches of Mornington Crescent tube station. After two months it was still cramped and overflowing with packing crates, most of which were filled with bubble-pac bags containing technical equipment. Once the system was fully set up and running smoothly, it would be possible to devote more time here to highly specialised investigations. Police stations like Bow Street and West End Central were filled with the daily distractions of round-the-clock petty crime. There were always colleagues asking for advice and reports waiting to be filled. Too many distracting demands were made, and too little advice was taken.

Here, above a busy junction noisy with the clamour of traffic pulsing into the West End, it would be possible to concentrate on complex cases serially, without outside interference or interruption. Only time would tell whether the new system worked or not. Failure would prove costly for the police and the public alike.

A series of piercing horn blasts caused John to tip his chair forward and watch from the arched window as, two floors below, another black diplomatic limousine was escorted through a red traffic light by police motorcycles. He'd read that Commonwealth delegates were gathering in London for next week's international conference. That meant the usual abuse of diplomatic immunity privileges, traffic accidents and shoplifting charges quietly forgotten. Momentarily distracted, he missed what Finch was saying.

'Repeat that?' he asked, pressing the receiver closer to his ear.

'Vascular dilation to an extraordinary degree, and tissue lesions you could poke your fingers through ...'

'Wait, backtrack a minute, Oswald, you're losing me.'

There was a sigh of impatience on the other end of the line. 'Really, John, it would be better if you came and saw this for yourself. He's laid out right in front of me. It's absolutely incredible.'

'God, Oswald, do I have to?' John grimly recalled the stench of formaldehyde and cheap after shave that always accompanied his meetings with the coroner. Finch was a brilliant man, but possessed the same gleeful enthusiasm for his job that evil children had for picking insects apart. His was a career chosen by those few rare individuals for whom death holds no terror.

'You know, autopsies usually only take a couple of hours, but so far I've spent over seven on this one. It's playing havoc with my timesheet. You really should see what I'm seeing, John.'

'All right. Give me fifteen minutes.' May replaced the receiver, checked the baleful sky beyond the window and reached for his raincoat. He needed to find his old partner, and he had a good idea where to look.

John May was now over sixty years old, but looked to be in his early fifties. The strength of his surprisingly handsome features, the straightness of his spine and the clarity of his eyes commanded immediate attention. Those unfamiliar with his profession would have marked him for a corporate head, a natural leader. He continued to dress fashionably, and although his immaculately groomed mane had long since greyed he continued to enjoy the fascinations of his youth, those fascinations being, in no particular order: police investigation, new technology, women and science fiction. Members of the fair sex no longer featured quite as powerfully as they once had in May's life, but he would always turn to appreciate an attractive face or figure, and would often be flattered to find his attention still reciprocated.

The girl standing behind the multi-coloured counter of the Brasilia smiled when she saw him enter. 'If you're looking for Arthur, he's back there,' she said, pointing to the rear of the steamy cafe. 'He's very gloomy this morning. It's about time you did something to cheer him up.'

'All right — I get the hint.' He threaded his way to the back of the room.

May's partner could not have been less like himself. Arthur Bryant was three years older, and appeared considerably more ancient than that. Perched on the end counter stool, he looked like a jumble sale on a stick. Shrunken tortoise-like within a voluminous ill-fitting raincoat picked out by his landlady, the small bald man had no time for the urgency of the modern world. Bryant was independent to the point of vexation and individual to the level of eccentricity. While his partner embraced the latest police technology, he proudly resisted it. He was a loner, literate and secretive, a deceptively sharp thinker whose mind operated — when it found something worthy of its attention — in tangental leaps and bounds.

It should have irritated Bryant that his partner was so

gregarious and popular. May was a methodical worker who grounded his cases in thorough research. For all that they had in common it was a friendship that should not have worked at all. They made a rather ridiculous couple, but then, they were little concerned with orthodoxy.

Although they had grown more like each other with the passing years, it was the clash of their personalities that remained the key to their success as detectives. Neither man had much regard for the politics of power, and none of their investigations ever followed the official line. They were tolerated, however, because of their extraordinary success rate in solving serious crimes, and were admired by the younger staffers because they had chosen to remain in the field instead of accepting senior positions behind desks. During the part of their week not taken up with teaching, the pair would arrive for work early so that they could filch the most interesting cases from other officers' files.

At least, that had been true until two months ago, when May had suddenly left the station to work in the new North London Serious Crimes Division.

'Want another?' May pointed at his partner's empty coffee cup.

'I suppose so,' said Bryant listlessly, loosening his scarf. 'There's been no sign of my acid-thrower.'

'Somebody must have seen him leaving the gallery. sounds as if he was wearing fancy dress. Obviously completely bats.'

'That's the point. I don't think he was.' Bryant's watery blue eyes remained on his cup as he passed it to the waitress. 'He searched out a particular painting for destruction. He knew exactly where to find it. The exhibition had only opened the previous week, so he must have visited it earlier to work out his escape route. Perhaps the opportunity didn't arise for him to inflict damage on his first trip. Also, this was faxed up from Forensics.' Bryant rummaged around in his overcoat and produced a crumpled note. His sleeves were so long that they covered the ends of his fingers. 'The acid used was a compound, ethyl chlorocarbonate, chloroacetylchloride, something else they can't identify — it was constructed to do the maximum amount of damage in the shortest possible time. And it did. The painting isn't salvageable.'

'Not at all?'

'A little at the edges. The canvas has been eaten right through. It would mean starting from scratch, and although there are transparencies of the work on file they don't reproduce the exact pigments used. Apparently we can't produce paints in the same manner anymore. Their reflective qualities are hard to reconstruct accurately. It seems the original has gone forever. I dread to think what will happen when the Australian government finds out.'

'Why?'

'Their arts minister is trying to get a number of aboriginal artefacts returned, but we've been refusing to give them up. The Aussies were extremely reluctant to loan us any Pre-Raphaelites at all. This will only prove that their fears were well founded.'

'Do you have anything to go on?'

'Not much,' admitted Bryant, sipping his coffee. 'There were no prints on the acid bottle, and no one in the surrounding streets saw him, despite his extraordinary appearance. The weather was terrible. People tend to keep their heads down in the rain. I'm one of the few reliable witnesses.'

'You were in the gallery?' said May, surprised.

'I was there purely by chance. I know the concept of looking at pictures is anathematical to you, but you should try it some time. The chap who put the exhibition together is an old friend of mine. I'm seeing him tomorrow. Come along if you want.'

'Not me.' May drained his cup. 'I have to go to the Savoy Hotel. Last night one of their guests dropped dead while reading his newspaper in the lobby. The house doctor thought at first that he'd had some kind of a haemorrhage.'

'And he hadn't?'

'Oh, he had all right. With a vengeance. They did an autopsy on him last night and found his innards in a state of complete liquefaction. Apparently the ambulance men were lucky to make it out of the foyer without their patient falling to bits. I'm told that there's absolutely no known medical condition which could account for such a thing. They wondered if he could have drunk some kind of chemical compound.'

'While sitting in the lobby of the Savoy? Anyway, wouldn't the taste have tipped him off? It's very hard to drink a poisonous liquid. The more potent it is, the more pungent it tastes.' Bryant's eyes took on a rare gleam. 'How very odd.' He drained his cup and set it down. 'Sounds like my kind of case.'

'It would be if it was in your jurisdiction,' said May. 'It could be — if you wanted to join me at Mornington Crescent.'

Bryant pointedly examined his hands. 'I was wondering when you were going to offer me a position.'

'I was waiting to be given full authority. Of course, it'll mean sharing an office for a while, until we get everything sorted out.'

'Are you still smoking those filthy cigars?'

'I'm afraid so.'

'Have they told you who the acting superintendent will be?'

'Stanley Marsden. I know you don't get on with him, but he'll only be there until a permanent replacement is decided on.'

'I'm not sure. I'll miss Bow Street.'

'Don't bullshit me, Arthur. You know very well they're closing it down any day now.'

'The word around town is that you'll be able to choose your own investigations. People are already getting jealous.'

'That's not quite true. It's strictly a high-profile murder squad. It'll include a lot of long-term unsolved stuff. That means research-heavy crimes.' They were Bryant's speciality.

Until now no permanent murder squad had ever been set up in Great Britain. This was partly because the country has a comparatively low per capita murder rate. Squads were only formed to solve individual murders, with superintendents drafted in from an Area Major Investigation Pool, supported by local detectives from other cases.

Now the system was changing. If the North London Serious Crimes Division worked out successfully, it would completely alter the structure of the Metropolitan Police. John May was aware that quite a few of his colleagues in the AMIPs were happy with the system in its present state, and would be glad to see the new division fail. Consequently, he needed all the friends he could get. More than that, he needed his old partner back.

'This office of yours,' said Bryant, 'does it have decent-sized windows?'

'Huge ones.'

'Good. I'm getting old, I don't want to miss anything. Could I have the room painted? I can't think clearly in tasteless surroundings.'

'Choose any colour you like. How's your present case-load?'

'I'll follow through this business with the National Gallery. The rest can be off-loaded. I must say your proposal isn't entirely unexpected. Still, it feels odd to be offered a fresh start at my age.'

May smiled. He knew how little the daily routine at Bow Street interested his old partner. At least in the new division there was no chance of Bryant's mind going to waste. As he rose to leave, the afternoon sun threw a lurid glare across the smeary windows of the cafe. Together, he thought, we have an opportunity to make a real impact on the system. He decided not to tell Bryant that they only had a two month trial period in which to do so.

'I made a standard Y incision from the shoulders to the chest and down to the pubis, as you can see,' Finch began, pointing at the splayed corpse in front of them, 'and I couldn't believe my eyes. The organic damage is phenomenal.'

Tall and thin, with spiky hair and bony raw hands, Finch's knee joints creaked like desk drawers when he sat down. A suntan gained on a recent holiday was all that prevented him from looking like Stan Laurel. As usual, the sickly smell of splash-on deodorant exuded from his pores.

'I don't see anything wrong,' said John, forcing himself to study the body. The whiteness of the skin contrasted shockingly with the crimson hole which had been formed by the pinning back of the victim's flesh.

'I've seen an awful lot of insides, John, and I know when something isn't right,' said Finch, wiping his hands on his lime green plastic apron. 'Tell me what you know about him.' He moved to the scales and made a note of the calibrations before removing a kidney from the tray.

May opened his briefcase and checked the report. 'Max Jacob, fifty-nine years old, five feet eleven inches, fourteen stone two ounces, partner of the law firm Jacob & Marks, based in Norwich. He checked into the Savoy last Friday. He was visiting London on unknown business — at least, he seems to have given his wife and partner two different stories for leaving town. No history of medical problems, nothing much out of the ordinary but we're still searching.' He looked back at the splayed corpse on the table. It seemed that the more cleanly a man lived his life, the harder it was to find anything out about him when he was dead. 'At the moment he's just a statistic, Oswald,' he said, 'I wish he'd been a criminal. At least we'd have somewhere to start.'

'Well, you know that someone hated Mr Jacob enough to want to kill him,' said Finch.

'Nobody has mentioned murder.'

'Then let me be the first. Take a look at this.' Reluctantly, May advanced on the cadaver. 'Jacob's stomach is a mass of dissolved tissue. Extensive haemorrhaging here, here and here.' Finch prodded beneath a bloody flap of flesh with the end of his biro. Thick streaks of yellow fat surrounded an abdominal incision. 'And here in the heart, the liver and lungs.'

'What are you putting down as the actual cause of death?'

'Cardial disfunction. The heart couldn't pump properly because the vascular bed surrounding it had become riddled with lesions. It had to be some kind of corrosive fluid, but as there were no burn marks in the mouth or trachea I ruled out ingestion and started searching for an injection site. It's not hard to see once you're looking for it. Here.'

He turned Jacob's head to one side and pointed to a

spot below the corpse's left ear. A swollen patch on his neck was pinpricked with coagulated black fluid.

'If you examine the wound closely you'll find not one puncture mark but two, you know, like a vampire.' He waggled his index fingers either side of his upper lip. 'And it's become gangrenous. The flesh around it has turned to diseased mush. I carried out the routine toxicology tests, checked for alcohol, cocaine, barbiturates and so on; nothing much there. I didn't want to run up a bill testing for more exotic stuff, but this had me beaten. I sent blood and tissue samples to the National Poisons Reference Centre for analysis, not expecting to hear back for several days.' Finch absently prodded the end of his nose with his biro. 'Instead, the results came through on the computer just over an hour ago. Seems this got them all excited. It's a cottonmouth.'

'Sorry, what?' John had been transfixed by the cadaver on the table. It was hard to believe that poor, putrifying Jacob would be stitched back together and buried beneath a headstone engraved with a soothing phrase like *Just Resting*. 'Foot and mouth?'

'*Cotton*mouth. That's the common name. Latin, *Agkistrodon piscivorus*, from the family *Crotalidae*.' Finch's speech was quick and excited. The pathologist's enthusiasm was always more pronounced when he had just discovered something in an opened body. 'It's called a cottonmouth because it threatens with its mouth wide open, and the inside of the mouth is white.'

'Oswald, what the hell is a cottonmouth?'

'That's the odd part.' He thoughtfully probed his left ear with the end of his biro. 'It's a North American snake.'

'You're telling me this man was bitten by a *snake*?' John threw his hands up helplessly. 'They must have made a mistake.'

'No mistake. The computer cross-checks the results.' Finch brought him over to the corpse and pointed. 'You can see the extraordinary effect it's had, even on the minor organs. This is a very particular venom, apparently found only in aquatic pit vipers.'

'Jesus, Oswald — a *water* snake? Does it bother you at all that this happened in the lobby of the Savoy Hotel?'

'I must admit it's a bit of a puzzle,' Finch casually conceded. 'The cottonmouth is more commonly found in marshland.'

'Don't you find that just a little bit strange?'

'Every unnatural death is strange, John.'

'Did they give you an idea of the reaction time between infection and death?'

'Oh, yes. Immediately after the bite, the wound turns itchy, then the victim gets irritable. After this he settles into a quiet aphasic state, and then he suddenly collapses and dies. Ten minutes in total. There's one other thing I wanted to show you.' Finch raised a plastic Ziploc bag and gently emptied the contents into a bowl. May found himself looking at Max Jacob's brain.

'As you probably know,' said Finch, 'the human brain has the consistency of a well-set blancmange. Fluid protects it from thumping into the skull wall. Look at this.' He touched his biro against a darkened patch on the frontal lobe of the brain. 'When you're hit on the head you get a bruise on the scalp, perhaps a fracture underneath it, and a bruise on the brain below that. All three are on top of each other; that's what we call a *coup* injury. Jacob's brain is marked at the front, but there's no corresponding damage to his scalp.'

'Why?'

'Instead there's a bruise on the back of his head. If someone passes out and the back of their head hits the floor when they collapse, the brain is driven forward and bashes itself on the inside front of the skull. That's a *contra-coup*, and that's what Jacob has. It looks like your man took a fall sometime shortly before his death.'

'Thanks, Oswald, you've done a great job.' May was forced to make his apologies and leave the room. The combined smell of formalin and anti-perspirant was starting to get to him.

'Let me know how this one turns out,' said Finch with a cheery wave as he turned back to the corpse. 'And John — don't be such a stranger in future. We're always happy to see you down here.'

The lobby of the Savoy was chaotic. Commonwealth delegates had begun to arrive in force, and stacks of expensive luggage stood in corners among the arrangements of dried plants like harvested corn bales. Jerry had spent the morning easing guests into rooms with the aid of encouraging smiles and pidgin English.

'He's no spring chicken, is he?' muttered Nicholas disparagingly. 'They could have sent someone a bit younger.'

'Shut up,' said Jerry, embarrassed. 'He'll hear you.'

'Intelligence is a compensation for the departure of youth, sonny.' John May removed a pocket dictaphone and set it on the counter. 'As even you may discover one day. I need to talk to this young lady for a few minutes, so perhaps you could busy yourself dealing with the minor grievances of your guests.'

Jerry smiled to herself. She instinctively liked the elderly detective. There was something very attractive about him. Sexy, even. He looked like a man who had retained much of his own youth by listening to the young. 'There's a room we can use behind here,' she said. 'It'll be quieter.'

Once they were seated in the small cream-painted staff room, May switched on his recorder and checked carefully through his notes. He obviously had a fixed method of procedure for this type of interview.

'I trust you've fully recovered, Miss Gates. It must have been a nasty shock for you.'

'I fainted, that's all,' she explained. 'He was spraying blood all over the place.'

'I've read your admirably lucid statement. There are just a few points I need to clear up. You checked Mr Jacob in last Friday, is that correct?'

'I took his filled-in reservation form and arranged for his baggage to be sent up. He was booked for a double room even though we had singles available.' She cleared her throat, more nervous than she had realised. 'Nicholas — the other receptionist — made a remark at the time. He handled the actual room allocation because he'd taken the original telephone booking.'

'You think Mr Jacob was planning to meet up with someone? A female companion, perhaps? He'd left his wife and family at home in Norwich. He didn't sign in as Mr Smith, did he?' The detective's friendly smile was designed to relax.

'Mr Jacob didn't look like an adulterer, if that's what you mean,' she said. 'You can tell them normally.'

'Oh?' May cocked an eyebrow, obviously intrigued. 'How?'

'Small things. Their clothes are too sharp. You know, dressed up for a date.' She thought for a minute, recalling some of the guests she had checked in. 'Often they're not at ease in a smart hotel. They don't tip at the standard rate, usually go over or under. Mr Jacob wasn't like that. He was old school.'

'How do you know that?'

Jerry shifted in her chair, trying to visualise the man who had walked toward her across the lobby last Friday. 'He had a club tie, done up with a small knot. Very neat. Starch in the shirt. A wet razor shaver.' She shrugged, hoping she didn't sound foolish. 'Well, it was late afternoon when he arrived, and he didn't have any stubble. Short hair, brilliantined. Expensive shoes, carefully polished. Ex-military, I imagine. He had the look.'

'You don't miss much, do you, Miss Gates?' May smiled again, and re-examined his notes. Jerry wished she could see what he had written down.

'Let's move on to Monday. You say he was sitting in the lobby for about half an hour. Did you see anyone approach him in that time?'

'No one. It was raining heavily, and hardly anyone came in or went out.'

'Before he fell asleep with the paper over him, did anything happen that was out of the usual, anything at all?'

'I don't think so ...'

'You seem like a bright young lady, Miss Gates, so I'll let you into a secret.' May beckoned with his fingertips. 'I have reason to believe that your guest did not die a natural death.'

Jerry had not considered the possibility of murder. The concept seemed so alien and theatrical. 'I thought he just had a heart attack,' she explained. 'I didn't know what to do. It was a hell of a shock.'

'Try to recall the evening in the light of what I've just told you, and see if you can think of anything else that happened. Mr Jacob came downstairs, sat down in the chair, and died half an hour later. Knowing what we do, something else must have occurred. Take your time about it.'

Jerry thought for a minute, pleased that the detective had turned off the tape until she was ready to speak.

'There was something wrong with the lights. They kept flickering. Because of the storm, I suppose. It didn't disturb Mr Jacob.'

'Anything else?'

'Wait a minute, I think he went to the toilet,' she said suddenly. 'He wasn't gone for long.' She hadn't mentioned this in her statement to the policewoman who had interviewed her yesterday. 'I guess it's not the sort of thing you really register,' she added lamely.

'I quite understand,' said May 'Under normal circumstances it's far too commonplace an event to take note of.' He had clicked the tape recorder back on.

'Can you recall any change in Mr Jacob's behaviour when he returned? Try to imagine him sitting back in the armchair ...'

'He was scowling,' said Jerry, surprising herself. She tried to picture the scene in the lobby. 'Fidgeting about. I remember looking up from the duty book several times. And he kept scratching his neck.'

'Thank you very much for your time, Miss Gates,' said May, closing his notebook with another twinkling smile and rising.

The abruptness of his leavetaking unsettled her. Having witnessed such a grotesque departure from life, she was anxious to know more, and to see what the police would do next. To them, it was just another unexplained death. To her, it was a window to a world she had no way of understanding.

# CHAPTER

Thursday dawned with an unnatural hazy warmth, steam rising from the soaked streets of East London to form pale obscuring wreaths of morning mist. Arthur Bryant paid the cab driver and dug into his jacket for his pocketbook, checking the Hackney address of Peregrine Summerfield. He was gradually realising that it would help to list his acquaintances in alphabetical order when the art historian found him.

'Up here, Bryant!' came a booming voice from above. He looked up and found Summerfield standing at the top of an extended ladder, his rotund form leaning precariously out to hail the passing detective. The ladder was propped against the end wall of a decrepit terraced house, where Summerfield was supervising the painting of an enormous mural. So far, only the lower third of the picture had been filled with colour, but the full scene was already discernible. Half a dozen schoolchildren armed with brushes and paintpots were working on the lowest portion of the design. Summerfield came thumping down the ladder, causing the surrounding scaffolding to shake against the wall. He pumped Bryant's hand with both of his, transferring a considerable amount of indigo paint in the process.

'This is a pleasant surprise.' He turned to the children. 'That's enough, you lot. Back to the shed for brush washing. You've done enough damage for one day.' There was a collective moan as tools were downed. Summerfield's dungarees were smothered in every colour imaginable. 'You'll have to excuse me,' he said, indicating his clothes. 'It's a community project. I didn't choose the subject matter.'

The wall showed a thirty-foot-high nuclear explosion, around which children of all nations were saluting with banners and clenched fists. 'I find its lack of imagination depressing, but the council reckons it'll encourage community spirit.' Summerfield lost his hand within his bushy paint-flecked beard and gave his chin a good scratch. 'I suggested a nice rural scene, lakes, trees, clouds, plenty of natural detail, something to cheer people up. They told me I was being reactionary.'

'Why are the banners blank?' asked Bryant, studying the mural in puzzlement.

'That's so local people can write in their own griev-ances. Interactive art. Some bright spark in the planning department came up with that one, I suppose. We've already had a few people write things in.'

'Oh really?'

'Yes, *Fuck The Arsenal, Tracy is a slag*, that sort of thing.'

'Hmm. I think I prefer your idea of the trees,' agreed Bryant. 'Can we go somewhere to talk?

'Certainly.' Summerfield examined the paint on his hands. 'Give me five minutes to get the lads cleaned up.'

He threw Bryant a set of keys. 'I live over the road, number 54, the one with the sunrise gate. Make yourself a cup of tea.'

Summerfield's house was cramped and cluttered, and surprisingly devoid of paintings. There were a great number of reference books stacked in untidy piles throughout the ground floor. The historian's knowledge of Victorian art placed him among the country's top experts, and he was frequently called in to help organise national exhibitions, but Summerfield had eschewed a permanent post in favour of educating young minds at the local primary school. Arthur had always appreciated his directness and lack of pretension when discussing art. He had just located a battered kettle beneath a pile of old newspapers when the historian returned.

'I can't spare much time today, Arthur,' he apologised. 'I've a life class at eleven. Their usual Christ is off sick, so I'm standing in. I've got the beard for it, you see. I don't mind, but it gets a bit tiring on the arms after a while.' He approximated the crucifixion, then searched around for a teacloth. 'Sorry about the mess. I haven't been able to sort myself out much since Lilian left.'

'I had no idea you two were separated,' said Bryant, looking for clean cups. 'My condolences.'

'Oh, none needed. We always had our differences. She was sick of me mixing paint in her Tupperware. I presume this visit concerns the vandalised Waterhouse?'

'That's right. You helped put the exhibition together, didn't you?'

'Indeed, and it was a pleasure to do so, just to spite the cynics.'

'How do you mean?' Bryant watched as Summerfield poured mahogany-coloured tea into a pair of mugs and led the way from the kitchen.

'Well, the poor old Pre-Raffs have had a pretty rough ride from the critics over the years. Too mediaeval, too gothic, too sentimental, too moralising; there's never been a school of painting so slagged off. Much Pre-Raphaelite art is narrative of course, and that's a form which has fallen from fashion. A lot of it is symbolic, and decorative, and they're undesirable qualities, too. Who wants art that looks nice these days? It's taken a long time for people to get past the Pre-Raff subject matter to the beauty within. Take a look at these.' He selected several volumes from a shelf and lovingly laid them open.

'Artists like Rossetti, Holman Hunt and Millais were reviving the poetic and spiritual qualities of fifteenth-century Italian art. Romance and colour for a drab old world. At first everyone took the piss out of them, but the movement was pretty much legitimised by its popularity. Having lots of tits helped, of course. Victorian nipples were always acceptable in a classical setting. Many a dull parlour wall was brightened up with a nice bit of repro-duction cheesecake.' He tapped a grimy forefinger on a colour plate entitled *Hylas and the Nymphs*. 'Look at Waterhouse and his horny ladies of the lake. Landscapes were popular, too, beautifully detailed by artists like Brett and Inchbold. And religious art, like Hunt's eerie *The Light of the World*, now hanging in St Paul's. Popular art's a bit of a dirty word today, though. The critics prefer "installations" that only other members of their little club can appreciate. A basketball floating in a fishtank, dead rabbits, that kind of thing.'

'Tell me about the exhibition.'

'It was a bugger to organise, because long periods of unpopularity helped to scatter the paintings into more private collections than usual. The sale prices were low enough for collectors, you understand. Manchester Art

Gallery has a sizeable amount of the decent stuff. The rest are all over the place. With Waterhouse, we still don't know where some of the paintings ended up. This is just a study of the one that was destroyed. The finished painting was much more detailed.

Summerfield tipped one of the volumes to the light. The picture was that of a young man seated on a throne, feeding pigeons from a salver while his councillors waited patiently for an audience. '*The Favourites of the Emperor Honorius*, an early piece, 1883. His first serious historical painting. Flavius Honorius, one of the forgotten Roman rulers. He was a bit of an arsehole by all accounts. Lazy, greedy, seen here too busy feeding his pet birds to grant his councillors any attention. Even in this crappy reproduction you can sense the genius of the painter. A moment of anticipation, captured forever. The title is ironic, and refers to the birds, not to the other men in the picture.'

'How did it end up in Australia?'

'At the end of the last century the big Australian

galleries were building up their collections. They bought quite a few Pre-Raffs. There are two oil studies for this picture, both in private collections. One had been mis-titled *Roman Emperor and Tortoises* for years. I've got a copy of the other one somewhere, but it'll take me a while to dig them out.'

'Can you think of any reason why someone would want to destroy such a painting?'

Summerfield pulled at the paint-daubed strands of his beard. 'Certainly no one could be offended at the subject matter. It's pretty innocuous stuff. It's more likely that your vandal wanted to cause some diplomatic damage. The availability of Commonwealth paintings is a very touchy subject at the moment.'

'So I understand. Are there any other pictures over here on loan?'

'Yes, two other Waterhouses, as a matter of fact. *Circe Invidiosa* from Adelaide and *Diogenes* from Sydney.' He located the prints in his book. 'You think these are in danger too?'

'We'll have to have them removed just in case. And I want you to keep thinking for me.'

'That's just it ...' Summerfield glanced from one print to the next. 'There's something odd which I can't quite—'

'Something about the pictures?'

'Not really. More the act of vandalism. There's a resonance here. Something very familiar. I'll need to think about it.'

'Well, if you have any ideas at all,' said Bryant, 'call me.' An electronic beep startled them both. 'It's this stupid gadget May makes me wear,' he explained, rummaging in the folds of his jacket. 'Can I use your phone?'

'Arthur, I know you're supposed to be shifting your stuff here today, but I need your help if you can spare the time,' said May. 'Oh, and there's a lead on your vandal.'

'Someone's had a sighting?'

'Better than that,' replied his partner. 'We have a clue to his whereabouts.

'Of course, the thing that puzzled me was not the snake itself,' said the detective as they crossed Camden Town's litter-strewn humpback bridge, 'but the bite.' A thin layer of grey mist drifted about them, settling on to the surface of the canal below. Bryant pulled his scarf over his nose.

'If you got bitten by a snake you'd run about shouting, warning people,' May continued. 'You wouldn't calmly go back to your seat and resume reading the newspaper.'

'You say he'd sustained a fall?'

'Backwards, according to Finch.'

'That could well be your answer.' Bryant's watery eyes peered over the scarf at him like a pair of poorly poached eggs. 'Suppose he was chloroformed. Once he'd fallen to the floor unconscious, his attacker could have induced the snake to bite his neck.'

'Don't be daft, man. That makes no sense at all. The only possible reason for using such a ridiculous murder weapon would be to frighten the victim first. Why go to all that trouble if your victim doesn't even get to see it?'

'I have no idea. It's not my case. What have you got on my vandal?'

'Seems he damaged something in his flight,' said May, savouring the imparting of his information. 'Our lads did a sweep of the gallery stairs and found this.' He removed a clear plastic sachet from his pocket and shook out a slender chip of black wood almost two inches long. Green flecks in the paintwork gave the ebony an iridescent sheen.

'It appears to have come from a cane of some description.

Not an old one, though. The varnish is a modern compound.' May had taken the chip along to a friend in the forensic lab who owed him a favour, knowing that this would be quicker than sending it into the system's Bermuda Triangle of evidence examination.

'Stokes remembered seeing a very individual cane under your vandal's arm, and confirmed that this chip has the same colouring. I had it sent out to a cane maker in Burlington Arcade. He agreed that it's a piece from a hand-made ebony walking stick. The green flecks are malachite, basic copper carbonate. He'd only heard of one company that makes them.'

'James Smith & Sons,' said Bryant, who had purchased one himself several Christmases ago. 'They're the only people I know who still produce traditionally styled canes.'

'Absolutely,' agreed May. 'Care to take a stroll down there?'

The brass-panelled store on the corner of Gower Street and New Oxford Street had sold canes and umbrellas for over a century. Impervious to the changing times, it survived with unmodernised decor and traditional service, a charming oddity from the past, shipwrecked in a fuming sea of traffic.

The two detectives stepped past the freshly polished nameplate and into a room filled with glistening wood. Walking sticks and umbrellas of every size and description hung in racks from the walls. The genial shop assistant required a single glance at the evidence to describe the cane from which it was broken.

'I think you'll find we have a record of this particular item, sir,' he said, turning the chip over in his hand. 'Canes with graining this richly detailed are rather expensive, and are only produced as special commissions, usually because the customer also requires an engraved silver top.' He pinched the wood between his thumb and forefinger, and gently sniffed it. 'Less than a year old, I'd say. I won't keep you a moment.'

He summoned an assistant, and they walked briskly to the rear office. A few minutes later they returned to the detectives bearing a single slip of paper.

'Here we are. We've only made two of these in the past year, one for a Japanese gentleman who is not, I assume, the person you seek. The other we engraved for an elderly gentleman.'

'What was the engraving he required?'

'A small symbol, a flame in a circle. The gentleman was very specific about the design. I served him myself.'

'Is there an address on the receipt copy?'

The assistant passed over the slip of paper. 'Looks like somewhere in Hampstead.'

'Do you recall anything unusual about your client?' asked Bryant.

'Most certainly,' replied the assistant. 'His manner of dress. I remember commenting to the cashier that his clothes were more suited to the year in which we opened for business.'

# CHAPTER

**Partial Section of Transcript # 170—49**
**Thursday 9 December**
Session with Dr Emil Wayland
Patient: Geraldine Gates

*Patient is a seventeen-year-old female named Geraldine Gates experiencing problems of emotional adjustment in relation to her parents, particularly her mother, for whom she shows a marked antipathy. Patient is affable and intelligent, but frequently antagonistic and confrontational.*

*In the past four years of treatment, her behaviour has shown a marked deviation characterised by alarming mood swings and antisocial acts (vandalism). She suffers from acute nyctophobia, possibly as the result of being shut in a cupboard by her mother when she was seven years old.*

WAYLAND:
Let's get back to the subject of your missed appointment.

GATES:

Let's not. I missed it, no big deal. I just wanted to get out of London for the weekend.

WAYLAND:

Why didn't you tell your parents where you were going?

GATES:

They would have tried to stop me.

WAYLAND:

Because you had planned to spend the weekend with a man?

GATES:

Gwen would have wanted to meet him first.

WAYLAND:

And you would have resented that?

GATES:

No. Actually, I'm sure they would have got on very well.

WAYLAND:

How do you know?

GATES:

Because he turned out to be a complete arsehole.

WAYLAND:

You seem very angry with your mother again.

GATES:

I'd say no more than usual.

WAYLAND:

We know where this leads, Geraldine. Let's move on. Do you want to talk about your attack?

GATES:

I suppose so. As Gwen's paying for the session and you always show the transcripts to her we might as well talk about something interesting.

WAYLAND:

You were on a country road when it began to get dark.

GATES:

Yeah. Very dark. Not like you get in the city. No light

anywhere. I started to panic. I ran until I found some light, then I stayed there until someone found me.

WAYLAND:

Can you remember the first time you ever felt a fear of the dark?

GATES:

(Pause approx. 1 min. 40 sec.)

I can't ever remember not being scared. The landing lights used to be on a timer. When I went to the toilet, I had to beat the timer getting downstairs. It was kind of a test.

WAYLAND:

What did you think would happen if you failed the test?

GATES:

Monsters would get me.

WAYLAND:

Is that what you thought would happen to you on Sunday night?

GATES:

I suppose so. I don't think when it happens, I just panic.

WAYLAND:

You know there are no such things as monsters, though.

GATES:

That's just it. I'm not sure any more.

WAYLAND:

Why do you say that?

GATES:

No reason.

WAYLAND:

(Pause approx. 30 sec.)

What else has happened to you this week? Has something upset you? Is there something you would especially like to talk about?

GATES:

No. No, nothing.

WAYLAND:
Hmm. How's your job coming along?
GATES:
Fine. It's been very quiet at work. Very dull.
WAYLAND:
And you're sure there's nothing else you want to tell me.
GATES:
Absolutely.
WAYLAND:
That will be all for today.

# CHAPTER

The uncharacteristic clemency of the day had produced a mist from the chill waters of the Thames which thickened and lingered with the passing hours. By 6.30 p.m. on Thursday evening it had obscured much of the South Bank promenade, providing London's few remaining tourists with a Turneresque vision of the city.

After her session with Wayland, Jerry caught a cab to Waterloo Bridge. From here she briskly descended the stone stairway in the direction of the hanging coloured bulbs that bedecked the National Film Theatre's cafeteria.

She had requested a serious talk with Gwen over dinner tonight, but at the last minute her mother had called to change the arrangement. It couldn't be helped, she had explained, as she was due to address a trustees' meeting at eight, and would only be able to spare an hour.

Jerry hoped she would be able to survive the full sixty minutes without getting backed into another pointless argument. Gwen's unhappiness with the choice of venue

63

was apparent in her facial expression. Carefully coiffured and preposterously out of place in her gold jewellery and fawn Dior suit, she was seated awkwardly at a counter near the window, surrounded by students and film buffs. She was trying to keep her attention focused on the fog-shrouded river beyond, but could not resist revealing her distaste for her surroundings at every opportunity.

As Jerry pushed open the door, her mother announced her presence with a violent coughing fit, pointedly waving away the smoke from someone's cigarette. As she herself was a smoker, the gesture was redundant. Jerry threaded her way to the table and pecked her lightly on the cheek before sitting opposite.

'I don't know why we had to meet in such a ghastly place, darling,' Gwen began, carefully shifting an empty coffee cup away from some imagined mark on the formica. 'Surely a few linen tablecloths wouldn't compromise their socialist ideals. If you want coffee, you have to serve yourself, apparently.'

Jerry bought two coffees and returned to the table. 'I'm sorry you don't have time for dinner,' she said. 'There's something I was hoping to discuss with you.' Gwen's eyebrows rose a fraction. Serious discussions rarely took place between them.

'If it's about the job, you already know my feelings,' she said. Jerry's decision to find work for herself was a source of great annoyance to her parents. They had assumed that she would automatically follow her father into one of his companies. There had been much talk of emancipation, of women holding top jobs in the city, but Jerry had announced her intention to forgo higher education. Since then, Gwen and Jack had been unable to conceal their anger and disappointment. To tide herself over while making decisions about the future — and to spite Gwen further — Jerry had taken what her mother described as 'a position in service'.

'I like it there, mother. It's not as if I'm about to make a career out of it.'

Gwen examined her coffee suspiciously and sighed. 'I suppose you're mixing with the right sort of people.'

'I'm serving them. There's a difference. That isn't even what I wanted to talk to you about.'

'Then what is it?' She set down her cup and searched her handbag for a cigarette.

'I want to move out.'

'Don't be absurd, dear, you're not even eighteen yet.' She tapped out a gold-tipped Sobranie and lit it.

'There's a flatshare going in Maida Vale. I could afford the rent, but there's a down payment to be made up front ...'

Gwen's attention crystallised. 'Share? You mean co-habiting? Have you met someone?'

'No, nothing like that. There's a guy at work who shares with two others, and one's moving out.'

'You know it's simply out of the question.' She spouted a column of blue smoke at the window. 'You must try to understand that I only want what's best for you, dear. There's absolutely no need for you to be stuck in some awful little flat somewhere when you have the complete run of the house. It's not as if we hold you back, or stop you from having friends over.'

Jerry knew the conversation would take this form. There seemed to be no way of avoiding the familiar cart-tracks of her mother's thought patterns. 'I want to be independent for a while, surely you can appreciate that.'

'But why must you be? Why can't young people accept the help of their parents with good grace? Other girls would be grateful for a helping hand.'

'I'm not a girl anymore, Mother.' She didn't want her father to find her a cosy position in the family business. Lately she'd been thinking about taking a foundation course at an art college. It had been a mistake to inform Gwen of her plans. 'Look, I wouldn't need to borrow any money after an initial loan. It won't be a large amount.'

'That's not the point, Jerry. You went behind our backs to get this job, and now you want to sever your home ties with us. You know what the doctor said about learning to deal with authority. Interaction with others is very difficult for you. Besides, art is not a career for a woman, it's a hobby. I'd be hard-pressed to name a single successful female artist.'

'That says more about the system than the artist, and anyway—'

'So now you're against the system!' Gwen shook her head sadly. 'No, I know these rebellious feelings, and believe me, they only last for a couple of years. Soon you'll want the things we wanted at your age …'

'I'm not like you and Jack. I don't have the same values. I don't even know what I want yet. I'm just trying to figure out what I don't want.'

'I suppose you think we're snobs,' replied her mother, stung. 'Well, I really have to put my foot down this time. I couldn't possibly allow you to leave home yet. I hate to bring this up …' She groaned inwardly, knowing what was coming. 'After your — illness — your father and I knew we had to do something to help you. That's why we set up the trust in your name. We wanted to help you make a start in life. That trust matures when you are twenty-one, and until then we are empowered to influence your decisions about the future.'

She reached forward and sealed her hands over her daughter's, artificial nails ticking on the tabletop. 'You know we love you. Darling, it's for your own good. You'll see one day that I was right. When you come of age, you'll be able to choose for yourself. Until then, carry on in this job if that's what you want. But think about your father's offer. Eventually you'll meet a nice boy. You'll want to settle down and start thinking about children. It's only natural. And hopefully by that time you'll be ready to assume your responsibilities in the business. You're lucky that girls are taken seriously in the workforce these days. Don't waste your life. You can be a mother and still have a marvellous career.'

'Like you, you mean.'

At the moment nothing seemed less desirable than following in her parents' footsteps. She knew there was no point in trying to explain her confusion to Gwen.

'Anyway, how is the dear old Savoy?' asked her mother, switching subjects to fill the uncomfortable silence.

'Someone dropped dead in the hotel foyer on Monday, and the police think it was murder. Apparently the newspapers are saying that he was a spy.'

'How dreadful! Is nowhere safe anymore? I hear there are homeless people sleeping in the Strand.' Gwen checked her watch and rose to leave. 'I have to go. You stay and finish your coffee, and remember what I said. You can try speaking to your father, but it won't make any difference. I know he feels the same way that I do. Can you believe this weather? I haven't seen fog in the city like this since the sixties.'

Jerry watched through the steam-slick glass as her mother paused at the door of the cafe to snap on her gloves before walking briskly away in the haze. She had always been this way, forever informing her of the wonderful future she had ahead, providing she followed their carefully planned path of least resistance. Did she realise how lucky she was, to have been born into a family with social standing and respect in the community? Did she understand how kind and generous her parents had always been to her? And how ungrateful she'd been in return?

The coldness that had arisen between them was the result of her nightmarish fourteenth year; a year of violence and misery, an unendurable sequence of fights and hospitals. After this there had been a reconciliation of sorts. But with it came a realisation on both sides that the older Jerry grew, the less like her parents she became.

She was increasingly uncomfortable with her mother's ostentatious displays of wealth, and felt unworthy of her cushioned, comfortable life. It was as if the three of them shared a secret: that she was a common foundling, a usurper to the throne of commerce and society whose presence would be tolerated for the benefit of both sides.

For a while Jerry had failed to see how the arrangement could possibly benefit Gwen, who had shown her scant attention in the first fourteen years of her life. She recalled an aimless, bored childhood spent in the old house at Chelsea, sprawled out on the untrodden pile of the midnight blue carpet in the drawing room, reading for hours on end, minded by a slow-witted nurse, waiting for her parents to return home. She remembered guiltily exploring the floors above, creeping about as if any minute now her parents would discover the scruffy cuckoo in their midst and throw her into the street. But of course there had been times when they fussed and fawned over her, Gwen especially — and finally she had come to understand.

She, Jerry, was the last piece in the creation of her mother's image. She was there to help her show a caring side to the world. Gwen's friends gathered to watch in warm indulgence as mother and daughter played happily together. Look at them, they seemed to say, what a perfect, loving mother she is. How does she manage it with all of her business commitments?

'Well, fancy meeting you here.'

She turned in her seat and looked up.

'Remember me?' said Joseph Herrick, smiling slyly. 'I mean, how could you forget?'

Jerry was stumped for a reply. She was suddenly thankful that Gwen had left.

'You're the receptionist at the Savoy, right? As I'm staying at your place, so to speak, I just wanted to thank you for your hospitality. Do many guests snuff it in your foyer? Is this some kind of common occurrence I should know about?' He lowered himself into the opposite seat and set down his coffee cup without waiting to be asked. He seemed to be wearing some kind of leather biker's outfit more suited to a science fiction convention than the NFT cafeteria. His straw hair was stuffed under his ever-present baseball cap. It was an odd look, but it somehow suited him. She had dressed conservatively, expecting dinner with her mother.

'Actually, that was the first corpse this week.'

'I'm sorry. I heard you found him.'

She smiled awkwardly, not really wanting to talk about it. The true effect of the death was impossible to share. 'How are you settling in?'

'Well, personally I'd have chosen something a little closer to the street if you know what I mean, but it's all right. I can't believe what you charge for a cup of coffee. I'm just glad I'm not paying the bills.'

'So you're here on business.' She watched as Joseph emptied four packs of sugar into his coffee. He was a little older than she had first thought, twenty-five or thereabouts.

'That's right. I'm preparing to start work on a show, set designing. This is my first big commission. They put me in the Savoy while we're meeting with the backers. You've got a bunch of Japanese blokes checking in tomorrow, haven't you?'

'I think so.'

'They're the ones putting up the money. Tasaka Corporation. Their boss is a man called Kaneto Miyagawa. In Japan he's considered to be a great patron of the arts, and now he's coming to London. That's why I'm here tonight.' He pulled a National Theatre brochure from his jacket pocket. 'I'm seeing a production at the Cottesloe. It's supposed to be terrible, but the sets are good. Big dreams on a small budget. How about you?'

Jerry pushed her fringe back from her eyes. Thanks to her sessions with Wayland, lying came easy. 'I was just having coffee with an old schoolfriend.'

'Listen, you want to come with me? They sent me loads of spare tickets.'

She laughed nervously. 'I couldn't, not tonight.'

'Why not? It'll be fun. Well, it'll be different. I'm alone and friendless in a strange land, many thousands of miles from home ...'

'Where are you from?'

'Edinburgh.'

Jerry started to laugh.

'Listen, I've travelled, I'm cosmopolitan, I've been to Europe. Ten countries in eight days, package tour, I can't recommend it. Now I'm going to the theatre. Are you coming?'

After trying to think of a way to turn him down, she realised that there was no reason at all why she should. She knew she should try to set aside the memory of Nicholas pawing at her.

'So, what's your name? If you don't tell me I'll have to try and guess it, and that'll embarrass both of us.' He studied her face with such an earnest expression that she gave in gracefully.

'Jerry,' she said, holding out her hand.

'Jerry, it's a pleasure to meet you. Is that short for Geraldine?'

'Damn,' she said, 'just when we were getting off on the right foot.'

'How about I never ever call you that again?'

'How about that.'

So they went to the theatre.

# CHAPTER

8

'My foot's gone to sleep,' complained Bryant, stamping experimentally on the pavement. For the past hour they had been standing in the mist-enshrouded garden beside their suspect's house. 'Nearly 11.00 p.m. I wish he'd hurry up. You're not much company.'

'I needn't have come at all,' said May. 'This isn't my case.'

'Yes, I suppose stakeouts are a bit beneath you these days. I like to keep my hand in. Look at this fog. The damp gets right into your bones. A real Victorian pea-souper. It's doing my chest no good at all. I'll need a vapour bath.' Bryant pulled down his scarf and peered over the sodden hedge. Dew had formed on his bald head and ears.

'Can you hear someone coming?'

A figure solidified from the surrounding haze. Bryant felt a chill forming in his stomach as he recognised the whiskers, cape and cane. Brass-heeled shoes clipped loudly on the street's sloping paving stones.

May tapped his partner on the arm and the two detectives stepped in front of the garden gate. Their quarry drew to a sharp stop before them, his eyes staring angrily beneath bushy eyebrows.

There was an overwhelming sense of the past about him, from the heavy cut of his clothes to the sharp smell of tobacco that suddenly pervaded the air. It was as if the man had stepped through the fabric of time itself.

'Mr William Whitstable?'

'Aye, and the appellation has me at a disadvantage.'

May unfolded his wallet and held it aloft. 'We'd like to ask you a few questions about an incident on Monday which occurred at the National Gallery ...'

'That was indeed my doing, but it remains no damned business of yours, sir.' Whitstable's hand tightened around the head of his cane.

'The destruction of a painting on loan to the nation is reason enough to make it our business, sir,' said Bryant angrily, 'and to apply the full penalty of the law.'

The figure facing them seemed to fall back a little. When he spoke again his voice was tempered with reason. 'My sympathy lies with Mr Waterhouse and with no other. *Nature has burst the bonds of art.* If I cannot remove the symptom of this sickness I must at least remind them of its root.'

He was starting to back away, one boot sliding behind the other. May moved forward, wary of the cane. 'Why did you do it?' he asked. 'Why this painting?'

'How would any other do?' cried Whitstable. 'To make it known that our ranks are broken, of course. They think they can get away with behaving as they please, but as God is my witness I'll owe no further allegiance and be gulled no more.'

Suddenly he raised the cane and struck out, catching

Bryant hard on the arm. May ran forward as their suspect turned and fled into the fog.

'I'm all right,' gasped Bryant, falling back against the garden wall. 'Go after him, quickly.'

John May was in reasonable condition for a man of his age, and soon gained on his quarry, but the night and the fog had settled in a concealing shroud across the brow of the hill. For a moment he caught a fleeting glimpse of a figure darting beneath sodium yellow lamplight, then it was gone, the clicking of boot heels lingering maddeningly in the murky air.

'Are you all right?' asked May, returning to his partner's side and examining his arm.

'Of course not,' complained Bryant, hauling back his coat sleeve and checking for bruises. 'I'm elderly. I've had a nasty shock. I need a brandy.'

'First we have to put out a call and bring Whitstable in. He can't get far dressed like that.' May waited while his partner wiped the wet leaves from his coat.

'A large Courvoisier,' said Bryant. 'He said he had to make it known that their ranks were broken. And what was all that about nature bursting the bonds of art?'

'I don't know. It sounded like a quote. That's your department.'

'It doesn't ring any bells, but my memory isn't what it was.'

'Let's hope your investigative powers are intact. I have a feeling we have our work cut out for us.'

On Friday morning, Bryant moved the last of his possessions to the new unit above Mornington Crescent station. Owing to the fast turnover of staff at Bow Street and the fact that most of his friends were operating double-shifts to cope with the criminal fraternity's run-up to Christmas, there was no time for a farewell drink, party or presentation from grateful colleagues. As Bryant left the office that had housed him for the last twenty years with a parcel of belongings under his arm, he felt more like a prisoner leaving his cell than a transferring officer of the law.

'You've an interview with the junior arts minister at ten,' said May as his partner entered the Serious Crimes Division for the first time. 'We'll have to move some of this stuff if you're going to base yourself here.'

He clambered between the packing crates of computer equipment that still lined the hallways of the North London SCD and covered the floors with anti-static styrofoam pebbles.

'Just find me a quiet corner to sit,' said Bryant, searching around. 'All I need for the moment is a notepad and a telephone.'

'You'll require your own terminal.' May indicated the computer on his desk, knowing full well that although Bryant had attended all the courses, he steadfastly refused to operate any technical equipment more complex than a fountain pen.

'I hardly think so, John, after all the trouble we had with that computer bacteria last year.' Bryant removed his overcoat and began to peel off a variety of woollen layers.

'I assume you're referring to the LAN virus that damaged our files.'

'Virus, bacteria, all I know is it cost a lot of man-hours to put right. Some jobs are more efficiently handled the old ways. Why is it so cold in here?'

'They haven't managed to connect up the central heating yet. I'll get you a bar radiator.'

'How Dickensian. Right, I'll settle here.' Bryant slapped the back of a chair and sat, staring straight ahead, his hands in front of him.

'Wait a minute, this is my office,' began May, alarmed.

'I thought we could share. You obviously have the best street view, and you can work the computer-whatsit for me on the rare occasions that I require its services.'

'But Arthur, I like to spread things around. You're too tidy for me. You alphabetise your toxicology manuals.'

'I'll have to put up with your vile habits too. Cleaning your nails while thinking aloud, I know what you're like. It'll be good for you to have someone in here to bounce ideas off.'

May knew that after a few weeks he'd be wanting to bounce more tangible items off his partner. Bryant was searching around for a wall socket. 'I hope you don't object to music?'

'Not the Mendelssohn,' groaned May. 'It must be worn out by now.'

'It helps me to think. Perhaps you could find me a three-pin plug. Do we have anyone assisting us?'

He had obviously acclimatised himself to the office. There was nothing for May to do but accept it. 'A new girl,' he replied, 'Christina Crosse, she's sitting outside.'

'Hmm. Reliable?'

'Judge for yourself.'

Bryant straightened the huge knot in his tie and stuck his head outside the door. 'Miss Crosse?'

An attractive young woman with tied-back fair hair looked up from her terminal. 'Your ten o'clock appointment is already here, sir. I thought you'd probably want to get settled in, so I told him you were in a meeting. Said you'd be free for just a few minutes.'

Bryant smiled approvingly. One look at Sergeant Crosse told him all he needed to know. She was specifically the type of officer with whom he found it a pleasure to work. Women like her were strong, decisive and not easily prone to emotion in a crisis. Inevitably, their personal lives were dovetailed to their work.

'The arts wallah? Show him in, will you?' He grabbed May by the sleeve as he attempted to slip out of the office. 'I'd like you to sit in on this, John.'

'We're sharing the room, not individual cases. I'm down for witness interviews on the Max Jacob death this morning.'

'You don't need to be there for that, do you? Just give me twenty minutes. Have you had the pleasure of Mr Faraday before?'

'I don't think so.'

'Mr Faraday is a pompous time-server, but curiously useful for all that. He's the British government's most pedantic civil servant, which is saying something, a professional junior-status minister. In a brief and unillustrious career he's been shunted all over Whitehall. First he was minister of snow, and managed to bring the road-gritters out in a national strike. Then he was appointed minister of sport, and sparked off a race row by inviting a white South African paramilitary leader to a Brixton Gaol cricket match ...'

'Then how is he useful?'

'Simple. He never forgets anything.'

A pudgy young man with slicked sandy hair appeared before them. Shaking his hand was like removing wet laundry from a washing machine. His suit was expensive but badly cut, so that his trouser bottoms were accordioned over his shoes. By his appearance it would have been hard to imagine a man less interested in any branch of the arts.

'Leslie Faraday,' announced the minister. 'We met two years ago, didn't we Mr Bryant? August 7 I think it was, nice and sunny but it clouded over a bit later. Shame, that.

I read about you in the paper last year, cracking secret codes in a multiple murder case. The *Daily Telegraph*, wasn't it? Someone fell out of a window and you were in trouble for hijacking a Porsche. This must be your partner. I wonder if I could possibly have a cup of tea? Brooke Bond will be fine, nice and milky, skimmed if you have it, two sugars if you don't mind.'

Bryant offered the minister a seat, noting the sweat that was beading on his pale forehead despite the chill in the room. 'What can we do for you, Mr Faraday?' He asked, anxious to shortcircuit the minister's time-consuming recollections.

'It's about this vandalised picture, Bryant, the Watermark thing. I know it was painted by a Brit but the Aussies seem to own it now and they're bloody furious, and not because it was worth a bob or two. To tell the truth, this is a relatively new field for me. I don't go much for your modern artsy-fartsy types. Their work is so inaccessible, not painting, just showing off. They're very good at building thirty-foot-high plaster models of their genitals but ask them to paint a decent duck in flight and see where it gets you. The trouble with artists is they're not businessmen. What's so terrible about giving the public what they want? Still, we can't all be Andrew Lloyd-Webber.'

May seated himself on a corner of the desk and watched, fascinated, as Faraday dabbed at his leaking brow with a handkerchief.

'The Waterhouse painting,' prompted Bryant, as the tea arrived.

'Yes, it seems that there's rather a lot at stake here,' explained the minister. 'Is that tea mine? Nice and hot, jolly good. As you know, the paintings were loaned against the wishes of the Australian government, whose talks concerning the return of aboriginal artefacts from the

Museum of Mankind have stalemated. HMG isn't prepared to negotiate for their return because a precedent would be set, and we already have our hands full with the Greeks. Certain aboriginal items were placed on display years ago as part of what has become a highly disputed permanent exhibition. Just some old mud masks, nothing to get excited about. I remember seeing them on a school field trip. Rained all day, although it brightened in the evening as I recall. The knock-on effect is that the Australian government is seen to be ineffectually responding to their lobbyists on a delicate high-profile issue. This chap Carreras is bellyaching and threatening to boycott the Commonwealth conference. Now, I under-stand that the painting can't be restored, but the next best thing is to find the culprit as quickly as possible.'

'We already know who he is,' said May.

'You do?' Faraday grew visibly agitated. 'Then why on earth hasn't he been arrested?'

'I am hopeful that he will be within the next few hours.'

'This is capital news.' Faraday slapped his hands together wetly. 'And you'll tell me as soon as you discover a motive for this malicious act?'

'Of course.'

'Well.' Faraday set down his teacup and rose. 'All in all, a good morning's work. Is it me or is it hot in here? I can see myself out.'

'What an exhausting man,' said May, closing the door. 'Why is he so interested in the motive?'

'He's hoping for a face-saver. Ideally his vandal would prove to be an Australian national protesting against the English, but I think there's little chance of that.' Bryant shifted his chair nearer the window and looked out on to the street below. 'It's almost as if Whitstable destroyed the picture because he somehow believes himself to be living within its time-frame. His speech was as archaic as his dress. He said he wouldn't be "gulled". It's an obsolete term. He may be mad, but he seemed sincere.'

'Mad people usually are. Have you had a chance to think about the phrase that sounded like a quote?'

'You mean nature and the bonds of art. I'll have to run a check.'

'He hasn't come home yet. The house is under surveillance, but so far there's been no report of any activity. He has a brother, Peter, registered as living in the same house, although we've had no sight of him so far. Obviously we'll interview William if and when he returns. I'd better let you get on with your unpacking.'

'Looks as if you have a bit of a backlog to deal with yourself.' Bryant gestured at the unsteady stack of cardboard folders propped up against his partner's computer console. It was characteristic of May to take on more work than he could handle.

While Bryant had remained at Bow Street to oversee specific ongoing operations, May had been staffing and organising the new unit. This was a chance for him to set up a division run on entirely new lines. The high-yield arrest rate resulting from their unorthodox working methods had been widely acknowledged by their superiors in the Met, but their techniques were impossible to incorporate on a wide scale in the existing Greater London network. A special unit designed to showcase new methodology was the logical answer; much to his surprise, May had been able to persuade the legendarily slothful Home Office and Her Majesty's Inspectorate of Constabulary that this was so. Now they had to prove their claim quickly.

Bryant was filling the last of his desk drawers with files

when the overhead lights began to flicker.

'Does that sort of thing affect your computer?' he asked.

'The machines have a back-up power source, and for safety's sake they run from a separate circuit,' replied May, glancing away from his monitor. 'The LEB have been warning us about power surges while they update their system, but this way it only affects the lights.' He looked back at the screen. 'Have you touched this in the last few minutes?'

'I've been sitting over here all the time.' Bryant rose and came around to the screen.

'What's wrong?'

'You haven't got a program running somewhere on the National Gallery case?'

'No, of course not. I've only just got here.'

'Well, I'll be damned. I don't believe it.' May tipped his chair forward and tapped the VDU with the end of his pen. The screen displayed the personal file of Max Jacob. 'Guess who we have listed as the largest clients at Jacob & Marks, and personal friends of Max Jacob?'

'Who?'

'Whitstable, P. and Whitstable, W., brothers currently residing together in Hampstead. It looks as if Max Jacob is their family lawyer.' He thumbed his intercom button and summoned Sergeant Crosse. 'The men on their way to question Peter Whitstable, call them at once. They're to observe the house and follow the occupant if necessary, nothing more.' He turned to Bryant. 'It would appear that our two investigations just became one.'

'I should have thought of it before,' said Bryant. 'Both events occurred around the same time on Monday evening.'

'At least it rules William Whitstable out as a murder suspect, unless he could be in two places at once.'

'You mean it rules out one of them. William can't go back to his house. If he tries to meet with his brother, I want to be there. Have the men radio in every half hour. It'll keep them alert.'

The call came through at 4.25 p.m.

'Peter Whitstable returned to the house a few minutes ago, and just left again on foot,' said Christina. 'Our car's following. Do you want to speak to them?'

'No,' said May. 'Tell them we're on our way.'

Bryant grabbed his car keys from the table. 'I'll drive,' he said casually. May well remembered their last nightmarish journey together. His colleague was usually more interested in the occupants of the cars around him than the smooth navigation of his own vehicle. Staying in lane, waiting for lights and signalling each move bored him.

'Thanks for the offer, Arthur,' he said, 'but let's wait until you've passed your test.'

'The traffic system needs a complete rethink,' said Bryant as the Vauxhall accelerated through Belsize Park on the outside of the traffic lane. 'Look at these road signs. Ministerial graffiti.'

'It's no use lecturing your driving examiner on the problem, Arthur. That's why he keeps failing you.'

'You're no better driver than I.'

'I don't hit so many things.' May circumnavigated the stalled traffic on Haverstock Hill by turning into a back street and staying parallel with the main road.

'Did you know that in 1943 the London County Council architects produced a marvellous road map for London that was so visionary it would have ended modern traffic snarl-ups as we know them?' said Bryant. This was the sort of bright snippet of information he was apt to produce while taking his test.

'What happened to it?' asked May, swinging from one side turning into another.

'One of their tunnels was routed under St James's Park. Well of course, it's royal ground. The councillors were scandalised and threw the plans out. There they are, just ahead.'

The unmarked police vehicle was two cars in front of them, at the traffic-blocked junction of Heath Street. On the left hand side of the road a portly middle-aged man was threading his way against the crowds exiting from the tube station on the corner.

'I bet the brothers are meeting inside the station. Pull over just here.' Bryant had opened the door and was out before the car had stopped. 'I'll stay close by. You get ahead of them.'

He walked past his subject and stopped by the magazine rack inside the station. It was already growing dark, and the lights were on in the tiled ticket hall.

Bryant glanced up from the magazines and studied the layout of the area. Hopefully Whitstable was meeting his brother from a train, which meant that William would have to pass through the narrow ticket barrier in order to leave the station.

Just then, Peter Whitstable walked into view. He physically resembled his brother in complexion and corpulence, but was dressed in modern-day clothes. Behind him Bryant could see May's car still stalled in traffic, but there was no sign of the unmarked surveillance vehicle. If it had turned the corner it would be caught in a rush-hour stream from several directions. The elderly detective hoped his partner would be on hand to help. He was in no shape to single-handedly tackle a pair of angry fifteen stone men.

Between trains, the ticket hall emptied out. Hampstead was the deepest station in London, and reaching the surface involved waiting for a lift. Bryant stepped back behind the racks as the younger brother approached. He asked the stallkeeper for the time, then took a slow walk over to the barrier.

His watch read exactly five o'clock. Bryant could hear one of the elevators rising, its cables tinging in the shaft.

The lift doors parted to reveal a carriage crowded with commuters. As they began to filter out he caught a glimpse of William Whitstable's stovepipe hat. He was still wearing the same clothes. Bryant looked around anxiously. There was no sign of his partner. What could have happened?

Peter had spotted his brother and was moving to the front of the barrier. As William reached above the railing and shook hands with his kin, Bryant moved aside to avoid the barrage of passengers, and in doing so revealed himself to both parties. William's eyes locked with his, and with an oath he launched himself back in the direction of the elevator. Just as the doors were closing he managed to slip inside.

Peter pushed away from the rail and into May's arms, while the two surveillance men ran past Bryant in the direction of the stairs.

'They'll catch him, Arthur,' called May from the entrance, but Bryant had already broken free to board the next arriving lift.

Below, homegoing commuters filled the northbound station platform. According to the destination boards, the first train was southbound and due to arrive in one minute, but as this platform was almost empty, their quarry would have to make a dash into a carriage just as the doors closed if he wished to avoid apprehension.

Bryant could see his men working their way up through the northbound platform crowd. A warm soot-haze filled the tunnel as the distant rumbling grew louder. Standing in the short bridging tunnel between the platforms, Bryant found he could monitor both without being seen.

Moments later the silver southbound train burst free from the tunnel and roared in, the few waiting passengers stepping back from the edge of the platform. There was a sudden commotion on the opposite side as William Whitstable was discovered by one of the policemen. Bryant could see arms flailing as people were pushed over like dominoes. Suddenly he knew that Whitstable would escape unless he did something to prevent it. Someone screamed as one of the constables fell backward from the platform. Bryant quickly stepped through the open doors of the stationary southbound train and found his way to a seat, watching from the window as Whitstable appeared running along the empty platform. With a sudden sharp movement he jumped between the closing doors three carriages further along.

As the train moved off, Bryant rose and began to walk the length of the train. He knew that passengers were no longer encouraged to pass between the connecting doors of the cars, but he was also aware that they had to remain unlocked for safety reasons. He had walked through the second carriage when he spied Whitstable standing in the aisle of the third.

The train was already starting to decelerate as it approached the downhill gradient to Belsize Park station. If he managed to alight before Bryant could stop him, he would be faced with the choice of journeying to the surface via the lift or the stairs. Bryant knew that if his quarry took the stairs he would never be able to keep pace with him.

The detective reached the door to the third carriage just as the train rattled over points and the carriage lights flickered ominously. He tried to twist the door handle, but it would not budge. Whitstable was turning to face the doors, readying himself to jump through at the moment they opened.

Lazily rocking, the train continued to slow down as Belsize Park's platform appeared. Bryant threw his weight down on the red metal door handle, but was unable to shift it. He stared through the glass at William Whitstable and caught his eye. They were immobilised, hunter and hunted, both unable to fix a course of action.

A muffled explosion slammed the tunnel air against his eardrums. He looked up to find that the window in the connecting door had suddenly become coated with something dark. For a moment he thought that Whitstable had thrown paint around the walls in an act reminiscent of his attack in the gallery. As Bryant fell from the slowly parting exit doors and stumbled towards the next carriage, he could hear screams and sobs as passengers fought their way free of the wrecked compartment.

A shocked young woman with gobs of blood smeared across her face and jacket tipped herself into his arms. Before he could ask what had happened, she turned and pointed back at the smoking detritus which had embedded itself in the walls of the train.

'He exploded,' she screamed at him and kept on screaming, 'he was just standing there and he exploded!'

# CHAPTER

9

The familiarity did not lessen the fear.

Leather soles slapped on familiar cobbles, slipping and splashing in shallow grimy puddles. Breath came in ragged gasps as the figure she pursued vanished around each corner, always tantalisingly out of reach. Once again she was running through high-walled alleyways, the flickering lantern held painfully aloft, illuminating the sweating brickwork as it passed.

As before, the figure in front was growing closer, losing ground to her.

With sickening familiarity, she found herself stopping dead in her tracks. He was turning now, laughing, proud, turning to reveal himself, wanting to be recognised. His hands and arms were thickly coagulated with blood, as if they had been plunged into a massive wound ...

And Jerry was awake, the pillow saturated in hot sweat, the house silent around her. In the corner of the room, a nightlight softly illuminated the walls. The glowing green numerals of the alarm clock on her bedside unit read 4.35 a.m. Saturday morning. Gwen and Jack were asleep in their suite at the end of the corridor, but still she felt the chill touch of the dream. She reached up and groped for the light switch, knowing that only brightness could dispel it.

She had returned home late to find that Gwen had left a rose and a glass of chilled Australian Chardonnay with her plated meal. It was the first time her mother had ever done that. Perhaps it was a gesture to show she understood that her daughter was growing up, even if she refused to allow her to leave home.

Jerry knew she meant well. It was a fact that made her mother harder to dislike. Angry with her underhand tactics in their ongoing war, she had deliberately slammed around in an attempt to waken the house, but no one had appeared to reprimand her. Her parents both knew that she felt like a prisoner. There was nothing either of them could, or would, do. Instead she had gone to bed, to lie alone in the gloom, cursing her mother and her insidious plans.

Gwen was contemptuous of her nightlight, and refused to countenance the reality of her fears. Her solution was to book her extra sessions with Wayland. Her father would explain his position on the subject by launching into one of his stories that began, 'During the War ...' During the war he could turn a Chieftain tank on a threepenny bit in pitch darkness with blackout curtains tied around it or something equally boring and stupid.

Back then, he would explain, nobody was afraid of the dark. Men were decent god-fearing chums who kept their chins up and their lips stiff whenever the Hun forced their backs against the wall. Not any more though, judging by the way good ol' Jack instantly obeyed his wife's every command. Gwen ruled the house with an iron first in a Gaultier glove.

Jerry sat up and flattened down her unruly black hair. She wished Joseph was staying at the house. What a great evening they had shared together. After the play he had taken her for something to eat, and they had squashed beside each other at a cramped corner table in a dingy Spanish restaurant, watching the red wax drip from the candle-bottle while they made loud small talk above piped guitar music.

Joseph had graduated from art college with a portfolio of designs that were about to be made real in the grandest way imaginable. For him it was a dream come wildly true. His work had been accepted over hundreds of designs from other young hopefuls. She found it hard to believe that someone like him would want to sit and talk to her when he could have been out having fun with anyone he wanted. The rest of the theatre's production team would not begin work until Monday, and until then he would be working alone in his room, revising his drawings, readying them to be transferred to computer.

Jerry had talked as little about herself as possible, painting a picture of domestic ease with her parents. She explained that she had taken the receptionist's job merely as a fill-in until she could start attending art classes full time. For a brief moment, as she watched the candlelight leaping in his dark eyes, the thought crossed her mind that he wanted to be with her all night. But the moment passed and they parted on the steps of Waterloo Bridge, and she supposed that tomorrow the status quo of guest and staff would be restored. It was a pity. She liked him because he was everything she wasn't. Most attractive of all was the fact that there was something vaguely dis- reputable about him, in the casual way he swung his arms as he walked, in the dirty chuckle he gave when he found something funny, in the careless looks he threw at strangers.

She was sick of being surrounded by men her mother approved as acceptable role models. It was time for her to choose her own friends.

The thought of Joseph dissolved her nightmares into harmless light. She knew now that she could find untroubled slumber with such a guardian angel to invigilate her dreams.

'You're in early. Couldn't sleep? Sign of a guilty conscience.'

May hung up his overcoat and took a look around the office. His new roommate had been hard at work. Crates of books had been unpacked. The shelves were now lined with forbidding procedural volumes, psychotherapy manuals and medical texts. There was a particularly nasty-looking plant on the window ledge, possibly the remains of an aspidistra. Bryant looked pale and out of sorts. He was trying to lever open the main window by wedging the tip of a screwdriver beneath the lintel.

'I don't sleep much any more,' he said, cracking a spray of paint chips from the window frame. 'When it gets this late in life, you don't want to waste time by being unconscious. Anyway, it's not every day a suspect explodes on you. Have you seen today's papers? It's been a godsend to the gutter press. All they had to report on was the latest royal divorce and the coming Commonwealth conference, then this landed in their laps. If I catch any of those weasels near my witnesses there'll be hell to pay. Give me a hand with this window.'

The press wasn't the cause of Bryant's anger, and May knew it. He had seen this mood too many times before.

'You couldn't have prevented his death, Arthur. Nobody knew he was carrying a bomb.' Together they shoved at the window until it burst open in a cloud of dust and dried paint.

'Are you sure it was a bomb?' asked Bryant. 'You read the statements coming in last night. Four witnesses saw a sudden ball of flame appear at Whitstable's midriff. What kind of explosive can kill a man in a half-full railway carriage without injuring anyone else? First his lawyer, and now him. Don't tell me it's a coincidence. Anything new on Jacob?'

May pulled out a handful of papers and checked them off. 'Some scuff-marks by the sinks in the Savoy toilet that the cleaners mercifully managed to miss, looks as if the polish we took from them comes from Jacob's right shoe. The pattern of marks will most likely confirm that he was attacked there. Some tiny scraps of linen at the site of the scuffle, a common Indian blend, possibly from a pocket lining. No fibre match with Jacob's clothing. One thing; the cottonmouth venom doesn't have to come from a live snake. It maintains its potency beyond the creature's living tissue, which means that it could simply have been injected from a syringe into his neck.'

'There were two puncture holes, like snake fangs.'

'The murderer probably tried to get the needle in once, and Jacob struggled so much that he had to jab it in again.'

'But he'd been rendered unconscious before the administration of the poison.'

May raised his hands in exasperation. 'Then maybe he wanted it to look like a snake had attacked his victim.'

'Why would he do that?' asked Bryant doggedly. 'Snakes aren't exactly a common sight in England, are they? Perhaps he thought he was in another country.'

'Right. The murderer must have mistaken Central London for India.' Sarcasm soured his voice. 'As for the rest of the findings, take a look in the papers. They seem to know as much as we do. The guards on Peter Whitstable will keep the journalists at bay for the time being.' May looked over at his partner and frowned in annoyance. 'Why do you want the window open, anyway? It's freezing outside.'

'I didn't want it open,' said Bryant testily. 'I wanted the option of having it open. There are about twenty layers of paint on the frame. It's like seaside rock.' He pointed at the crate blocking May's path to his desk. 'That's the last one I have to unpack.'

May knew that his partner would not settle to a comfortable work pace until he had made the new office his own in some way. He reached down into the opened crate and pulled up a bony brown object inlaid with silver. Turquoise gems returned sight to its eyeless sockets. 'Where on earth did you get this?' he asked, turning it over in his hand.

'A friend of mine brought it back from Tibet,' explained Bryant. 'It's an engraved human skull. As the Chinese government has systematically destroyed Tibetan culture over the last forty years, it stays on the shelf to remind me of the evil and injustice in the world.'

'You only have to take a look at the overnight crime figures to be reminded of that,' said May, holding the skull at arm's length. 'It smells terrible.'

'I don't think they emptied out the brain cavity properly.'

May watched his partner as he carefully unwrapped a china Wade figurine, a woman dancing in a delicate green dress, and placed it on his desk. It was strange being part of a team again. Arthur wasn't looking too steady on his feet these days. He hoped the old fellow hadn't lost his touch.

'Who's interviewing the brother, you or I?'

'I'll take Peter Whitstable,' said Bryant. 'He's a major, fully decorated and highly respected. Let's hope he's capable of providing some kind of explanation for his brother's behaviour.' Sergeant Crosse entered the room with a small plastic bag in one hand. Her shift had finished four hours late, at 3.00 a.m. Makeup hid the dark crescents beneath her eyes.

'I'm sorry you were pulled in on your day off, Christina,' said May. 'Marsden's worried that the investigation is getting too much of a public profile. He's cancelled all leave for the foreseeable future.'

'That's okay, I was only sleeping.' If she was annoyed, she had no intention of showing it. She dropped the bag on May's desk and displayed its tag. 'Doctor Land came by a few minutes ago and left this for you.' She sniffed the air. 'What's that awful smell?'

'You'll have to talk to Mr Bryant about that. Wasn't there a message with it?' He held the bag to the light and slowly rotated it. Tiny metal shards glittered within, like crystal formations.

'He said he'd call you once you'd had a chance to examine it.'

'Is Land based full time in the division?' asked Bryant.

'He has the office right at the end of the hall.' Raymond Land was an excellent forensic scientist, but his meticulous manner and air of superiority did little to endear him to his colleagues. He was particularly irritated by Bryant, whose elliptical, unorthodox approach to investigations infuriated him.

May unzipped the plastic bag and carefully shook out its contents. He separated the curving slivers of gold with his forefinger.

'What do you make of this, Arthur?' he asked. Bryant searched in his drawer for a magnifier and approached the metal splinters.

'Looks like old gold. Victorian, I should say. Much purer than the stuff you buy these days. Quite red, and very soft. There are some markings ...' He slid one of the pieces beneath the magnifier and turned up the light. 'Roman numerals. Calibrations of some kind? I've seen something like this before.'

'Could be pieces of a pendant,' suggested May.

'No, it's something more technical. One of these fragments isn't gold. Looks to me like good quality silver.' He turned the metal over in his hand. 'There's a tiny hinge on one side. It's the lid of a container.' The telephone rang. 'That'll be Land. He's been sitting at his desk timing you.'

'Well, John, what do you think?' asked Raymond Land, speaking too loudly into the mouthpiece.

'I'm not sure. Where did you get it?'

'Finch removed the pieces from your man, the exploded Whitstable. They weren't inside his stomach to begin with; the force of the blast drove the pieces in. I assume it's part of the movement from his watch.'

'Tell him it's not,' said Bryant in a loud stage whisper. He held one of the gold shards between his thumb and forefinger. 'Give me the phone.' May passed the receiver over.

'Hello?' Bryant shouted back. 'This is part of the mechanical device that killed him.'

'That's ridiculous,' replied Land. 'You don't build a bomb out of precious metals.'

'Why not? They used to in the past. The craftsmen of the nineteenth century were prepared to inlay just about anything with elaborate metalwork.'

'This is the end of the twentieth century, Bryant,' snapped Land.

'I'm aware of that,' replied the detective. 'Still, I'd like you to spectrum test the shards for chemical residue.'

'I really don't see what use—'

'No, but I do,' said Bryant rudely. 'If you would be so kind.' He hung up.

'I'll have a lot of friends left around here by the time you've finished, I can see that,' said May. 'Let's find out if Peter Whitstable has anything more to say.' They had questioned the major on the night of his brother's death, but he had been too upset to be of help to them. Now it was time for some real answers.

# CHAPTER

## 10

Nearly a week had passed since she had witnessed the murder, but Jerry could still feel death on her hands. She turned them over in the light, trying to remember where the blood had stippled the whorls of her fingertips, attempting to recall the exact spot on the carpet where the old man had collapsed.

'I wonder how the police knew it was foul play,' she said aloud, studying the red leather armchair from her place behind the reception desk.

'It wasn't any such thing,' said Nicholas. He felt that their discussions of the last few days had exhausted the subject, and Jerry's obsession with it was beginning to bore him. It was bad enough that he had been forced to take a Saturday shift with her, but with Commonwealth delegates arriving in force everyone was working overtime. 'The police don't have any idea what happened. There was a complete expose of their incompetence in *The Guardian* yesterday. They're trying to hush the whole thing up.'

'It wouldn't work though, would it? There's been too much publicity about the case. The truth will have to come out eventually.'

'I suppose it will, so long as you're alive to talk about it,' said Nicholas. 'There's another batch of delegates being greeted at twelve thirty. Leaders of emerging nations. A lot of unusual headgear, the national anthem played on logs, that sort of thing. You'll have to check them in by yourself because I'll be off duty by then.' He smoothed a long curl of blond hair back in place and returned to his bookkeeping.

'If it wasn't murder,' she persisted, 'why haven't they taken the police seal off Jacob's room?'

'They have.' Nicholas looked up from his monitor, exasperated. 'We're putting someone in there today.' He checked his watch. 'In about fifteen minutes.'

Jerry wasn't sure why, but it suddenly became important for her to see the room. Removing the pass key from the wall compartments behind her, she excused herself from the desk and took the elevator to the fourth floor. The room at the end of the corridor had been electronically tagged along the doorframe to prevent anyone else from entering. Now the tag had been removed, and the maids had been allowed to make up the beds.

There was nothing left in the room to reveal anything of its previous occupier. Had she honestly expected there to be? The police would have removed Jacob's belongings and forwarded them to his family. The room would have been searched, but their forensic team would have had no reason to examine it. After all, it wasn't the murder site. Instead they had concentrated their efforts on the ground floor men's washroom.

Jerry walked into the bathroom and flicked on the light.

Her pale reflection stared back, black hair flopping in pale blue eyes. She looked around, pulling back the shower curtain and checking the ceramic soapholder. Jacob had risen and showered on Monday morning, not knowing that this was to be the last day of his life. Why had he come to London? How had he spent his final hours? Presumably the police already knew the answers to those questions. Could she call the detective and ask him? She still had the number. Wouldn't they think it odd that she wanted to know?

She could hear rain hitting the windows in the bedroom. The morning had begun as dimly as last Monday had ended.

She knew there was something wrong with the way she felt; that something had been triggered by witnessing an act as private as dying. To see an actual life depart, it was all so sudden and unfinished.

If it was murder, Jacob could have suspected nothing. He had come to the front desk earlier that day and chatted pleasantly to Nicholas. He had certainly not been in fear of his life then.

Jerry reentered the bedroom and searched through the desk drawers. The hotel stationery had already been replenished, and lay neatly prepared for the next resident. If Jacob had left behind any sign of his occupation, it had since been removed by the police and the maids.

She pulled open the bedside drawer, and was about to close it after a cursory glance when she noticed the bible. It was not one of the standard copies that were supplied to each of the rooms. Opening the volume, her eyes travelled down the page to find a passage heavily underscored.

*John 19.3. And men loved darkness rather than light, because their deeds were evil. For every one that doeth evil*

*hateth the light, neither cometh to the light, lest his deeds
should be reproved.*

A scrap of paper had been used as a bookmark. It bore a
number: 216. She flicked back through the pages, noting a
number of heavily marked passages.

*Psalms 139.11. Even the night shall be light about me.*

*John 12.35. Walk while ye have the light, lest darkness come
upon you.*

*Genesis 1.16. And God made two great lights; the greater
light to rule the day, and the lesser light to rule the night.*

There were dozens of other pencilled references, all of
them offering advice on matters of light and darkness.
Presuming Jacob had marked the passages himself, he
obviously believed in practising his religion. But that
made no sense. Surely the name Jacob was Jewish? She was
about to check that there was nothing more of interest in
the room when she heard the lift arriving further along the
corridor. Checking her watch, she realised that the room's
new occupant could well be arriving. She slipped the bible
into the pocket of her jacket and closed the door behind
her, briskly walking around the end of the corridor
without glancing back.

If anyone was to ask why she had suddenly developed
the urge to involve herself in the affairs of a stranger, Jerry
would have found it hard to explain her motives. It had
become essential to know more, as if new knowledge
could have personal consequence. She had caught sight of
death, and the brief glimpse had darkened her world. She

returned to her place at the reception desk, ready to consider her next move.

John May rang the doorbell and stepped back.

A constable stood guard beneath the large sycamore at the end of the front garden. Water was running from his cape, soaking the knees of his trousers. There was no sound save that of the rain falling into the trees in the deserted Hampstead avenue. Bryant trudged through the bushes at the side of the house, pushing aside the wet leaves to peer in through dirt-spattered windows.

Finally there was the sound of muttering, and footsteps shuffling in the hallway. The gentleman who laboriously unlocked the door was indeed a little younger than his brother, but was in every other way his double. The heavy-set face, with bulbous crimson nose and pendulous lower lip, recalled to mind any number of Hogarthian caricatures. Peter Whitstable's outfit of heavy winter brown woollens was barely of the present era. He seemed to be having trouble opening the door. Finally he managed to pull it wide, whereupon he looked up at May, stumbled on the step and fell into his arms.

'Good God,' said Bryant, returning to the doorstep, 'he's completely drunk.'

'Help me get him into the kitchen.' May hooked his hands under the Major's arms and hauled him across the hall, enveloped in the sour scent of whisky. 'He's no use to us like this.'

'Give him a coffee, by all means,' said Bryant, 'but let's ask him a few questions. We might get some honest answers while he's in this state.'

The house smelled of lavender polish and old scotch. As they passed the lounge, Bryant peered in through the open door. None of the furniture could be dated after the late 1900s. Oils and watercolours of every size and description filled the walls, butted frame to frame. It was as if they had stepped into a typically cluttered Victorian home from the previous century. Heavy velvet curtains kept light and time at bay. Bryant's eyes grew brighter as he examined the gilt-framed photographs on the walls that lined the kitchen corridor.

'The past has been well preserved here,' he commented.

'How dare you, sirrr,' slurred the Major suddenly, raising his head and fixing Bryant with a bloodshot eye. 'To men of enlightenment this is the present, not the damned past!'

May sat their man on a straight-backed chair while Bryant made strong coffee. Beneath the sink were more than a dozen empty whisky bottles. Peter Whitstable had not turned to alcohol to numb the news of his brother's death. He and Johnnie Walker were old friends.

The kitchen was immaculate in the old-fashioned manner of having been scrubbed and polished. A vast iron hob dominated the room. Copper saucepans hung in gleaming rows. A Victorian ice cream drum stood beside a rack of spoons and ladles, and looked as if it were still in use. Whitstable didn't seem capable of organising this himself, the brothers most likely had a housekeeper.

'Jus' put a shot in it, there's a good chap,' he said as Bryant passed him a steaming mug. When no such action was forthcoming, he removed a silver flask from his jacket, unscrewed the cap and tipped in an ample measure before either of the detectives could stop him.

'We have no desire to impose on you in a time of grief,' began May, 'but some urgent questions must be addressed.'

Whitstable's eyes hooded over as he slumped back in his chair. 'I can't believe he's gone,' he said. 'Or rather, I can.' He promptly fell asleep. Bryant nudged him awake, none too gently, and prised the spilling mug from his hands.

'Th' bastards won't get away with it this easily,' he suddenly cried, swinging his great head from one face to the other. 'We're not the only ones against this, you know.'

'What happened to your brother?' asked May. 'Why should someone want to kill him?'

'S'obvious,' said Peter Whitstable, making a half-hearted attempt to sit up. 'Enemies. Anarchists. Sybarites and sodomites. None of us are safe!'

'We're not going to get any sense from him,' whispered May.

'Let me try.' Bryant moved his chair closer. 'Major Whitstable — Peter — may I call you that? I know you'd like to be left by yourself. If you want we can take the guards from your house and leave you alone, in peace.'

'God, don' do that!' he shouted, terror clearing his drunken stupor. He sat forward, his eyes widening. 'We're in terr'ble danger, dreadful things could happen!'

'Then you think whoever killed your brother will come after you?'

'I do believe that. Yess.' He patted his pockets for the whisky flask. 'And you too, if you get in the way. Darkness is rising.'

'Explain what you mean,' challenged May.

''S'plain, yes. Follow me.' He lurched to his feet and beckoned to the detectives. 'Have to come upstairs.'

At the first landing, Bryant had to move fast to stop the Major from falling backwards. A gloomy room opened from the hall. Here the smell of furniture polish and dead air was stronger than ever. The thick floor-length curtains were parted no more than a foot. Photograph frames and military trophies cluttered the green baize-covered mantelpiece, and more dingy watercolours filled the walls. The Major weaved his way over to a walnut sideboard and searched among the decanters.

'Take a good look around at this lot,' he said. 'We are a dynastic fam'ly. Came over on the ark. Aristocratic British stock. Traditional values. We obey the landowners' creed. If it's attractive you shoot it, if it's ugly you marry it. William and I ... poor William. I don't s'pose there's enough left to bury.'

'We can catch the people who did this if you help us,' said May, but the Major was not listening.

'We knew what was expected of us in those days,' he was saying. 'Have a herd of children, marry the daughters into money, stick the bright sons in business, the dim ones in the church and the mad ones in the army. O' course you make enemies. S'only natural.' He sat down heavily with a decanter between his knees. 'I s'pose you want to know who.'

'Yes,' said May, relieved that their purpose was finally being understood. 'You could start by explaining why your brother destroyed the painting.'

'Oh, I don't know why he did that. Our family has a long association with—' he paused for a breath, ready to take a run at the sentence '—the sponsorship of art, so you can imagine my s'prise when I heard what he'd done. I called on him to explain hisself, but he told me I should already understand the reason for his action.' He unsteadily filled a tumbler and lost the decanter to Bryant, who managed to snatch it away. 'But I *didn't* understand. William was so attached to the past — how could he be responsible for destroyin' part of it?' May made a lunge for the filled whisky glass, but Whitstable clasped it to his chest with both hands.

'Poor confused William. Our enemies are laughing at us, but we'll be avenged by our ancestors, see if we won't.' His cheeks became suffused with an angry crimson as he began to shout. 'They hate the power of the light because they will be damned by their foul deeds! You should have asked Max Jacob, slimy little weasel, he could have told you.'

'He's off again,' said May from the side of his mouth. 'Take his glass away, quick.'

But Bryant was not fast enough. Whitstable managed to snatch it up and drain it.

'Was Max Jacob killed by the same person who murdered your brother?' asked May.

The Major thrust his large head forward and stared wildly at the detective. 'Don't be bloody daft, man. My brother was not killed by a 'person', and neither was the Israelite. It was not a Who that killed them, Mr May, but a What. And a bloody frightening one at that.'

'Then if you know, tell us,' begged Bryant. 'You can avenge William's death.'

'William, William, William.' He shook his head violently. 'There'll be plenty more joining him now.'

'What do you mean?' asked May. 'Are more people going to die?'

'Lots more, lots and lots, blood and bodies everywhere, Armageddon, all the way to the end of the light. If you try to do anything, you'll die too. For without are dogs and sorcerers and whoremongers and murderers.'

Bryant was torn between leaving him to sleep it off or questioning him further now. He felt sure that the Major would not answer their questions when he was sober. 'We can't understand you,' he said. 'You have to explain what you mean.'

'To know what killed William you must understand our

family, and the families of others like us.' He reached out for the decanter and found it missing. 'You have to face the true darkness, if you can find it anymore, which is bloody doubtful these days.'

Bryant released a hiss of frustration. The Major was never going to give them a straight answer. 'If you don't help us, Peter,' he warned, 'I'll have the guards on duty removed from your house.'

'Then remove them!' He suddenly shouted. 'I'll take my chances. After tomorrow I'll be safe.'

'How?'

'Why, Bella is arriving to take care of me.'

Bryant looked across at his partner and mouthed 'Who's Bella?'

The Major tipped his head back and dropped the glass to the floor. 'My beautiful Bella,' he sighed, as he allowed his eyelids to fall. 'The grace of our Lord Jesus Christ be with you all, Amen.' This time he descended into an unshakeable sleep, and was snoring loudly before the detectives could find a place to lay him down.

# CHAPTER

Jerry slowly turned the bible over in her hands. She was walking through the garden, exhaling clouds into the frosty air, watching as the last dusk-bound starlings left the sky. The peaceful Chelsea backwater in which her family had lived since her birth was green and damp enough to feel like countryside. Trees rustled constantly, sounding like an off-air TV channel. It was hard to believe that beyond the darkened beeches lay the electric brilliance of the King's Road.

Behind her, the house was filled with bright, dead light. Gwen and Jack had gone for their usual Sunday night game of bridge, and as always had turned on every bulb in the house, mistakenly thinking that this would deter burglars. Jerry reached the verdigris-covered bench in the small brick arbour and seated herself, turning her attention back to the bible.

When she had seen it laying there in the drawer she had almost been fooled by it, because of the binding.

Although it was much older and in poor condition, it was similar to that of the standard Concordance copies kept in the hotel rooms. But it wasn't one of the Savoy editions. One of those had already been placed in the right-hand drawer of Jacob's bedside table. She had found this book to the left of the bed. Now she reread the unfamiliar name on the flyleaf, *W. Whitstable, St Peters, Hampstead*, and turning the dry, semi-transparent pages within, saw that the bible was older than she had at first realised. There was a particular smell that exuded from its pages, of church pews and still, ticking rooms. The printing mark read 1872. It felt as if it had been given as a gift, something which Mr Jacob had valued greatly. She knew that she should take it to the police, but felt sure that if she did so, she would never know the outcome of her discovery.

Instead she withdrew the cordless telephone from her jacket pocket and extended the antenna. The phone book had yielded thirty-one Whitstables in Central London, seven starting with the initial W, three of them roughly in the Hampstead area. She would call each of them in turn.

She unfolded the notepaper on the knee of her jeans, marked off the first number with her thumb and began to dial.

Her first two calls failed to net a reply. Third on the list was Whitstable, William, of Mayberry Grove, Hampstead. By now the sun had fully set and the garden lay in pale darkness. It was never truly dark in the city. Even in deepest night it looked as if the sky was made of tracing paper. She studied the illuminated numeral panel of the receiver and waited for her connection to be completed. Instantly, she was sure that she'd called the correct number. The elderly male voice at the other end was filled with suspicion, as if in anticipation of such a call.

'Why are you ringing here? What do you want?'

'Have I reached the home of Mr W. Whitstable?' she asked in her best Savoy telephone manner.

'William?' There was confusion now. 'There's no one here ...'

'I have something to return to him. Something I believe he's lost.'

'Well, what is it?' The speaker was agitated. His words were sliding into one another, as if he was drunk. She decided that she had nothing to gain by holding out. 'I have a bible belonging to a gentleman named Mr W. Whitstable.'

The single word again. 'William.' And a hushed silence.

Bingo. Jerry smiled in the shadows. 'I was wondering if I could return it to the gentleman.'

'He's no longer here,' said the speaker hastily. 'You can send it to me instead.'

'I couldn't possibly trust the post office with something as delicate as this,' she replied. 'But I'll bring it to you, if you like. I have your address from the telephone book.'

'I don't think — no, not tonight, I can't have visitors at night, not now ...'

'Then tomorrow,' she pressed. 'I'll call by in the morning. Your name is also Whitstable?'

The line went dead. Jerry switched off the receiver, puzzled. At least she had located the bible's owner. She considered informing Mr May, just in case there was any trouble, but decided against it. The voice had belonged to an old man. She could handle it. She rose from the damp bench and rubbed warmth into her arms as she left the dark arbour. She would go to bed and think about tomorrow's meeting, and her confrontation with a possible murderer.

The fluctuating weather had once again produced a mist.

It clung to the hedgerows of the quiet streets like milk settling in water. Jerry left Hampstead tube station and followed a winding residential road on the left hand side of the hill.

Mayberry Grove was a slim cul-de-sac filled with solid Victorian red brick houses, each one hidden behind swathes of greenery. They were houses built by confident men, whose calloused hands had toiled in the belief that an Englishman's home was his castle, and whose minds could not imagine the twilight of the empire. As Jerry approached the house she was surprised to find an unfriendly-looking police constable standing in the front garden.

'I've come to see Mr Whitstable,' she said loudly, pushing back the wet gate. Having been given no information to the contrary, she was still guessing that the name was correct.

'Oh yes? And who are you, then?' The constable was not that much older than her, but had already developed an antagonistic attitude.

'I spoke to Mr Whitstable last night. I'm returning something that belongs to him.'

'He can't have visitors.' The constable rocked back on large polished boots and gave the top of his walkie-talkie a wipe. 'Give it to me and I'll make sure that he gets it.'

'He told me I should give it to him myself.'

'Not possible, lovey.' He gave a dim smile and shifted his gaze away as if he had sighted something in the middle distance, as policemen do when they have finished listening to you. Jerry was just about to start arguing when the front door burst open behind them and there stood a florid-faced man in an ill-fitting checked suit and crooked tie. He seemed vaguely familiar, and was arguing with a second older constable, who had appeared at his side from somewhere within the hall.

'I don't give a good goddamn what your superior officer says,' shouted the man Jerry presumed was the one she had spoken to the previous evening. 'It's where I've been the second Monday in every month since the end of World War Two, and no blasted low-ranking officer is going to stop me now.'

'Then you must allow us to accompany you,' reasoned the officer, trying to keep pace as they marched down the garden path. 'It may not be safe for you to go out.'

'I am well aware of that,' snapped the Major, whirling on the young officer. 'D'you think I should change my life for the sake of some cowardly sniper who can't show his face in the light? Is that what my brother went to his death for? Is that the spirit that made this country great? Never, sir! I shall face up to the foe with a strong heart and a—' He forgot what the other thing was, and switched metaphors. '— Spring in my step,' he finished vaguely, pushing the second constable from his guard duty at the gate. 'And I shall be back within the hour.' He slipped the latch and passed into the street.

'For God's sake go after him, Bimsley,' said the first policeman. 'If we lose him there'll be hell to pay.'

'Where is he going?' asked Jerry, looking toward the rapidly retreating figure.

The officer had seen her in conversation with the other constable, and surrendered the information easily. 'For a haircut,' he replied, throwing his hands up helplessly. 'The Major's a possible murder target, and he has to go to the Strand just for a bloody haircut.'


Jerry caught up with the Major in an alleyway leading into Haverstock Hill. The younger constable was trailing a hundred yards or so behind them, pausing only to listen to

the crackle from his handset. Peter Whitstable reached the
main road and turned right in the direction of Belsize
Park. Jerry hung back, dipping into the doorway of a
chemists as the Major looked back at the corner. So the
man they were following was being kept under surveillance because his brother had been killed? A second death,
separate to Jacob's? This was too bizarre-stroke-
interesting to be true. Nothing like it had ever happened
to her before.

Major Whitstable's life couldn't really be in danger,
otherwise the police would have put him in protective
custody, wouldn't they? What if he wasn't going to his
barber at all? What if he was about to give them all the slip?
Perhaps the police had deliberately let him out to see
where he would head.

Perhaps they were just incompetent.

Because now the Major had sidled between the stalled
traffic on the hill and was heading into another of the still-
misty alleys on the far side of the road. Jerry glanced back,
and saw that the constable had missed the move. It was a
good job one of them had been watching. As the traffic
lights flicked to amber, universal British driving code for
'pedal to the metal', she darted between revving engines
to the opposite pavement and ran into the alley. At first
she thought that there must be an old barber shop tucked
away here, but all she saw was the usual collection of effete
Hampstead shops selling Provence pot-pourris and patch-
work cats.

At the end of the passage she could hear the throb of a
taxicab, and as she ran forward she was just in time to see
the Major's ample rear disappearing into the vehicle. By
the time she had reached the kerb, the cab had pulled
away, U-turning past her as it headed for an unknown
destination. As she walked back to the hill she passed the

befuddled constable, who was shouting into his squawking handset.

Where would someone like the Major still be able to have his hair cut in such a severe military style? Simpson's? Harrods? She was trying to think of as many places as possible when she remembered the constable's complaint; his charge was insisting on visiting the Strand. There was only one place he could possibly be heading for — an illustrious hotel she knew only too well. Jerry flagged down an empty cab and leaned in at the window.

'The Savoy, please. As quickly as possible.'

'Right you are, love.'

In less than ten minutes they were pulling up beneath the shining metal letters of the hotel entrance. The steel canopy on the front of the building reminded her of a Rolls-Royce grille. The barber shop within was timeless and traditional, just right for a man of the Major's appearance.

Inside, the foyer was already crowded with newly arrived delegates for the Commonwealth conference, due to start in Whitehall this morning. Jerry made her way through the groups, ignoring Nicholas's puzzled look as she headed upstairs to the barber shop. There, within a gentleman's world of monochromatic tiled walls, stainless steel fittings and chromium-trimmed leather shaving chairs, she knew there was a chance of locating her quarry. And perhaps he could be persuaded to explain the link between a Victorian bible and a poisoned lawyer.

One question had occupied Peter Whitstable's mind since the police had informed him that his brother was dead. How could it have happened? *How?* These days, of course, they had many enemies. That was only to be expected. The world was changing so quickly. There was simply no time left for chivalry. What was the point of trying to do the decent thing when your adversaries seized the moment to steal a march on you? Nobody cared for the subtleties of honour any more. He had always loved his brother dearly, but the sad fact was that William had lost touch with the modern world.

As the taxi left the Aldwych he saw the homeless wrapped in cartons of corrugated cardboard and thought, My God, there are people actually sleeping in the streets again. What had their high ideals done for these people, and the thousands like them who arrived at the stations looking for a city that would somehow work miracles? In a hundred years, nothing had changed. The city's underclass still consisted of thieves and addicts and whores, men and women of good intent, people who had been systematically robbed of their ideals and their self-worth as they were forced to the gutter by their masters.

Major Whitstable's eyes were blinded by tears as the cab turned into Savoy Street. He kept his head turned from the driver as he paid the fare. Bad morale for the servants, he thought from habit, then tried to adapt the thought to modern times, the end of the twentieth century. No more servants, he told himself. We are all equal now. Try telling that to the kids in the shop doorways, he thought as he walked through the congested foyer of the hotel. To the well-heeled guests here the homeless, the disenfranchised, the teen runaways were just faces looking in on a world to which they had no claim. We are all equal now, he thought bitterly, if you don't count the judges and landowners and politicians and diplomats. If you don't count families like the Whitstables.

He ascended the curving stairway and pushed open the glass doors at the top. The smell of fresh soap and hot towels restored his humour a little. Surprisingly for a

Monday morning there were no other customers, and even Maurice seemed absent. A barber he had never seen before was honing an open razor on an orange leather strap.

'Good morning, Major,' said the man cheerily. On second glance, perhaps he had seen him before. The brilliantined hair combed across the tanned bald patch and the tiny waxed moustache were certainly familiar, but this chap seemed to be wearing makeup. His face was painted an unsubtle shade of orange, and the colour ended at his grey neck. How odd.

'Good morning,' said Whitstable testily, removing his overcoat. 'What's happened to Maurice?'

'Believe there's a bit of a bug going around, sir,' said the barber. 'I'm Eric.' He didn't look like an Eric. To be honest, he looked like an Indian, and a very sickly one at that. The major decided to let it pass.

'Well, Eric, I suppose we'll have to start from scratch.' He studied his watery red eyes in the bevelled wall mirror.

'Not at all, sir,' said Eric genially. 'I had the pleasure of shaving you once long ago, and Mr Maurice informs me that nothing has changed in the way of your personal ablutions. Please take a seat.'

As the barber leaned close he became aware of an odd smell, perfume over something rotten. It was vaguely familiar. Old meat. What had the fellow been eating? He frowned.

Eric flapped out a white apron with a crack of fresh linen that sounded like gunshot, and swirled it over Whitstable's head like a matador preparing to antagonise a bull. The Major closed his eyes and listened to the sounds he had heard all his life. Fresh shaving foam slapping in a ceramic bowl, the rhythmic stropping of an open blade. He felt the stiff bristle of the badger flowering foam across his cheeks, and the years melted away.

'Where did you shave me before? Not here, surely?'

'No, sir. In India.'

The lights above the mirror dazzled and flared through his half shut eyes as he felt the first sharp prick of the blade upon his throat. Even in the desert, in Rommel's darkest days, he had never shaved himself, and nor had William. Such times were gone forever.

'Won't take long now, Major,' said Eric soothingly.

The searing steel cut a swathe of bristles from below his jawline to the base of his ear lobe. The blade was rinsed clean, and returned to his face hotter than ever.

'Whereabouts in India?'

'Calcutta, sir. 1958, I believe it was.'

'That's right, I was stationed in India then.'

'And so was I, sir.'

'Well I never.'

The blade ran lightly across his chin and bit into the bristles at the top of his trachea — a little too deeply, he thought.

'I say, steady on.'

The edge of the razor lifted, caressing his throat with its edge, then suddenly pushed forward, a streak of flame crossing his throat. He was sure he'd been nicked. It was unforgivable!

'Look here—' he began.

With a sudden application of pressure, the honed steel blade popped the skin like a bayonet and smoothly parted it in one wide sweep. He raised his arms as a torrent of blood burst forth over the white-hot wound, flowing around his chin and down his neck. He tried to call out but the blade was sawing back and forth, deeper and deeper, severing his vocal chords as the demented barber whose name was not Eric worked on, his wild eyes rolling and glittering in a livid orange face.

*

'Where do you think you're going?' asked Nicholas, grabbing her sleeve. 'You were supposed to be on duty over an hour ago.'

'Couldn't you cover for me?' Jerry pleaded. 'This is really important.'

'Why should I? This isn't the first time you've been late when we've had a rush on.'

Jerry looked desperately towards the doors of the barber shop. 'You're right,' she said, 'I'm sorry.' Nicholas released his grip. 'I'll be back in just a minute.' She ran off up the stairs, leaving her protesting colleague behind.

The doors were locked. She looked at her watch. 10.15 a.m. The shop should have opened at 9.30. Besides, Maurice never kept the entrance locked. She could see no movement through the frosted glass. The room seemed to be empty.

She knelt down on her knees and peered under the crack of the door. There was a large figure slumped in one of the shaving chairs. One arm hung down toward the floor. The white sheet covering the body was splashed with crimson.

Then she was on her feet, hurling herself at the door until the wood splintered and the old glass panels cracked from top to bottom. She shoved aside the shattered door and stepped into the salon. The figure lay back in the chair with its throat untidily slashed into a second grimacing mouth. Its face bore a look of disbelief, the eyes protruding in stark surprise. The mother-of-pearl handle of an open razor jutted up from between the victim's teeth. Only the polished army shoes which poked out beneath the encompassing cape reminded Jerry that she was looking at the brutalised remains of Major Peter Whitstable.

# CHAPTER

12

One side of the heavy wooden lid slammed back in a cloud of fibrous dust. John May raised his head above the lintel and shone the torch inside. The attic ran the entire length of the house. The rafters of the pitched roof were clean and cobweb free, and a new wooden floor had been laid across the boarding joists to turn the area into a practical work-space.

May slid the torch-beam across the end wall, and located a light switch. The single mercury vapour lamp was bright enough to illuminate the central part of the room. He wiped the dirt from his palms and sat back against a packing crate. This was going to take a lot longer than he'd thought. There were at least twenty sealed tea chests here, plus stacks of books, dust-sheeted pieces of furniture, carpentry equipment, an old litho press, plaster statues, an upright harpsichord. The Whitstable brothers had hidden away a large part of their past, and all of it would have to be searched.

He rolled back the dustsheet from an open-topped crate and shone his torch inside. A soot-blackened Victorian dinner service, complete by the look of it, and a number of Staffordshire figurines lay unwrapped and unprotected. He raised a pair and studied them. Characters from the Crimean War, he imagined. A commander mounted upon his steed, his helmet beneath his arm, another beside the barrel of a mobile cannon. Bryant would know who they were. He gently set them back in the crate, trying to imagine just how much the contents of the attic were worth. By the look of it, the brothers had been sitting on a fortune. He wondered who in the family stood to benefit the most.

It was the theatricality of the investigation that bothered him more than anything else. This kind of carefully planned upper-class murder belonged to the end of the last century. Such deaths were virtually obsolete nowadays. An average week in the West End could yield half a dozen killings of particular official interest, but they all fell into the standard categories. A young Chinese man shot in Gerrard Street, broad daylight, possibly a triad connection, bad gambling debts. A punter leaving a club on Saturday night, found dead in an alley, seen flashing cash by a group of kids who waited for him to leave. An altercation outside a bar that left one dead and one in critical condition, knives and drink and a row over nothing much at all. Bryant was right — the common run of city crime was vicious and pointless, and more than likely fuelled by alcohol. From the business end, it was rarely worthy of attention.

Most murders still take place at home. Women are more likely to die there than men, nearly half of them suffering at the hands of a husband or lover. Men are slaughtered by acquaintances and strangers, simply because they get out of the house more often than their partners.

May knew that the statistics of death were woefully inaccurate; doctors were pulling more victims through, lawyers argued over terminology, constantly shifting the boundary lines. He and his colleagues could be certain of just two facts. Murders were more likely to be committed within the family. And every passing year brought rising figures.

But as for this ...

He looked around at the accretions of more than a century, relics of the past, overflowing from every corner. There was an odd Wilkie Collins flavour here, the sense of a long-standing family feud reaching a flashpoint. Over what? A contested inheritance? A missing will? That sounded unnecessarily gothic but promising, especially as the family lawyer had also been killed. What other possibilities were there? An unrighted wrong? Stolen virtue? A debt of honour? The investigation was being forced to gather speed, and the danger was that they would overlook the answer in a rush to pin the blame.

The senior officials were already aiming for a fast arrest. Yesterday morning Stan Marsden, in his capacity as acting head of the unit, had paid a visit to May's office, knowing that even though it was Sunday the detective would be found there. The case had a political dimension, he explained. The Whitstables weren't just off the street. They were an ancient family, well connected. Peter was more than a passing acquaintance of Field Marshal Mont-gomery, whose patience and solid, cautious strategy he had long admired. He'd been there with the Eighth Army on the east coast of Italy. He had been decorated for his part in the Normandy invasion. Brother William had been introduced to the Queen at Sandringham, although Marsden was unsure of the reason for this.

But if William Whitstable was such an establishment figure, May had asked, why would he have wanted to risk damaging the Commonwealth conference by attacking a politically sensitive painting? Could it — a long shot here, thought May — could it be that someone in government circles had taken revenge for the act?

As Marsden had virtually accused him of treason, the meeting was adjourned.

The political dimension of the case had allowed them to limit press damage to a certain extent, but the journalists wouldn't be held at bay for long. Speed was of the essence, Marsden had explained, emphasising the point by jabbing his finger against the door as he took his leave. This was the new division's first full-scale investigation, and everyone was watching for results.

Nothing like a little pressure from above to help a case along, thought May, as he raised the lid of another packing crate. This box was filled with books on heraldry. Wedged along one side was a slim mahogany case with a small brass key still in its lock. Strictly speaking, they had not yet been granted clearance to search the house, but work had to continue until the next of kin arrived.

According to his information, Bella Whitstable, the younger sister, had been abroad on a business trip for the past six weeks. She had apparently left a forwarding address with Peter, and had been informed by him of the tragedy that had occurred to her brother. What she did not know, as a British Airways flight returned her from Calcutta, was that her remaining sibling had also found death from an unknown hand.

By all accounts they were not a close family, but with Christmas approaching Bella had planned to stay with her brothers for a few days. Now she would find herself facing a double funeral. May hoped she was a strong woman.

There was nothing so disturbing as coping with death at Christmas.

He turned the key and opened the case, examining its contents. Inside was a robe of thin blue silk bearing a woven shield, guarded by unicorns. Underneath, the words *Justitia Virtutum Regina* had been stitched in dark golden thread. He felt sure that these were the symbols of one of the City of London guilds. It seemed logical that the brothers belonged to such an organisation. He gently closed the case and returned it to the crate. The collected contents of the attic would help them build a picture of the Whitstable family. Still, he somehow doubted that they would provide a clue to their killer.

He returned downstairs and placed a call to Raymond Land.

'They've just got back to me on your bomb,' said the doctor. 'Your partner was right. It's not the traditional sort, but an extremely effective device nevertheless. Can you call by when you finish up there?'

By late Monday afternoon the barber shop at the Savoy had been examined by forensic experts, cleared and somewhat restored to its former pristine condition, with the exception of a six-foot area ribboned with demarcation tape. Arthur Bryant stepped over a section of freshly dusted floor and stood studying his reflection in the tall bevelled mirrors above the sinks. *What a scruffbag*, he thought. *I need some better-fitting dentures and a decent winter coat, one without threads hanging from it.* He needed a haircut too, but places like this weren't his style. The gleaming chrome and ceramic sinks, stencilled with the manufacturer's name in smudged blue like old tattoos, the iridescent tiling and hard white towels all belonged to a prewar world of manservants and valets, and Bryant knew where the class system of the time would have placed him; on the side of service.

His own father had been a head butler, and proud of it. He had kept his family well provided for, and had always maintained his dignity. It had certainly never occurred to him that he might be every bit as worthy as those upon whom he waited all his life. In later years it became a constant source of conflict between father and son.

Bryant turned away and examined the black leather barber's chair. Someone had done a good job; after being dusted for fingerprints it had been buffed to a fierce shine. You'd never think that just a few hours ago someone had been murdered in it.

The girl was slouching guiltily by the towel-rail, contriving to act suspiciously even when there was nothing to be suspicious about. She had a habit of looking down at the ground as she spoke, so that her dark hair fell across her face, obscuring her eyes. She was an attractive sort. It was a pity she didn't bother to make the most of herself.

'Well?' asked Bryant, settling down in the barber's chair and raising his shoes from the floor. 'You walked in and there was Major Whitstable with the razor sticking out of his mouth. Where was the barber?'

'He must have only just left the room,' said Jerry. 'He could have attacked me as well, you know.'

'I realise that,' said Bryant. 'Has someone warned you about not speaking to the press, by the way?'

'I wouldn't want to.'

'And you're absolutely sure you saw no one other than the Major in here or outside?' Jerry shook her head and stared at the door. Thank God the young were so resilient, thought Bryant. The poor kid had witnessed two deaths in less than a week. She looked shaken, but intact. Still, there was a chance that she was holding something back. There was a tradesman's entrance to the salon leading into an alleyway behind the hotel. Whoever attacked the old man had done so with a perfect escape route at his rear.

'Which brings us to the big question; what were you doing up here at all?'

'I was going to ask Maurice if he would give me a free haircut,' said Jerry. 'What happened to him?'

'It doesn't matter.' The less the girl knew, the better. Apparently someone with an Indian accent had rung Maurice on Saturday and told him not to come in on Monday. He had warned the barber that they were closing the salon to refit some water pipes. Maurice had gladly accepted the day off. Bryant swivelled the chair around to face the girl. 'Why do I think you know more than you're telling me?'

'I don't know, sir.' Jerry hung her head, swivelling a shoe.

'If you remember anything else, no matter how insignificant it may seem, will you be sure to inform me or Mr May first?' asked Bryant, rising. 'Every sudden death is tragic, but brutality on this level must be stopped before any further tragedy occurs. It can also destroy the reputation of a hotel, even one as venerable and respected as the Savoy. You must come to me before speaking to anyone else.'

'Mr Bryant?' She raised her eyes to him.

'Yes?'

'Is this to do with Mr Jacob?'

'I don't know. So far the forensic evidence hasn't—'

'It must be, mustn't it? I mean, they knew each other.'

'I admit it's a bizarre coincidence. In my heart I'm sure the deaths are connected. But we deal in hard facts, and those seem to have been carefully removed. Until they can be established we have to wait—'

'I want to help,' she interrupted. 'I'm already involved. I can find things out for you.'

'I'm afraid that's not really allowed.'

'But you're in an experimental unit. It's been in all the papers. You're working outside the system. If you wanted me to do something, nobody would be able to tell you otherwise.'

'Thanks for the offer.' He patted her on the arm. 'I'll bear it in mind. You'd better get back to work. I'll probably need to speak to you again.'

He led the way out. The shattered door was the last remaining sign of the disturbance, and was already being removed for repairs. The salon would have to remain shut for the rest of the week. As Bryant made his way upstairs, he checked the waistband of his voluminous trousers and tutted with annoyance. May would kill him if he'd lost another bleeper.

Making his way back to Mornington Crescent, he tried to connect the events of the past week. The fact that the deaths were related was enough to elevate the case into the arena of the extraordinary. The speed with which they were occurring rendered the situation quite unique.

'Watch this.'

Raymond Land handed the experiment over to a pasty-faced young man in a lab coat, who produced a small test tube of what looked like liquid mercury and a paintbrush. Carefully dipping the brush in the solution, he painted a thin strip of liquid on the side of a child's building block. Bryant withdrew a pair of smeary reading glasses from his top pocket and put them on. May was sitting on the only chair in the room.

'We have to wait a few moments for it to dry,' said the young lab technician. 'It's something we haven't seen for years. A form of silver acetalide. You titrate it through ammonia and it comes out like sludge.' He held up the test tube. 'While it's in liquid form it's fine. But if you let it dry out ...' He picked up the child's block and checked the line of paint. Satisfied, he tossed the block on to the desk. There was a loud bang, and the clearing smoke revealed a blackened pit in the wood.

'... it becomes totally unstable,' said the technician, somewhat unnecessarily.

'That's my desk,' said Land angrily, examining the damage.

'What would a device designed to make the most of this property look like, do you reckon?' asked May. 'How big would it have to be?'

'Not large at all, just so long as the drying area for the liquid was maximised sufficiently. Here.' He produced a pad from his pocket and began to draw. 'Working from a reconstruction incorporating the slivers of metal we found in William Whitstable's stomach, we get something like this. The liquid is contained in a section here ...'

'I wondered why one piece was silvered,' said Bryant. 'It was part of the liquid chamber.'

'A preset clockwork mechanism could release it into a flat drying chamber that might work from, say, the heat of the body. As soon as it's dry, the device is armed and lethal.' He held up the finished drawing to reveal a metal chamber the size and shape of a cigarette case.

'Just the sort of thing that a smart Edwardian gentleman would carry upon his person,' said Bryant. 'Thanks for the demonstration.' He tapped May on the shoulder with the back of his hand. 'Come on, you. We've an appointment to keep.'

By 8.30 p.m. the concourse at Victoria Station had only a

light groundswell of homebound commuters passing between the trains and ticket windows.

Bryant stood at the barrier watching the arriving passengers. 'You realise if she's anything like the rest of the family, she'll be wearing a crinoline and bustle.' He looked across at May, who was checking his watch.

'That must be her.'

Bryant followed his partner's pointing finger. Bella Whitstable was a pleasant surprise. Broad and stocky, neither smiling nor serious, she came at them with a purposeful gait and sensible shoes, a county woman with city edges. The practicality of her winter jacket was lightened with a sprig of lapis lazuli, and gold earrings balanced the severity of her haircut. Unsurprisingly, her handshake was firm and dry, her manner direct.

'I don't want you to mollycoddle me,' she told the detectives. 'It's no secret that we didn't get along, William, Peter and I, but of course it horrifies me that they met such terrible ends.'

'So you know about Peter,' said May, surprised.

'It would have been hard to avoid items like this,' replied Bella, holding up a copy of the *Evening Standard*.

## DEATH RIDDLE OF SAVOY SHAVE
Dead man was brother of tube explosion victim

The press were well and truly on their tails now. As Peter Whitstable's identity had yet to be divulged, May wondered how the hell they had managed to link the two deaths so quickly. The official line on the Hampstead tube bombing was that a technical fault had occurred in one of the carriages. The subterfuge had been necessary to prevent the public from thinking that the IRA were renewing their Christmas attacks on the city.

'I'm sorry you had to find out in such a manner,' said

May, taking her bag. 'There was no way we could contact you in time.' They had planned to send someone to meet the arriving flight, but were too late to do so.

'I quite understand,' said Bella, with considerable coolness. 'It will take me a while to fully appreciate what has happened.'

'Under the circumstances I wouldn't advise staying at the house.'

'I'm sure you wouldn't, but that's where I need to be. There are some items belonging to me in the attic. I'm not fond of London, and intend to spend as little time here as possible.' They made their way to a waiting squad car.

'You can ask me anything you like,' said Bella, seating herself. 'I have just returned from a city where sudden death is part of everyday life. I won't get sniffly on you.'

'Why didn't you get along with your brothers?' asked Bryant.

'There were feuds between us that went back a long way. It all seems so trivial now. I couldn't bear all that living in the past. It seemed so unhealthy. William didn't approve of me finding a beau so soon after our mother died, and put an end to the relationship. I could not forgive him for that. There were other things, financial arrangements that caused problems. It's hard to be specific. You'll have to give me some time to think.'

'We will need details of the beneficiaries to the wills. I suppose Peter told you that their lawyer, Max Jacob, is also dead.'

'Yes, it seems so extraordinary. I wonder if any of us are safe. I wish I could throw some light on all of this, but I simply don't know where to begin.'

'There is the question of the funeral,' said Bryant, gently. 'Although perhaps you'd like to discuss this later ...'

'William and Peter will be interred together. We have a

family vault at Highgate,' said Bella, looking out of the window at the retreating station. 'It would seem to be the best thing.'

'We want your permission to maintain a high police presence at the service,' said May. It was not uncommon for a murderer to attend the burial of his victim.

'I understand. Do you have any idea of the kind of person you're looking for?'

'We're hoping that you can help us there,' said Bryant. 'Why do you think William lived so much in the past?'

'Oh, we're an old-fashioned bunch. The family's history is the history of England.' Bella rummaged in her bag, produced a huge linen handkerchief and gave a brisk honk into it. 'I think William chose a period he particularly liked and stuck with it. Of course, the late nineteenth century was our grand time, so to speak. Our ancestors' fortunes grew with the Empire, and so did the family. Sons and daughters in every outpost. It's the same with all the old families. Now they're like us, in sad decline. Although I don't suppose they're disappearing in quite the same lurid manner. I wonder if we have any business rivals at the moment. You should check into that, Mr Bryant.'

'We're trying, although it will be harder to do so now that Peter has died. Both of your brothers were retired, presumably?'

'Apart from a bit of dabbling on the Stock Exchange. I heard about William and the painting. What an appalling thing to do.'

'You have no idea why he might have done it?'

'None at all. I can't imagine that either of them had any real enemies. And who would want to kill them over a painting? It wasn't even famous, from what Peter told me.'

'How well did you know Max Jacob?'

'Not at all, I'm afraid. He handled the family estate and

all of its financial dealings, but he only ever dealt with William.'

'He lied to his family about coming to London,' said May. 'If he met up with William, we have no evidence of it.'

The car had reached St John's Wood. Bella was momentarily distracted by a passing apartment building. 'Look at that,' she said, pointing to a sign on the wall. 'Tadema House. What a marvellous painter Alma-Tadema was. How we all loved the Pre-Raphaelites, Peter included. Mother owned several, you see. All donated to galleries now, of course.'

'Did she own any paintings by Waterhouse?' asked Bryant.

'No, I don't think so. Why, is that what my brother destroyed, a Waterhouse?' Bryant nodded. 'What could he have been thinking of?' Bella blew her nose again. As the car arrived in Hampstead, a light rain began to fall.

'We're keeping a twenty-four-hour guard on the house,' said May as they turned into the crescent. 'If you're planning to go out, you'd better let me have an itinerary.'

'I have to attend a meeting of my society tomorrow night,' said Bella, alighting from the car. 'I know that William and Peter would have wanted me to keep the appointment. I suppose someone will have to come with me.'

'Who is the meeting with?' asked Bryant.

'The Savoyard Society,' said Bella, closing the door. 'Gilbert and Sullivan. I'm the president. Don't worry, I can see myself in.'

'Well,' said May as they drove back to Mornington Crescent, 'what did you make of her?'

'She seems to have an alarmingly calm attitude to all of

this. Either she's genuinely undisturbed by what's going on, or she's lying about how much she knows.' Bryant looked out at the rainswept night. 'I hope to God she can tell us something.'

'I'm not too sure that she wants to,' said May. 'If there's anything the Whitstable family members share in common, it's that none of them knows how to behave like a normal human being. How can we ever be expected to establish a motive?

# CHAPTER

**Partial section of Transcript # 170-51**
**Monday 13 December**
Session with Dr Emil Wayland
Patient: Geraldine Gates

WAYLAND:
We hadn't scheduled an appointment for this afternoon, you realise.
GATES:
I know. I wanted to see you, and the nurse said you were free.
WAYLAND:
Should I look upon this as some kind of breakthrough?
GATES:
No.
WAYLAND:
Was there anything in particular you wanted to talk about?

GATES:

You once explained something to me. About schizo-phrenia.

WAYLAND:

What did I say?

GATES:

About it being present in everyone to various degrees.

WAYLAND:

Well, that's true. As we live our lives we learn to cover up many of our emotions. If you look at a baby, you'll see its moods change by the second. As civilised adults we find such behaviour unacceptable, so we channel our feelings.

GATES:

But even when they're hidden away, they're still there, aren't they?

WAYLAND:

Certainly. Most of us come to terms with ourselves, but some people are at war with their hidden emotions. For example, someone living in an excessively repressed environment may experience strong sexual desires. They may sublimate these feelings into aggression, and deliber-ately hurt those who have sexual freedom. They become resentful and phobic about their own buried natures.

Another example. Kids sometimes start behaving badly to upset social conventions, although in fact they're seeking ways to gain the attention of their parents.

GATES:

You're talking about me now.

WAYLAND:

No, we're just generalising.

GATES:

What if you just grow up in a normal environment?

WAYLAND:

There's no such thing. Every family raises its offspring in a highly specialised manner.

GATES:

All right, say you grow up in an *average* family—

WAYLAND:

Like yours.

GATES:

I'd hardly call it average. My mother had me committed when I was fourteen, for fuck's sake.

WAYLAND:

You know very well that she wanted you to have special care, Geraldine. I thought you were satisfied with the way we'd covered this.

GATES:

(Pause approx. 45 sec.)

What I'm trying to get at — you think you know yourself, right? Then you see something new, something you can't explain or understand, and it changes the way you look at things.

WAYLAND:

You want to be more specific?

GATES:

I didn't say it had happened to me. I didn't mean *me*.

WAYLAND:

Then who did you mean?

GATES:

It was hypothetical, that's all. I'm scared of the dark. But I'm drawn to it as well. I want to understand why it frightens me.

WAYLAND:

And this feeling has intensified since your recent — experience.

Your mother told me what happened. Seeing a death. At our last session I asked you if there was anything wrong. Why didn't you tell me?

GATES:
Because nothing is wrong.
WAYLAND:
But you've been thinking about death since.
GATES:
Aspects of dying.
WAYLAND:
Have you reached any conclusions?
GATES:
Yes. It's like the dark. It interests me.

# CHAPTER

She was startled to find blood on the pillow.

She had bitten her lower lip in her sleep. The dream had returned again, its effect unblunted by familiarity. But now that she was awake, eyes turned to the growing stripe of daylight bisecting the pale blue ceiling of her room, she felt the dread of those endless dark alleys dissolving within her.

In the past week she had seen worse, and it had been no dream. For the first time, reality had proven more disturbing than her imagination. She thought of the swathed body in the barber shop yesterday and her skin prickled hotly. It was as if she had succeeded in stepping beyond the comfortable safety zone provided by her parents, and into an area of real danger. Worst of all, the thought excited her. Wayland had ended their impromptu session with a warning about the harm of allowing what he termed 'negative aspects' of her nature to the fore. Well, the good doctor could go fuck himself. His main concern was to keep Gwen's monthly cheques rolling in.

Jerry checked the alarm clock and rolled out of bed. At 8.00 a.m. the house was still silent. In the time-honoured manner of the well-to-do, Jack and Gwen had a way of effortlessly maintaining a fragrant lifestyle. Neither of them would be awake for another half-hour. Wait until the papers arrived, she thought, they'd be able to read about the latest gruesome discovery at their only child's place of employment. Gwen would probably find a way of implying that she was somehow to blame.

Her parents' friends were all vines from the same noble tree, and shared an approximate social standing. The men were higher-echelon professionals, and their partners were wives before they were women. In the uppermost branches above them were the families fortified by generations of old money, and the minor royals. Below were the twisting creepers of the nouveau riche.

Jack and Gwen were locked into a very precise level of British life, sparkling ammonites in the strata of society. They lived in London, (too *cosmopolitan* for some of their ilk) with the mitigating factor that Chelsea was an enclave of select families like themselves. They had a house in Warwickshire, and a small, comfortable cottage in Provence. As was proper these days, Gwen worked, both as an active board member for her husband's businesses, and as a hostess on the many charity nights their friends arranged for each other to promote this year's fashionable cause.

Here in the upper-middle reaches, the rules for social climbing had to be strictly adhered to. Jack's money was not yet old enough for them to be allowed to behave as they liked.

Further complicating the family's position was the fact, due to her traumatic past, that Jerry had not received the 'right' education. Instead she had been enrolled at a small private school in Chelsea which enjoyed a fine reputation as a clearing house for the problem children of the comfortable classes.

Jerry looked around the room, at the home computer and stacks of unplayed games, the TV, video and CD systems she ignored in favour of perusing unkempt stacks of books. She had never had to tidy the room herself, but she was not allowed to put posters on the walls because of the pin-marks they left.

She wondered what would happen if she told Gwen what she had witnessed, and how she had talked to the police. Her mother would probably drop dead from sheer embarrassment. She had a sneaking suspicion that people like her parents lived in fear of their children developing strong imaginations. In their eyes it encouraged creativity, and that prevented young people from becoming productive. It was important to them that she did something useful.

She wondered if they would ever truly allow her to choose her own course in life. She wanted to discover their exact level of interest in her own happiness.

As Jerry showered and dressed, she marvelled at how much could happen in the space of a single week. She had glimpsed death and conspiracy, had spoken to the men who dealt with it as part of their daily routine, and now she wanted to know more, although she was unsure how far she could pursue her own investigation without the approval of the police. She still had the bible in her possession. She would have to consider her next move very carefully.

As she wiped condensation from the mirror and combed back her wet hair, she thought about Joseph Herrick. She knew he had been busy drawing his plans for the theatre, but the next time he came past the reception desk she would definitely ask him out on a date.

For the first time, it seemed that anything and everything was possible, so long as she kept her own counsel.

*Daily Mail, 14 December*

*Exclusive*

## STARTLING NEW LINK IN WHITSTABLE DEATHS 'DENIED BY POLICE'

According to a source close to the police teams working at North London's experimental murder investigation division, vital evidence linking three bizarre deaths in the past week is being deliberately ignored.

From its inception the Serious Crime Division has drawn charges of élitism, and faces heavy criticism for its proposed work methods, which encourage experimentation over traditional investigative procedure.

Now, however, it is being suggested that a vital clue common to all three deaths has been discounted in favour of obscure 'alternative' theories.

William and Peter Whitstable, together with their lawyer Max Jacob, have died in circumstances bearing no common link — save one. *The Daily Mail* has learned that police know of a symbol common to each victim which had deadly connotations.

The sign of a sacred flame is popularly used by members of the Whitstable family and their business associates. But during the Second World War this very symbol had a sinister meaning. It was a code used by highly trained German assassins to mark predetermined British targets.

Between 1941 and 1944 no less than thirty-seven English men and women who were perceived to be a threat to the German invasion were coded with the sacred flame symbol, and were subsequently eliminated in a variety of elaborate scenarios. The sacred flame has a mythological origin connected to German Olympian ideals.

Few now remember the terror that this sign once inspired. The re-emergence of the flame's use, timed at the start of a groundbreaking Commonwealth conference, suggests the return of powerful right-wing German interests.

It is common knowledge that the Whitstable family have profitable export connections with German delegates who were invited to attend the conference in an advisory capacity. Recently their Hamburg office suffered extensive damage and two members of staff were injured after a firebomb was hurled through a ground-floor window.

Confronted with this fresh evidence, a police spokesperson denied any link with recent German troubles, suggesting that the connection of the sacred flame was 'spurious at best'.

On the morning of Tuesday 14 December, Bryant and May began the second week of their investigation by facing up to two major problems in their search for information.

The first was a lack of available manpower. Theirs was the only division ranking above the existing Area Major Investigation Pools in Britain. These pools were divided by areas, and handled the majority of homicide enquiries. Typically, they were overworked and understaffed. In theory the new unit was supposed to receive help from the pools' senior investigating officers, or SIOs, but in practice it was not possible to free them from their essential 'caretaking' duties within the AMIPs. This left the division with a single acting superintendent, Stan Marsden, two sergeants, of which Christina Crosse was one, the other being answerable to Marsden, and an inadequate footforce.

Their second problem was one of time. It was commonly recognised in the force that the first seventy-two hours following a homicide were the most vital. At the end of three days, a strong sense is gained of whether the case will be solved quickly or not. This period of time had already passed in the cases of Max Jacob and William Whitstable without any agreement on motive, opportunity or circumstantial evidence. Little had been established beyond the fact that they were dealing with three cases of unlawful homicide with malice aforethought. Now the detectives both realised that they were in for a long haul. Consequently, they decided to divide chores according to each other's specific talents.

Bryant was to question Bella Whitstable about her brothers, while May spent time with the forensic team appointed to the case. The properties of all three victims were in the process of being searched and catalogued, and Jacob's family was being questioned for the second time. Witness statements were being correlated by Sergeant Crosse, who added them to the steadily expanding database at Mornington Crescent.

Faraday, the junior arts minister, had called twice to find out why no arrests had been made, and an expert from the National Gallery had faxed a detailed report on the problems that would beset anyone attempting a restoration of the Waterhouse painting.

Forensic information was starting to arrive on Major Peter Whitstable's death, but no one could spare the time to correlate it to the rest of the investigation. Their personnel situation was scandalous, May reflected. Worse still, their detractors on the force might well have arranged for it to become so.

Equally frustrating was the fact that it was impossible to find time to follow up this morning's suggestion by the *Mail* that German business interests were to blame for the deaths. The theory was as plausible as any other, perhaps more so, but Christina had been forced to publicly dismiss it until a team could be freed to investigate the allegation. And who knew how long that would take?

When he arrived at the morgue, May found Oswald Finch tabling results from his autopsy on William's younger brother into the micro-recorder that sat on his bench. The air in the white tiled room was chill and antiseptic, but still could not hide the smell that surrounded the clinical study of death.

'I'm glad you came back,' said Finch, rising to offer a thin, clammy hand. 'How are you getting on with your snake man?'

'Not very well,' admitted May. 'It would have helped if they'd managed to get a few readable fibres from him.' Forensics had laser-searched all three corpses and had failed to find any common substance matches. It seemed obvious that the murders were linked, but so far they had found no way of proving it.

'You know, the methods of death we're dealing with must be symbolic of something,' said May. 'They're intended to have a theatrical effect. There's no other reason for going to so much trouble.'

'In Jacob's case you could be looking at suicide,' said Finch, crossing the room to the banks of grey steel drawers set in the far wall. 'It's possible that the wound was self-inflicted. It would explain why he calmly returned to his seat and continued reading the paper. The same with your bomb man. He might have accidentally triggered his own device. Something has cropped up that I thought you might be interested in.' He unlocked a drawer and rolled it out, deftly unzipping the pale plastic bag in which the mortal remains of Peter Whitstable were housed. 'This was an assault of quite incredible force,' said Finch.

'What do you mean?' May attempted to avoid looking at the dry, broad slashes on the major's throat and the split wounds to his mouth.

'If the attack had resulted from an altercation, or had been motivated by hatred, I would have expected to find a fair bit of damage to the face. But you say no cries were heard outside the barber shop. His attacker could have armed himself with any number of sharp instruments, but he chose the razor. He was very fast, with powerful strokes through the vocal chords here, across the throat and down into the mouth. This chap had no time to struggle. It's actually an execution-style killing. There are a couple of other things I wanted to mention. We found some odd flakes of skin on the Major's arms. Dead tissue, most likely human in origin. There were traces of grease-paint or makeup on his apron, probably transferred from the killer. And then there's this.'

He thumbed open the inside of the corpse's upper arm and shone a high density narrow beam torch on the exposed flesh.

'As we're dealing with a lifelong military man I wasn't surprised to find that he had a tattoo,' said Finch. 'It's the placing of it that's odd. I've never seen one on the inside of an arm before. It's only a few centimetres below the armpit. No one would ever see it.'

John May found himself looking at a familiar aqua-marine smudge. The flickering flame symbol was the same as the one he had found on William Whitstable's cane.

'Did you find this on either of the others?'

'No, only on the Major. Perhaps it has military signi-ficance. There must be a way of finding out what it means.'

'Yes,' May agreed half-heartedly, all too aware that he could spare no one for the task. 'If the newspapers are to be believed, we're under attack from modern-day Nazis protecting their business interests. The journalists are securing information faster than we are.'

'I don't know where to begin,' said Bella Whitstable, standing at one end of the angled seventy-foot corridor that constituted her brothers' attic. 'I doubt either of them could remember what had been stored up here.' Judging by her neat makeup and smart appearance, she appeared to have passed a good night. She certainly hadn't sat up for hours crying.

'There are some ceremonial robes,' said Bryant, removing the mahogany box and unlocking it. 'Perhaps you know what they represent.' He had a good idea himself, but he wanted confirmation.

'Oh, that's easy,' said Bella, removing the blue silk gown and holding it to the light. 'It's William's guild robe. Peter has one as well. Most of the men in our family do.'

'What kind of guild does this represent?' He looked into the box and removed an ermine-trimmed collar. He expected to find a heavy gold chain somewhere, and here it was at the bottom of the box.

'It's part of the Goldsmiths Company. We're a craft guild family. That's originally where the Whitstables got their money. A long time ago, they were all craftsmen. Gold and silver. I believe our ancestors can be traced back to the foundation of the guild in 1339.'

Bryant himself had attended a school financed by the Worshipful Company of Leathersellers, and knew a little about the ancient network of guilds that still operated a system of patronage, performing charitable works within the city. His old school had become private in the mid-eighties. Kids from his background were no longer welcome.

'Did William and Peter still keep up their contacts, attend meetings, that sort of thing?'

'I doubt it. Neither of them were particularly sociable. They were always too suspicious of others to make many friends. It wasn't much fun growing up with them.'

'So there's no chance that their deaths might have resulted from some past transgression here.' His fingers traced the stitched livery on the robe.

'I don't think that's very likely, Mr Bryant.'

For a moment he'd had a vision of the ageing guild members quarrelling over a fraudulent deal, a distant betrayal. The arcane circumstances of the deaths somehow seemed to fit.

'I have to leave soon,' said Bella. 'I'm meeting my Savoyards at seven.'

'I should come with you,' said Bryant. 'You say this society is connected with Gilbert and Sullivan?'

'Indeed,' said Bella. 'We're attending the new production of *Princess Ida*. Tonight is the first night.'

How could he have forgotten? Ken Russell's new version of this work had received a surprising amount of praise at its previews. Bryant had promised to buy himself a ticket, but the events of the last week had ended any thoughts of leisure.

'I'm sure we'll be able to find you a spare seat,' Bella told the pleased detective.


An innovative programming policy at the Coliseum had resulted in a surprising change in the English National Opera's audiences. Fans of all ages now congregated beneath the illuminated globe of London's largest theatre. The purists still attended the Royal Opera House, leaving the ENO free to return a sense of fun to opera-going. It was one of Bryant's greatest pleasures to attend most of the productions here, and it pleased him greatly to see so many students in attendance. Unlike some of his colleagues, he welcomed the chance to be in the company of the young, and was usually prepared to listen to their opinions.

Tonight, the chill evening air had forced most of the arriving audience into the foyer of the theatre. Bella had changed into an alarming black-beaded dress for the event. The heavy symmetry of her body was accentuated by the geometrical cut of the dress, to the point where she looked like a man in drag. Bryant thought that this was often the way with county women. They failed to adapt from the field to the foyer. The elderly detective was not in a position to criticise his escort, as he was sporting his usual battered brown overcoat topped with another of his landlady's unnecessarily prolonged scarves.

'They should be around here somewhere,' said Bella, searching the crowded vestibule from the steps. 'You can't miss them.'

'Oh, why is that?' asked Bryant, seconds before he caught sight of the most extraordinary group of people he had ever seen. They all appeared to be in fancy dress. One of them, a short, bespectacled man clad in doublet and hose, came over and pumped Bella's arm.

'Oh, well done,' he cried, examining her gown. 'A perfect revival Lady Blanche!' He indicated his own clothes. 'I've gone for the James Wade 1954 production. The original's too laden down with fur and chain mail, unless you're King Hildebrande. I was supposed to be Cyril, but the chap taking Florian fell off his exercycle and landed on his keys, so I took his place.'

Bryant touched Bella's arm. 'You mean they're all dressed in character?' he asked.

'Certainly,' said Bella. 'The Savoyards differ from other

Gilbert and Sullivan groups. They live out the parts of each opera. Actually it's not as crazy as it sounds.' She pointed to the motley group now assembling around them. 'Our functions raise a lot of money for charity, and pay for the preservation and restoration of related artefacts.'

'I take it your brothers had no connection with the group?' asked Bryant.

'Good heavens, no. In our family, theatre is something for the men to sleep through.'

Noting the size of some of the ladies' headdresses, Bryant tried to imagine how the rest of the audience would feel about this added embellishment to the evening's programme. Then it was explained to him that the Savoyards had reserved Boxes G and H on the right side of the theatre, where they would be able to enjoy themselves in relative privacy.

As they reached the boxes, Bryant examined the faces of the assembled Savoyards, and found himself searching for possible suspects. With fifteen minutes to go before curtain up, champagne was opened, and several members approached Bella to offer awkward condolences. One of the Savoyards was sitting on the far side of the box in a visored steel helmet which hid his face. Bryant excused himself from Bella's side. It was important to ascertain that there was no danger here, and that began by knowing everyone's identity.

'Hello there.' He pulled up a small gilt chair. 'Mind if I join you?' The man in the plumed helmet said something he could not understand and pointed helplessly to the side of his head. Bryant loosened a wing nut and worked the visor free. The face revealed was sweaty and russet-coloured.

'Phew, thanks,' said the knight gratefully. 'Damned

thing keeps jamming. I should have picked someone else.'
He held out a hand. 'Oliver Pettigrew. I'm not normally
dressed like this. I'm an estate agent. You're the police
chap.'

'That's right,' said Bryant, unwinding his scarf and
placing it on the back of the chair. Below them the heat
and sound levels rose as the auditorium filled up.

'What do you make of this business, then? Both her
brothers gone in a week, and yet she's here tonight. What
a trouper.' He shook his head in wonderment.

'How often do you meet?' asked Bryant.

'Once every six weeks for a costume reading, usually in
a church hall, every G&S revival of course, and at a variety
of charity functions. Save the Children, London Light-
house, things like that. And we provide funds to keep
original manuscripts and props in the country. There's a
great interest in the operas throughout the Commonwealth, and of course in America. We even have an official
chapter of the Savoyards in Chicago.'

'Extraordinary,' said Bryant. 'I've long been a Gilbert
and Sullivan fan, but I had never heard of you before Bella
told me.'

'It's all rather out of fashion over here,' said Bella,
picking up the conversation. 'There's always been a critical
reaction against anything popular in this country, don't
you think? People rather tend to forget that Gilbert and
Sullivan's satirical targets — the judicial system, the police,
royalty — are just as relevant today.'

'That's right,' agreed Knight Pettigrew, fiddling with his
wing nut. 'They ridiculed affectation, snobbery and
nepotism. Gilbert's rude lyrics kept him from receiving a
knighthood until he was nearly dead. The Victorian age
died with them, you know. Lewis Carroll, Ruskin,
Gladstone, William Morris, D'Oyly Carte, Oscar Wilde

and Queen Victoria herself — all gone with the end of the century.'

'Mr Sullivan's music is the music of the common people,' said Bella. 'It's a direct descendant of the folk songs that once bound the country together.' She refilled their glasses. 'That's why the guild supports it.'

'The guild?' Bryant's ears pricked up. 'You mean money from the Goldsmiths helps to run the Savoyards?' he asked.

'Sometimes,' said Bella. 'It works both ways. There are many common charities involved. I think it's about to start.'

The main auditorium lights began to dim, and everyone took their seats. Bryant was reasonably familiar with the plot of *Princess Ida*, a rather heavy-handed, patronising satire on women's rights, but he had never seen it performed. Indeed, its awkward recitative was the reason why it was rarely produced at all these days. This was a pity, for it contained what was known as 'Sullivan's String of Pearls' in the second act, a sequence containing some of the composer's finest work.

The opera consisted of three acts, with two intermissions of fifteen minutes each. At the first of these, the Savoyards turned to each other with the falling of the curtain and chattered excitedly. The production had obviously found favour with them. The location had been updated to futuristic London with reasonable success, just as Jonathan Miller had once shifted the action of *The Mikado* from Japan to Brighton in the 1920s.

This new version allowed for a variety of jokes surrounding the women's liberation movement, but it was the singing that elicited the group's enthusiasm. Bryant caught Bella Whitstable heading for the door of the box and called her back. 'If you want to go to the bathroom,' he suggested, 'take someone with you.'

'I was only going to fix my face,' she replied somewhat archly.

'Then do it here,' said Bryant. 'I don't want you out of my sight.'

Knight Pettigrew had removed his helmet and was refilling his champagne glass. Several more Savoyards had entered from the other box. The bejewelled outfits of the women and the polished silver gilt of the men's armour glittered in the soft red gloom, although someone dressed as a ragged beggar in a floppy hat seemed to have gotten the raw end of the deal. Bryant had to admit that it was an extraordinary sight, admirable in a slightly dotty way.

Pettigrew tapped him on the arm. 'You know, people don't realise how much of Gilbert and Sullivan is buried in the national consciousness,' he said. 'Take *Princess Ida*. The lyrics owe a considerable debt to Tennyson, did you know that? The BBC was playing the first act on 3 September, just before Neville Chamberlain announced that we were at war with Germany. And you know the last lines that were heard that fateful day before they faded out the music? "Order comes to fight, ha ha, order is obeyed."'

Bryant glanced at his friend's eager face and had no doubt that he possessed hundreds of similar pieces of anecdotal trivia. People like Pettigrew were harmless enough, but it was usually dangerous to show too much of an interest. As the estate agent prattled on, Bryant wondered how many of the others had told their friends and work colleagues about the way they spent their leisure time.

The house lights flickered and dimmed for a moment, presumably to notify the audience that it was time for them to return to their seats.

He became aware of a commotion on the other side of the box. Several of the women were bent over another in a chair. He made an excuse and rose, crossing to find one of the women fanning Bella with a programme.

'She feels faint,' she explained. 'It's very warm in here. Do you think we should take her outside?'

'I'll be fine, really,' said Bella. 'I just feel a little strange.'

'She was complaining that her limbs were stiff,' said her friend. 'I wondered if—' She got no further, because Bella suddenly jackknifed forward as if every muscle in her body had contracted simultaneously. Everyone jumped back in shock as her arms and legs began to spasm.

'Oh, my God!' Pettigrew was pushing into the knot of horrified onlookers. 'She's having a fit.'

Bryant grabbed the two largest men he could see. 'Hold her down,' he said, snatching up the handset attached to his belt. It was the one piece of equipment he had not managed to lose.

'Put something soft between her teeth that she can bite on,' said Pettigrew. 'Something she can't swallow.' Bryant called for an ambulance and watched Bella's back arching in agony as she thrashed on the floor of the box. The men were fighting to hold her arms and legs, but the power of her involuntarily flexing muscles was kicking off their hands. Someone was hammering on the door behind them.

'Get them to stop banging,' shouted Bryant as one of the women scurried to the door. He had a good idea what had happened, and knew that sudden light or noise would only increase the intensity of her spasms. 'Has anyone got any Valium?' he asked.

'I have,' said several of the women simultaneously, rummaging in their handbags. Bryant had seen a sealed bottle of Highland Spring on the floor of the box. He twisted off the cap, accepted a Valium bottle and shook several capsules into his hand. Bella's face, twisted in an agonised muscular rictus, was beginning to turn blue. 'You're going to have to force her lips apart,' he said. By emptying the entire litre bottle of water into her mouth, they managed to make her swallow several of the pills.

The ambulance men entered the box to find that Bella's convulsions had begun to lessen, but the protuberance of her startled eyes and the frozen grimace of her mouth suggested that her time was running out. As he helped to fasten the stretcher's restraining straps, Bryant caught a brief glimpse of the audience reseating itself below, oblivious of the real-life drama unfolding above their heads.

# CHAPTER

15

'You're late,' said Nicholas. 'Another batch of delegates have already been moved out this morning.'

Jerry stowed her bag beneath the reception desk and took her place. Half a dozen security officers were standing in the reception area awaiting the departure of another Commonwealth dignitary.

'With the amount of security we've got, you'd think they'd feel safer staying here than anywhere else.'

'People remember the bombing of the Grand Hotel in Brighton,' said Nicholas. 'Suppose this whole thing turns out to have a political cause? According to the *Telegraph*, the chap who got his throat cut was some kind of government spy.'

'You shouldn't believe everything you read,' said Jerry.

'I suppose you know better.' Nicholas swept his hair back disapprovingly and turned his attention to the computer billing system. Jerry looked off across the lobby. She was about to answer a guest's enquiry when she saw

Joseph descending the main staircase. He smiled short-sightedly in her direction and headed off towards the breakfast room.

'Be a pal and deal with this gentleman for me, Nicholas.' Jerry slid out of her seat, straightening her shirt. It was now or never. She ran her fingers through her hair, flicking her fringe forward. 'I won't be long.'

'Look here,' complained Nicholas, 'you've only just arrived. Where do you think you're going?'

'I fancy a spot of breakfast.' She knew she could take liberties with him, just so long as he continued to study her breasts from the corner of his eye when he thought she wasn't looking. His recent humiliation at his parents' house was obviously beginning to wear off.

Joseph had seated himself against the tall glass wall overlooking the Embankment, and was staring out at the grey expanse of the rainpocked river. As she approached the table, she coughed to warn him of her arrival. The smile of recognition on his face suggested that he would enjoy her company. He was dressed in black jeans and a black sweater. So far she had seen him in no other colour.

'Mind if I join you?'

'Not at all,' said Joseph, indicating the chair opposite. 'Do you normally take breakfast with your guests?'

'Oh, all the time. It's part of the service.' She seated herself and unfolded a napkin in her lap. 'I'm surprised you're still here. All the Commonwealth delegates are checking out. They're being moved to a high-security residence.'

'Well, two deaths in the same location — it's not exactly an advertisement for healthy living, is it?'

'It's hardly our fault,' said Jerry. 'The security's as strong as ever. They weren't muggings. They were, you know — proper murders.'

'I see. You can be killed in a robbery and that wouldn't be a proper murder, is that it?'

Jerry waited while one of the waiters took their order. 'I mean a murder with a motive,' she explained. 'Malice aforethought, with intent, everything carefully worked out.'

Joseph took a bite of buttered toast and chewed it slowly, regarding his breakfast companion with an indulgent smile. 'You mean like Sherlock Holmes. Red-headed League, Sign of Four, stuff like that.'

'Well — if you like, yes.'

'Forget it, Jerry, it doesn't happen. Death is sordid and simple. I saw it on the telly. People kill to satisfy sexual compulsions or violent urges, or both. They get drunk and rape women, or they bash each other up when they're pissed. QED. There aren't any carefully planned crimes anymore.'

'You're wrong,' she said vehemently. 'Girls go for non-existent job interviews, make appointments with fake estate agents and vanish. Serial killers are on the rise. Murderers are getting cleverer.'

'And you think the Savoy has a clever murderer? You think he could even be staying here?'

'I don't know.' She looked down at her arriving plate, embarrassed. 'Maybe.'

He was smiling again. He wasn't taking her seriously. 'Have you spoken to the police about this theory of yours?'

'Not exactly.' This was going all wrong. She had come to talk to Joseph, to ask him out. Instead, he was questioning her. She needed to take control of the conversation. 'How's your show coming along?' she asked.

'Good,' he replied, pouring tea. 'I began work in the theatre for the first time yesterday. 'It's still pretty much of a mess. The refurbishment is running behind schedule. It's taking longer than anyone expected.'

'Which theatre are you talking about? There are loads being done up.'

'I thought you realised.' He passed her a cup. 'I'm right next door, at the Savoy. It burned down over three years ago. The Japanese are paying for the renovation. They've appointed me as the set designer for their first production. We're opening with a new Gilbert and Sullivan staging, very post-modern and irreverent. Actually, it's not exactly new. It's been touring the country for a while, but the production is getting a facelift for its London debut, and that's where my designs come in. I can get you tickets for the first night if you like.'

Beneath the table she clenched her fists tight. Now or never. 'Perhaps I — could see you before then.'

'Sure. I'm here right through to the opening.'

'I mean, perhaps we could go out one evening.'

Joseph smiled and leaned forward, his voice dropping as he beckoned her. 'It's very nice of you to offer,' he said, 'but just to set things straight between us, you should know that I have a girlfriend.'

Her stomach dropped uncomfortably. Of course he had a girlfriend, how could someone like him be single? She was probably intelligent and beautiful. And sadly, still alive.

'Where is she?' she asked, drawing back slightly.

'She's studying at Oxford, but she's gone home to her parents in Edinburgh for Christmas. Listen, it doesn't stop us from being friends. I'd still like that.'

Her instinctive reaction was to withdraw the offer, but she realised that this would be childish. 'All right,' she agreed reluctantly. 'Friends, then.'

Joseph seemed genuinely pleased. 'Now we've defused

that particular timebomb, perhaps you'd like to tell me more about your murder theory.'

'Sure, you see ...'

He laid a slim finger against his lips. 'When you get off this evening,' he said with a smile.

May had woken to the sound of rain pounding against the bedroom skylight, and one look at the dark turmoil beyond the glass had told him that it was settling in for the day. Yesterday he had taken his overcoat to the dry cleaners. Coffee was called for, but a routine check for messages quickly pushed the thought of breakfast from his mind.

As he ran from his car to the entrance of Gower Street's University College Hospital, the shoulders of his jacket became soaked. At 6.05 a.m. on Wednesday morning the hospital foyer was populated only by an elderly floor polisher. A word with the duty nurse sent him along the corridor to the overnight admissions rooms.

Here he found Bryant bundled up on a green leather bench, asleep. He had sunk down into his voluminous coat like a tortoise vanishing into its shell for the winter. May's shoes squeaked on the polished linoleum as he approached, and Bryant's bald head slowly emerged at the sound.

'What happened, Arthur?' asked May. 'Why on earth didn't you let them page me?'

'There was nothing you could have done to help,' said the detective wearily. 'There were quite enough people here. You would only have been in the way.'

May looked toward the closed door. 'How is she?'

'She died at three o'clock this morning. Due to the unusual nature of the death I asked the doctor if she would put down her findings in some kind of off-record preliminary report. Marsden's going to go crazy when he finds out what happened and I need all the information I can get.'

May sat down beside his old friend. Bryant looked done in. 'What did happen?' he asked.

'She suffered some kind of seizure. Violent convulsions, uncontrollable muscle contractions consistent with poisoning. It was terrible to watch.' He looked along the deserted corridor, listened to the distant clatter of the awakening hospital. 'She seemed like a good woman,' he said sadly. 'What on earth is happening out there?'

The administering doctor was about to go off duty, and stopped by to see them. 'I wouldn't want these notes to be used as a basis for any kind of evidential document, Arthur,' she explained, holding the file against her bosom, 'but you'd better have it.' Bryant imagined that the last thing she had wanted to do after a long shift was fill in paperwork as a favour to the police, but the young Irishwoman had helped him a number of times in the past, and always did so without complaint.

'It's very kind of you, Betty. I'll leave you something in my will.'

'You'd better leave your friend your overcoat,' said Betty, glancing at May. 'He's going to catch his death dressed like that.'

As they walked back along the corridors, Bryant thumbed through the neat handwritten pages. 'At first they thought it was tetanus, but it looks like strychnine poisoning,' he said. 'I thought it would have to be. She died of asphyxiation and exhaustion. There's only so long the body can stave off a total attack on the central nervous system before it gives in. The reaction time of the poison is normally ten to twenty minutes, but it was slowed down because she'd eaten earlier, and because I was able to administer valium to reduce the spasms.'

He checked a page of detailed operational procedures. 'There was no point in pumping her stomach because the symptoms had already begun. Instead they intravenously administered succinylcholine to slow down the convulsions and take the strain off her heart. I suppose it didn't work.' He closed the folder.

'What did she eat?' asked May. 'Did you see?'

'It can't have been anything from the restaurant. She only ate from the salad bar. And she sat through the whole of the first act without showing any symptoms. She was just a few feet away from me.'

'Did she eat anything during the performance? Chocolates?'

'No. There was champagne, both before and during the intermission.'

'Did you see any of it being opened?'

'There were quite a few bottles, but as far as I know they were all sealed. I kept an eye on the one Bella drank from. She uncorked it herself and we all had a glass. John, we need to get everyone back to the box and recreate this thing while it's still fresh in their minds. And I want the press kept out, although I suppose they'll catch wind of it soon enough.'

They ran through the rain to the waiting car.

Chief Acting Superintendent Stanley Marsden was not a man who enjoyed life, and today he was enjoying it even less than usual. His narrow shoulders rose and fell as he fidgeted with frustration behind his empty desk. His hand frequently rose to pat the wispy grey hair combed in thin bands across his head. He did not want to be here, at all, but if he had to be here, he wanted his stay to be a quiet one. The new unit was not for him. It was too experimental, too innovative, not regulated by the rulebook enough for his taste. Providing the work paid off, Detective Chief Inspector Ian Hargreave would arrive to handle overall responsibility for the division in three months' time. Until then, there were no other inspectors in the area with sufficient experience for the job.

Marsden did not look up when Arthur Bryant entered the room. Instead, his restless grey eyes regarded the waterlogged world beyond the window.

'I know that you and your partner have evolved your own methods of working,' he began, attempting to keep his voice at a calm and even level, 'but we have an exceptional investigation on our hands.' He stood up suddenly, aiming for maximum effect. 'Four people, Bryant!' he exploded. 'This latest death somehow managed to make the late morning editions. The press are having a bloody field day. The *Sun* is running a "Solve It Yourself, Win A Mini Metro" competition. I don't think you need me to tell you that we've never seen anything like this before.' He stood by the window with his index fingers pressed into the bridge of his nose. 'We live in a fractured time. People are uprooted, unemployed.' He hiked a thumb at the window. 'They're losing their wives, their families, their jobs and their homes at an unprecedented rate. And the reasons for murder are becoming as convoluted as the times.'

Bryant was well aware of this. Indeed, he had attended Marsden's recent lecture on the subject at Hendon Police College.

'Numerically speaking, we're catching fewer murderers. You know as well as I do that a murder file can only stay open while we receive help from the public. We can't be expected to search for eternity. And we're marking more and more homicides unsolved. Now we have three members of the same family dead in eight days, and so far no forensic indications, no decent witnesses, no outside information. These aren't random acts of violence, for God's sake. Someone is playing a deliberate, arrogant game with us. What I want to know is, how can so much happen with so little result from this department?'

'Our problem lies in the evidence,' explained Bryant, 'or rather the extraordinary lack of it. It's as if there was a team of people cleaning up after each act of violence, removing everything that might be turned to our use. Then there's the problem of motive.'

'What about this German business the *Mail*'s been talking about, tying the deaths to the Commonwealth conference?'

'The design of the Whitstables' sacred flame is admittedly similar to the wartime assassination symbol, but I'm positive it's just a coincidence. There are no other corroborating factors.'

'You're positive, are you?' How did you manage to protect Bella Whitstable so well that she died while she was in your care?'

'As we have yet to discover how she died, I consider that an unfair remark,' replied Bryant, stung. 'And I'd like to point out that in a murder investigation of this sort I would normally have expected as many as sixty men to be drafted on to the case. May and I are working with barely half a dozen staff. It's essential that we talk to the surviving partner at Jacob & Marks, but because their office is in Norwich neither of us have had time to go there yet.'

'I know,' said Marsden angrily, 'and at the moment there's not a damned thing I can do about it. It's this place you've built for yourselves. Until it's fully operational, how do you expect anything to be organised? There seems to be no order of seniority here ...'

'That was intentional.'

'And assuming your information is fully collated, which I doubt, there's nothing you can do with it because your computer system isn't set up to HOLMES yet.' HOLMES was the Home Office Major Enquiry System designed to cross-reference every piece of information received by the police. (Someone had added an L for Large for the sake of a more appropriate acronym.) HOLMES was capable of transmitting the files of all those suspects conforming to the statistics provided.

'We have many lines of enquiry that need to be followed,' said Bryant wearily. 'What we need is greater manpower.'

'I'll see what I can do,' said Marsden, picking up a folder and removing its contents. 'But I don't need to tell you that there's a lot of resentment about this unit. Extra staff are simply not being made available to us. Quite a few people think you're being élitist, that the old system isn't good enough for you anymore. They're waiting for you to hang yourselves. But unless I receive positive proof that someone is physically trying to hinder the investigation, there's nothing I can do.'

As much as he didn't care for the superintendent, Bryant knew that he was a reasonable man, and at the moment represented their only path to increased resources. It was important to have him on their side. 'At least I've had a chance to go over your report,' said Marsden, brandishing a sheaf of paper. Bryant was pleased that he had found the time to do so; he'd been up most of the previous weekend assembling it.

'Before you go through it, I need to explain something to you,' said Bryant, seating himself opposite the superintendent. 'It's something I haven't put in that document. Little more than a feeling, really. I think we're looking for

something extremely unusual, more than just a clever
murderer. The timing of the deaths seems odd to me. This
is someone who knows the value of political embarrassment, a real-life Moriarty. He has a working method but
it's complex, and we have to understand it before we can
proceed. His approach is highly theatrical, as if he's killing
for attention. It's controlled — and yet it feels as if
anything could happen. Tell me, do you believe there is
evil in the world?'

'Yes, of course. I've seen enough of it.'

'Then you believe, as I do, that there are truly evil men.
I know it sounds vague and unprofessional but I think
we're looking for something very, very evil. The standard
investigation procedures cannot apply here. It's quite
unprecedented in my experience.' He imagined that even
Marsden would be surprised to hear him admit that.
Almost everyone was aware of the breadth of Bryant's field
knowledge.

'Do you have any information on the woman's cause of
death yet?'

'I'm afraid not.'

Marsden was clearly dissatisfied with his own powerless
role in the proceedings. He stood at the window picking a
flake of paint from the peeling ledge. 'I want our backs
covered with this one,' he said carefully. 'There are
rumours that the Australian delegates to the Commonwealth talks have been sent death threats. It's already been
confirmed that their arts minister, Carreras, has deliberately scheduled another press conference complaining
about the lack of security he's experienced in order to
embarrass our government into official action.'

'We haven't established a positive connection between—'

'Did you know that, until this morning at least, the
minister was staying at the Savoy?'

'Yes, I was aware of that.'

'Were you also aware that he was attending the theatre last night?'

Bryant felt a crawling sensation in the pit of his stomach. 'At the Coliseum?'

'The very same. Box L.'

The box exactly facing the one in which Bella Whitstable was taken ill. Anger rose within him. There was a grotesque pattern emerging here. Why could he not see it?

'We'll step up our enquiries,' he promised. He knew that it would now be necessary to call a damage-limitation press conference. He would schedule it for late this afternoon. But first, there was a murder to reconstruct.

On his way out of the office, he walked into Jerry Gates. She had come up to the Mornington Crescent unit in her lunch break, and was still wearing her hotel uniform. It was luck rather than judgement that had set her on collision course with the detective. She had been searching the building for him.

'What are you doing here?' He frowned at her in displeasure.

'You said you might need to talk to me again.'

'I said I'd call you when I was ready. How did you get in?'

'Sergeant Crosse admitted me. I wanted to be of help, and I thought if you'd just listen to me for a minute—' She hadn't meant to ask like this, but now she found it impossible to stop herself.

'Miss Gates, neither I nor my partner has a moment to spare right now.' He stopped and turned to face her. 'We really haven't. You've probably heard that there's been another one.'

'Oh my God, another murder?'

'So you can see that I don't have time to waste. Please, go back to work and leave it to us to take the appropriate steps.'

He strode off along the corridor, leaving her behind. Fine. She'd beat him at his own game. The police obviously weren't making any progress. She would do better on her own. And if anything bad happened, they'd only have themselves to blame for not listening to her.

They met in the foyer of the Coliseum with their outfits bundled into carrier bags, a forlorn, dripping crowd in suits and raincoats, like a party of tourists gathered for a particularly unrewarding walking tour. Bereft of their finery they seemed smaller and less significant. They awkwardly offered their condolences to Bryant as if attending the wake before the funeral.

'I'm afraid I must ask you all to come back to the box, and it will be necessary for you to don your outfits once more. It seems morbid, I know, but it's necessary to recreate the exact circumstances under which Bella Whitstable died. It may help us to catch her killer.'

Below them, rehearsals continued as the Savoyards struggled back into armour and hose. Bryant stood patiently at the rear of the box with a smirking police photographer while the group dressed. Then he directed them back into their places, marking the seat in which Bella collapsed.

'All right,' he said, raising his hands for silence. 'How many members do we have here?'

'There are twenty-two of us,' said Oliver Pettigrew. 'There are more in the society, but we vary in number according to each production. Principal cast members can't be duplicated, and the main cast of *Ida* is fifteen.'

'So what does that make the rest of you?'

'Courtiers, Soldiers and Daughters of the Plough.'

'I want everyone to take the positions they held last night at the time when it was first noticed that Mrs Whitstable was feeling unwell,' Bryant requested. There followed much shuffling and pulling free of snagged cloaks.

'Wait,' said Bryant, 'there's somebody missing.' The Savoyards looked at one another, then back at the elderly detective. 'There was a little beggar in a hat standing against the wall.'

'Are you sure?' asked Pettigrew. 'There aren't any beggars listed in the cast of *Ida*.'

'I distinctly remember seeing him there,' said Bryant, walking to the spot. 'A tattered man. I didn't get to see him close up, but surely someone else must have noticed him.' He searched the surrounding faces, positive that the assassin had been discovered, but the Savoyards rubbed their chins and shook their heads. He looked back at the empty chair where Bella had collapsed, and the spot beside it where she had stood down her handbag. What could the beggar have done to cause her death? An absurd idea began to form in his head.

As he moved toward the door of the box he turned back to the assembled group, who were still watching him and waiting for guidance.

'Thank you for coming,' he told the semi-circle of baffled faces. 'Please check that the constable here has your personal details written down correctly, and we'll get back to you if there are any further developments.'

And with that he hastily left the theatre.

'They found no trace of strychnine in the champagne?'

'None whatsoever,' said Raymond Land. 'What's on your mind?' Bryant had blasted into his office like a rainy night and was proceeding to soak everything with his umbrella and overcoat.

'I was thinking about strychnine,' he explained. 'It's a fairly fast-acting poison, so it had to have been administered within the theatre box. It seemed to me that the murderer was making things unnaturally difficult for himself. Why pick a drug with such a startling effect, and risk capture by still being on the premises when she began to convulse?'

He dumped a large opaque plastic bag on Land's desk. 'You'd have to be very sure of your method of administration, wouldn't you?'

He carefully opened the ziplocked evidence envelope and withdrew Bella Whitstable's handbag, still covered in fingerprint dust. 'When I saw her initial symptoms, severe facial grimacing,' he continued, 'I knew that something was paralysing her muscles. Strychnine poisoning always starts in the face and neck.' He fished about in the bag and withdrew an object in a bony fist. 'How does it look if you were buying it in the form of, say, rat poison?'

'It's a powder,' said Land. 'Crystalline and colourless.'

'And it can kill on contact with the skin or the eyes.' He opened his hand to reveal a powder compact. 'She applied it herself when she freshened her makeup in the intermission. It was a simple matter for our tattered man to dip into her bag and doctor the compact while we were watching the first act.'

Land took the compact from Bryant's outstretched hand and carefully opened it. Beneath the face pad lay a pool of granules which appeared slightly more crystalline than the fine pink powder below it. 'Well, I'll be damned,' he said, amazed. 'Someone's been reading Agatha bloody Christie.' He looked up at Bryant. 'Who did you mean when you mentioned a tattered man?'

'That's what I'd like to know,' said Bryant.

# CHAPTER

Joseph shone the torch across a paint-streaked brick wall, then up into a network of distant blackened rafters. 'Come on. It's quite safe.'

'I have a problem with the dark,' she said, peering ahead. 'It's a stupid phobia. If there's a light somewhere I'm okay.'

'There's a junction box here that controls the lights, such as they are.' The torch beam picked up a grey steel cabinet with electrical warning stickers pasted to the doors. 'All the structural repair work has been completed, but I'm still not supposed to bring anyone else in here. If you fall through the floor you're not covered by the insurance.'

They had entered the site of the Savoy Theatre through the wooden surround that encased the red brick and portland stone of the building's ground floor. Joseph wrenched open a door of the cabinet and flicked a row of switches. A handful of dim emergency bulbs threw amber pools of light across the auditorium. She tried to relax her breathing, not daring to think about the surrounding darkness.

Part of the interior of the theatre was still blackened and fire-ravaged, but the proscenium arch and the stage beyond it had been fully restored, and waited under sheets of heavy plastic to be unveiled once more before an audience.

'You wouldn't think we were just two weeks away from opening, would you?' he said. 'It doesn't look as if the paintwork's going to be dry by the time they admit the paying public. Theatres and restaurants — I've worked in both and they always leave things to the last minute.'

Many of the surrounding seats had been newly installed, and were wrapped in plastic. As Jerry followed him down the side aisle, she could hear distant rain falling on glass far above them.

'Richard D'Oyly Carte was a very modern man,' he called back. 'His theatre was designed for all-round visibility, no matter what you'd paid for your ticket. He abolished tipping the attendants and gave them decent wages instead.' He turned before the scaffolded stage and opened out his arms. 'Best of all,' he explained, 'there was the incredible decor. Carte ditched all the dingy dark walls and heavy velvets favoured by the Victorians. This whole place was a blaze of yellow satin, white and gold paintwork. The seats were bright blue and the boxes were red. And the vestibule floor was paved in black and white marble. It was a monument to light, luxury and elegance. You know, the mediaeval palace of the Princes of Savoy used to stand on this site. I think Carte was trying to recapture that spirit.' He pulled himself up on the stage and beckoned for her to join him. She wanted to simply sit and talk, but the lack of light unsettled her and she was nervous about saying something stupid. His knowledge and energy made her feel dull.

He rose and dusted down his jeans. 'The Tasaka Corporation are paying for most of the restoration,' he explained, walking to the rear of the stage. 'They'll also help to decide management policy.'

'It doesn't look like you're even half-ready to open,' she said, clambering up on to the front of the stage. If he had managed to climb up without using the steps, so would she.

'But we will be open, just after Christmas. It will be a Japanese-British co-production, and they'll have touring rights for the East. Mr Miyagawa is hoping that the Savoy will become a forum for world theatre. I still can't believe he wants me to design his first new set.'

Jerry watched as he strode back and forth across the stage, a tall figure dressed in black with a knotted mess of bouncing straw hair. She wanted to run up and press her fingers over his heart, to feel the life pulsing inside him.

Somewhere in the rear of the shadowy auditorium there was a soft sound, like a roll of rope uncoiling. Jerry paused on the stair and listened. The slithering was lost in the renewed drumming of the rain on the roof. Ahead, metal drums and tangles of wiring blocked the way.

'Where are you?' she called. 'Be careful you don't fall over.'

'It's okay,' he replied, his voice muffled by the charred curtain that still hung at one side of the proscenium arch. 'I already know my way around pretty well.'

The sound which reached her ears this time was much nearer. A metallic rasping, as if steel cables were being dropped on one another.

'Joseph,' she called, 'are we the only people in here?'

There was no reply. The hanging lights strung across

the stage flickered momentarily, causing shadows to jigsaw between the pipework and the walls.

'Joseph?' she squeezed through the gap between a pair of steel stanchions and walked deeper into the stage area. The wings were dark with equipment and debris. Above, boards creaked as if a weight had been gently laid across them. She glanced up, but could see nothing. The lighting rigs had mostly been removed. Surely he wouldn't just have left her here? She walked slowly toward the orchestra pit, moving between deep pools of light. The chill air pricked at the flesh on her arms, like ghosts of the theatre passing by. It felt as if someone was watching her. She smiled at the thought; after all, she was standing on a stage.

There was a ping of metal, and a small steel bolt bounced on the floorboards beside her. She looked into the wing and up at a gantry still half-covered in dust-sheets. She sensed the figure before seeing it. A small man, dressed in the manner of a stage character, wrapped in the tattered rags of a Victorian footpad, was crouched in the gantry like a motionless brown insect, staring silently down at her.

Jerry's most irrational impulse took over, and she cried out in fright as the figure suddenly jumped to its feet and kicked away from the wall. With a creak and a groan the gantry began moving toward her. Several planks cascaded to the floor in a series of timed explosions. As she turned to run, she knew that the steel stack had been shoved free of its moorings, and was about to land on top of her. Ahead lay the orchestra pit, its depth impossible to calculate, its floor lost in shadow.

As the gantry crashed down above her head she jumped out into the darkness, praying that there was nothing sharp below.

The pit was shallower than she had realised. As she hit the ground hard, the gantry slammed flat on the floor of the stage and broke into clanging steel sections with an impact that rang in her ears. Above her lay a twisted network of galvanised pipes. One of the fallen emergency lights was shining across her eyes. She raised herself on a bruised elbow as the tattered figure scampered on to the scaffolding and peered down at her.

Jerry rolled to one side and thrust herself through the gap at the side of the pit, scrambling back into the aisle as the figure, shocked to see that she had survived, darted ahead and through the door marked with an emergency exit symbol.

She gave chase and found herself in a red-painted passageway leading out to the rear of the theatre. The bar of the external door slammed up with a hard echo, and she turned the corner to find it swinging shut on her. Seizing and kicking it wide, she ran out into the downpour and caught sight of the ragged figure lurching away toward the Thames.

The rain-slick street impeded her progress as she slid on to the Embankment just yards behind the tattered man. She could hear her attacker wheezing as he tried to stay ahead. They crossed the road to the river, where aureoles of light sparkled around the illuminated globes lining the embankment, marking the path to the sea.

The walkway in front of her was deserted. There was nowhere for the fleeing beggar to escape or hide. Rain flicked rhythmically from his rags as he loped ahead, his head concealed beneath a dirty brown hat, his body twisting dementedly to one side. His hands flapped back and forth, as if they were broken at the wrists.

For a moment Jerry was reminded of the dream. The

enclosing brick walls were absent, but the tattered man was just as deformed as her nightmare creatures. The image was far too close for comfort, and her pace momentarily faltered. What the hell was happening to her?

A crippling stitch in her side caused her to drop further back in her pursuit. The beggar veered out into the roadway and darted through the traffic to the far side, nimbly vaulting the fence into the park. Jerry doubled over in pain, her breath coming in hot gasps. There was no point in going on. She couldn't believe that she had been outrun by what appeared to be a tramp. Pulling her shirt-tails above her belt, she examined her stomach and found the cause of the trouble. A long red welt was already darkening across the lower part of her ribcage. She had landed badly in the orchestra pit.

Suddenly fearful for Joseph's safety, she reversed her direction and made a painful journey back to the theatre. She arrived to find him waiting outside for her. He was covered in dirt and dust.

'What happened to you?' she asked, slapping his shoulder angrily. 'Why didn't you answer me when I called?'

'I couldn't. Someone shoved me into one of the bloody property cupboards.'

'What do you mean? Who?'

'How the hell should I know? I just felt his hands in the small of my back. The next thing I knew, I was in complete darkness.'

'You're big enough to take care of yourself. Why didn't you do anything?'

'I was caught by surprise, that's all.'

'Then why didn't you call out?'

'I did, but the damned thing was filled with dustsheets. I nearly choked to death. There was an enormous bang, clanging metal, God knows what. I managed to get the door open, but I couldn't find you anywhere. He'd turned all the lights off.'

'Then there must have been two of them. There was someone on the scaffolding. He tried to kill me.'

'Oh, come on . . .'

'You didn't see him, but I did. He tipped the gantry over, nearly squashed me flat.'

'It couldn't have been intentional, surely.' Joseph looked back at the silent theatre, wiping corkscrews of hair from his eyes. 'What did he look like?'

'A tramp, I guess. No, more like an actor in a play, someone's idea of what a tramp should look like.'

'That's it, then,' said Joseph. He brushed at his sweater, but only succeeded in matting the dust into wet wool. 'We just disturbed a couple of tramps, probably scared the hell out of them.'

'This was no ordinary dosser, Joseph.'

'There are lots of homeless people in the Strand looking for somewhere to sleep. Maybe they managed to break into the theatre.'

'Why is it no one ever listens to me?' she asked, looking up at the sky. 'This was deliberate. He pushed the gantry over intentionally. And there was more than one — you were locked up to keep you out of the way.'

Joseph folded his wet arms and studied her. 'Listen to yourself, you're saying that someone tried to murder you.'

'Why not?' Jerry shouted. 'They're dropping like flies around this place, or did you forget? I'm a witness to two violent deaths. Outside of a few prison warders I'm probably unique in the whole of the British Isles.'

'If you were a real witness you'd have seen who did it,' said Joseph calmly. 'And you didn't, did you?'

'That's not the point. If other people can be attacked,

why not me? The management's called a security meeting for all hotel staff. They think we're in danger. Maybe someone deliberately followed me into the theatre.'

'It's preposterous, Jerry.' He began to make his way back toward the polished steel facade of the Savoy. 'You're a hotel clerk, you're not selling Commonwealth secrets to the Soviet Union. Why would someone pick on you?'

She felt a knot of rage hardening in her stomach. It was the familiar anger of not being taken seriously, of being dismissed as insignificant, the feeling that had dogged her ever since she was a child.

'Why wouldn't they?' she cried. 'What's so different about me?'

'You make it sound like you want to be part of it, like you've got some kind of victim complex.'

'I just want—'

He turned to go. 'Jerry, I've a really big day tomorrow, and I have to get some sleep. This is completely fucking nuts. Can we talk about it some other time?'

'Well, I'm pleased that you've got such a wonderful career ahead of you,' she shouted pointlessly, desperately. 'I'm glad everything's so damned perfect in your life. You're not the only one who's going to do great things, Mr Ego. You'd be amazed at what I could do.'

'Probably,' he called wearily, 'I don't know. I don't want to know. It's been a weird evening and I'm going to bed. Goodnight, Jerry. Get some rest.'

She kicked out against the wooden casement surrounding the theatre, kicking again and again until stinging tears of fury were forced from her eyes. Above the darkened theatre, the rain descended on the city in stippled, glittering sheets.

# CHAPTER

The offices of Jacob & Marks smelled of age and affluence. John May, newly arrived in Norwich on a windy, ragged Thursday morning, found himself surrounded by the burnished parquet and marquetry of fine old wood, and smart young employees who hurried past sporting fashionably conservative suits. Legal firms of this calibre dealt only with large companies and old families. Shopkeepers, he had no doubt, were encouraged to go elsewhere.

May had been kept waiting in the law office for half an hour, and as the train's buffet car had been inexplicably missing, he had so far made up for his lack of breakfast by consuming two cups of tea and a plate of biscuits.

Outside the sky was raw and bright, the colour of a summer sea, and leaf-churning breezes sucked at the windows, rattling the panes. May told himself he should make the effort to get out of London more often. He had forgotten the glorious gentility of the English countryside. Even in December the low hills and bare trees appeared to offer a welcome, yielding their verdant contours to the lowering winter sky.

But for the detective there was little call to visit the country. Most of May's family were dead, and the few friends with whom he bothered to keep in touch were citybound, so there was no real call to travel further. He took the odd trip to the south coast to visit his sister, but this pleasure was mitigated by the fact that she had three outrageously spoiled children to whom Uncle John represented a combination cashpoint and climbing frame.

Bryant, of course, reacted to the idea of visiting any area beyond the M25 with a kind of theatrical horror. Whenever May suggested visiting the countryside, his partner would convulse in a series of Kabuki-style grimaces meant to convey revulsion at the thought of so much fresh air and so many trees. The farthest he ever travelled these days was Battersea Park, and as his apartment overlooked this it could hardly be counted as an excursion. Bryant had been happy to leave this particular visit to his partner.

At 10.05 a.m., Leo Marks blew through the doors exhaling apologies, ushering May into his office while simultaneously firing off complex instructions to a pair of tough-looking secretaries.

The detective had expected to meet a much older man. Marks appeared to be in his late twenties, although his excessive weight and dour dress had added age to his appearance. Seated opposite him, May found himself disconcerted by the fact that the grey pupils of the young lawyer's eyes turned slightly outwards, so that it was hard to tell if he was looking directly ahead. After asking his secretaries to redirect his calls, he adopted a look of professional grief and turned his full attention to the visiting detective.

'We were terribly upset to hear of Max's death,' he

began in measured tone. 'It's been awfully hard on Anne—'

'His wife.'

'You probably know their children no longer live at home. Anne spent all her time with Max. All this speculation in the papers has been having a terrible effect on her. There was talk of a snake attacking him—'

'Somebody injected Max Jacob with a lethal amount of poison, a rare venom. We found a needle bearing traces of the substance in the corridor beyond the washroom.'

'Someone should have told us, Mr May.'

'I'm afraid it's only just turned up. It had been trodden into the carpet and missed the earlier searches. Am I right in thinking that Max and your father were partners?'

'Actually, it was my great-grandfather who set up the firm with Max's grandfather.'

'So your families have been close for a very long time.'

'We still are. There are loyalties here which go back well over a hundred years.'

'Does your father still work here?'

'Only part-time since his heart attack, although he hasn't come in at all since Max died. It's been a terrible blow for him. The worst thing is not knowing.'

'Not knowing who killed him, or not knowing what he was doing in London?'

Leo Marks swivelled a look directly at May. 'I think I can tell you why he was visiting the city,' he said. May sat forward, waiting. 'He had arranged to see Peter Whitstable.'

'Why would he do that?' asked May. 'Peter's sister told me that all financial arrangements were conducted through William. And surely Max would have informed his wife where he was going.'

'Well, it wouldn't necessarily have been official business.

They were old friends, you see. They were all at Oxford together.'

'Was Max Jacob in the habit of taking off for London to visit the brothers without telling anyone?'

'Not really, but he had mentioned the idea of making the journey.'

'When was this exactly?'

Leo turned back the pages of his diary and checked the dates. 'The previous Thursday,' he said. 'That would have been on 2 December. He spoke to Peter several times during the course of that week. The brothers were arguing over something — they always were — but this time I understand it was rather more serious.'

'You have no idea what they argued about?'

'No. But it wasn't over money, I can tell you that.'

'Why wasn't it?'

'Their finances are tied up from here. We acted as their stipendiaries, allowing each a set annual amount, the revenue from certain investments and so on. They were quite happy with the arrangement.'

'Who stands to benefit financially from their deaths?'

'No one, immediately. You have to understand that the Whitstable financial empire is so absurdly complex that half of the family beneficiaries won't see a penny for years to come.'

Thanks to the lawyers who set up the system in the first place, thought May. 'What about Max Jacob?'

'That's straightforward enough. His will appoints Anne as his trustee.'

May checked through the notes on his pocket computer, marking off the queries to which he had received answers. He felt as if his questions were leading him around in a circle. 'I'll be honest with you, Mr Marks ...'

'Please, call me Leo.'

'The more I find out about the Whitstables, the less I understand them. The brothers were financially comfortable, established, settled in the most old-fashioned ways. I'm informed that they did nothing more adventurous in their dotage than read the *Daily Telegraph* and listen to the radio. They bothered no one. They were not powerful men. If they had once wielded influence in the City, they certainly did so no longer.' May closed the computer and slipped it back in his pocket. 'Then,' he said, 'one day, for no apparent reason, William commits an act of vandalism and is subsequently exploded, while Peter gets a open razor pushed down his throat. Concurrent with the first act, their family lawyer is injected with the venom of a watersnake, and now their sister is paralysed with strychnine. Bombs and knives and poison. It's all rather Grand Guignol, don't you think?' He leaned forward, carefully watching the young lawyer.

'I must ask the obvious question, Mr Marks. What on earth were these people hiding? They weren't random victims; their deaths were carefully arranged, and must therefore serve a purpose. The killer can't have been looking for some physical object. He's shown no desire to search their homes. I have to conclude that the goal is knowledge of some kind, knowledge that was also intimated to your father's partner. Something so important and so secret that Max Jacob went down to London without even telling his wife where he was going.'

'I see your problem,' said Leo, who didn't look as if he could see much at all. 'Could someone be trying to humiliate them by associating the family with scandal?'

There must be an easier way of humiliating people than blowing them all over the Northern Line, thought May, and sensibly kept the thought to himself.

'Tell me more about the Whitstables.'

Leo thought for a moment, massaging his florid jowls with the tips of his fingers. 'They trace themselves back to the founding members of one of London's craft guilds, as I'm sure you know.'

'The Goldsmiths, isn't it?'

'Actually, no, the Watchmakers in Blackfriar's Lane, although I believe there are strong affiliations with the Goldsmiths. There are still many such companies in existence, the Cordwainers, the Coopers, the Haber-dashers and so on, many of which have their own boards, schools, trusts and benevolent funds scattered throughout the capital. Inevitably, there are strong masonic ties. Peter and William were both masons. So was Max.'

'Is that common? Are there other masons in the family?'

'Quite a few, I believe. The Whitstables made and lost fortunes through the decades, but I understand that the bulk of their present income derives from alliances forged in Victorian times ...'

May shifted in his chair. His hopes of returning by a mid-morning train were fast disappearing. 'I need to know much more about the family itself,' he explained. 'Their businesses are presumably still active. Surely there are some younger members around?'

'A few perhaps, but like so many old dynasties, the Whitstables are dying out. There was an unhealthy amount of intermarriage in earlier centuries, but I imagine the partial breakdown of the class system did the most damage. We do have a rather incomplete family tree for them, and some of their current addresses. I could let you have a photocopy.'

'That would be a great help.'

'You'll have your work cut out if you're planning to contact them all. Their last big population boom was a hundred years ago. Most of the grandchildren have long since married, divorced or departed the country.'

'I still need to speak to as many of them as I can,' said May. With three members of the same family dead there was no telling how many other lives were in danger.

'I understand.' Leo rose and summoned one of his sturdy young secretaries. 'There was one other thing.' He pushed a red leather appointment book across his desk and turned it around. 'On the day Max went down to London there were no engagements marked in his diary, but there was this.' He tapped his finger at the top of the page, where a number had been written. '216. Does it help in any way?'

'Not that I can think of,' said May, who had already noted the doodle which encased the number. A burning flame, drawn in the exact style of Peter Whitstable's tattoo.


'I never said they deserved to die,' exclaimed Arthur Bryant indignantly. 'How dare you put such words into my mouth.'

'You more or less suggested as much,' said May, unrolling the Whitstable family tree and pinning it to the noticeboard beside his desk. Back in London the winter sky was the colour of gutterwater, the clouds marshalling themselves around the damp buildings in preparation for another stormy assault.

'I merely said that I disapproved of the way the Whitstables made their money. The British upper crust exploited their colonies and destroyed their workers to preserve a status quo not worth clinging to. They deserve everything they get.'

'Including murder? I might remind you of your humanitarian oath at this point.' As he spoke, the two workmen who had entered the already overcrowded room a few minutes ago began to fire up an ancient blowlamp.

'What the hell are they doing?' May shouted above the din.

'I'm having the room returned to its original colours,' said Bryant brightly. 'You saw the paint on the sill.'

'Do they have to do it right now?'

'If we don't do it now, squire, we won't be able to start until after Christmas,' said one of the workmen, shifting a crate to reach the window.

'We need to make contact with all the surviving relatives listed on the chart,' said May, attempting to concentrate on the business at hand. 'I want every available staff member on this.'

'I've requested a source list for the strychnine,' said Bryant. 'According to Land, the granular fineness is very unusual. That's not the way it's usually made commercially available.'

'Good. Christina has found a two-man team to check out the visiting members of the Australian Art Commission, and I'm afraid we need to make another appointment with Mr Faraday. It's essential to pinpoint a connection between the deaths and the destruction of the painting.'

Bryant walked over to the unfurled family tree and began to study it. 'Why did Max Jacob come here?' he wondered aloud. 'What did Peter Whitstable tell him that was so important he had to drop everything and come to London?' He scraped thoughtfully at his chin. 'There's some terrible principle at work, John. I can feel it. Everything's out of alignment. There's the cause and effect of each murder to consider.'

'What do you mean?'

'Well, you can usually see who a murder affects the most. But these crimes are free of motive, and more important, they have no real effect. They don't change anything. They're deaths with no sense and no suspects. I ask myself, how does Jacob's murder benefit anyone? How on earth does Bella's? Unnatural death is usually linked to sex and money. Why not in these cases? Take a look at this.' He tapped a name on the family tree. 'Bella Whitstable never married. She's the end of the line.'

'How many remaining family members are still living in this country?'

'There are certainly more than fifteen, possibly as many as thirty. Peter Whitstable had a wife who divorced him in the late sixties, so she's not represented on the tree. There are two sons from the marriage, but they live abroad. There's also a Charles Whitstable living somewhere overseas. The rest are up here.'

'If Jacob looked after the fortunes of the whole family, it shouldn't be hard finding a motive for his death.'

'*Cherchez la femme,*' said one of the workmen, wiping his hands on his blue overalls and relighting the blowlamp. 'You can bet there's always a woman involved.'

'Thank you very much,' said Bryant icily. 'If we need your help, we'll ask for it.'

'I reckon you could do with a hand, judging by what the papers are saying about you lot,' said the other workman.

'Perhaps you'd like to handle the investigation while we do the window frames.' Bryant turned to face the door, where Jerry waited awkwardly. The girl had wet shoulders and a pale, anxious face. Right now she looked much younger than her seventeen years. 'Jesus, will you stop appearing like that?' he cried. 'You nearly gave me a heart attack.'

'Well, come in then,' cried May, exasperated. He gestured to the chair behind his desk. 'You might as well ask whoever else is outside to join us. We could probably get the Dagenham Girl Pipers in here as well.'

'I brought you some evidence,' said Jerry, embarrassed to be speaking in front of the workmen, who had stopped tackling the paintwork and were watching the proceedings with satisfaction.

'What sort of evidence?' asked May.

Jerry withdrew the bible from her jacket and set it on the desk.

May carefully opened the book and studied the flyleaf. 'Where did you get this?'

'I found it in Mr Jacob's room. The police missed it.'

'Why do you think it's of any interest to us?' asked Bryant.

Jerry looked momentarily nonplussed. 'There are some passages underlined,' she said. 'They might meant something.'

'You mean you've been withholding evidence?'

'No,' she said indignantly, 'I was looking in the room and—'

'Suppose his murderer had been looking for this?' said Bryant. 'You could have put your own life in danger. Did you stop to think of that?'

'No,' said Jerry softly, bowing her face. Suddenly Bryant saw how much of a toll her recent experiences had taken. She had knotted her pale hands over each other to keep them still. Death could have extraordinary unseen effects on the living. He wondered about the nature of the discovery it had brought to her.

'She keeps turning up like some kind of awful wraith,' said Bryant as the squad car turned into another waterlogged avenue lined with sycamores. 'You can tell she has some kind of morbid fascination with the case. I know she's witnessed two fatalities, but she's starting to give me the creeps. I wish she'd smile occasionally.'

'You can't blame her for wanting to be part of the investigation,' replied May. 'The hand of death has given her a good old shaking.'

'It can't hurt, can it? You taking her around with you?'

'I wouldn't have thought so. She's bright enough, and I can do with the help.'

May steered the car over to the kerb, braked to a halt and killed the engine. The sound of rain continued to drum above their heads, an ever-present backbeat to their conversation.

'If you need anything, you can call me on this number.' He handed his partner a slip of paper. Bryant reluctantly accepted the note and made a show of pocketing it as May watched him with suspicion.

'You haven't got it, have you?' he said finally.

Bryant gave him a wide-eyed innocent look, saw that it wasn't going to work and gave in. 'Er, no,' he admitted.

'What is the point of me providing you with a portable phone if you don't remember to bring it with you?' he asked.

'I put it in my jacket this morning,' he explained earnestly, 'but it, er, ruined the cut of the pocket.'

'What are you talking about?' May studied his partner, who had owned four second-hand suits in the last twenty years, all of them brown and shapeless. 'You've lost it again, haven't you?'

'Not lost, John, mislaid. Anyway, they don't work properly.'

'They don't the way you use them, filling them up with water and soup and fluff,' said May, unclipping his own and passing it to his partner. 'Take mine. If you lose this one, you're a dead man.'

Bryant climbed out of the car and watched as May

drove away. Then he walked in the shadow of the dripping sycamores to the front door of Bella Whitstable's house.

On her own admittance, Bella had rarely stayed here in the past few years, preferring the relative peace of the country. Until recently she had allowed a lodger to stay rent-free in return for looking after the property. Bella's house was situated in a quiet Chiswick sideroad, a pleasant part of suburban West London where only the double-parked company cars gave any hint of the area's recent invasion and renovation by young professionals. It seemed to be one of the few large properties in the street that had not been converted into flats.

Bryant pushed open a wrought-iron gate and crossed the overgrown garden. A sudden change in light caused him to look up at the gabled roof. The sun, invisible during the course of the day, was making a faint embarrassed flourish through the fluctuating rain before dropping dismally behind the encroaching cloud of night.

When he had managed to fit a key to the front door lock, he entered the hall and tried the lights, but nothing happened. The electricity had already been turned off. He dug out a small plastic pocket torch and switched it on.

Bella's house proved to be a distaff version of her brother's, decorated in a gloomy, spartan manner which suggested that the owner was little interested in comfort or the vagaries of fashion. The rooms were uncluttered by all but the simplest furniture, the walls adorned by a handful of sporting prints. Only the well-stocked kitchen cabinets provided signs of a woman's occupation, and only the graceful decor of the bedroom gave any hint of femininity.

Wardrobes and cupboards proved mostly empty. A single unlabelled key lay beneath the lining paper in the empty chest of drawers. The belongings Bella Whitstable required for daily use were presumably stored at her house in the country.

Bryant shone his torch to the end of the landing and up at the ceiling. There was no sign of a loft. The design of these houses would not allow for much storage space. The elderly detective carefully descended to the floor below, pausing at the landing window to listen. Incredibly, it had begun to rain again. The sound suggested the start of a long, dank winter filled with harsh saffron sunsets and flooded footpaths. It was the season of murder.

Bryant pulled his scarf tighter to his throat and shone the torch across a set of ugly Victorian hunting prints. For a brief second, his reflected face flared back at him. Perhaps there was a basement. Upon reaching the kitchen, he cast the torchbeam across the walls, searching for a door.

He soon found it — a narrow wooden panel painted gloss white, but it was locked, and no key on his ring fitted the lock. Digging into his coat pocket he withdrew the unlabelled key from Bella's bedroom and inserted it, turning the handle. The damp wood had swollen in its frame. Jerking it hard, he unstuck the door and peered inside.

Below him, a flight of stone steps led off into pitch blackness. Beneath ground level, the temperature of the cellar was several degrees lower than in the rest of the house, and there was an unhealthy, mushroomy smell.

As he descended, Bryant could see his breath condensing in the beam of the torch. Gardening equipment stood at one side of the steps. Behind the rakes and shovels were fence posts and bales of wire, presumably for use on Bella's country property. Somewhere in front of him, water dripped steadily on to sodden wood. There was no such thing as a completely dry Victorian house in London.

The torch beam showed the side of a large packing crate. Bryant picked his way across the wet floor and examined it. The top was open, and several old playthings protruded from it. Here were stacks of forgotten games that touched off childhood memories of his own. Setting down the torch, he reached in among ruptured teddy bears, grotesque china dolls with missing limbs and eyes, pandas and golliwogs with their stuffing protruding, and withdrew a sepia photograph in a mildewed frame of grey cardboard.

Three children stood arm in arm on a manicured lawn, tentatively smiling, as if they had been instructed to do so by an impatient parent. The girl, pale and heavyset, wore a lumpy linen frock decorated with large, unflattering bows. The two boys were older, and were dressed formally in suits and gaiters, like adults in miniature. There was an air of sadness about them, as though the photograph had been taken moments before its subjects' incarceration. Behind them, the ground floor of an imposing country residence could be glimpsed.

On the flyleaf of the frame was handwritten in white ink: *Will Whitstable, aged 11. Bella Whitstable, aged 8. Peter Whitstable, aged 13. Summer, 1938.*

The composition of the portrait was awkward and stilted. It exhibited a lack of warmth that Bryant had so often seen in photographs of the upper-middle classes. He closed the picture and pushed it into his pocket, vaguely aware that it might provide some future use.

Behind the crate was another identical box, similarly filled to overflowing but harder to reach. The beam of his torch was growing softer. He would have to replace the batteries and return for a better look.

It was then that he heard the sound of soft, shallow breathing in the dark beside him. Someone, or something, had just woken up.

He must have disturbed a sleeping tramp. That was it, a tramp had somehow gained entry to the house and had fallen asleep in the cellar. He swung the torch around and tried to trap the nearby figure in its barely visible beam, only to hear a rapid shift of movement to the far side of the room.

At the top of the steps a dim light fell from the kitchen. As the torchbeam fluctuated once more, darkness pressed in. Bryant inched his way across the cellar floor. There was an odd, perfumed smell in this part of the room, a scent which masked something sickly and decayed. As he reached the stairs, he sensed the change in air pressure rather than hearing any movement; it was all that saved him from being knocked unconscious.

Armed with a wooden club of some kind, his assailant only succeeded in grazing his shoulder and thudding the weapon against the wall. His remaining hand grabbed the detective's coat, trying to pull him over. Bryant held tightly to the torch, shining its pulsing beam in his attacker's face. Wide brown eyes stared back as the figure released a guttural cry. Bryant swung the torch hard and connected with flesh and bone. With another shout the hand clutching his coat suddenly released its grip.

Bryant stumbled to the stairs and was halfway up when he was tackled from behind. This time, strong arms pulled his legs from under him. He felt himself falling, the torch beam flaring and whirling across the ceiling as he crashed over the side of the steps into a pile of cardboard boxes filled with bedding. The worst of his fall had been broken, but by the time he had righted himself his attacker had climbed the stairs and slammed the door behind him, turning the key in the lock.

Bryant groaned, more in fury than in pain. If he ever managed to get out, he would never live this down. He thumped the side of the torch, but the batteries were now completely dead. Somewhere above a door slammed shut, then another. No one knew he was here except May, and his partner was used to not hearing from him for days. He pulled himself from his perch on top of the squashed boxes and felt in his pockets for the matchbox he carried. Although he was a non-smoker he always kept a light on him because of the name of the match company. Bryant and May were the bearers of illumination; it was an old joke, and one which still brought comfort. He removed the box from his pocket and struck a light.

In the flair of the burning splinter he found himself sitting opposite a four-foot-high painting in an ornate gilt frame. He realised that he must have dislodged it from its packing crate as he had fallen.

Now the painting, in turn, began to topple forward. As it did so, in the moment before the match burned Bryant's fingers, he saw the figure of a Roman emperor feeding his pigeons. *The Favourites of the Emperor Honorius.*

The sulphurous smell of the burnt match filled his nostrils, and he was in darkness again. Bryant fumbled another from the box, struck it and held his hand high. Even in the dim flickering light that was afforded, he could see the signature that proved the authenticity of the canvas before him.

It was the mark of John William Waterhouse.

# II
# THE COMING OF THE NIGHT

Judgement drunk, and brib'd to lose his way,
Winks hard, and talks of darkness at noon-day.

*William Cowper*

# CHAPTER

The last thing she wanted to do was talk with him in front of Nicholas, but here he was striding across the hotel lobby to the desk, tufts of blond hair bobbing from beneath his baseball cap. Jerry laid down her ballpoint, ready for a fight.

'Before you say anything, I just want to apologise for being rude to you last night,' said Joseph. 'You have to admit, it was a pretty damned weird evening.'

Just as she had been gearing herself to attack, he had breached her defences. Jerry was left speechless. She was used to arguing with people.

'So, by way of a goodwill gesture, I wondered if you wanted to have something to eat with me.'

She was aware that she was staring at him. No man had ever apologised to her before. She tried to close her mouth but it wouldn't shut.

'Close your mouth,' he said, reaching over and raising her jaw with a finger. 'You'll catch a fly.' He handed his room key to Nicholas with a smile.

'You can't leave yet, Gates,' said Nicholas. 'You're on late duty tonight, and there's still half an hour to go.'

Without saying a word, Jerry collected her bag from beneath the desk and swung it on to her shoulder.

'If you walk out now,' hissed Nicholas, a vein starting to throb furiously at his temple, 'I'll see that this is reported. You'll be out of a job when you get back. I won't stand for it anymore.'

His words were wasted. She was prepared for anything he might try to do. Moments later she had passed through the revolving door with Joseph and was out on the street.

Back at the reception desk Nicholas looked down at the key in his hand, and hung it back on hook 216 as he began to plot his revenge.

John May stood at the foot of the Staircase Hall and carefully refurled his wet umbrella. On either side of him stood white marble statues, offering chilly representations of the four seasons. Overhead, a gigantic electrolier hung suspended from the gilded central dome. The supporting spandrels bore the arms of Richard II, by whose charter the Goldsmiths Company had been incorporated in 1393.

The Goldsmiths Hall stood behind a pair of discreet iron gates in Foster Lane, and nothing outside had prepared him for the dazzling sights held within. Golden heraldic mouldings shone down from every wall. Mirrors held an eternity of reflected crystal. A sense of pride in craft glowed through each ornamental carving. Displays of modern silver and ornate ceremonial plate filled the discreet glass cabinets which lined the corridors. He had made an appointment to see Alison Hatfield, the public relations officer representing the Worshipful Company of Watchmakers. Having provided him with a potted history of the Goldsmiths Company on the telephone, she was now about to take him through to the hall of the Watchmakers, situated a little further along Foster Lane.

He heard her heels ticking across the marble floor as she approached, slipping into a raincoat as she walked. Miss Hatfield had large pale eyes set in a slender face, and all the excess energy of someone underweight. She had taken great pleasure in describing the philanthropic duties of the guild, but much of this had been wasted on May, who was more interested in discovering the extent of the Whitstable family's dealings with the Watchmakers.

'The front rooms were badly damaged by bombing in 1941,' said Miss Hatfield, smiling generously, 'and of course, much of the building isn't open to the public. Mostly, that's the part involved with the day-to-day running of an active livery company. The craft guilds still support their own trade, of course.'

'I was admiring the silver plate,' said May, attempting to keep up with his guide.

'It's not just for display, you know,' she intimated. 'It serves a practical purpose. Many of the silver pieces were created to act as a reserve fund in times of need. I'm afraid much of it was sold off in the sixteenth and seventeenth centuries.'

They left the building and stepped into the grey, rainswept street. 'It's not very far.' Miss Hatfield marched on, unbothered by the downpour. 'The Watchmakers are a relatively new organisation, of course. The first portable timepieces didn't appear until shortly after 1500, when a German locksmith figured out how to replace weights with a mainspring. The guild wasn't formed until 1625, after iron movements had been superceded by brass and steel. Quite late, as craft guilds go. Here we are.' She stopped before another iron gate and rang the bell. A buzzer sounded in reply, and she pushed open the gate. They had arrived in a similar but smaller hall to the Goldsmiths.

'I'll hand you over to my opposite number,' she said, leading him briskly along a richly decorated corridor lined with Corinthian columns of scagliola. 'Well, he's actually the Company's general secretary.'

'Would the Watchmakers have a list of members readily available?' asked May.

'The guilds maintain entirely separate identities,' Miss Hatfield explained. 'I'm afraid you'll have to ask Mr Tomlins about that.' She ushered May into a small modern office which contrasted starkly with the elaborate embellishments outside. Seated behind an absurdly large desk, a rotund man in a tight grey suit was speaking softly into his telephone receiver. His hooded eyes made him appear half-asleep.

'He'll be with you shortly,' said Miss Hatfield, clasping her hands together.

'Thank you very much, Miss —'

'Please, call me Alison.' She plainly felt that she was trespassing on alien terrain, and took her leave with a nervous smile. May studied the bare room as Tomlins continued to ignore him. Finally, the receiver was replaced, but the official made no attempt to offer his hand.

'I understand you want to know more about the Watchmakers,' he said in an alarmingly high voice. 'May I ask why?'

Something about his manner instantly annoyed May, who decided to divulge as little as possible. 'We have an ongoing investigation that may indirectly involve the guild,' he said. 'I am collecting background information that may throw some light on the matter.'

'If I'm to provide that, surely I need to know the exact nature of the investigation.'

'I'm afraid it's out of the question at the present time,' said May. 'But you could help by showing me around.'

Tomlins was clearly reluctant to provide anything but the most minimal service. This was surprising, considering he acted as the guild's main contact with the public. As they walked from room to room, each one filled with display cases of gold and silver watches, he only spoke when he was asked a direct question.

'What is your company's link with the Goldsmiths?' asked May, genuinely interested in what had always been, for him, a hidden side of the city.

'The Goldsmiths were founded nearly three centuries before us,' Tomlins explained. His small, highly polished shoes squeaked as they walked. 'The craft of watchmaking is one of ornamentation as well as mechanics. When it first became so, the Goldsmiths helped our members to become adept in the use of rare and precious metals. Obviously, gold and silver are still the most popular materials for watchcases.' They passed a pair of matching portraits, Queen Victoria and the Prince Consort, unrecognisably youthful.

'There seems to be a lot of symbolism in the decoration of these items,' said May.

'Indeed. Craftsmen have always included certain personal images and signs in their engravings.'

'Have you ever seen one like this?' He produced a piece of paper from his pocket and unfolded the circled flame symbol they had first traced from William Whitstable's cane.

'I don't think so, no.' Tomlins shook his head, but May was unconvinced.

'Do you all meet socially?'

'Who do you mean?'

'The guild members. The old Watchmaker families. You still hold regular meetings?'

'There are certain annual functions to attend, yes. Whether we wish to meet outside of these engagements is entirely up to individual members. Many of our members are also masons, and naturally some of these gatherings overlap.'

'But you probably know the Whitstable family through direct contact?'

There was a brief flicker behind the hooded eyes. 'I believe we have met on occasion.'

'I imagine you've heard about the deaths of William, Peter and Bella Whitstable?'

'Only what I've read in the papers, Mr May.' He turned, tapping at one of the display cases. 'This contains some of our finest fob watches. Although two were traditionally worn, one either side of the waistcoat, one of them was usually false.'

'That one would make a nice wristwatch,' said May. 'When did you last see any of the Whitstables?'

'Wristwatches were not invented until the First World War, Mr May. There was a gala mayoral dinner in June. Members of the family would probably have been in attendance. Perhaps you'd like to see the Court Rooms now.'

'So you personally have not spoken to any of them,' pressed May. 'What about their business dealings with the Company? Do they play an active role in your daily financial affairs?'

'That sort of information is restricted to the Company's managers and accountants. I should hardly think it's of any interest to outsiders. It certainly has no bearing on their unfortunate deaths.'

May had the distinct impression that he was being misdirected. Any further pressuring on the subject of the Whitstables would no doubt bring about a sharp closing of the ranks. The close ties they maintained with various masonic lodges had taught them the value of secrecy. He would have to tackle the problem from another angle.

'What I'm trying to establish here, Mr Tomlins, is who profits and who loses by their deaths.'

Tomlins came to a halt and turned to the detective. 'If you're trying to infer that a member of the Watchmakers is somehow responsible ...'

'I didn't say that. I need to understand every aspect of their lives, and I'm afraid that doing so means going beyond the usual boundaries of privacy.'

'But they were the victims of violence, not the culprits. Surely they deserve to be treated with decency. If you're going to go prying into their affairs —'

'Mr Tomlins, I have to know where their money went, who they were involved with romantically and financially, what their hopes and fears were for themselves and for each other. Now you can make this an easier process for me by asking the other guild members to cooperate. All enquiries will be treated in the strictest confidence. We know that William and Peter had recently argued, and that Bella had virtually severed her ties with the family. Someone here must know why the Whitstables weren't on speaking terms with one another. I need you to set up a meeting for me.'

'With whom, may I ask?'

'There must be guild members who knew the brothers well. They, and presumably several other members of their family, have been lifelong fellows here. You take care of your other members. At the very least, the Whitstables deserve to have your help.'

'Very well,' said Tomlins finally, 'I'll see what I can do.'

As May saw himself out, he turned to see Tomlins moving away from him at great speed, taking small fast steps, like a secretary in a tight skirt. Something seemed to have urgently summoned him back to his office.

The cellar door was sealed fast. Bryant's eyes were trying to adapt to the dark, but there was nothing to focus on. He was finding it hard to draw his breath. His chest felt tight, and he was starting to hyperventilate. He was below ground level in a darkened house, sealed into the night. Normally the darkness did not disturb him, but the violence of his earlier encounter had left a strangeness in the stifling air.

He forced the unease from his mind and carefully felt his way back to the top of the cellar steps. He swung an experimental kick at the door, but it was made of heavy old oak and fitted well in its jamb.

He tried hard to remember where he had set down May's portable telephone. He recalled taking it out of his pocket at the first available opportunity. It was some-where here in the cellar, but he had no more matches left and the room was completely filled with junk.

He was considering the problem when the distant sound of an opening door reached his ears. Muffled conversation followed. Someone else was in the house. Bryant began to shout out. He kicked the base of the door until his foot was bruised. He no longer cared whether he was to be confronted by friend or foe.

'Is that you, Mr Bryant?' The voice was vaguely familiar.

'Of course it's me!' Relief overwhelmed him. It was as if he had been pulled from the sea at the point of sinking for the third time.

'Stand well back from the door.'

An axe head appeared through the splitting wood, and drove Bryant to the edge of the steps as the centre panel of the door collapsed. One of their patrol officers stuck his head through the open space.

'Blimey sir, this is no time for you to be creeping off for a nap,' said the constable, offering his hand.

Bryant was so pleased to see a friendly face that his customary rudeness deserted him. Remembering his discovery, he returned for the painting and began to haul it up.

'We have to take this,' he explained. 'It's vital evidence.' As if determined to remain hidden in the shadows, the painting pulled from his grip and fell back down the steps.

The Arizona Bar and Grill off Camden High Street had wide misty windows and tables covered with crescent-shaped dents from a thousand slammed tequilas. A harassed young waiter led them to a miniscule table in the corner of the room and waited while they perched themselves around it.

In the evenings, Jerry liked to leave the West End to the tourists and head for the alternative entertainments of North London. Making friends in the status and fashion-conscious nighteries of Chelsea had proven impossible and undesirable. She had little in common with the posturing teens who filled the King's Road bars with talk of their latest shopping accessories. Travelling to North London was like coming home. She much preferred the brash bad behaviour of Camden Town street life. Joseph certainly appeared more at home here.

'God knows how we're going to balance burritos on this thing,' he complained. 'Why do we always get such tiny tables? Are you hungry?'

'I'm always hungry. I maintain a level of hypertension

that can burn off a four-course meal in an hour.' Jerry picked up a menu and studied it as Joseph made a grab at the retreating waiter. Glancing hastily at the main course list, they ordered enough food for three and sent him off to the kitchen.

'Is there any chance that you're going to tell me something about yourself this time?' he asked.

'What do you want to know about me for?' She brought her chair in closer. 'You already have a girlfriend.'

'Things aren't that black and white, Jerry. A man can be interested in a woman without having to jump into bed with her.'

'How caring and nineties. Doesn't sound like a good arrangement to me.' She thought for a moment. 'You want family history or what?'

'That'll do for a start.'

'Okay. The personal CV; my parents are quite old, but not as old as their money. We don't have a great home life. Gwen goes to so many committee meetings I've been wondering if she's having an affair. She loves the trappings of power, you know, sitting around those boardroom tables. She lives in the hope of rare animals becoming threatened with extinction so that she can chair committees to save them. Jack still thinks it's 1944. Maybe he was happy then. My mother prefers to throw parties rather than cook, because her parties are always catered. I grew up thinking that a meal with the family meant finger food for fifty. Actually, we get along fine just so long as we don't talk about my future, which is all they ever want to talk about.'

'How come?'

'I wanted to go to art school and they wanted me to enter the family business. But war had been declared between us long before then.'

The food had started to arrive. Joseph dug into a plate

of nachos as if he'd just been rescued from a lifeboat, licking melted cheese from the tips of his fingers. 'What kind of business do they have?'

'Import—export, gold and silver. Mostly shuffling paper and arranging shipments. I don't know the details and I'm not really interested.'

'Why not? Sounds like there's a lot of money to be made.'

'Great, I get to be an executive, wear boxy black suits and do coke in the toilets of fashionable restaurants.' She picked peppers from the cheese chips and ate them. 'I wouldn't fit in. I've seen the kind of people Gwen and Jack mix with. I never wanted to be part of the old school network.'

'How come they didn't try and send you to one?'

'They had my name down. But when I was fourteen, I had some problems ...' She had never discussed this with anyone, and she wasn't too sure of starting now. The memory of that time was still fresh in her mind. To talk about it was to lower her guard, but maybe it would do some good. The past wasn't meant to be bottled away, to ferment in the dark.

He was quick to sense her discomfort. 'We can talk about something else if you'd rather.'

'No, it's okay.' She took a swig of her beer and set the bottle down. 'Basically I screwed up my parents' long-term plans by getting expelled from school. Gwen went berserk. Told me I'd let her down. How could she face her friends, all that kind of stuff, so I smashed the house up and accused her of some pretty terrible things. I didn't know what I was saying. It was kind of a breakdown.'

'So what happened?'

'I got sick. They put me in therapy, and the doctor tried to blame my behaviour on all kinds of revolting stuff, so I hit him. The blow ruptured a blood vessel in his nose. Jack had to settle out of court. Gwen had me sent away to a special care centre. I wouldn't stay there, kept running away. Eventually we reached a truce, Gwen and Jack and me. If I learned to control my behaviour, they'd allow me to follow my own course. There's money held in trust, which I'm supposed to get when I'm twenty-one. I had to agree to be the model daughter. At that point I even promised to go into the family business.'

'So how did you end up as a receptionist?'

'I guess I broke the promise.'

'And they're upset with you for doing so?'

'That's putting it mildly. Now tell me about you.'

'Don't change the subject.'

'It's depressing talking about it. Tell me something.'

'It's very ordinary. I get on well with my folks. I'm very close to my sister. I went to college in Edinburgh. This is my first job after getting my degree. I've always been interested in set design. Now the Tasaka Corporation have given me the chance to put my ideas into practice. I've already begun the preliminary work on their next production. It's jumping the gun a little, but a show of enthusiasm can't hurt. They're paying my hotel bills plus a retainer, but I'll rent a flat as soon as my first real salary cheque comes through. Believe it or not, I hadn't expected to meet someone involved in a murder case. Have you heard anything more from the police?'

'Well, I'm involved but it's not as if I'm related to the deceased or anything. I've bullied them into letting me help out. I want to see where this thing goes.'

'Why? I mean, what's the interest?'

She faltered. It was not a question she wished to ask herself. 'I don't know, exactly. I think it has to do with the things that scare me.'

To her surprise, he took her seriously. 'I guess it's a reasonable way of coming to terms with your fears.'

She studied his face as he ate. Joseph was just the kind of person she wanted to be, self-assured and purposeful. 'I'd like to see your designs,' she said. 'Will you show them to me?'

'I'd be happy to,' he replied, smiling. 'The most detailed plans are with the construction team, but I can show you the rough sketches. Come up and see my etchings; I'm only on the second floor.'

'I don't know,' replied Jerry, 'I may be busy. Nobody's been murdered in the hotel for a few days; the management probably want me to be around in case something violent and disgusting happens.' She stopped chewing. 'I thought you were on the fourth floor?' She remembered seeing his room number on the reservation card.

'That's right, I was supposed to be but your colleague made some kind of mistake. I thought you knew. There was a mix-up with the rooms. He was very apologetic. I'm in 216.'

'216?' The number inscribed on the bookmark in Jacob's bible. If it was a coincidence, it was a damned odd one. 'I'll come back to the hotel with you,' she said.

They arrived at the Savoy reception desk just as Nicholas was reaching a state of panic. The function suites were full, despite the adverse publicity the hotel had been receiving in some quarters, and security arrangements for the rooms were constantly being rearranged by the handful of remaining Commonwealth dignitaries. Nicholas reluctantly explained that he was prepared to forgive Jerry if she agreed to work overtime. The foyer was crowded with couples in evening dress.

'You can help out now,' he began, 'but it's no use begging me to keep quiet about your timekeeping. This has happened once too often for that. I'll still have to report you.'

'Have you met my friend?' said Jerry, introducing Joseph. 'This is Nicholas. He can crack walnuts with his sphincter. Why did you change Joseph's room, Nick?'

Nicholas looked over his shoulder at the leather-clad designer. 'What?' he asked, thrown by the question. 'Oh, you can't blackmail me about that because it wasn't my fault.' He waved his hands ineffectually, as if the idea was stuck to his fingertips. 'It was the telephone booking that threw everything out.'

'What do you mean?'

'The lawyer, you know — Max Jacob,' said Nicholas, lowering his voice. 'He made a telephone booking two days before he arrived in London, asking specifically for room 216.'

'Then why didn't you give him the room?' she asked.

'I made a mistake when I typed in the request. I had a lot on my mind, and the security guards for the delegates were swarming all over the place. I told Jacob that his room had been allocated to someone else. He was extremely pissed off about it. I promised to have a word with the new occupant and switch the rooms back, but he didn't want to change. What more could I do? Then Jacob died.'

I searched the wrong room, thought Jerry. 'Do you often give guests incorrect reservations?' asked Joseph.

'He has a point,' she agreed. 'A dissatisfied guest. I'm going to have to report you.'

'All right, Gates, that's enough,' snapped Nicholas. 'I'll forget it this time, but this is your absolute final warning.'

'Let's go and see those etchings,' she said, heading for the stairs.

'I don't understand what you expected to find in here.'

Joseph unlocked the door to his room and switched on the lights.

'I don't know either. Why would Jacob have insisted on this particular suite?' asked Jerry, looking around. 'It's no better or worse than his other one. They're virtually identical.'

'Perhaps it had some sentimental significance for him.'

'He was a lawyer, Joseph.'

She walked into the bathroom and checked under the sink. 'Suppose it was some kind of drop point?'

'Hey, wait a minute.' Joseph followed her in. 'Doesn't personal privacy count for anything these days? Do you always check out new friends like this?'

For the next ten minutes she pulled the bedroom apart while Joseph looked on. By the time he had decided to stop her, she had finished. 'There must be something hidden here,' she told him. She was sure that if Jacob had come to London to collect something from 216, it had to still be in the suite. 'No one else has come into the room except you.'

'What about the maids? The staff have pass keys. Anyone could have — what is it?'

She was on her knees, feeling the white tiles at the rear of the washbasin pedestal, when one came away in her hands. Beyond it was a square hole six inches across. Joseph crept forward. 'What's in there?'

She carefully pulled out a beige envelope, noted the jagged tear along the top and turned it upside down. 'Looks like we're too late to find out,' she said. She shook the top section of the envelope again, and a slim torn segment of Xeroxed photograph fell out where the paper had been ripped apart.

'Whoever took this stuff was in a hurry to check the contents. I bet it was drugs. I bet the lawyer was a dope fiend. They often are, you know.' She checked the envelope for residue, but found none. Instead, when she examined the piece of paper she found herself looking at two pairs of bare legs, a bottom, a breast and part of an unappealing erection.

'*Pornography?*' she said, confounded.

# CHAPTER

'How are you feeling?' asked May, seating himself on a section of the Moroccan bedspread that wasn't covered in the Saturday morning newspapers. His partner's eyes were red and swollen, his face the colour of a supermarket chicken.

'Oh, wonderful. That's all I needed right now, on top of everything else, a cold.' Bryant fixed him with a beady, suspicious eye. 'Have you eaten all the grapes?'

May looked around guiltily. It seemed that he had. For someone who wasn't feeling very well, his partner didn't miss much. 'There were only a couple left,' he said. 'You had a nice rest yesterday. You'll be back on your feet by Monday.'

He looked across to the window of Bryant's apartment. If he stood, he'd be able to see the muddy grasslands of Battersea Park and the wind-stippled river beyond. It had disturbed him to find his old friend in such a frail and frightened state. He wondered if Bryant's cold had appeared as a psychosomatic result of being shut in the cellar. Thank God he had not been left down there for longer. Friday had proven a wasted day of paperwork and procedures, without any discernible progress. He needed his partner back in full health.

The rescued Waterhouse painting had been placed against the far wall. The bedroom was a reflection of Bryant's mind, its tidy shelves filled with games and puzzles stacked in ancient boxes, statues and mementoes competing for space with books relating to every subject imaginable, from *Sensation and Perception in the History of Experimental Psychology* to *Illustrated British Ballads* and *A History of Indian Philosophy*.

'What are you reading at the moment?' asked May.

'*Batman*,' said Bryant. 'The drawings are terribly good.'

'Your landlady said you weren't to be disturbed, you know.'

'Alma's always looking for an excuse to get me alone. She brings me bowls of foul-smelling broth on the hour and perches on the bed like some overweight Florence Nightingale, prodding at my orifices with a thermometer. No wonder her husband died. You realise how close we came to never finding the painting at all?' Bryant pushed himself down into the blankets. 'It's the key to this whole business, I'm sure of it. I wanted you here because Summerfield's on his way over to check its authenticity. My trousers got torn. One leg of my suit is ruined.'

'I realise the thought of buying new clothes fills you with horror, Arthur, but you should be glad you're still in one piece.' He drained his teacup and set it down. 'Are you thinking of getting up at all? It is only a cold, after all. You'll be pleased to hear that Christina and I have put calls out to every surviving member of the Whitstable family.

We're bringing them all together for a meeting tomorrow afternoon.'

'On a Sunday? We won't have enough staff to take care of them.'

'I've agreed to let Jerry Gates give us a hand. The Sunday idea is to stop them from using the excuse that they have to be in their offices. I need you there, if you're feeling up to it.'

'I'm not malingering, you know,' said Bryant indignantly. 'Not like you, and that so-called heart attack of yours.'

May knew that his partner was thankful for being rescued, but didn't suppose he would ever say so. Finding Bryant's bleeper down the back of his passenger seat and knowing that he would never remember how to use the cellular phone, he had radioed a request for one of the patrol officers to keep a discreet check on the house. If the boy hadn't looked in when he did, he wondered if Arthur would have survived for much longer.

The doorbell rang, and May went to answer it. Peregrine Summerfield entered, his bulk filling the narrow door frame. He waved a bottle of cognac in a meaty fist. Red and yellow gouache still speckled his beard, as if he'd been using his chin to paint with. Perhaps he kept the pigments there as a way of presenting his credentials.

'Where is the old malingerer?' he asked, studying May. 'You must be John. I've heard a lot about you.'

'Oh, good things I hope.'

'Not really, no. There he is!' Summerfield walked into the bedroom and was about to shake his friend's hand when the sight of the painting stopped him in his tracks. 'Jesus Golliwog.'

'I thought you'd be interested,' said May, propping himself up. 'Is it the real thing?'

'Oh, yes.' Summerfield crouched down and examined the canvas carefully. 'That's the beauty of Waterhouse,' he said softly. 'He went straight from the idea to the paintpot. No endless squared-up sketches or chalk studies for him. He rolled up his sleeves and got stuck in. It's the real thing, all right. This is the intermediate study for the painting. I knew it was in a private collection but had no idea where. Waterhouse did a small oil sketch to start with, then this.'

'Would you like to tell my friend here a little about it?' asked Bryant.

'With pleasure,' said Summerfield, unable to remove his eyes from the canvas. 'It's a very dramatic subject. Flavius Honorius was the sole ruler of the Western world at the tender age of ten. With his empire overrun by invading tribes, and Rome captured by the attacking Visigoths, he sat on the throne sodding about with his pet birds. His army took all the shit while he married a couple of bimbos and did bugger-all for the collapsing empire. On the few occasions he did get involved, he cocked it all up. Weakest of all the Roman emperors, and a total wanker. Seen here ignoring the desperate pleas of his statesmen to grant them an audience.'

'Is there much of a difference between this and the finished painting?'

'Indeed. The central character was removed completely for the final version. The attendant in the middle of the canvas was felt to be too dominant, so he came out. Where did you find this?'

'It would seem to have belonged to one of our victims.'

'So Bella Whitstable lied to us,' said May.

'Not necessarily,' Bryant countered, levering himself from the bed and pulled a dressing gown over his pyjamas. 'We have no reason to assume that she knew which

Waterhouse painting her brother had vandalised. These are the sort of people who ferret away valuable items and forget all about them.'

'On a world scale, this isn't particularly valuable,' said Summerfield. 'It's an unfinished study of a neglected picture, primarily of academic interest, although it is rather beautiful. Waterhouse's fame rests on later paintings, particularly *The Lady of Shalott*, painted five years after this. The first one, where she's in the boat looking dead miserable, not the second one where she's got a fat arse and looks like she's breaking wind. It's in the Tate, I think.'

'Thank you very much, Peregrine,' said Bryant. 'You have a way of bringing art history colourfully to life.' He turned to his partner. 'Unless I'm mistaken, that will be Alma Sorrowbridge's heavy foot on the stair. Unless you want to be forcefed chicken-flavoured Bovril for the next half hour, I suggest we head for the West End with all possible dispatch.'

'The other day you mentioned that there was a resonance,' said Bryant. 'The act of vandalism reminded you of something. Did you remember what it was?' They were squeezed in the back of Bryant's rusty blue Mini Minor. May was driving, although he had barely been able to fold his legs beneath the steering column.

'Yes, sorry, I should have called you. It was Whistler.'

'What, the one with the sour-faced mother?'

'James Abbott McNeill, the very same.' Summerfield was pressed against the roof of the car. When he turned his head, his beard cleared the condensation from the window. 'You know, the famous action against Ruskin.'

'I don't remember the details, Peregrine. Explain please.'

'Whistler brought an action against John Ruskin for

saying that his painting *The Falling Rocket* was "flinging a pot of paint in the public's face". It made me think that your man was doing the same thing in reverse. You know, a member of the public hurling back an indignant reply, sort of thing. Whistler wrote about London: *When the evening mist clothes the riverside with poetry, the poor buildings lose themselves in the dim sky, and the tall buildings become campanili, and the warehouses are palaces in the night.*'

'That's very poetic,' said Bryant, 'and completely un-enlightening. What on earth are you talking about?'

'With the study of the painting held by his own family, it's possible your bloke wanted to increase its worth by destroying the finished article.' Summerfield stared absently from the window. 'But I think he was performing some kind of symbolic act.'

'Symbolic? Of what, for God's sake?'

'Well, that's what you have to find out isn't it?' replied the artist with a smile.

# CHAPTER

The second floor conference room of the Mornington Crescent SCD had been planned as a site for future press briefings, but on Sunday afternoon it had been filled with folding chairs and reserved for a different purpose. Jerry stood in the doorway, pulled her sweater sleeves over her hands and surveyed the group gathering before her.

The disparate branches of the Whitstable family had been brought together and assembled in the high-windowed room, so many having turned up that some were left standing around the edges. Everyone was talking at once, to each other, to the authorities, to anyone who would listen. Gathered together in this fashion, Jerry could now see that the Whitstables possessed certain physical characteristics, including bad teeth, large ears and a profound blotchiness in moments of stress.

'If I could have your attention for a few moments,' said Bryant, facing the group with his arms raised. 'The sooner we get started ...' He turned back to May, who was seated on an orange stacker chair behind him. 'I don't believe it. They're completely ignoring me.' Admittedly the cold had blocked his nose, but he could barely be heard above the swell of so many simultaneous conversations.

'You'll have to shout,' said Jerry. 'I don't think they're used to being ordered about.' Bryant unclipped a microphone from its stand on the table and held it close to one of the wall speakers. The resultant squeal of feedback caused everyone to clap their hands over their ears. Over thirty indignant men, women and children turned to face the low stage at the front of the room.

'Thank you, ladies and gentlemen,' said Bryant, returning the microphone to its stand. He studied his audience like a teacher confronting an unruly new class. Here they were, thought Jerry, the Whitstable clan en masse, well shod and well connected, the cream of British society — if magazines like the *Tatler* were to be believed. In gathering the Whitstables together, the detectives had been unsurprised to find the family's arrogance and sheer bad manners matched only by their disinterest in anyone outside themselves.

'I'll try not to keep you here too long,' he promised. 'It will help if we get to know each other.'

'Isn't there anyone younger looking after this investigation?' shouted a catarrhal young man on the end of the first row.

'We are the senior officers to whom you may direct your questions.' Bryant introduced himself and May, accompanied by a chorus of derisive snorts. A baby started crying and a woman stood up to leave.

'I'd like you all to stay seated until the end of the briefing,' Bryant requested.

'I have to feed my parking meter.' The woman glared defiantly at him and remained standing.

Dealing with the Whitstables was going to be a lot harder than they had realised. Now was the time to take a stand, before the whole family ran roughshod over them. 'You should have thought of that earlier, madam. I am not prepared to commence the proceedings until every one of you is seated,' said Bryant. The woman made a noisy, dissatisfied show of sitting down.

'Who's she?' shouted someone else, pointing at Jerry. 'She's not a Whitstable.'

Thank God, thought Jerry, resisting her natural instinct to run from the room.

'Miss Gates is directly involved in the investigation, and is assisting us,' replied Bryant. 'You should all have been given a typed brief by now. Although many of you already know each other, I understand that some of you have not met face to face before. We thought it better to bring the family together like this so that we could explain more clearly —'

'What do you intend to do about this disgraceful state of affairs?' shouted a cultured male voice from the rear of the room.

'Perhaps you could identify yourself and your relationship within the family when you address the group,' said Bryant. 'I'll be able to place you more easily in the future.'

'Royston Whitstable,' came the disgruntled reply. 'Alec and Beattie's son, although what that has to do with ...'

'My colleagues and I will endeavour to explain the course of the investigation to you, Mr Whitstable,' said Bryant. 'Or perhaps I should call you Royston, as all of you here bear the Whitstable name.'

Relative hush had fallen in the room. Bryant faced his audience squarely, fixing his eye on each member in turn. He could cut an imposing figure of authority when he wanted to, she thought, thrusting her hands into her jeans pockets and leaning against the wall.

'Some of you knew William and his brother Peter. I understand that many of you were fond of Bella Whitstable. We thought it would be of more practical use to bring you together like this, rather than speak to you individually. The first thing that's important for you to do is forget what you've read in the papers.' Bryant eased his tie loose and seated himself on the edge of the press table. 'Today's conversation is, of necessity, a frank one. If anyone would like their children to be absent from the room, we'll be happy to take care of them.' As arranged, Jerry gestured to the open door. Much head shaking. Nobody moved.

'We have not been able to trace everyone yet, but hopefully you'll be able to assist us in that task. I understand that some family members no longer live within the British Isles. They will be contacted in due course.'

'Who's going to pay our travel expenses?' asked a heavily made-up woman in the second row.

'We'll be happy to discuss reimbursement for any inconvenience caused to you,' said May. 'Our purpose in meeting today is two-fold. Firstly, you should all know by now that three members of this family have died in unnatural circumstances. No culprit has yet been identified, so we must warn you of the possibility that others may still be in danger. If you wish to be provided with police protection, we'll try to come to some arrangement. Secondly, the biggest problem we face is in pinpointing a common enemy of the Whitstable family. Peter, William and Bella were murdered under highly unusual circumstances. Their encounters with the killer required preparation and careful timing. Their deaths were more than just premeditated; they were intended to be symbolic. But of what? To discover that, we must understand the true intentions of your enemy.'

'You want us to do your bloody job for you,' complained a sour-faced elderly woman.

Bryant pointed sharply. 'Your name, please?'

'Edith Whitstable. The daughter of Charles and Rachel.' She looked about her for signs of approval and found none.

'What I am trying to do politely, madam,' said Bryant, 'is remind you that the withholding of information is a grave and punishable offence. While Mr May and I will attempt to respect your privacy, we need personal details from you that you may not wish to give — details of business feuds as well as family arguments.' He knew that his request ran the risk of opening files on all kinds of malicious gossip and hearsay, but it could not be helped. There was also a strong possibility that their business interests infringed certain areas of political delicacy, and might well be protected from legal access.

'In return for your assistance, we'll undertake to keep the press away from you. At this point, certain assumptions must be made. First, that one or more of you must know the murderer personally. Second, that one of you may even be the person we're looking for.'

The room quickly filled with indignant chatter. Bryant knew that, from a legal standpoint, he and his partner were treading on very thin ice.

'Now look here.' A thin young man with narrow features tapering to a feral, pointed nose pushed back his chair and pointed a threatening finger at Bryant. 'As I see it you've managed to put up a pretty piss-poor show so far. The papers say you were with Bella when she was killed. You're supposed to be public servants, but I don't see much service. You're not doing anything at all to put this chap away.'

He had a point. At the moment, it would be hard for

the Whitstables to see that the police were doing anything at all. 'And you are —?' asked May.

'Oliver and Peggy's son, Luke Whitstable.' As they quoted their lineage, Bryant tried to mentally locate them on the family tree. They all sounded so damnably sure of themselves. Perhaps it was a common trait in wealthy old families. He had no idea. He was from Wapping.

'Well, Luke, at the moment it's true that we have no way of knowing how, or when, or why this person strikes. Normally in a murder investigation, progress is made in the hours immediately following the victim's death. Connections are completed by talking to family members. Suspects are quickly eliminated. Certain names recur. A culprit is pinpointed, and tied into the crime with corroborative forensic evidence. But this has not happened in our investigation. Why?

'Because, despite our endeavours, evidence has not been forthcoming from yourselves, and no forensic signposts have been discovered at the crime scenes. Now, we need you to help us eliminate the unknown elements at work here by attending a further series of interviews, and by providing us with any documentation we request. On two separate occasions the murderer has been seen by witnesses. He certainly seems intelligent enough to devise a series of successful disguises and escapes.

'It's no use pretending that we can completely protect you from him. With someone this devious at large, no one is ever one hundred per cent safe. That's why we need to know everything you can tell us, no matter how insignificant or how absurdly inconsequential it may seem to you. The only way you can be made completely safe is by putting this person behind bars. Until then, think carefully about our questions. I personally witnessed William's awful death. I fought to save Bella Whitstable's life, and saw her die in terrible agony instead. This brave young lady was present at Max Jacob's death and saw Peter lying with his throat cut from ear to ear. Both of us have since been physically attacked. Remember, I want this ended every bit as much as you do.'

Bryant blew his nose and sat down. The audience sat in stunned silence. Finally, a small girl in the front row ran up and kicked him hard on the shin.

Before everyone began talking at once, May took over from his partner. 'No one is saying that this murderer *will* strike again, but you must be vigilant. Don't let your children talk to outsiders. Don't allow neighbours to become familiar with your daily routine. If you'd like to see us individually after this briefing, we'll try to help you further.' Instantly, a scrum of furious relatives formed around their desk as questions and insults filled the air.

For the rest of the afternoon the detectives remained seated in the conference room. The Whitstables were argumentative, imperious, secretive, and Jerry suspected, naturally misleading in their information, but most of all they were scared. Their bravado was a reflexive action, a family trait that failed to mask their fear. None of them seemed to agree with each other, or even have anything in common.

The detectives distributed a complex questionnaire to each member of the family in the hopes that they would turn up a common suspect. There were still several cousins, uncles and aunts left to track down, but as none of them were based in London within the present radius of the murders, their safety was of secondary concern.

At 8.30 p.m. after nearly five hours of half-hearted promises and vague accusations, they terminated the session. The logging of the information would be undertaken at once by the new night shift, and would be fed into a central databank of information to be referenced and annotated by May and Sergeant Crosse.

For now though, May took Jerry and his partner over to the saloon bar of the Nun and Broken Compass for a cheese roll and a pint of best bitter.

The small backstreet pub had been overlooked in the area's recent rush toward modernisation. Unable to attract a young upscale clientele with videojukes and karaoke, it had given up the ghost so completely that its only amenities were a hairy dartboard obliterated with overuse and a moulting resident dog of especially peculiar breed and odour.

'I've never met anyone like them,' said Bryant, seating himself in a worn armchair and taking a sip from his pint. 'The backbone of England. They're more concerned with losing face than losing each other. Jerry, you're from a posh family. Are they all like that?'

'You should see the people my mother has over for bridge,' she replied, sipping her juice. 'They're exactly the same. This afternoon was just like being at home.'

'Leo Marks says they sustained a certain amount of inbreeding in the last century,' said May. 'Life would have had a very different set-up for them then. Arranged marriages, the protection of name and honour. An exaggerated sense of duty, both to the nation and to the family escutcheon. A smattering of titled heads, all gone now. That's rather unusual. Families like the Whitstables cling to their nobility beyond anything else.'

'I understand that they're frightened, but I can't cope with their damned condescension,' said Bryant.

'They can't help it,' replied Jerry. 'They're used to being deferred to.'

'They've got powerful government connections,' agreed May. 'Two in the foreign office, three high up in the DTI. On the boards of all the major charities. Friends of nobility. They're not a family to be trifled with.'

'Do you think we could be dealing with a series of political assassinations? They've no doubt made their fair share of enemies abroad.'

'It would be tempting to think that,' May conceded, 'but it feels more personal, don't you think? It's odd, but I get the feeling that none of them can imagine why they've been singled out. If they could, they probably wouldn't tell us. Something should have come to light by now. At the moment we have their co-operation and we should be thankful for it. So let's have none of your customary rudeness when dealing with the upper echelons.'

'How dare you,' complained Bryant. 'I was a paragon of civility. Even when that devil-child kicked me.'

'You were fine today. Let's see how you behave when the Whitstables exert pressure on Marsden. Or start demanding action from the Home Office. Because they will, you know.'

'I'm sure you're right,' said Bryant, gloomily. 'And they'll get away with it because their social standing will make sure that the right people listen to them. It's not fair. Class has nothing to do with intelligence.'

'Arthur, they're different to the likes of you and I.' May nodded in her direction. 'Jerry, you agree with me, don't you?'

'They like to think they're better,' she said. 'They think badly of other people. That makes them different.'

'Nonsense,' snapped Bryant. 'In all my years, I've found that the only real difference between one person and the next is what kind of biscuit they like. Everyone has a favourite biscuit. It should be individual personality that separates people, nothing else.'

Some of Bryant's theories left Jerry behind. This was

one of them. 'Excuse me a moment,' said Bryant suddenly. 'There's something I really must find out.' He rose and took the empty glasses to the bar, catching the landlord's eye. 'Why is this pub called the Nun and Broken Compass?'

'It's a long story,' said the landlord, pulling a fresh pint. 'And it's rude. You know. A bit Rabelaisian. I don't want to offend the young lady.'

'Tell us anyway,' said Bryant. 'It's been a long day.'

After leaving Mornington Crescent, Jerry called in at the Savoy on her way home. She had tried calling Joseph's room all afternoon, but there had been no reply. Just as she was leaving the lobby, he entered through the revolving doors. He looked terrible, as if he'd just been informed of a death in the family.

It was 9.40 p.m., and the foyer was finally quiet. The remaining Commonwealth delegates had left to attend a formal dinner at the palace. Joseph dropped his bags beside the reception counter and rummaged in his voluminous black jacket for his wallet. 'I didn't think you were on duty.'

'I'm not. What's wrong?'

'It looks as if you have to make up my bill,' he replied. 'I'm leaving first thing in the morning.'

'Why, what's happened?' She came around from the counter and lightly held his arm. 'You want to walk for a while?'

The lights on the Embankment swayed like ropes of pearls, reflecting in the empty wet streets that led toward Blackfriars.

'I can't believe it,' she said. 'How could it have happened so suddenly?'

'You tell me. The Japanese just pulled out, without a

word of explanation. Miyagawa called me into his office this afternoon and explained that the Tasaka Corporation were returning to Japan at the end of the month. They've cancelled their plans for the production and all subsequent events, and they're selling the theatre to a British consortium. The deal has already been completed. They've fired the entire production team. They were very apologetic.'

'Why couldn't they have told you earlier?' asked Jerry.

'Perhaps they thought we might jeopardise their deal somehow. I'm right back at square one.' The thought of him leaving so suddenly chilled her.

'What are you going to do now?' she asked.

'Head back to Edinburgh, I suppose. Try to get commissions for next year's fringe.' He looked up at the starless sky, his voice betraying the hurt he felt. 'There'll be other times. Other opportunities.'

'How are you off for cash?'

'They paid me for next month. It wasn't the money. It was the chance to do something I believed in.'

'I'm so sorry, Joseph.' She thought for a moment. 'Why don't we find out who they've sold it to? The Savoy's a listed building. I bet it can only be used as a theatre. Maybe you can get a job with the new company.'

'I was wondering about that. It's worth a try.'

'Of course it is,' she said, looping her arm through his. 'You give up too easily.'

'And you don't, I suppose?'

She narrowed her eyes in what she hoped was a sexy look. 'Hey, I'm still here with you, aren't I?'

The hand he slipped around her waist took her by surprise, but as his lips pressed against hers she yielded, allowing her mouth to slowly open and his tongue to enter.

# CHAPTER

Jerry watched the platform posters slide from view as the crowded tube train lurched on toward Chelsea, and her mind turned to fresh murder theories. She was determined to push Joseph's lingering kiss from her thoughts, but it was so damned easy to allow him in. As she recalled the contours of his mouth, his hand resting lightly below her breast, she wondered how it would be if they made love, and how they would feel about each other afterwards. Joseph would apologetically return to his patient girl-friend in Edinburgh. She would remain stranded in the Château Despair at Chelsea. It was best to forget the possibility.

Instead, she forced herself to think back to that rainy Monday night two weeks ago, then to the prior Friday when Jacob had appeared at the Savoy, summoned by one of the Whitstable brothers. Could their summons have concerned a legal problem connected with the damaged painting? Maybe William Whitstable had wanted to turn himself in and was taking some professional advice.

Or suppose Peter had called his lawyer and told him to collect the package hidden in 216. What the hell was a respectable member of the legal profession doing skulking around with a pile of dirty photographs? Was that why he was murdered?

This was something she should be able to help the police with. She was glad she had been able to talk Joseph out of quitting London. He would be able to find a cheap hotel in Earl's Court, a bit of a comedown after lodging at the Savoy, but at least he could then leave town with the satisfaction of knowing who had taken over the theatre.

She removed the folded envelope from her pocket and carefully opened it, the single damaged piece of photograph sliding face down into her palm. The damned thing was burning a hole in her pocket; she wanted to study it on the train, but figured it wouldn't appeal much to the woman seated next to her. It was only when she looked at the reflection of the carriage lights on the sheen of the photographic paper that she realised she was seeing the indentations of a row of digits.

She held it closer, at an angle to her eye. Someone had sealed the pictures in the envelope, then written out a telephone number on a sheet of paper placed on top of it. The soft padding provided by the pictures had picked up a clear impression. In a few moments she had worked out the sequence, seven numbers and part of a name, the letters *And*, possibly *Andy*? *Andrew*?

As soon as she alighted from the train, Jerry checked the pencilled number and rang it from a callbox at the corner of Sloane Square. The recorded voice of the operator told her to redial adding the prefix 081.

'Andy?'

'Who's calling?'

'A friend of his.'

'Hang on, I'll get him.'

The receiver was set down and taken up a few moments later.

'Who's this?' The voice had a heavy Jamaican accent.

'My name is Jerry.' She saw that there was more chance in gaining his confidence by being honest about it. 'I'm a friend of one of your clients.'

'Yeah? Which one?'

She cleared her throat. Time to take a chance. What the hell, he couldn't hurt her. He was on the other end of the line. 'I saw the set of photographs you left at the Savoy. Very impressive stuff. Did you take them yourself?'

'I dunno what you're talkin' about. I didn't take no photos.' Andy was indignant, or feigning it, at least. She was sure his reluctance to talk wouldn't hold up for very long if money was mentioned. The recession was far from over; jobs were competitive on both sides of the law.

'I have some of them in front of me right now, and one has your telephone number written on it.' She tried to sound as friendly as possible. 'I thought you might be available for another job. I'll make sure you're well paid.'

'So, what have you got there, then?'

Jerry turned the piece of photograph over, trying to see it in the dim light of the booth. Two bodies, naked, a full breast, buttocks, and a sausage-like erection. The man was still wearing black socks. No light in the room apart from the camera flash. Judging by the odd angle of their limbs, the revellers hadn't expected to be captured for posterity. As there was nothing in focus above their shoulders, their identities could not be discerned. Perhaps that was why the picture had been torn and discarded — it couldn't do enough damage.

'Well,' said Jerry casually, 'the first one shows a

gentleman enjoying himself with a very young lady in one of the suites, 216 I think. I'll pay you double the amount you were paid before.'

She held her breath and pressed her ear hard to the receiver. For a moment there was only the silence of the open line.

'What, you want some more done?'

'That's right, of the same couple. Could you do that?'

The voice at the other end remained guarded. 'I can't get hold of the girl again. It'd have to be a different one.' So he supplied the woman, too. Handy service. 'I don' reckon he's gonna go for it twice though.'

'Leave that part to me,' said Jerry. 'I want you to get whoever you think he'd like.'

'Well, the Japs love blonde girls. I could ...'

'Kaneto Miyagawa.' Suddenly it was obvious. Jerry drew a slow breath as the realisation dawned.

'Wait a fuckin' minute, who is this —?'

She quickly replaced the receiver and left the booth, walking briskly down to the river. She needed to think. Andy's girl had arranged an assignation with the Japanese executive at his hotel. It meant that Miyagawa had arrived in London earlier than Joseph had realised. The Tokyo executive had been careful enough. Others knew of his libidinous nature, and had exploited it.

She tried to reconstruct the order of events. Miyagawa had gone to his room with the girl, and she had presumably arranged to leave the suite door unlocked. Ready for someone to burst in and take pictures.

Which meant that someone had paid to have Miyagawa set up. Suddenly a reason for the murders began to emerge. Was it possible that the Tasaka Corporation had been blackmailed out of the Savoy deal by the lawyer Jacob? Had he been instructed to do so by the Whitstables?

Suppose Peter Whitstable had made all the arrangements, and had then called Jacob to London to carry out
his bidding. Had the lawyer been brought down to ensure
that the photographs reached a target where they would
do the most damage? And suppose her assumptions were
all correct. What happened after that?

Outrage. The respected head of the Tasaka Corporation, caught red-handed and blackmailed into dropping
his plans for the Savoy. By doing so he would avoid a
scandal that would shatter company confidence and slump
share prices. But could the Japanese have hit back by
taking their revenge on Jacob and his employers?

And if this was true, why go to the trouble of killing the
lawyer with a needle full of snake venom? Perhaps it was a
ritualistic thing. Her head buzzed with crazy thoughts.

Could an honest-to-God conspiracy have been going
on without anyone noticing it? Why not, she thought, it
happens all the time in the City's square mile.

One thing was certain. What she knew now set her
ahead of the police. She would go to them with the
information, but first she'd put her theory to the test. She
could enlist Joseph's help. It would be a good excuse to
continue seeing him.

The decision was made. She would call him as soon as
she reached home.


Michelle carefully disentangled the headset from her hair
and detached it from the Sony Walkman at her waist.
She listened for a moment, but no sound came from
upstairs. Daylight was starting to fade from the lounge,
and it was only a little after three. From the window
overlooking the lawn she could see low clouds shielding
the weakening sun, like pages protecting a dying monarch.
The garden was empty, the bare branches of the cherry

trees clicking in the rising wind. Christmas was only a few days away. The weather was all wrong for the season. Far too wet.

'Daisy, what are you doing?' she called. Small footsteps crossed the ceiling, then stopped.

'Playing.'

'Do you want a glass of milk?'

'No, thank you.' A tiny clipped voice, precise and polite. Michelle shrugged and headed for the kitchen to make some tea. At the age of twenty-three she had retained the plump figure and bad complexion of her late teen years, and was resigned to the fact that unless she lost some weight she would be unlikely to ever find a boyfriend. Not that she particularly cared. It was only the magazines that went on about finding a partner.

Michelle preferred the company of small children. The pleasures of tending them had been bred into her by years of babysitting her younger sisters, and in the last few of those she had become highly valued as a childminder. Her responsible attitude reflected the genuine warmth she felt for her young charges. Still, she had never met a child like Daisy. A pretty little thing, thin and blonde, with translucent pale skin and large blue eyes that stared flatly and observed instead of seeing. At the age of seven, Daisy seemed to have no friends at all. She never returned from school with the other girls in her class, and spent her free time alone in her room, watching from the window or sitting on her bed.

Not that her parents seemed to give two hoots about her or her brother Tarquin, who was now eleven and had been packed off to boarding school. Daisy was quite used to being alone. Her mother and father were hardly ever at the house. He was something important in the City, and she was always organising charity events for one of the children's leagues. It seemed to Michelle that Mrs Whitstable spent so much time worrying about fundraising for needy children that she failed to notice how introverted her own offspring had become.

She switched on the kitchen lights, momentarily alarmed as they buzzed and dimmed before returning to their full capacity. As the electric kettle clicked off, Michelle opened the caddy and dropped a teabag into her mug. She poured boiling water over it, and while she waited for the beverage to brew slipped her earphones back in place, plugging the jack back into the Walkman on her jean-belt. As she tuned the radio to a phone-in, she failed to hear the wavering song which sounded from the street beyond.

Daisy rose from the floor of the playroom and listened. The tune was different to the normal one that played. Usually it was 'Greensleeves'. Michelle had told her that. The new one was much prettier. And fancy him coming around at Christmas! She looked up at the mantelpiece, and the plastic money-bear that sat there.

'Michelle, can I have an ice cream?' she called, but quite softly, so that Michelle might not hear her. It was too near tea-time for her to be allowed an ice cream.

Outside, the pretty tune played on. In the summer the van parked at the end of the street, but today it sounded as if it had stopped right outside the front door.

Daisy ran to the head of the stairs and looked down. The lights were already aglow on the Christmas tree in the hall, and it was growing dark beyond the frosted glass of the front door. She wasn't allowed out of the front of the house by herself, because of the traffic. But Mummy and Daddy had gone to London, and Michelle was in the kitchen, probably making more tea.

It wasn't fair. She could eat an ice cream and still be

hungry for dinner. In the street, the tinny song came to an end. Her mind made up, she reached for the money-bear and opened his secret door, releasing a single pound coin into her palm. Then she returned the bear to its place, tugged her skirt down, and descended the stairs.

She could hear crockery being moved about in the kitchen. Michelle was probably foraging for something to eat. No wonder she was so fat. Daisy quietly opened the door and slipped the safety latch on, praying that she would not be too late. The van sat silently at the kerb. It was different from the one that visited in the summer, white instead of blue, and there was no man serving at the window. She walked to the edge of the pavement and looked up, puzzled. From within came a delicious smell of chocolate. Just then, the melody began its warped tape-loop again and the van slowly started to roll out into the street.

'Wait, please. Wait!'

Daisy ran forward with the pound clutched tight in her hand. The van rolled slowly toward the disused railway arches at the end of the road, its distorted tune tinkling on. Daisy looked back at the house, and the opened front door. It had grown cold and was raining lightly, and there were no customers to be seen. The van driver hadn't spotted her. Now that she had looked forward to it, she wanted the ice cream more than ever. The van rolled to a stop beneath the darkness of the railway arch, its red tail-lights glowing.

Daisy could see the driver moving from his seat to the counter window. Perhaps he had seen her after all. Inside the archway the song echoed eerily. Daisy stood beneath the window, her money-hand raised in a pale fist. The interior of the van was in darkness. She wanted a Ninety-Nine. How could the man see to fill the cone properly? As he leaned forward, she gasped. White stuff was leaking from his eyes, like he had a really bad disease or something. What was wrong with him?

She was about to ask him when he suddenly moved forward in the gloom and leaned down from the window, scooping her up in one swift motion and clamping his hand across her mouth. The counter panel slammed down, sealing the van shut, and the vehicle rolled quickly away into the darkness of the tunnels beyond.

# CHAPTER

22

So much for her determination not to think about the newly unveiled sexual possibilities of their relationship. As soon as she reached home, she called Joseph with an argument that quickly won him over. Why pay for another night at the Savoy? If he checked himself out now, she could help him find a cheaper — if less luxurious — hotel tonight. He agreed, providing they could share a late supper. They both knew that any further meeting would be complicated by their new interest in each other.

Earl's Court tube station was cluttered with more bags and backpacks than a hotel foyer, a symptom of the area's year-round transience. The Victorian apartment buildings that surrounded it were ports of call for visiting Australians, Greeks and Asians of every caste and creed. The formerly fashionable squares were lost behind an array of neon-lit twenty-four-hour kebab and falafel shops.

Joseph's new room was so small that she could sit at one end of the sickly pink candlewick bedspread and see traffic moving sluggishly through the rain on the Old Brompton Road. It wasn't smart, but at least the narrow-windowed boarding house was warm and dry, and reasonably priced.

Joseph rose from the bed and placed his hands against the chill glass. It was late now, but time had little relevance in this part of London. Night seemed to suit the area, and the streets remained almost as busy as they were during daylight hours. Above them, dank underlit clouds glowed like wet oilskin, brushing across the red brick and slick slate of a hundred rooftop turrets.

'I've never met anyone like you.' He turned to face her. 'There's something about you that's very — disturbing.'

'Oh.' She smoothed out the bedspread, disappointed. The room was poorly lit, and made her uneasy. 'Can you put another light on?'

He came to the bed and sat beside her. She could smell shaving soap, and a musky trace of perspiration from his black vest. 'No, let the night come in.' He ran a finger along the seam of her jean-clad thigh. 'There's nothing in the dark that can hurt you. I'm here to make sure of that. Perhaps we can get over the problem together.'

Everyone thought she could just wish away the fear. She wanted to explain that rationalising it had no effect. 'It's a clinical thing,' she explained, 'a kind of gut panic that blots out everything else. It's not just in my mind. I feel it hitting every muscle in my body.'

He brought himself nearer, shadow closing over his face. 'Do you feel it now?'

'No.' Not strictly true, she thought. The light on the far wall seemed to be dimming, blurring the pattern of the wallpaper. He softly kissed her shoulder, her neck, her throat. His body pressed her back against the bed cover, the heat from his chest warming her breasts. She closed her eyes and allowed him to envelop her, his arms sliding around her back, one hand slipping into the waistband of her jeans. They lay on the counterpane with their bodies lightly touching, exploring each others' mouths, their hands establishing the contours of their arms, their thighs, their stomachs. A warmth spread inside her as as his fingers crossed the buttons studding the front of her jeans.

His hands rose and covered her hardening nipples as she brushed the solid pectorals masked by his vest. The burr of night traffic buzzed like static beyond the window-panes. He opened her shirt, kissing the tops of her breasts, moistening her flesh with his tongue, and slowly she allowed her mind to drift. But in its eye she saw not Joseph, not the man whose room she had entered this night, but the stalking figure in the alleyway, the hunching creature of her nightmares. She opened her eyes. The faulty wall-light had gone out completely. It was as if she had suddenly been struck blind.

And shoving down on top of her was a half-human creature, anxious to devour her body, exposing her breasts, pressing his fingers down towards her sex, clamping his hot foul mouth over hers ...

She pushed him aside with such force that he fell to the floor, cracking his head against the skirting board, pulling down the lamp from the bedside table. She could not hear beyond the pounding of her heart, could not breathe the suffocating air, could not see in the filthy, stifling room. Her only thought was to locate the door and open it.

He found her slumped on the landing, wheezing asthmatically, grimacing as she clutched at her chest with both fists, as though she was trying to suck in the light from the neon strips above her.

'Christ, are you all right?' She gave him no answer. 'I didn't know it was that serious.' He crouched before her, offering his hand. She stared at the upturned palm, unable to accept it. She saw the truth now, that his comfortable affinity with the darkness made him an agent of the night, someone to pity and distrust, not someone to love.

She gathered her coat and left the room without apology or explanation, unsure of her loyalties — or indeed, her sanity.

'He's keeping me awake, Mr May, boots tramping back and forth across the ceiling all night. I don't know what's wrong with him. I hope he's not having another one of his brainstorming sessions. He already gave Boadicea a nervous breakdown.'

It was true. Every time her tenant opened the front door, the mongrel cat fell over in fright. Alma Sorrowbridge moved along the hall with theatrical delicacy, her plump hands raised, elbows moving in opposition to her broad hips. As always, she wore red washing up gloves and an apron dotted with tiny blue cornflowers; he had never seen her attired in any other fashion.

John May had brought the bad weather in with him. His umbrella trailed pools on the polished linoleum floor as the landlady led the way to the stairs. He had been visiting his partner here for many years, and Alma had always insisted on seeing him up. He suspected that, knowing she housed a detective, she had decided to cast herself as a bizarre South London version of Mrs Hudson to Bryant's aged Holmes.

'Arthur was telling me that he doesn't sleep so much these days,' said May as they edged past a stuffed kestrel squatting beneath a glass dome at the corner of the passageway.

'I don't mind that, but he plays his music all the time. Gregorian chants, The Gondoliers, Madonna, you name it. And last night, the clattering! Like he was throwing

crockery about the room!' She held the landing door
open. 'My bed's right underneath. Could you have a word
with him?'

'I'll do my best, Mrs S.' He raised the Victorian brass
demon head set in Bryant's door and let it fall. Beyond, he
heard a muffled curse and the sound of breaking china. A
burglar bolt was withdrawn, and Bryant peered around
the lintel, a disgruntled tortoise head fringed with short
spines of umcombed grey hair.

'Oh, it's you. You'd better come in. Am I supposed to
be somewhere?'

'No, but I wanted to talk to you.' May stepped into the
hall, looking around at the framed panels which covered
the walls. Here were displayed the sheet music and first-
night programmes of a variety of Victorian entertainments. Further along stood a particularly horrible plaster
bust of the composer William Walton; why it was in
Bryant's possession he had no idea, but it had sat there
undusted for years. May ducked before the hall mirror and
smoothed his hair into place. His partner was a collector
but not a hoarder, and not much of a materialist, either.
Everything here was owned for a reason. Often Bryant had
taken something into his apartment simply in order to
preserve it from harm elsewhere. He had once told May
that he was conforming to the natural traditions of
maturity. 'We spend our youth attempting to change the
future,' he explained, 'and our dotage trying to preserve
the past.'

The rising wail of the kettle sounded in the kitchen and
Bryant went to deal with it, pulling a patched green
cardigan around his shoulders. 'You're just in time, John.
Go into the lounge, but be careful where you tread. I see
the weather's still disgusting. We might as well be living in
Finland. What brings you here so early?'

'One of the Whitstable children has gone missing.'

Bryant appeared in the doorway with a teapot in his hands. 'Which one?'

'Daisy. She's seven years old. Walked out of her house between three and four yesterday afternoon and hasn't been seen since.'

'Yesterday? Why on earth didn't someone —?'

'The nanny says she was only out of her sight for a few minutes. I'd like you to talk to her. Naturally, she's distraught. West London has over a hundred staff and civilian volunteers out searching the area. The call didn't come through to Mornington Crescent until this morning. Apparently nobody made the connection with our case. Either that, or they deliberately chose to ignore it.'

'Then how did you find out?'

'I was in the incident room when some of the sweep details turned up on the computer.'

'Someone's obstructing us. I hope to God this isn't part of the Whitstable vendetta. It wouldn't be, would it? Not a child? How are her parents?'

'Mother's under sedation. They're both at home.'

'And her brother, Tarquin?'

'He's only just been — how did you know she had—?'

'I told you, go in the lounge.'

When May did so, he found every cup and saucer, plate, vase and bowl standing arranged across the floor like pieces in a scaled-up chess game. Different coloured lengths of string connected them. Every item of crockery had been given a name and dates with a blue or a red felt-tipped pen. The dining room chairs had been shifted back against the wall, beside a walnut-faced grandfather clock that ticked sharply.

'It's the Whitstable family tree,' Bryant explained,

entering and setting down his tea tray. 'It's the only way I could get it sorted out in my head. I had to see them properly laid out, who was descended from whom. Daisy Whitstable's bottom left-hand corner, by the fireguard.' He pointed to a milk jug. 'Next to her is the egg cup, brother Tarquin, stepbrother actually, from Isobel's first marriage.'

In the centre of the china maze stood two upturned vases and a cafetière — two deceased brothers and a sister, May noted, reading off their dates. He had done something similar himself by tracking the family across a computer spreadsheet.

'What are the blue and red tags?' he asked. Some pieces had scraps of paper attached to them.

'Family members killed in the First and Second World Wars. It's not a modern crime, John. The answer to this has no home in the present.' Bryant seated himself and leaned forward with his elbows on his knees, surveying the mapped floor.

'What do you mean?' asked May, dropping into the opposite chair. Outside, fresh squalls of rain began to batter the glass.

'Doesn't this feel like an old score being settled to you?' asked Bryant softly. 'William, Bella and Peter, one after the other, an entire branch of the family tree pruned away for consciously — or unconsciously — committing some past offence.'

It had crossed May's mind that his colleague might be allowing his own interest in the past to colour his perception of the case. For the moment he decided not to voice his concern.

'You mean it's some kind of long-term family revenge?'

'Well, it's certainly not for financial gain. This particular branch of the tree was pretty bare. None of them had any heirs, and there wasn't much ready dosh about. As far as I can gather, they have little to leave beyond a small lump sum each, some stock portfolios and some nice furniture. The pictures, of course, but no one has tried to claim them. On the contrary, nobody even seems to have known of the existence of the Waterhouse study. Now, pass me Marion and Alfred Whitstable over there.'

'What's their significance?'

'We need them to drink out of.'

As they sat back with their teas, Bryant produced a sheaf of handwritten notes from behind his chair. It irritated May that his partner had continued working without consulting him, but he knew this to be Bryant's preferred methodology. At least by now he was used to it.

'William, Bella and Peter Whitstable had no individual or collective power, financial or otherwise,' explained Bryant, donning his spectacles. 'The only thing that could be gained by killing them was personal satisfaction. But is the culprit within the family dynasty or beyond it? It might surprise you to know that every single Whitstable, past and present, is cared for by the Watchmakers Company. That is to say, they would be awarded an annual stipend in the event of personal injury. Relatives to be compensated in the event of bereavement, and so on, although there's no case for compensation here. Murder makes the claim exempt.'

The remark brought something to the fore of May's mind. 'You don't suppose the Whitstables' collective wealth is being stockpiled by these deaths?' he asked. 'You know, concentrated, like a tontine?'

'You mean the holdings eventually falling to the last surviving family member? I wondered about that. If one of them was knocking off his relatives, it would soon become obvious who was doing it.'

'Would it? The lawyer might have been killed because of his awareness of the family's legal structure.'

'The Whitstables' financial arrangements aren't secret. Nor are the dispositions of their wills. Leo Marks has already arranged for me to inspect all documents pertaining to the investigation.'

May was exasperated. 'Why didn't you tell me this?' he asked.

'I only spoke to him yesterday. But this business with Daisy Whitstable changes everything. Someone wants to get back at the family very badly if they're prepared to take a child.'

'Perhaps it's all because William damaged a painting. Or because they all belong to the Watchmakers Company. If there's a rivalry going on, it certainly isn't in any of their statements. I'm trying another tack. The guild owns a lot of Central London property. There's big money at stake. We need to speak to a member, or better yet, someone who's been thrown out. Unlike the masons, they're allowed to talk to outsiders. Tomlins is the general secretary, but he's not returning my calls. We need a warrant to search the guild. It'll take time and a decent reason, and at the moment I don't have either.'

'Then we need to talk to Mr Lugsea.' Bryant drained his cup and returned it to the tree. 'He'll be able to provide us with some information.'

'Who is he?' asked May, 'one of your mediaeval historian friends?'

'No,' replied Bryant. 'He's my butcher.'

The formica sign read *Reginald Lugsea, Your Friendly Battersea Butcher*, but the man hooking up rabbits in the window looked far from it. Glowering beneath a sweaty red brow, his expression changed as soon as Bryant removed his trilby and made himself known.

'Blimey,' he shouted to his apprentice, a pale young man with spectacular spots who stood disconsolately weighing mince at the rear of the shop, 'we don't often see Arfur in 'ere, do we, Phil?' He turned back to the detective and grinned as he hoisted a chicken onto the counter. 'We was beginning to fink you'd gawn vegetarian.' He raised one of the chicken's legs and pointed with the tip of his knife to an elderly lady who stood nearby. 'This a bit on the big side for you, missus?'

The old lady looked up from beneath her woolly hat and smiled through perspex-thick glasses. 'Ooh, no, luvly, ta.'

'So, what can I do for you gents?' asked Reg, smacking one of the chicken's feet off with a quick thud of his blade. 'A nice bit of beef?'

'Heraldry of the London craft guilds,' said Bryant. 'What do you know about it?'

Reg looked at the ceiling as he chopped off the other chicken foot. 'The Tudor company halls in general, or did you 'ave a specific trading family in mind?'

'The Watchmakers.'

'Late arrivals, first quarter of the seventeenf century. Cos yer first halls were fruit and fish, round the docklands. Then yer Dyers, Plumbers, Vintners, Cordwainers, Wood-mongers, Girdlers, Plasterers, Waxchandlers, one for every profession.' He held the chicken up by its neck and shouted at the old lady. 'You want the giblets, luv?'

'Ooh, yes please.'

He laid the bird down and hacked off its neck, then thrust his hand up its behind. 'Course, they were able to take advantage of the Dissolution of yer Monasteries and the Reformation, cos guilds were able to move into the empty nunneries, like the Leathersellers did in St Helen

Bishopsgate round about 1542. Not the watchmakers, though, cos they was looked after by the Goldsmiths, and shared part o' their fancy halls.'

'They all had their own heraldic badges, didn't they?' asked Bryant.

'That's right,' said Reg. 'The Skinners had crowns and feathers on their livery, the Fishmongers had herrings with hats on, no lie. Watchmakers was fobs and gold chains, orange on blue if memory serves.' He yanked at the chicken's interior and produced a handful of innards, which he proceeded to drop into a plastic bag. He reminded May of Oswald Finch, the coroner.

'What about a radiant flame, red outlined in yellow?' asked Bryant. 'That's not part of the Watchmakers' livery?'

'Don't fink so,' said Reg slowly. 'Although I seem to remember seein' it in their colours somewhere.' He thoughtfully knotted the bag and wiped his blood-covered hands, smearing chicken guts down his striped apron. 'I got a feelin' it's a recent addition to the Watchmakers. By recent I mean maybe only 'undred years old. Sometimes merchants formed special "inner circles" with new symbols to separate them from their parent companies. Yeah, that's prob'ly it. You'll need to talk to someone on the inside, though.'

'Thanks, Reg,' said Bryant, touching the brim of his hat, 'you've been very helpful.'

'Always a pleasure, Mr B,' said Reg with a smile. 'You sure you don't want a nice pig's trotter while you're 'ere?' He picked one up and walked it along the counter. 'Nice an' fresh. Was gallopin' round a field last Thursday.'

'Not today, Reg.'

May hiked his thumb back at the butcher as they left the premises. 'How did you ever get to know about him?'

'I talk to people,' replied Bryant. 'You should try it

sometime, instead of spending your life in front of a computer screen.'

'Why does he know so much about heraldry?'

'Reg is rather famous.' Bryant gave a knowing smile. 'He won the Mastermind competition two years ago, specialist subject Tudor Mercantile history, self taught. It never pays to underestimate the arcane knowledge of the public. This flame symbol, is it common to all of the Whitstables I wonder, or just some of them?'

'An inner circle within the guild. I don't think I'm going to get anywhere further with Tomlins without scaring him. Not to worry, though.' May unlocked the passenger door of his car and ushered Bryant in. 'I think I may have found a mole.'

'What do you propose to do?' asked Bryant.

'Go back to the Watchmakers. Which unfortunately leaves you to deal with Daisy Whitstable's childminder.'

'Why do you say that?' asked Bryant, fastening his seat belt.

'I just heard that Daisy's parents are planning to sue us for something called protective negligence.'

Michelle Baskin was sitting awkwardly on the orange plastic chair in the hallway when Bryant arrived. Sergeant Crosse emerged from her office and drew him aside, handing him a sheaf of papers. 'I've given her some tea,' she said quietly. 'She's been crying a lot, so you'd better go easy. The workmen are still in your office, I'm afraid. And you've an urgent message to call a Mrs Armitage. She wouldn't say what about, said you knew her.'

'I'll handle that, thanks.' He turned to the distraught childminder, who sat miserably kneading her hands in her lap. 'Miss Baskin, would you come with me, please?'

Inside his office, the two workmen were clearing paint

from the far wall with their blowlamp. Two distinct bands of colour were discernible beneath the top coating, green, and below that brown. The room stank of petrol. Bryant asked them to wait outside, and opened a window.

'We'll soon have the air cleared,' he said, ushering Michelle into a seat with a smile. The girl pulled the remains of a wet Kleenex from her cardigan and wiped her nose, head bowed. She was clearly in great pain. 'I understand that there's been no news yet.' He pulled a fresh linen handkerchief from his drawer and passed it to her. 'You know, children have gone missing for much longer periods than this, and have turned up safely again.'

'Mrs Whitstable warned me to be extra careful with Daisy, just before she left,' said Michelle, sniffing hard.

'Why did she say that?'

'Because of what happened to her uncles and her auntie.'

'You mean William, Peter and Bella?'

Michelle nodded, pushing her lank hair back from her face.

'Did they ever visit their niece? Were they friendly with Mr and Mrs Whitstable?'

'Never, to my knowledge. Luke — Mr Whitstable — hardly knew them at all. Isobel — Daisy's mother — sometimes saw them.'

'How would you describe Daisy?'

Michelle composed herself and sat up, thinking for a moment. 'I s'pose you could say she's a true Whitstable. Like her cousins, very pale, bit small for her age. Inclined to be moody. She's a direct descendant from the original Whitstables, like her mummy, and her grannie, Peggy, so they share the same blood.'

'I'm a little confused,' said Bryant, seating himself on the edge of his desk. 'Did Isobel retain her maiden name upon marriage?'

'It's something most of the Whitstable ladies do. So long as they stay in the family business.' *So long as they stay in the guild*, thought Bryant.

'I suppose it has its advantages.' Bryant checked the statement in his hand. 'It says here that Daisy was wearing a light summer frock. It was very cold yesterday. Why do you think she'd have gone outside dressed like that?'

'I don't know,' said Michelle. 'It was warm in the house. Too many radiators.'

'The doors and windows, were any of them kept open, just to help cool the rooms down?'

'No, sir. And Daisy wasn't allowed to go out of the front door by herself.'

'But you found it open when you went into the hall.'

'That's right. Someone had put the latch up.'

'You didn't hear her go out?'

'No, sir.'

'I want you to think back carefully, Michelle. I want to cover everything that happened from the moment you last spoke to Daisy, whether it has any relevance to her disappearance or not.' Michelle nodded sadly.

'Let's start with the last time you were aware of Daisy's presence in the house. You were standing in the kitchen, making tea. You'd taken off your Walkman ...'

It took them an hour to cover the events of the previous afternoon. Michelle cried at several points in her explanation. Minutes after she had found the front door open and searched the street, Daisy's parents had arrived home, and an argument had ensued. Later, Mrs Whitstable had angrily accused her of incompetence and negligence in her duties. Then she had fired her. Michelle explained that it was more than just a job, that she really loved her charges, even the difficult ones, that she was more worried for Daisy's safety than for her own future.

Bryant tapped her former statement with the end of his pencil. 'There's a point here I don't understand,' he said. 'You boiled the kettle. You removed your headset. Then you say you heard Daisy run across the floor upstairs above the sound of the music. It says here —' he squinted at the sheet, readjusting his bifocals, '*I could hear her footsteps above the music.* But by this time you'd removed the head-set and presumably turned the music off at its source. Or did you leave it on?'

'No, I turned it off.'

'Then how could you have heard music?'

Michelle thought hard. 'There was a song playing.'

'Somewhere else in the house?'

She thought for a moment. 'No, not in the house.'

'Next door? In the street? What kind of music?'

'Tinkly. I don't really remember.'

'What, a car radio?'

'No, more like an ice cream van. Only they don't come 'round at this time of year.'

'Did Daisy like ice cream?'

'Very much, but she was forbidden to eat between meals.'

'Did she have money in her room?'

'Yes, a little bank. You don't suppose —'

'She put the door on the latch herself. You don't happen to know how much money she had in her room exactly?'

'Not right now, but Daisy kept a written note of it. She's a very practical girl.' Bryant placed a call to Luke Whit-stable, then made an internal call to have someone check the area's ice cream companies and van registrations.

Within the hour he received two return calls. The first from Daisy's father, confirming that his daughter's account showed a discrepancy of a pound from her bear-bank. And the second from an officer reporting that the ice cream van allocated to the road where Luke and Isobel Whitstable lived was not due to return until next April.

With a sinking heart, Bryant was forced to acknowledge the possibility that the family had lost another member, and this time, surely, a blameless one.

# CHAPTER

23

**Partial section of Transcript # 170—53**
**Monday 20 December**
Session with Dr Emil Wayland
Patient: Geraldine Gates
(Note: Patient arrived unannounced in a state of severe agitation.)

WAYLAND:
I'd like you to keep to our scheduled appointments if you can. This isn't fair on my other patients.
GATES:
I needed to talk to someone. I can't face Gwen about something like this. I don't care if you show her the transcripts. There's nothing she can do.
WAYLAND:
Tell me what has happened.
GATES:
Okay. Recently I met someone at the hotel. One of the guests.

WAYLAND:

A man.

GATES:

No, a fucking giraffe.

WAYLAND:

There's no need for this attitude, Geraldine. If you want me to help you—

GATES:

I'm sorry. Let me — I liked him a lot, he says he has a girlfriend but she's in Scotland, anyway he kissed me and I liked that and I went back with him—

WAYLAND:

Wait, slow down. You did what?

GATES:

I. Went. Back. With. Him. Is there someone else I can see?

WAYLAND:

I can't help you if you're going to be like this. This man, is he just visiting London?

GATES:

Yes. No — he's here for a while, I don't know.

WAYLAND:

All right, you're attracted to him and you kissed.

GATES:

Then we started to make love. It was getting dark. I couldn't see him any more and *it* appeared—

WAYLAND:

The nyctophobia.

GATES:

It came back in the weirdest way, like the nightmares. It came through him.

WAYLAND:

All right, we'll skip the fact that you've never mentioned this man to me before. What do you mean, it came back through him?

GATES:

It's kind of hard to explain. It wasn't just a panic-sweep, like I usually get. This time *he* was the darkness. The enemy. I had to get away, so I ran from the room.

WAYLAND:

Tell me something. While this was happening had he actually begun to make love to you?

GATES:

(Pause approx. 22 sec.)

What, you mean—

WAYLAND:

What I'm asking is, had actual penetration occurred?

GATES:

No. No, I—

WAYLAND:

So I assume you haven't lost your virginity.

GATES:

I don't think that's really any of your—

WAYLAND:

Don't you see? You equated your fear of the dark — actually, your fear of the unknown — with your fear of this man.

GATES:

I'm not scared of men.

WAYLAND:

It's quite normal to be nervous about sex. Contrary to what you may have been told, the first time is rarely the best. The pleasure is mitigated by apprehension. As the darkness deepened so did your fears. Control was taken from you, and you didn't like that. All acts of sex involve a struggle for dominance and assertion. In the dark you have no authority. In the act of sex — something you have no experience of — you were frightened of the same thing, losing control. Do you love this man?

GATES:

That's not — I don't know.

WAYLAND:

Then why not wait until your feelings are clearer? You say he already has a girlfriend. Isn't he behaving in an irresponsible manner? You may feel threatened by this, yet remain drawn to him. Wait until you are clear about your duty to one another. When you're sure of his intentions, you'll no longer be scared of relinquishing control.

GATES:

If I get crushed by a bus in the high street tomorrow, I'll die a virgin. At least that would please Gwen.

WAYLAND:

Sounds like you're back to your old self already.

# CHAPTER

24

It was time for Joseph to start looking for another job. He had reached a decision. He'd stay on in London for a while longer, just until the money ran out. To return home now would be to admit defeat. Jerry needed help, although he wasn't sure what kind, or how he could be of use to her. She was already seeing some kind of shrink. She suffered from an overactive imagination, and her insistence on turning everything into a mystery irritated him. She seemed drawn to the morbidity of the police investigation. He just couldn't figure her out. When she spoke of her parents, or the supposed conspiracy she imagined surrounding them, it was as if she meant something else entirely; as if her true intentions lay just beneath the surface, and he had yet to bring them into the light.

He was unlocking the door, about to leave the room when the telephone rang.

'I wanted to apologise about last night.'

'None needed, I assure you.'

'Yes, there is. I wanted to — but—'

'Listen, I think we both have some things to work out first. Are you at work?'

'Yes. Something just came up on my screen, in the daily schedule. There's a meeting arranged for this morning in one of the small conference rooms. Savoy Theatre Shareholders. Have you ever waited on tables?'

'Yeah, a couple of times—'

'Is it easy, I mean could I do it? All I have to do is stand beside the coffee pot and serve them when they take their break, right?'

'Jerry, what are you talking about?'

'The refreshment area is just outside the main room. Hopefully I'll be able to hear every word they say.'

'Now, wait a minute,' he protested. 'You're going to dress up as a waitress just so you can—'

'It's all above board. Why not? I think I can arrange to switch shifts for the day, although Nicholas is being a real creep. I even get paid. I already checked it out.'

'That's not the point—'

'Why, do you want to do it?'

'You're taking this too far, Jerry.' He paused. Hadn't he wanted to help her? 'I don't know, it's industrial espionage or something. What's the point?'

'People are being murdered and blackmailed and you ask me about the point? Things like this go on all the time and nobody stops them.'

'That's conspiracy theory bullshit.'

'No one ever bothers to find out if it is or not. What about wrongful prosecutions, they happen, don't they? It's not until individuals take matters into their own hands—'

'All right, if you have to do this, promise me something.

If you don't hear or see anything suspicious, drop it, leave the damned thing alone and let the police do it their way.'

'It's a deal. Come on over.'

As he replaced the receiver, he had to admit he was intrigued. If he'd lost his job because Miyagawa had been set up, he had a strong case for wrongful dismissal.

PC Colin Bimsley was at the very end of the Metropolitan Police chain of command. When orders filtered down from the top, when reprimands were issued and disagreeable duties were passed on, they were usually dumped in Colin Bimsley's ample lap. If restaurant dustbins had to be searched for a discarded weapon, if a decomposed body part stuck in a drain had to be raised and wrapped in plastic, people in power would turn to each other and say, 'Let's get Bimsley to do it.' At least, that was how it seemed to the young constable.

Today was no exception, as Bimsley was one of the thirty or so foot soldiers handling door-to-door enquiries in the pouring rain, asking householders about the disappearance of little Daisy Whitstable. So far the response had been low, the progress slow. It was no surprise, thought Bimsley as he pushed open yet another garden gate. The area was host to a particular strand of upper middle class family. Most of the residents worked during the day, their houses minded by an army of cleaning ladies, nannies and gardeners, few of whom spoke English.

As Bimsley rang the bell and surveyed the tailored front lawn, he wondered if his dislike of the neighbourhood stemmed from the fact that he would never have the money to live in such an area.

'Can I help you?' The elderly woman who answered the door was staring suspiciously at him, despite the fact that he was wearing a uniform. She demanded to see formal identification before letting him start the questionnaire. Bimsley impatiently ran through the opening paragraph explaining that he was trying to establish the exact time and whereabouts of a rogue ice cream van.

'I remember it clearly enough, you don't have to go on,' she snapped. 'When I heard it passing I went straight to the window and looked out.'

Apart from the hazy recollections of a Portuguese gardener in the next street, this was the first positive identification Bimsley had received. 'Would it be possible for you to describe the vehicle or its owner?' he asked carefully. The rain was falling in heavy sheets now. He could see his breath. 'Perhaps I could come in for a minute,' he ventured.

'You stay where you are. Muddy boots on my Axminster, the very idea. Shut up while I think.' She pushed past him on the porch and looked along the street, narrowing her eyes.

'A little girl was abducted in this area yesterday,' he asked, 'possibly by the driver of the van we're seeking.'

'I don't much care for children. Too demanding. I don't have a television and I don't read the papers. Too depressing.' She pointed in the direction of the Whitstable house. 'It stopped up there,' she said. 'I remember thinking at the time that it was odd to hear an ice cream van at Christmas, especially one like this.'

'What was different about it?' asked Bimsley, turning over the questionnaire and taking notes.

'It was plain white, more like an ambulance. Then there was the man inside.'

'You saw the driver?' This was too good to be true.

'Only through the windscreen. He didn't have a coat on, you see. The regular man always has a white coat. This one didn't.'

'Is there anything else you recall about him?'

'He was dark.'

'Black?'

'No, more — tanned. He had long hair, most unhygienic where the preparation of food is concerned. And pale eyes, very pale.'

'You didn't see the girl?'

'I just took one look, then closed the curtains.'

Bimsley thought for a moment. 'Why did you look out in the first place?'

'As I said, it was too late in the year for the van to come around,' she explained, absently twisting her loose wedding ring. 'And then there was the tune. They normally play "Greensleeves". This one was playing something jolly from an opera.'

'Can you remember what the tune was?' asked Bimsley.

'No,' replied the old lady, shaking her head at the floor, 'but I can tell you it was something by Gilbert and Sullivan.'

'You're usually on the desk downstairs, aren't you?' whispered the young girl standing beside her. 'My name's Sandra.' She held out her hand. Jerry shook it and smiled back.

'I'm just filling in for today,' she explained. 'They're short-staffed.'

For the past ten minutes they had been standing sandwiched between stainless steel tea urns, behind a low table filled with clingfilm-covered plates of sandwiches. Until now, neither of them had spoken. Sandra seemed shy and overawed by the guests. Jerry wanted to say something that would put the girl at ease, but realised uncomfortably that to do so might be patronising. A nasty little class gap lay between them like a concealed mine.

Jerry wasn't in awe of these people. She saw them every day at home.

Ahead of them, across acres of crimson carpet, the shareholders sat beyond oak-panelled doors which had been pulled tightly shut. The only sound that could be discerned from within was a thickly muffled murmuring.

The whole exercise had proven to be a waste of time. Jerry dragged at the hem of her ill-fitting waitress outfit, trying to work it below her knees. The least the duty manager could have done was to find her some clothes that fitted properly. It had taken her ages to pin her unruly hair beneath the white cap. She looked over and found Sandra smiling apologetically.

'It's difficult keeping your legs warm in this weather, isn't it?' said Sandra, ducking her head. 'Then you come in here and it's so hot. I've got these heavy wool tights and they're itching like mad. They should be coming to an end about now.' She nodded toward the conference room in reference to the group rather than her underwear arrangements.

'Who are they?' asked Jerry. 'Do you know?'

'Friends of the Savoy, something like that,' said her new friend, her voice barely above a whisper. 'Something to do with the theatre next door.' From within came the sound of chairs being shoved back. The meeting had been concluded, and Jerry was no wiser than she had been before.

As the oak-panelled doors were folded open and the committee members filed out toward the refreshment table, she examined their faces, trying to see them as conspirators, but it was impossible; a less sinister group of people would have been hard to imagine. They looked like an average church congregation, with the exception that there were rather more of them. Most of the ladies

were middle-aged and wore firmly pinned hats. The
gentlemen were besuited and spectacled, conservatively
dressed by their family tailors.

As she began filling coffee cups and passing them out,
Jerry strained to catch exchanges of dialogue within the
group. After ten minutes she gave up. Beyond the odd
phrase referring to investments and healthy rates of
return, there seemed to be very little business being
discussed. Of the two couples nearest to her, one was
airing the problem of waterlogged lawns and the other
was complaining about a recent play at the National. It
was hopeless. She could have spent the morning resolving
her difficulties with Nicholas instead of wasting time like
this.

After a further ten minutes the room began to clear, and
Sandra started packing away her end of the table.

'I wonder if I have time for another cup of tea?' asked a
pink-cheeked old dear in a ratty-looking fur coat.

Smiling wanly, Jerry took her cup and refilled it.
'Thirsty work in there, was it?' she asked.

'Oh no, not really.' The old lady accepted the cup and
began heaping sugar into it. 'But it's all very exciting,
nevertheless.' She leaned forward secretively. 'We're
buying a theatre,' she confided.

'Really?' Jerry joined her halfway over the table, a fellow
conspirator. 'Who's *we*?'

'Cruet,' replied the old lady. Jerry frowned. Was she
looking for the salt?

'I'm sorry?'

'The Committee for the Restoration of West End
Theatres,' she replied. 'CROWET.'

'Oh, I see. And you're taking over the place next door?'

'That's right. Two years ago I helped save the otters; last
year it was typhoid; but this is much more interesting.

How did you know which theatre we've purchased? It's supposed to be a secret.'

'Oh,' she replied airily, 'we had a Japanese gentleman staying here who was going to buy the Savoy.' She waited while the old lady stirred her tea. 'But I believe the deal fell through.'

'Apparently, yes. I understand he changed his mind at the last minute. The yen isn't strong at the moment, or something like that.'

'Rachel, dear, we're going via the Brompton Oratory, do you need a lift?' called one of the remaining men. The old lady smiled vaguely at her and pottered away to join the group.

CROWET, thought Jerry. It wasn't much to go on, but at least it was a starting point.

# CHAPTER

John May strode along the marble-faced corridor, his grey mane bouncing at his shirt collar. He had had enough of Tomlins' refusal to return his phonecalls, and had decided to pay a surprise visit to the Goldsmiths' hall.

He pushed open the door at the end of the main chamber and entered, passing a pair of startled secretaries. Tomlins was seated at his desk, fountain pen poised above a sheaf of documents. His eyes bulged in his florid face as he recognised the detective.

'Mr May, I told you I'd call you once I had found someone you could talk to,' he said, attempting to pre-empt May's complaint.

'And when might that be?' asked May. 'As I see it, you're deliberately attempting to obstruct an investigation.'

'It's not as easy as you think,' he said calmly, recapping his pen with deliberate care. 'I mentioned the fact that you would like to discuss certain aspects of the Whitstable family's lives with someone who knew them, but I'm afraid I've had very little response. Perhaps people have no wish to speak ill of the dead.'

'Why would anyone speak ill?' May moved into the room and seated himself in the only other chair. 'Weren't they liked? You told me you barely knew them. How many guild members do you have here?'

'Oh,' Mr Tomlins waved his hand airily, 'it would be hard to estimate ...'

'Mr Tomlins, let me make things simpler for you.' May was beginning to lose his patience. He had seen men like the general secretary in every walk of life, 'clubbable men' who used the privilege of membership as a class weapon. 'I want exact figures from you right now, this morning, or I'll have you brought in and your files sequestered as evidence. I want to know how many members of the Worshipful Company Of Watchmakers there are, and how many of those belong to this little inner circle of yours, the one which uses the symbol you couldn't recognise, the sacred flame. Then we'll start going through names and if necessary we'll publicly interview every single person on your list.'

Tomlins' sanctimonious half-smile froze on his face. 'You must understand that this is information we never give out ...' he said, his voice climbing to a falsetto.

May waved the objection aside. 'You send your members mailings, every organisation does. The names and addresses are presumably in your secretary's computer. I passed her IBM on the way in. I'll use it myself if you like.' May placed his hands on his knees and rose.

'All right, I'll get you the list,' said Tomlins hastily, 'but I don't know what you mean by an inner circle.'

'We'll go through the names first,' said May, 'then we'll come back to the sacred flame. I'll have a number of other requests in due course. Until then, I suggest you make yourself busy, because you wouldn't believe some of the things I'm going to be asking you to do for me tomorrow.'

Alison Hatfield was waiting for him at the foot of the main staircase, dwarfed by the white statues of the four seasons. As May approached her through the temple of chalced marble, he wondered if she had come to a decision. Last night he had called her and asked for her help. As she was employed outside the Watchmakers Company but within the same system, he figured that she would be the ideal person to assist him.

'Thanks for meeting me, Miss Hatfield,' he said, as she led him to the deserted Court Room in the north-west corner of the building, 'I need a guide through all of this.' He showed her a folder filled with computer paper.

'Please, call me Alison. We won't be interrupted in here.' She pushed open a pair of heavily carved doors. May's mouth fell open as he gazed upon the elaborate gold and silver cornices of the Court Room.

'Impressive, isn't it?' Alison pointed at the far wall. 'That piece of stone behind the Prime Warden's chair is a Roman altar from the second century. Some workmen discovered it in the building's foundations about a hundred and fifty years ago. The figure on the side is Diana, or Apollo, we're not sure which.'

'Extraordinary,' he agreed. 'It makes you wonder how much more of London is still hidden away from public view.' They seated themselves at the mahogany banjo-shaped table which dominated the room. 'I thought it was supposed to be classless, all of this, wasn't it? I mean, the guilds were for artisans and their families.'

'The guilds still carry out a massive amount of work for charity,' said Alison absently.

'So does the royal family.' God, thought May, I'm

beginning to sound like Arthur. That's what sharing an office with him does. He emptied the folder on to the leather surface of the table.

'I'll be honest with you, Alison,' he said with a sigh. 'There are unusual pressures being brought to bear on us, and I'm desperate for some outside help. The murders occurred within a respected family during Commonwealth fortnight. Could Peter Whitstable have died when an incendiary device of his own making exploded? I know the whole family belongs to the Watchmakers; their ancestors are men with mechanical minds. Did they do this to each other? If so, why the hell would they abduct a small child? Are the Whitstables members of some private club which exists within the Watchmakers? How can I find out if they are?' He sat back in his chair and turned to her. 'You see my problems.'

'What can I do to help?'

May reached forward and patted the papers. 'I need you to look through this lot and find me the name of anyone who can tell me the truth about the Whitstables. Tomlins is either too scared to talk, or genuinely knows nothing about what's going on. I fear it's the latter. Can you honestly say that no one here has ever seen this sign?' He held up the picture of the sacred flame once more. He didn't want to tell her that the only person to recognise it as a guild symbol was Arthur's butcher.

Alison took it from him and carefully examined it. 'Actually, I have seen it somewhere,' she said slowly.

'Where?'

'I think it was on a brochure. We help the Watchmakers send out their mailings. I don't know whether it was to do with them directly; there are many associated companies. I think it was something connected with their charity work.'

'Would you have any of these brochures left?' asked May.

'There are bound to be some in the basement. All the leftovers are packed in boxes. We never throw anything away.'

'Can we go and look?'

'It'll be very cold and dark. A real mess. No one ever goes down there.'

'I really need your help, Alison. Please, it'll be easier than trying to find them by myself.'

'All right,' she said finally. 'I'll take you down. But we'll have to get a couple of torches.'

The ancient trellis goods lift shook and rattled as they descended into musty darkness. Bare concrete walls rose around them. It was as if they were leaving the guild hall for the ruined Temple of Diana which lay buried far beneath it.

'Why aren't there any lights down here?' asked May, watching his breath turn grey in the chill air.

'I don't know.' Alison pointed to the tiny dim bulb set in the ceiling of the lift. Standing in the gloom with her nose tilted and her hair brushed to the back of her long neck, Alison looked like a Pre-Raphaelite heroine. He wanted to touch her skin, to see if it could really be that soft and pale.

'There are a few emergency lights,' she explained, 'but they must operate on a separate circuit. I think it's a different voltage or something.'

'Great,' said May, remembering his partner's dictum that bad things happened when the lights went out. The elevator stopped with an echoing thump, and Alison pulled open the trellis. She clicked on her torch and shone it along a faintly lit corridor.

'This way,' she said, holding back the gate for him. They passed nearly a dozen darkened doorways before she turned into a tall, windowless storeroom and shone the torch beam over stacks of boxes.

'If the brochures are down here at all, they'll be in one of these.'

'Okay, you start at one end and I'll start at the other,' said May. For the next half-hour they tore open the lids of damp-smelling cartons and checked the mildewed contents. May was just resealing one of the boxes when he heard a scuttling noise in the darkness beyond the room, like tintacks skittering across tiles. 'What was that?'

Alison looked up at him, her pale eyes catching the light like some kind of nocturnal animal. 'I think there are rats,' she said calmly. 'Hardly anyone ever comes down here because of the leak.'

'What leak?' May looked down at the torch. The beam had begun to falter.

'One of the tributaries of the River Fleet runs right under here. Sometimes, after a very heavy rainfall, you can hear a dull rumbling underneath the floor. It's a really creepy sound. There's a leak in one of the corridors below, and the rats get in. They breed in the river. They're supposed to be as big as cats.'

'There's another floor below this?'

'Yes, but they dammed it up with cement because of the danger from the river.'

May found himself listening for the rush of the underground current. The torch flickered again. He tapped the glass with his hand. On the other side of the room, Alison ripped open a carton and emptied it. 'I think I've found them,' she called.

May clambered over the boxes and joined her just as his torch beam dwindled to nothing. She held one of the brochures high and shone her light on it.

The back page bore the stamp of a golden flame

burning in heavenly light. The words LUX AETERNA were written in neat Tudor script beneath it, and beneath this were printed the words *Alliance of Eternal Light*. May took the brochure from her and turned it over. The headline across the front read: *Renovating London's Most Beautiful Theatres: How You Can Help*. Below was a reproduction of a Victorian painting showing an excited first night audience. May opened the front cover and found himself gazing at a pair of photographs, smartly bordered in gold.

One showed the late William Whitstable. The other was a portrait of the family's founder, James Makepeace Whitstable, a man who had been dead for the best part of a century. A man, thought May, studying the stern face in the photograph, who still exerted such power over his descendants that nothing, not even death, would allow them to share their secrets with the outside world.

# CHAPTER

*The Guardian, 21 December*

## POLICE INCOMPETENCE BLAMED FOR DAISY DELAY

The search for little Daisy Whitstable, aged seven, taken from her Chelsea home on Sunday afternoon, got off to a poor start after a fourteen-hour delay because police missed vital information.

Daisy's disappearance had not been connected to an ongoing investigation of several mysterious deaths among the little girl's distant relatives. Because the crucial link had been overlooked, investigative work was set back at a time when it was most needed.

*Daily Mail, 21 December*

## NO CHRISTMAS CHEER IN MISSING DAISY HOUSEHOLD

Pretty Christmas stockings hang above a merrily burning log fire, waiting to be filled. A saucer of water stands beneath the sparkling, bauble-covered tree, a child's thoughtful offering for weary reindeer. But unless a miracle occurs, there will be no joyous Christmas laughter in this house, only anguished tears.

For this is the home of little Daisy Whitstable, abducted on Sunday evening last. Instead of the welcoming sight of a jovial red-faced Santa stacking presents at the foot of the bed, there has been a grimmer, not-so-jolly uninvited visitor — and instead of emptying his yuletide sack, he has filled it.

*Letter to the Independent, 21 December*

Dear Sir,

Your recent suggestion that the 'sacred flame' symbol associated with the victims in the Whitstable murders has a connection with a secret Nazi assassination bureau is utter hogwash.

The symbol that is currently being flaunted in the national press bears no resemblance whatsoever to the one which made a brief appearance toward the end of the Second World War. It is, however, very similar to the sacred flame of certain Victorian occult societies.

These societies harboured no murderous intent, being merely gathering spots for clubbable men who welcomed the occasional chance to escape from the wife and summon up Beelzebub in the company of a few friends.

Yours sincerely,
Rev. George Bartlett.

'I want to see John May,' she said, trying to regain her breath after having galloped up the broken-down escalator at Mornington Crescent tube station.

Christina Crosse looked up from a stack of reports and regarded her coolly. 'Good morning, Miss Gates. You're early today.'

The desk clock read 07.43. Jerry had not slept well, and knew she had dark smudges beneath her eyes. The sergeant looked as if she had been working all night.

'However,' she said, 'Mr May was even earlier. You just missed him. He's doing some more interviews. I'm expecting him back at noon. Do you want to leave a message?'

'No — it can wait.'

She was desperate to share her findings about CROWET, but forced herself to hold on until she could speak to the detectives in person.

'Jerry.' Christina was tapping her pencil against the desk and frowning at her.

'What?'

'If you don't have anything specific to do here, can you come back later? We're really busy.'

'Sorry. I thought I could, you know, help or something.' She was about to leave when she noticed the damp-stained theatre brochure on the sergeant's desk. The front cover showed a painting of the interior of the Savoy Theatre. May had obviously been following the same lead. So much for promising to keep her in the picture.

'At least let me buy you a coffee, Christina.' She offered an inspirational smile.

'Actually you could do that,' said the sergeant. 'I can't get away from this desk.'

'I've only got pound coins. Do you have change?'

'Let me see.' Crosse turned to the raincoat hanging on the stand behind her and fished through the pockets as Jerry slipped the brochure neatly inside her jacket. She felt that she had every right to do so. Joseph had been cheated out of his job, and the police would doubtless be unable to help him. Now it was up to her.

'You said to drop it if I didn't find anything out, but I did,' she insisted, setting her tray on the counter. She was annoyed about having to justify her actions to Joseph.

They were seated in the coffee bar opposite the Savoy, where she was supposed to have started her shift ten minutes ago.

'I'll just go to her house and talk to her. What harm can possibly come of that?' She stared into a cup of scalding, foamy tea and sighed. 'I can't get hurt, if that's what you're worried about.'

'You're out of your depth,' Joseph insisted, not for the first time this morning. 'The police are prepared to let you help them out. You've virtually got your own hotline to them. Why not be content with that?'

'It isn't enough, Joseph. They may never discover the truth. Lots of murders remain unsolved. I can do interviews they'd never be able to get.'

'If you think you can make a difference, fine.' Joseph threw his hands up in defeat. 'You stole evidence from a police station and it's not even 9.00 a.m. yet. Imagine what you can accomplish by lunchtime. Go and see this woman, pretend you're from the press or whatever harebrained idea you've come up with, see where it gets you. I can't stop you.'

If she didn't have Joseph's blessing, it couldn't be helped. She was determined to see the thing through, and that meant finding out more about CROWET. Peggy Harmsworth was William Whitstable's co-director on the theatre committee, and the only other person to be listed by name in the CROWET brochure. Reading the printed biographies, she had found Mrs Harmsworth named as a Whitstable, the wife of Oliver Whitstable and grandmother to the abducted Daisy, in what proved to be yet another uncharted branch of this interminable family.

'I won't get into trouble,' she promised. 'Would you do me one small favour? Tell Nicholas I have a cold and can't come in to work?' She reached across the counter to touch his hand. Even before he replied, she knew what his answer would be.

The rain was still falling in a fine mist as Jerry pushed open the gates of North London's exclusive Holly Lodge estate, on the West Hill leading to Highgate. The twenties mock-tudor houses, recessed from the gravelled streets beyond billiard table lawns, reeked of secret wealth and functioned as the Bel-Air of London.

Peggy Harmsworth didn't get to live in a place like this by giving much away. She had agreed to be interviewed at short notice only because she had been offered a bargain. Jerry knew how to handle the Peggy Harmsworths of the world; she had been around such people all her life.

Her plan was a simple one. She had rung Mrs Harmsworth and offered her money for a series of interviews in a fictitious magazine. A small fortune would change hands on one condition — that an impromptu preliminary discussion this morning went well. That was her escape clause. Okay, it was a scam, but Jerry saw no reason why it shouldn't work. She smoothed out her skirt and rang the doorbell. Her Savoy uniform was smart, and would add an aura of respectability. It was a good job Peggy's choice of surname had kept her away from the crime unit on Sunday, or else she might recognise her visitor.

Peggy had been seated in the lounge awaiting her arrival. She was a well-preserved fifty, smartly dressed in a grey suit, a white silk blouse, and a single rope of flawless pearls. She had the look of a practical woman, and even sat purposefully. Her sleek dark hair was pulled back and fixed with a discreet gold clasp. At her feet lay a small, hypertense dog of the kickable variety. She did not look as if she was about to countenance any nonsense. Nor did she look entirely sober. After a shameless discussion about money during which Jerry lied through her teeth, they settled down to work.

'I do like your fringe,' Peggy cried in a theatrical voice. 'I suppose the thirties look is back.'

'Matched by your wall decorations, I see,' said Jerry, looking around at the dusty animal heads which peered forlornly down at them. 'Did you kill them yourself?'

'I can't be responsible for the mistakes of my ancestors.' She ground out her cigarette in an antelope-foot ashtray.

No tea and biscuits here, thought Jerry gloomily. She walked over to where Peggy Harmsworth was seated and examined the smouldering ashtray-foot. 'I assume there are three others like this.'

'I thought you came here to ask impertinent questions about my family. It's a little late to give me lessons in ecology. I'm a major consumer.' She tapped out another cigarette and lit it. 'For God's sake sit down. You're making me nervous.' She exhaled a cloud of blue smoke. 'Well, come on. Interrogate me.'

Jerry cleared her throat. 'As I explained on the telephone, Mrs Harmsworth, my articles will present the family's side of the story regarding your recent tragedies, and I'd like you to be as frank as possible. Do you think the abduction of your granddaughter is connected to the recent deaths?'

'Of course I bloody well do!' Peggy exploded. 'The most hopeless idiot can see that we're being decimated.'

'But who hates you enough to do such a thing?'

She tipped back her head and fountained smoke at the ceiling. 'That's rather the question, isn't it? All import—export businesses make enemies. When your main aim is to throttle the life from the home competition, you're bound to tread on a few toes.' She studied her cigarette, addressing the end of it. 'Of course, these days nobody behaves in an openly vicious fashion. Rivals don't get obliterated, they get gently squeezed out, like spots. We're not the Krays.'

She fanned smoke away from her face. 'Don't misunderstand me. The financial world is as nasty as ever, but in subtler ways. The Whitstables haven't stitched anyone up in years. Our grandfathers behaved like bastards, but then so did everyone else. The East India Company had set a fine example at the start of the last century, exporting opium to China, monopolising the drug and fostering the addiction of the Chinese so that Britain could profit from imported tea and silks. They had always had to fight for their trading rights. Nearly one hundred and fifty people were shoved into the Black Hole of Calcutta at Fort William. I don't suppose they teach you this sort of thing at school anymore.' She peered suspiciously through the smoke at her. 'With the government approving company plans like these, no wonder there has always been so much bad behaviour in the City.'

'Let's get back to the present day,' said Jerry. 'What about the CROWET symbol? Where did that come from?' By asking questions about the theatre organisation, she hoped to detour around the familiar roadblocks she had seen the Whitstables set up whenever they were asked something personal. But Peggy seemed ready to talk about anything.

'It's the symbol of the Alliance of Eternal Light. It's not as grand as it sounds, merely an organisation founded over a century ago by some of the Watchmakers Company members.'

'Who, specifically? James Makepeace Whitstable — the chap on your brochure?'

'Yes, it was James's inspiration. No doubt the name came to him in one of his evangelical moods.'

'What are the modern-day duties of the Alliance?'

'These days it's a philanthropic trust mainly involved in charity work, although I don't think that was always the case.'

'You mean it used to be a profit-making organisation?'

Peggy exhaled another plume of smoke and closed her eyes, working her thoughts back. 'I think it was originally started as some kind of get-rich-quick scheme. The family coffers were empty and James came up with a plan to fill them. Whatever he did, it worked for a hell of a long time. Much of the family fortune can be traced back to around that period. Finally it evolved into a holding trust for organisations like CROWET. We've just taken over the restoration of the Savoy Theatre. A Japanese consortium was handling it, but we successfully managed to buy them off. It was rather odd.'

'How so?'

'A few days ago the Japs suddenly dropped out, leaving us with a successful bid for the building. It was almost too good to be true.'

'Why do you say that?'

'Because we've always wanted the Savoy. Now, with the Alliance's help, we'll be able to ensure that the theatre reopens this Christmas. It's a pet project of mine.'

'Who runs the Alliance now?'

'We've all helped out from time to time. It's a private family concern. There are no outsiders involved.'

Jerry was disappointed to hear that the guild's inner organisation was nothing more than a charity. 'Would the Alliance have kept records of its history?'

'I suppose so,' said Peggy, reaching down to box the dog about its ears. She was starting to sound suspicious about the tone of the interview. 'They're probably at the guild, but I don't see why you need to look at those.'

'I was just curious. By the way, why theatre restoration?'

'What do you mean?'

'Why is it of such particular interest? I mean, why not battered wives or sick children?'

'The Alliance has been connected with the London stage since its inception, don't ask me why. I'm not sure anyone remembers now.'

'One last question. This brochure.' Jerry removed it from her pocket. 'Who designed it?'

'We have freelance people we call upon for printing and suchlike,' she said, clearly disinterested.

Jerry flipped through the booklet, folding it open. 'I couldn't help admiring the paintings that illustrate the copy. Holyoake, Sickert, Chapman, Crowe, enchanting stuff. And a lot of them R.A. Any particular reason for that?'

'Of course. We never do anything without a reason. The Royal Academy had a strong link with the foundation of the Alliance, and the connection has been maintained. James Whitstable was some kind of honorary Academy member. I'm not sure why. You'd really have to ask them. All of the interesting things that ever happened to our family happened a long time ago, and all in the name of duty. Now, if there are no more questions, I think it's time for a cocktail. When would you like to send me your cheque?'

# CHAPTER

Bryant insisted on driving his battered blue Mini Minor to their appointment in South London. Although his skill in negotiating major intersections had marginally improved in the last few years (the only useful by-product of endless failed tests), he still refused to obey any traffic sign he considered superfluous, and that included most of them. Weaving through the heavy lunchtime traffic in Victoria proved to be a logistical nightmare, as Bryant remained oblivious to the shouts and honks of dumbfounded fellow motorists. Even highway-hardened truck drivers blanched and braked when faced with Bryant's blithe disrespect for the road.

'Leo Marks has sent down a mass of documents pertaining to the financial history of the Whitstable empire,' said May. 'Christina's having most of the facts and figures transferred to our database, but it's a laborious job. I want you to go through it with me when she's finished.'

'Couldn't I just look at the documents?' asked Bryant, peering through the windscreen for an all-clear, then stamping down on the accelerator.

'You'll be able to collate facts more clearly from the screen,' assured May. 'The database is being assembled with a cross-referenced index. A brief overview of the various holding companies — and there are hundreds going back across the century — suggests that the whole family is slowly going broke. Nothing precipitous, just a gentle decline of fortune. Their philanthropy is well established and beyond reproach, although their business practices throughout the early years show a lot of very nasty tarnishes. Lawsuits, maltreatment of workforce, exploitation of minors, racial discrimination, restrictive practices, stuff like that.'

'The Victorians weren't too fussy about how they expanded their empire,' said Bryant. 'They thought God was on their side. It's always a big mistake mixing religion and business. We need to find somebody who's been burned by the Whitstables in their financial dealings. We might hear a few home truths then.'

'Trouble is, they've closed ranks against outsiders, ever since we began conducting interviews. Their answers are too similar to each other's. They sound rehearsed.'

'Then we'll conquer by dividing them up.'

He and his partner were walking briskly along the river footpath at Vauxhall, a dismal part of the Embankment barely cheered by the thin winter sunlight refracting from the dirt grey waters of the Thames. Daisy Whitstable had been missing for over thirty-six hours. There had been no new developments in the search for the bogus ice cream van, and now that the capital had begun emptying out for the Christmas holidays, interviewing for witnesses had become even less rewarding.

May kicked out at a stone, sending it skittering against the wall of the Embankment. He had never felt so helpless in his search for a common enemy, and the strain of the past two weeks was beginning to tell on him. 'I think they've been told not to speak to us by a member of the family,' he said, 'someone they all respect. But who?'

'They're just naturally secretive,' offered his partner. 'We've interviewed virtually all of them.'

'No family is impregnable, Arthur. There must be a weak link. We can't just wait until someone breaks from the party line.'

'No, but we can keep talking to the older members separately.' On the previous evening, the detectives had attempted to speak to Mina Whistable, the bedridden mother of William, Peter and Bella. For the last five years the old lady's grip on reality had been tenuous at best, and the deaths of her children had provided the final push into mental aphasia. They were now pinning their hopes on Edith Eleanor Whitstable, a contemporary of Mina's and something of an outsider, judging by the rest of the family's comments about her.

Edith was an irascible sixty-seven-year-old matriarch who owed little loyalty to those around her. Referring to her earlier interview with Sergeant Crosse, May saw that she had been frequently and volubly critical of the running of the Whitstable's business empire, in which she had long taken an active role. Three months ago she had suddenly moved out of the district where she had spent most of her life, choosing to live instead on a small private estate by the river. May was interested in finding out why. Bryant tapped him on the shoulder and pointed to a number of large red-brick buildings with arched windows.

'I must have written the address down wrong. This is the old Sarson's vinegar factory.'

'Not any more,' said May. 'Looks like it's been converted into town houses.'

'This sort of property is built for single professionals, not dowagers. Why on earth would she want to move here?'

'Perhaps her old house was too large for her to manage.'

They were buzzed in through a pair of electronically controlled iron gates, and found themselves in a large mock-Elizabethan courtyard of herringbone brick.

'How did she sound on the phone?' asked May as they searched the video-register for the old lady's apartment number.

'Nervous. Certainly not the dragon I was expecting. We might find out something useful. Here we are.'

Edith Whitstable resided in a medium-sized ground floor apartment on the far side of the estate. She had a small manicured garden lined with conifers, and brass carriage lamps set in the front wall. The setting seemed out of place with the Whitstable character. Bryant gave his partner a puzzled look as he rang the doorbell and loosened his scarf.

The heavyset woman who answered the door looked younger than her age, and welcomed them in with an easy warmth.

'You found us,' she said, taking their coats. 'I've already made tea, or would you prefer a scotch on a raw day like this?'

'Good idea, it's cold enough to freeze the—' said Bryant before a look from May stopped him. 'Tea will be fine.'

The apartment had the sparse decoration of a newlyweds' home. If Edith Whitstable had brought any of her old furniture with her, it wasn't in evidence. A number of iron crucifixes lined the hallway, and there were several more austere religious icons of varying size in the lounge.

'I understand you wish to ask me more questions,' she said, setting down a tea tray and starting to lay out the cups. Her plump hands sported pale indentations from wearing rings that had now been removed. Her dress was floral, cheap, off the peg. Around her neck was a large silver cross. Bryant supposed that she must have fallen upon hard times. Yet, when they had met en famille at Mornington Crescent, he remembered that she had been wearing a pearl choker and a mink coat.

'That's right, Mrs Whitstable. It shouldn't take long.' May checked his notes. 'Your husband Samuel died two years ago, is that right?'

'Yes. Cancer of the spine. He was in pain for a long time. The children were a great help.'

'You have two boys, don't you? Jack and Harry?'

'Hardly boys, Mr May. They're in their early fifties.'

'What relation were you to William, Peter and Bella Whitstable?'

'They were my cousins. All of the modern-day Whitstables stem from James and Rosamunde somewhere along the line, starting around the middle of the last century. I suppose you know all about them?'

'No, our investigations don't go back quite that far.'

'Oh, but they should! James was a fascinating man, kind, charming, a devout Christian. He carried out so many wonderful works, as did his children. Alfred, his oldest son, founded several charitable missions in the East End, you know.'

'What about Daisy Whitstable?'

'A terrible business,' said Edith without hesitation. 'Her grandparents are also my cousins. Her paternal grandfather was shot down in the Second World War.'

A clang of metal sounded in the next room, followed by a grunt. Whatever had made the noise, Edith chose to ignore it.

'I understand you've recently moved house,' said Bryant, looking about. 'You must miss the old place, seeing as you grew up there. The recession can't have been favourable to family fortunes.'

Edith showed surprise at the question. 'Selling up has had its good and bad sides, Mr Bryant,' she said, nervously brushing the fingers of her right hand over her cross. 'It has brought our family closer together. And it has helped me to rediscover my devotion to Our Saviour.'

'I should imagine the money helped, too,' added Bryant crisply.

'It's no secret that we've had financial difficulties since Samuel died. With the house up for sale I will at least be solvent once more.'

'Couldn't you have borrowed from someone else in the family?'

'Neither a borrower nor a lender be, Mr May. Besides, none of us are as wealthy as we used to be, so we can't lean on each other for financial support.'

Another clang and grunt sounded from the next room.

'You say you've been brought closer together as a family, Mrs Whitstable. A cynic might suggest that it's because of the recent assault. No one has any relevant information about your cousins' deaths. No one has anything to gain by their collective demise.'

'You're not suggesting that one of us killed them?'

'You tell me,' said Bryant irritably.

'It's quite impossible,' said Edith, clearly affronted, her hand now clasping the cross at her throat. 'We may be larger and a little more eccentric than the average English family, but at heart we get on very well together. It's in our nature to react with a certain coolness. We are not demonstrative in our loyalties and affections. Nor do we believe in hysterics or histrionics. We quietly set about doing our duty. In that respect we're really very normal.'

Bryant looked doubtful. A clang and a shouted oath boomed through the wall. Edith smiled peacefully. May threw his partner a look. 'Is there somebody in the next room, Mrs Whitstable?' he asked.

'You must forgive the boys,' she explained. 'I'm living with my grandchildren, my Harry's sons. They're working out on their gym equipment.' She turned in her chair and called out. 'Steven, Jeffrey, would you come here please?'

Two muscular young men entered the lounge. They were identical twins, both blond, both broad, both narrow-eyed and feral-featured. They had been lifting weights, and were out of breath. Both had silver crosses fastened around their necks. One of them lowered a vast arm to his grandmother's shoulder.

'Is everything all right, Edie?' he asked, looking sourly at the detectives.

'Fine, boys. My friends were just leaving,' she said with a frightened smile. The detectives rose awkwardly and were ushered from the lounge. Bryant tried to see into the other rooms as they were being returned to the hall, but one of the twins threw his arm across the corridor, barring the way. 'We'll help to see them out for you if you like,' he offered.

'That won't be necessary,' said Edith firmly. 'Everything's fine.'

The boy caught his brother's eye and held it, smiling. 'Praise the Lord,' he said.

'Just like any normal family,' snorted Bryant as they marched back along the Embankment path.

'Well, she doesn't look as if she's been abducted,' replied May. 'She's not being held there against her will.'

'Maybe not, but she's half scared to death. I'm willing to bet that her children have installed her there to keep a watchful eye on her.'

'I don't know, Arthur. We have to be able to trust *somebody*. She sounded perfectly innocent.'

'When it comes to the Whitstables,' said Bryant, '*innocent* is not a word that readily springs to mind.' Talking to Edith about James Makepeace Whitstable had confirmed his suspicions. Although the family's allies and enemies had been created in the past, their influence reached forward to the present. Connections were maintained. Dues were paid. Duty was seen to be done. That was the common link, an all-pervading Victorian sense of duty.

He was sure that even now, after so much time had passed, the trail was far from cold and the danger far from over. The abduction of Daisy Whitstable was firing up press attention to ever-greater heights. God forbid the little girl died, for there would be a public hue and cry of such proportions that it would threaten the entire investigation. It was like facing the aftermath of a terrorist attack. They were expected to produce a culprit, and fast. But how could they when such a person might not even exist?

For Bryant was now convinced that they were seeking no modern-day murderer. Far from it. The answer lay buried in the convoluted lineage of the Whitstable family, and was still waiting to be unearthed.

# CHAPTER

28

'I'm still hungry.'

Daisy Whitstable sat back on the bench and wiped the chocolate from her mouth. Her dress was filthy and crawling with lice, and even though the tunnel door was shut she was shivering in the bitter winter air. She had eaten nothing but ice cream since her capture. The wet brick arches were gloomier since the van's headlights had faded with the dying battery. A neon tube had been plugged into the wall, and threw just enough light across the floor to keep the rats at bay.

Daisy could no longer tell if it was day or night. Her ankles were loosely tied with a piece of nylon cord, and as she was sick of scraping her knees on the rough concrete floor she had given up trying to move about. She had also given up crying. Tears only seemed to make her captor more upset.

'Can't I have something that isn't ice cream?' She looked about and was glad she could not see him. He was there, though. He was always there among the oil cans and coils of rope, crouching in the darkest corner with his head resting on his knees. Sometimes he made strange moaning sounds and frightened her. There was something terribly wrong with him.

The tunnel smelled of his sickness. When he touched her, his skin dented wherever she pressed it, like putty. It seemed to slip on his bones, as if unanchored by muscles. Whenever he came toward her she tried to move away because the smell was so bad. She had stopped trying to understand why her mother and father had not come to take her home. Perhaps she was being punished for something. Suppose she never saw them, or her brother, ever again? Against her will, she began to cry.

In the corner, her captor stirred and rose slowly to his feet. She tried to stifle her tears but it was too late. He was shuffling toward her now, making the shuddering little moan in his throat that she had come to fear so badly. He would reach out and slide her back into the corner of the sack-covered bench, pushing at her with his awful fingers.

Or so she thought, until she saw that this time he was carrying a rusted carving knife in one hand.

Maggie Armitage's face had been created specifically for smiling. She beamed reassuringly at her clients, her eyes waning to happy crescents, and massaged their hands consolingly as she provided conviction enough for both of them. This was an important part of her function, for as the Council Leader of the Camden Town Coven she was often the harbinger of bad news.

Every Monday night, she and the six remaining members of the sect met in the gloomy flat above the World's End public house opposite Camden Town tube station, and attempted to provide some psychic balm for the city's wounds. Evil could not be stopped, merely held at bay, but at least its victims could be helped, and if possible, forewarned of harm.

*John will be furious if he finds out I've agreed to this meeting*, thought Bryant. May had no belief in the Hereafter. Neither did he, if truth be known, but he attempted to keep a more open mind than his partner. In past consultations, information provided by the cheery white witch had proven to be significantly correct, and had helped to close a number of longstanding police files. This good work went unacknowledged by the force, who regarded fringe operators with the same distrust doctors reserved for practitioners of alternative medicine.

Bryant surveyed the ground floor hall of the Victoria and Albert Museum, wondering why Maggie had specifically asked to meet him here, in this sturdy edifice of marble and stone. He turned to find her striding briskly between the glass cases, her spectacles swinging on an amber chain at her bosom. In keeping with the approaching holiday season, she had enough dangling plastic ornaments about her person to decorate a medium-sized Norwegian pine.

'Dear old thing, how well you look!' she cried, causing several members of the public to turn disapprovingly. 'I hope you didn't mind coming here, but I'm with Maureen and daren't let her out of my sight. She's sitting her Witchcraft exams and I said I'd help with the research, but she's a bit of a klepto and tends to heave open the cases when I'm not looking. She's liable to have Aleister Crowley's soup spoons up her jumper before you know it.'

Bryant beamed jovially, catching her energetic mood. 'So you're in here uncovering obscure necromantic rites, eh?' he asked.

'No, actually I was over in the gift shop admiring

their casserole covers, but I'm on a diet so let's not dwell. Maureen's doing her Fellowship of Isis and Dion Fortune — always sounds like a fifties singer, don't you think? — and lately she's developed the habit of dropping into trances so she needs some looking after, especially when we're on her moped. Anyway.' Maggie paused for a breath, and donned her spectacles. Her eyes swam at him from sparkling plastic frames. 'I wanted to talk to you rather urgently as it happens. Nigel is the coven's resident numerologist. I think you've met him.'

'I remember meeting a jolly Jamaican girl a couple of years ago.'

'Oh, Katherine's still with us, but she's called Freya now and won't talk to anyone who doesn't acknowledge her god, Odin. Her husband's not pleased because he's on night work and he sometimes forgets. No, Nigel's very good at Chaos Theory, which is just as well because his maths is terrible, and at the moment he keeps coming up with sevens. Sevens, sevens everywhere, and it all seems connected with you. Or rather, with your investigation. You'd better follow me.'

She led the way back between glass cases of Victorian fans, canes, calling cards and snuff boxes, as high above them late afternoon rain pattered steadily on the angled skylights.

'Very few people bother with this part of the museum,' she explained, turning into a smaller corridor which had been partitioned off from the main floor. 'There's something I want you to see.'

Here the overhead lamps were spaced further apart, and the occultist's multi-coloured sweater sparkled like the scales of a tropical fish as she moved from one pool of light to the next. 'We've been following the case in the papers, of course, and you know how one makes these connections. It was Nigel who remembered reading an obscure Victorian text about the powers of light and darkness.'

At the end of the corridor, a red velvet rope separated them from a dark flight of stairs. Maggie slipped the hook off and beckoned Bryant through. She flicked a switch at her side and a dim radiance shone from below. 'The documents kept here are extremely sensitive to the light,' she explained as they descended. 'As a special interest group we're allowed access to them. Nigel was checking some numerological data when he got to thinking about the sevens. Do you know anything about the power of numbers?' They reached the foot of the stairs and she looked across at him, her eyes lost in shadow, less comical now.

'No,' Bryant admitted. 'I assumed they were all pretty much the same.'

'Not at all.' Maggie paused to sign her name in a visitor's book which lay open on an unmanned reception desk, then walked ahead between dimly illuminated cases, checking each one as she went. The sound of the rain was lost far above them. 'Seven is a very special number. It traverses history like a latitude, always appearing at times of great upheaval. It's a schizophrenic number, Janus-faced, often representing both good and evil, a grouping together and a tearing apart. There are many bloodstained sevens in history: Robert E. Lee's Seven Day Battles in the American Civil War, for example; the destruction of the Red River settlement in the Seven Oaks Massacre; and the battle of Seven Pines. There's the Seven Weeks War — that's the Austro-Prussian war of 1866 — and of course the Seven Years War which involved just about the whole of Europe in 1756.

'There are everyday sevens, like the seven-note scale,

the Seven Hills of Rome, the days of the week, the seven-year itch, then there are lots of legendary sevens: the seven Greek champions who were killed fighting against Thebes after the fall of Oedipus, the Seven Sages of the Bamboo Grove, the Seven Holy Founders, the Seven Gods of Luck, the Seven Wonders of the World, the Seven Golden Cities of Cibola, the Seven Wise Masters of ancient Arab myth, and the Seven Sleepers of Ephesus, soldiers who were resurrected from the dead ...'

'I think I get the idea,' said Bryant. 'What have all these sevens to do with the Whitstable murders?'

'Well, they don't directly — but this does.' She stopped before the end case and wiped dust from the glass with the end of her sleeve. Bryant joined her and peered down. Pinned open in the case were several pages from a Victorian guild booklet that had been damaged by fire. The pages were edged with gold leaf, a tribute perhaps to the Goldsmiths to whom they owed their origin. The watercoloured illustrations had faded badly. Still, the central photograph was clear enough.

It showed a sour-faced man with bright, menacing eyes and bushy eyebrows, standing in the centre of an ornately carpeted room. On either side of this commanding presence sat three men. Each man had a handwritten phrase marked beneath his person.

Bryant donned his spectacles and leaned against the glass, attempting to decipher the titles. A chill draft blew at his ankles as he read, from left to right, *Arathron, Bethor, Phaleg, Hagith, Ophiel, Phul.* The nomenclature beneath the sinister central figure was *Och.*

'The names pertain to the Seven Stewards of Heaven,' said Maggie, tapping the glass with a painted nail. 'God governs the world through them. They're also known as the Olympian Spirits, and can be invoked by black magicians.

Each has a certain day associated with him, as well as a particular planet in our solar system. This central figure here, the tall man, is the Master of the Sun, Bringer of Light, and he governs Sundays. I wondered if you'd come across him yet in your investigation.'

'Oh Margaret,' said Bryant, finally standing and wiping his glasses. 'I most certainly have. I saw his picture only yesterday. What is he doing here?'

'I'd say that these finely dressed Victorians were practising some kind of obscure ritual, wouldn't you?' said the occultist with a dark smile. 'Look at the arcane instruments set on the table beside them. There's no date to the picture but I'd say it was 1880 to 1890. And there's no way of identifying who six of the fine gentlemen are, but we know the identity of the seventh.' Her finger moved over the central figure of *Och*, then to the accompanying panel of text below. The name in the box was that of James Makepeace Whitstable.

'The Victorians were up to their ears in strange sects and movements,' she explained, pulling the top of her sweater up to her chin, 'but the Stewards of Heaven had an ancient and very powerful belief system connected to the secret powers of darkness and light.'

'Presumably this particular sect is no longer in existence?'

'It hasn't been for centuries, but it looks like your victims' ancestor was trying to revive it. As the Seven Stewards are hardly familiar in everyday conversation, I assume he failed to draw a large number of converts.'

'It may not have completely vanished,' murmured Bryant. 'It could simply have remained dormant until now.'

'That's what I wondered,' said Maggie, turning from the display case. 'As alternative belief systems go this one operates on a pretty grand scale. Such organisations have a habit of reviving themselves when conditions are right. Their reappearance and decline occurs in a regular cycle.'

'How long would each cycle last?'

'It could be any timespan of up to one hundred years. In fact, century cycles are rather common.'

'Good God,' said Bryant softly. The image of the Waterhouse painting had sprung into his mind. *The Favourites of the Emperor Honorius.* Seven men.

He took another look inside the glass case, mentally superimposing the painting over the watercolour drawing. Seven acolytes in both. Cold draughts now filled the room, and he gave an involuntary shudder. 'One hundred years,' he said. 'That brings James Whitstable right back into the 1990s.'

'This is a very powerful occult force,' said Maggie. 'It looks as if your troubles are only just beginning.'

PC Steven Burridge was reconsidering his decision to join the Metropolitan Police. His lanky body was numb with cold, and the freezing rain was starting to leak through his sou'wester. His beat was dark, dismal and depressing. It had never felt less like Christmas.

*Be observant,* they had always told him, *be ever vigilant.* But there was nothing to observe beneath the arches of the Embankment except the occasional forlorn tramp, and vigilance was a matter of course at this time of year, when bombs were planted in the West End. No wonder they call us Plods, he mused, as he plodded heavily through the tunnel and emerged in a deserted sliproad at the side of the Mermaid Theatre. What would it be like to have a job that afforded some recognition for his talents?

A thin, echoing wail forced him to break from his thoughts. The sound came from the tunnel at his back.

Now he turned and re-entered it, looking around. It sounded like a cat. Perhaps there was something trapped in one of the recesses of the dripping wall.

The constable stopped and listened, but the sound had ceased. Suddenly it began anew, the cry rising in pitch. He screwed up his eyes and stared into the gloom. He could just make out a bedraggled cat, sitting beside a bundle of coloured rags.

As he walked further into the tunnel the cat ran off, and he saw that the bundle was a small body.

Placing his arm around the child to pick her up, PC Burridge knew that his pleas for recognition had been perversely heard. From now on, he would be known as the policeman who discovered the butchered corpse of Daisy Whitstable.

# CHAPTER

29

All hell had broken loose at Mornington Crescent.

The press were doorstepping the building and the phones were ringing off their hooks. The late edition of the *Evening Standard* had already gone to bed, but the papers wanted the Daisy Whitstable story for Wednesday morning's first editions. The child's parents had been informed, and Isobel Whitstable was being treated for traumatic collapse. It was 11.00 a.m., and Bryant had yet to make an appearance, leaving his partner to face the wrath of their acting superior.

'Where the hell was she all this time? Her clothes were bone dry. Her body was barely cold, so she must have been kept alive somewhere. It doesn't look as if she's been interfered with. The poor little thing has no heart left in her chest. What kind of animal would do such a thing? Why the hell was she taken at all?' Stanley Marsden flopped heavily on to the sofa and lit yet another cigarette. In the last few minutes his face had flowered with red blotches. May wondered if the acting chief was about to have a heart attack, but the effect slowly waned as he calmed down.

'We can't assume anything until forensic tests have been carried out on her clothes. The autopsy will cause trouble.'

'Do we have any further information on the ice cream van?'

'It seems to have vanished off the face of the earth. We're searching all the contract garages and storage arches in London.'

'This could be an entirely separate killing,' said Marsden. 'Have you considered that, or are you just shoehorning it into your current investigation?'

'Sir, it seems unlikely that two murderers are targetting the Whitstable family simultaneously. Daisy's death must be connected. Her dry clothes suggest she was dropped off in the arch, perhaps so that the body could be discovered.' He shifted to avoid the fountains of smoke funnelling from the chief's flaring nostrils.

'I've had nothing from you or your partner in two days,' complained Marsden. 'And now we have another death, the worst one yet. Instead of constructive reports all I get is a list of complaints, first from the Whitstables about your unhelpful attitude and the non-advancement of the case, and then from that whinging twerp of an arts minister who just wants us to shove the whole thing in a file marked *Solved*. Now, though, we've really stepped up into the big time.' He pulled so hard on his cigarette that it crackled. 'They're going to throw us to the lions, do you realise that? It's more or less the end of our careers. The Home Office have called twice in the last hour. I'm having to hide from them. Don't you have anything at all for me?'

May had seen the look on Marsden's face before, a look of panic under pressure that could only bring more trouble. He was begging for something to release to the media, but how could they help him? They had nothing so far that would stand up as substantive evidence.

Earlier that afternoon, Bryant had hesitantly described his discovery at the V&A. He could imagine the look on Marsden's face when he informed him that their only suspect was a man who had been dead for nearly a hundred years.

'Bloody cold out,' said Bryant, suddenly breezing in behind Marsden. 'Oh, hello Stanley, what are the barbarians doing at the gates of Rome?'

'What?' asked Marsden, momentarily nonplussed.

'Journalists.' Bryant waved his hand at the window. 'They're everywhere, bullying receipts out of taxi drivers, crawling all over the place, shouting their heads off.'

'Daisy's been found dead, John,' said May quietly. 'They took her into St Thomas's about two hours ago.' He recounted the preliminary findings of the admitting doctor. Bryant listened in silence, then seated himself at his desk.

'I need to know if you have anything for me,' said Marsden. 'Whatever I tell the press can't be worse than what they're capable of making up. I can't afford to alienate them any further.'

'It's a little late to worry about now,' cried Bryant. 'They've been accusing us of incompetence for the past fortnight. I suppose John must have mentioned our new lead.'

'I've been explaining that we're following a new line of enquiry,' said May, signalling to his partner to shut up, 'but that we're not quite ready to present it.'

'What line of enquiry is this?' asked Marsden, confused. 'If you're keeping anything back from me I'll ...' Just then the office door reopened and the two workmen entered armed with cans and buckets. Marsden turned to glare at them. 'Christ on a bike, do they have to be here all the time?'

'We do if you want these offices finished,' said the older of the two workmen. 'We pack up on Friday for two whole weeks. Do you know how many layers of paint we've still got to strip off before we can do your sills?'

'Oh, for God's sake,' said Marsden, grinding out his cigarette and rising.

'At least we're making good use of our time,' said the younger decorator. 'Leave it to the working classes to handle all the shitty jobs. At least we've got a sense of duty.'

'Yeah,' agreed his mate. 'Try catching a few criminals instead of towing taxpayers' cars away.'

'I can't delay speaking to the Home Office any longer. I'm going to tell them that this whole thing will be wrapped up by the end of the week,' said Marsden, heedless of the breach in security represented by the listening workmen. 'And I'll say the same thing at the press briefing if I have to.'

'Why not give them a hypothetical sequence of events?' asked May. 'Release plenty of facts and figures, all the exact times and dates we've held back, and let them draw their own conclusions. There can't be harm in that. They might even be able to help us.'

'That's not a bad idea,' agreed Marsden, mollified. 'You'd better talk to them. If you can't arrest anyone, at least you can come up with a plausible explanation as to how this whole damned mess occurred. We must explain that whatever triggered this ... explosion of violence ... is finally over and done with.'

'He's going to try and shove it all under the carpet,' said Bryant after the door had shut, 'wait and see.' He unwound his scarf and dropped it onto his chair. 'Five deaths now, and he doesn't care about getting to the truth so long as he keeps himself off the hook.'

'He's panicking because someone's pressuring him to put a lid on the whole business,' said May. Understandably, the death of a child was a highly emotive issue, and the media would wring every last drop of coverage from it.

'It's a government cover-up, innit?' said one of the workmen, heating up his blowlamp. 'Stands to reason. Just like Jack the Ripper.'

'Thank you, Fabian of the Yard,' said Bryant, surveying the mess beyond his desk. Half of the office was now a sickly hospital green, the colour of the paint beneath the surface. The workmen were scraping this off to reveal a layer of impenetrable twenties lincrustre wallpaper.

'This room is starting to make me feel sick,' said May, tossing his partner's hat over to him. 'Let's go.'

'But I've only just come in,' complained Bryant. 'It's thick fog outside.'

'It's not much better in here,' replied May, noting the filled ashtray that Marsden had left behind. 'Come on. We'll slip out the back and I'll buy you a pint over the road.'

'It's much too early for me.'

'We have to talk where no one can find us.'

The saloon bar of the Nun and Broken Compass was mercifully deserted. Only the disgusting dog which lay half in the fireplace ceased clawing clumps of hair from its ears to briefly register their arrival.

'Two days to make a breakthrough,' said May, returning from the bar with pints of Old Peculiar. 'Forty-eight hours. The chances of coming up with something in that time are pretty slim. The city's already half empty.

Have you found out anything more on James Whitstable's little group?' Bryant's first appointment of the morning had been to conduct further research on the Alliance of Eternal Light.

'Only that his family denies any knowledge of his activities,' said Bryant, relishing his first sip of beer. 'There was a biography of him written in the twenties but the British Library has no record of it, so Christina is searching through private collections.'

'Everything about this case is upside down,' complained May. 'We eliminate all the suspects, only to resort to digging through the past. None of the traditional methods of investigation work, and any evidence that turns up seems to appear by accident.'

Just then the saloon bar door opened and Christina Crosse stuck her head around the door. 'Mr Bryant, there you are,' she said, relieved to see him. 'Your friend Mr Summerfield called. He wants to see you urgently. He says he's made some kind of discovery.'

The Kawasaki 500 sat beneath a dripping plane tree, its engine quickly cooling. Joseph slid from the pillion and massaged his rump as Jerry kicked up the stand. She had managed to borrow the bike from a schoolfriend. Neither of them were insured to ride it.

'You haven't given me an answer,' Joseph said, shoving his sweater further into his jeans. 'What are you going to say when she opens the door?'

'I don't know, I'll figure something out. I could introduce you as the photographer who works with me. She's the only lead I have and she certainly knows a lot more than she's told me so far.' Jerry turned to face him. She had slicked back her hair to make herself look older. The ruse had not been particularly successful.

There was no point in explaining that it was a hopeless idea for him to accompany her. He didn't understand her obsession with the murders, but he obviously couldn't stand by and watch her land in trouble.

She checked her watch. Nearly 9.30 p.m. The street behind them was fog-shrouded and silent. The lights were on in Peggy Harmsworth's house, but they had no proof that she was even home.

'I don't see how you expect to extract any more information from her without arousing suspicion. I mean, look at the bloody time. Nobody makes business calls at this hour.' He pulled the sleeves of his leather jacket over his hands. The freezing fog had turned the overhead branches crystalline. This was no night for them to be standing around outside. The Holly Lodge Estate took on the unreality of a film set when perceived through the dim aureoles of the surrounding streetlamps.

Joseph was right. Her impatience had brought them here, but Peggy Harmsworth would have to be insane to believe she was simply revisiting the area.

'Either knock on her door or turn around and go home,' he said finally. 'Make a decision. My blood's slowing down.' He watched as she stared across the glittering lawn, grinding her teeth. 'Maybe I should go with you.'

'No, I can handle it by myself.' She made a fist.

'So tough. What are you doing to do, fetch her a punch up the bracket when she questions you? Assault and battery. Great.'

She was about to reply when they were surprised to see the front door open. After pausing in the hallway for a moment, Peggy Harmsworth stepped on to the drive in a full length mink coat and scarf. The couple pressed back into the shadows of the tree as their quarry set off across the estate on foot.

'That's her,' whispered Jerry.

'Get on the bike,' Joseph hissed back. 'We can follow her with the engine off.' He kicked away the stand and they mounted the bike, rolling silently into the road. Mrs Harmsworth marched purposefully to the far side of the street, then turned into the thickening fog that rolled within the cul-de-sac.

'She can't get out of there,' Joseph whispered over her shoulder.

'Maybe she's visiting a neighbour.'

When she reached the end of the road, Peggy Harmsworth skipped between two tall mock-Tudor apartment buildings and faded from sight.

'Shit, there's an alleyway.' He rolled the bike forward and guided it along the tarmac. After several hundred yards the path opened out onto a hill. On the other side of this stood the iron gates of Highgate Cemetery.

'Where the hell is she going?' Joseph rolled the Kawasaki to a standstill. 'They must have closed the boneyard hours ago.' Ahead of them, Mrs Harmsworth rattled a padlock in her hands and let it drop, passing through a smaller gate set within the large entrance. 'Jesus, she's got her own keys.'

The padlock was refastened on the other side of the railings, and the figure in the mink coat began to retreat once more into the mist.

'We'll lose her if we're not quick,' said Jerry, helping to lean the motorcycle against a tree. She stowed her helmet in the rear panier and pocketed the ignition key. Then she headed for the gates.

'Wait a minute,' said Joseph. He had agreed to go with her to ask the woman a few friendly questions, not follow her into a graveyard. 'We can't get in there, and even if we could ...'

It was too late. Jerry could no longer allow him to hold her back. She was already halfway over the lower gate when he ran for the wall and began to climb after her.

Heels clicked on cement as the mink coat moved through the thickening fog with a powerful strength of purpose. They followed as closely as they dared, the cemetery gates lost somewhere behind them. The main path was illuminated to deter vandals, but the light was sucked into the surrounding trees and barely reached the ground.

Mrs Harmsworth certainly knew where she was going. She switched from the main route on to a smaller path which led uphill, through a less accessible part of the cemetery. Jerry and Joseph could barely keep pace with her. Here, small new graves gave way to the older family tombs.

Despite their general air of neglect, fresh wreaths lay at the feet of several monuments. As she passed, Jerry glimpsed the half-eroded epitaphs. There were Germanic Victorian names and grim little platitudes carved in stone, children 'Joyously Accepted into the Bosom of the Lord' as if death were a privilege, adults 'Departing This Vale of Tears For Eternal Peace'. She sensed lives of dutiful toil passed in the anticipation of acceptance into a welcoming golden kingdom. She saw crumbling monuments to the Victorian conviction of everlasting life. And ahead she watched as Peggy Harmsworth stopped before an ivy-stranded mock-Grecian mausoleum of disproportionate immensity.

Instinctively she dropped from sight, kneeling behind a gravestone. Seeing her, Joseph did the same. Mrs Harmsworth descended the few stone steps and produced another key, inserting it into the portal, which appeared to have been fitted with a standard Yale lock. She quickly shoved back the door, stepped inside, and pulled it half-shut behind her. Jerry turned around and mouthed 'Now what?', throwing up her hands.

'Wait,' he signalled back.

The chill settled about them. Water droplets coated her jacket in a gelid frost. Far in the distance a lorry laboured up the hill, engine noise fading in the encroaching silence. She raised her body, unbending aching knees. A light showed faintly through the doorway of the crypt. Joseph came over to her.

'What the hell could she be doing in there?' he whispered. Somewhere nearby, a branch broke beneath a shoe. They looked at each other and dived back behind their respective gravestones. A figure appeared along the side of the crypt, moving with a spider-like gait, a man wearing a brown slouch hat and a tattered matching greatcoat. He could easily have been mistaken for a tramp, but for the odd theatricality of his attire. As he paused before the door, Jerry looked over at her accomplice, puzzled.

After waiting for a moment or two at the entrance, the tattered man stepped through the gap, entering the crypt. Barely able to contain her excitement, Jerry ran over. 'That's the man,' she said, confidently pointing back, 'the one who attacked me in the theatre. It has to be.' But uncertainty nagged at her.

'Well, is it or not?'

'He's dressed the same, but — he's a lot taller.'

'Great,' said Joseph, 'A murderer who changes height. Why not?' He rose, exasperated. 'Why not add it to the rest? Add it to the blackmail and the poisonings. What *is* it with you, anyway? If you're so scared of the dark, what the *fuck* are we doing in a *graveyard at night*?'

Before she could think of a reply there was a guttural moan followed by a disturbing squeal, like a peal of hysterical laughter, and the door of the crypt was shoved open. As they ran toward it, the tattered man emerged. They could both see that Peggy Harmsworth had fallen backwards on to the floor of the mausoleum and was moving from side to side. Joseph ran down the crypt steps toward her, only to slip over in the blood that had been smeared across the flagstones.

The tattered man threw something aside as he ran, an instrument that shone with a glinting steel edge. Jerry closed in behind him, running hard. The figure in front was light on his feet, and moved quickly across the slick grass between the gravesites, his coat-tails flapping behind. For a moment the tunnel of trees and the fleeing dark figure threw her back into the searing panic of her nightmares and she stumbled, slamming her pelvis against an eroded memorial slab, landing hard on her stomach.

By the time she had pulled herself back up and resumed her pursuit, the tattered man had almost reached the main gate. She ran back onto the path and limped toward the cemetery entrance, just as the frayed figure flew at the lock with a kick that smashed open the small gate through which Peggy Harmsworth had entered.

Jerry could feel the joint of her thigh already starting to bruise and swell. As she drew nearer, the ragged figure abandoned its attempt to reseal the gate and dashed across the road, hauling itself into a small white van parked at the side of the road. Seconds later, Jerry reached the Kawasaki and painfully straddled it, keying the ignition.

The van pulled away down the hill with a squeal of slipping tyres. Jerry jerked out into the road, her crash-helmet still locked in the rear panier. She was trying to think clearly but the bitter wind tore at her skin, blasting aside all rational thought. Although she'd borrowed the bike before, she hadn't ever ridden it at high speed. She tried to keep the van in her sight, but the fog grew thicker with their descent until she could see no more than a few feet in front of her.

Van and motorcycle shot across one junction, then another. London was a deserted city this close to Christmas. The season, together with the poor visibility had kept traffic from the night streets. For the moment no other vehicle appeared in their way. Then the van swung right into a main road, so hard that it seemed it would topple over, and cut across the path of an oncoming bus.

Sounding her horn, Jerry skidded in an arc around the vehicle, mounting the pavement on the far side but holding her position behind the van. Together they raced over Dartmouth Park Road and down toward the city.

She tried to pull out ahead of the van, intending to force it over, but dimly appearing traffic islands and the blinking amber lights of open roadworks warned her back. Her quarry was still picking up speed, racing toward the busy junction at the top of Kentish Town.

Jerry knew that if she jumped the lights there, collision with another vehicle would be unavoidable. The only way to cut off the van would be to do it right now. She twisted the throttle, opening it wide, praying that her tyres would keep their grip on the shining surface of the road.

In the next moment she had drawn alongside the van. The figure within had opened his window and was waving something in his hand. As soon as she saw the shotgun, Jerry's grip on the bike throttle instinctively relaxed and the Kawasaki fell back as the barrel flashed with a muffled thud. She swung back in behind the vehicle, her wheels skipping as they tried to bite on wet tarmac.

They hit the junction above Kentish Town Road at seventy-seven miles per hour. An oncoming Peugeot and a

BMW were forced aside as the van burst from the fog, catching the first car by the front bumper and spinning it into the path of the other. Jerry pushed ahead as the van struggled to right itself, taking to the oncoming lane of the road as she raced toward the red and green Christmas lights of Camden.

The Kawasaki drew along the inside of the van, and then into the lead. Easing the bike over she relaxed the throttle, attempting to decelerate the vehicle behind. As the van's radiator grille buckled her rear mudguard, she knew that the driver had called her bluff and was planning to ride her out. The grille slammed against her back wheel as the van driver accelerated harder.

A crowd of pubcrawling revellers scattered in their path, jumping for the sides of the road. Jerry tipped her handlebars and swung the bike aside, resuming her position at the rear of the speeding vehicle. It was a stalemate.

The van could conceivably drive right across town. Where the hell were the police when you actually wanted to be pulled over? They were usually swarming all over the West End at Christmas, coming at you with their breathalysers. Jerry's face and hands were dead, her fingers locked and frozen, her eyes stinging from the intensity of staring into the pulsing fog. She was surprised at how well she handled the bike, but knew she would have to stop before she killed herself or someone else.

The van perceptibly slowed.

Jerry eased back as it cut through the red lights of a gridmarked intersection, following the one-way system to the right, then left, finally ploughing across Camden High Street into Delancy Street. He was trying to shake off his pursuer. Why? Jerry suddenly realised that the driver was lost. The tattered man had missed his turning somewhere and no longer recognised his surroundings.

As she tore into the deserted streets that ringed the railway lines above the city, Jerry knew that the van would have to stop. Here in this corner of North London, all the streets were effectively sealed off by the tangled network of rail tracks fanning out fifty feet below them. There was no way to safety. The triangular area beyond was known to locals as the Island, hemmed in on each side by Regent's Park, the railway and the canal systems.

With another squealing left turn she knew that the van was in trouble. Following raids, getaway cars usually turned left because they followed the traffic flow. Her quarry was doing the same thing. They entered the dimly lit street at fifty-two miles an hour, and Jerry knew that it was over. Ahead was a solid brick wall, a hump-backed pedestrian bridge and a long drop to the railway tracks. There was everything but a road.

The van slammed its brakes on hard, to no avail. The vehicle continued to charge forward, fishtailing over the glistening tarmac as if the brakes had not even been applied. It hit the metal fencing beside the wall and uprooted two concrete posts. For a moment Jerry thought that the chickenwire might hold. Then the van tore through, the fence screaming over its roof, and slid down the steep embankment to the lines below.

She had just pulled the bike over and dismounted, planning to head down into the cutting, when blue lights reflected on the building walls ahead, and she turned to find herself facing a pair of arriving squad cars.

As Joseph ran down into the Whitstable family crypt to attend to Peggy Harmsworth, the door was pulled shut behind him and an oppressive darkness closed over his senses.

For a moment he heard and saw nothing, nothing at all,

and became aware of how Jerry must feel in the dark. There was someone else breathing right next to him. With a shrill shriek of laughter Peggy thrust out her hands, raking her fingernails across his face, spinning him away from the faint light of the entrance. His legs slipped from under him and he hit the stone floor heavily. As he tried to rise he realised that his ankle was sprained, possibly fractured. With an ear-gouging squeal she leapt on to his back, pulling at his hair, trying to dig her fingers into his eye sockets.

He lashed out at her throat, or where he imagined it to be, and hit stone instead. He tried to force her body away from him and move towards the door, but his sense of direction had been confounded.

Before he could think further she was upon him again, shouting laughter in his face, digging her nails into his skin, sinking her teeth into his shoulder until they met through the flesh, kicking and screaming and lashing him with her hair like an inmate of Bedlam.

As he fought for the door, blinded by his own blood, carrying the ranting maniac on his back, it seemed that he had departed the public realm of the sane to enter someone else's private hell. He fell painfully to his knees as the madwoman dug deeper into him, screaming and crying and piercing his flesh in an echo chamber of her own insanity.

# CHAPTER

30

'Welcome back, Miss Gates,' said May sarcastically. 'We had begun to miss you.'

Jerry wanted desperately to lie down and go to sleep. It was after midnight, and her battered pelvis ached like hell. A few minutes ago she had rung Gwen from the station payphone, and the call had quickly disintegrated into a shouting match. The last thing she wanted now was an official interrogation as well as a parental one.

'Where's Joseph?' she asked, her voice rising little above a croak. She felt as if she was coming down with a cold.

'Your friend is in the next room being taken care of. He's fine, no thanks to you. My congratulations. We don't often find you in the company of live people.'

'Can I have a cup of tea? I can't talk.' May studied her for a moment, then pulled open the door and spoke to someone.

'This had better be good,' said Bryant, scowling as he entered with a tray of teamugs a few minutes later. 'It's nearly one o'clock. I was just about to go home. Old people need extra sleep.'

'Oh, this is good, all right,' said May, pulling out a chair for his partner. 'We've been looking for you everywhere, where the hell were you? Peggy Harmsworth was attacked at the family vault in Highgate Cemetery—'

'My God, is she dead?'

'No, but she's of no use to us as she is.'

'Why?'

May pursed his lips and perused the ceiling. 'Let's see,' he said, 'how can I best put this? She's taken a detour from the highway of mental health. They took her away tied to a stretcher.'

'How? What the hell was she doing there?'

'I really have no idea, but guess what? This young lady was on hand to apprehend her murderer. In case you're not keeping score, this is the third life-threatening experience Miss Gates has managed to witness.' He turned to her. 'If you ever lose your job at the Savoy, you might consider becoming one of the Four Horsepersons of the Apocalypse. Perhaps you'd like to tell us about it in your own words.'

Jerry tried to explain how she and Joseph had come to be there, but to do that adequately she found herself having to backtrack to the blackmailing of Kaneto Miyagawa and the withdrawal of the Japanese from the Savoy to make way for Peggy Harmsworth's theatre society. This meant explaining everything that had happened to her, including the assault in the theatre.

May looked angrier the more he heard. Bryant nodded every once in a while, suggesting that he had guessed as much already.

'You mean to say you withheld this information deliberately from us, when you knew that it was exactly the kind of thing we were seeking?' asked Bryant. 'When we first met I thought you had more brains than this.'

Jerry sipped her tea sheepishly, her fingers wrapped around the steaming mug. She should have taken Joseph's advice, and told them everything days ago.

'Mr Herrick is quite surprised by the events of the evening,' said May. 'He doesn't want to see you for a while.'

'What happened to him?'

'He spent the last part of his evening shut inside a family mausoleum being attacked by a madwoman. The poor bloke thought he was helping you by going along with your half-baked plans. Instead he was left in the dark with a raving lunatic. Luckily one of the bolts was out and the door couldn't swing completely shut, otherwise no one might have known he was inside. There's a keeper living on the premises, and he came running when he heard all the screaming and shouting. God help us when the tabloids get hold of this.'

'You should both be thanking me,' said Jerry hotly. 'I caught your murderer. He's the one. We saw him run out of the crypt seconds after he attacked Mrs Harmsworth.'

'You think he also murdered Max Jacob?' asked May.

'Yes.'

'And Peter, William and Bella Whitstable?'

'Well — yes.'

'What about abducting and slaughtering Daisy Whitstable? He did that as well?'

'Probably. Ask him.'

'You reckon he's also the one who assaulted you at the theatre?'

'I suppose so.' Jerry faltered.

'You don't sound too sure.'

'Well, he's much taller than I remember. Different looking, somehow.'

'Good,' said May, draining his tea. 'I'm glad we've found a fault in your argument. I thought for a minute you'd solved the entire investigation and we could all go home.'

His sarcastic tone bothered Jerry. It seemed out of character. They had been accused of incompetence, of dragging their feet, even of deliberate obstruction. They were clearly at the end of their tether.

'You're holding him in custody, aren't you?' she asked. 'You didn't let him get away?'

'He couldn't exactly run off,' replied May. 'Seeing as both his legs were broken. He fell out of the van as it bounced down the embankment, where it finally came to rest on his head.'

'He's not dead, is he?'

'Well done.'

No wonder the detectives looked so hacked off.

'Was he a member of the family?' Jerry asked nervously. 'Was he a Whitstable?'

'No, he was a gentleman from Pakistan. A window cleaner.'

'*What*?'

'You obviously didn't read the side of Mr Denjhi's van.'

Jerry was aghast. Could he be joking? 'You mean he didn't do it? But I saw him—'

'We won't know what he did until the body has been blood-typed and fingerprinted, and his clothes have been subjected to forensic testing. There's a bit of a queue these days. Right now, Daisy Whitstable's in the line ahead of him. But there's certainly no reason to assume that he has any connection at all with the Whitstable family.'

'He *has* to be the one,' said Jerry desperately. 'It said in the papers that the guy who abducted the little girl was driving a white van. I saw him leave the crypt, we both did. It *couldn't* have been anyone else.'

'What I fail to understand,' said Bryant, 'is what you were hoping to achieve by following Peggy Harmsworth. All right, you thought you could get your friend compensation of some kind for losing his job. There had to be an easier way of doing that, surely? The motorcycle isn't registered in your name. Then there's a charge of reckless driving. Do you have insurance?'

'No.'

'How about a licence?'

'No.'

'How foolish of me to ask. You really think you can piss us about, don't you? That you're superior to all of us? Is your friend in on this as well?'

Jerry shifted uncomfortably on her seat. She set down the tea mug.

'I don't know what you're talking about.'

'We know you're playing a joke, Jerry, so why don't you just admit it? Then we can charge you with wasting police time.'

'I really don't know what you mean,' she pleaded. May looked at his partner, then returned her gaze with a frown.

'I'll spell it out for you. Mr Denjhi was not merely dead. The body we found on the embankment had been dead for *over a week*. The skin was turning leathery. It had been kept somewhere dry, but it had started to decompose. There were needles through his jaw, wiring it to his head, for God's sake. You're trying to tell me that the van you chased through Camden Town was driven by a rotting corpse.'

'But he was alive! I saw him! I swear to God, he tried to kill me!'

'Could you describe this man?'

'No, not exactly. His head and shoulders were in shadow.'

'Tell me something,' said Bryant. 'What is it that keeps you coming back? You always manage to be in the right place at the wrong time. What is it you're after? Is this merely a ghoulish interest in police procedure, or were you planning to trap the killer by yourself?'

Jerry wanted to describe how she felt, but in the harsh light of the crime unit office she knew that her explanation would sound foolish.

They were just sitting there, watching her, waiting for her to speak. 'What is it about your family, Jerry?' asked May.

'My family,' she finally whispered. 'If you've met the Whitstables, you've met my mother. They probably attend the same parties. Gwen's been following the whole thing in the papers. I think she really admires them. Christ, my father's company has even worked for the Whitstable family. They have similar ideals and aspirations. And I'm supposed to be like them.'

'Then why aren't you?'

'I don't know. I'm just different — I feel like I'm adopted or something. The Whitstables are secretive. They're protecting themselves from something they don't want to face. I keep wondering what it is.'

'And if the Whitstables are discredited, your parents won't admire them any more,' said May.

'Maybe, I don't know.'

She felt sure that if she had allowed herself to be pushed into the family business, she would have been used as some kind of asset, an indication that her difficult upbringing had been successful after all. She could hear Gwen now. *Look at my daughter, she was a problem child but now she has a real business head on her shoulders — she has real family spirit.*

She wanted to see the Whitstable family disgraced and discredited. Then perhaps Gwen and Jack would have to put their faith in her, the daughter who had exposed them.

'In a traditional investigation, we'd be concentrating on forensic evidence and statements. We know that such an approach would have led us nowhere. We've been forced to follow alternative methods. My colleague is convinced that the family knows why this is happening to them.'

May reseated himself on the edge of his desk. 'He thinks it has something to do with their distant past. Nobody will talk openly to us. At first I thought they were simply unwilling to share details of their private affairs with the authorities. Now I believe that they're deliberately hiding knowledge of something — some event — that has caused all this to happen. We need inside information.'

'And I could get it,' said Jerry suddenly, sitting forward. 'If you give me half a chance.'

Bryant was about to dismiss her remark when he stopped short, his eyes narrowing. 'Out of the question,' he said unconvincingly.

'You said they won't talk to you, but they might to me. Provide me with the credentials and I'll feed you the information. It's just the sort of thing I'm good at.'

'We can't risk anyone else's life, Arthur.' May shook his head. 'It goes against every rule ...'

But Bryant was slowly warming to the idea. 'I haven't heard a better proposition. We could monitor her ...'

Jerry was quick to agree. 'Joseph can make sure I don't get into trouble.'

May thought for a moment. 'You reckon you can trust him?'

'Absolutely.' She searched their faces for signs of approval. 'What do you want me to do first?'

'Go home, get some sleep, and let us think about it,' said May, rubbing his forehead wearily. 'If we decide that we want you to move, we'll dictate *exactly* what you're to say and do. Right now you should be thankful we're not pursuing a reckless endangerment charge.'

Bryant watched the girl leave the office and faced his partner. 'This is our last chance,' he said, 'She may be able to get to them even if we can't. Besides, we're already in so much trouble that one more broken rule isn't going to make much difference.'

'You know it could be dangerous using her.'

Bryant waved the suggestion aside. 'We're running out of time, John. She'll be fine. She'd continue whether we sanctioned her or not. Whatever's really driving her, it's something she's probably not even aware of, and certainly has no power to control.'

'You can't guess what people hide inside themselves,' said May. 'Identity comes from the heart, not the head.'

The problem of Jerry Gates could wait for a few hours. He could see that there was no point in going off duty when the body of Peggy Harmsworth's attacker waited in the morgue. As he rose, his bones cracked. He couldn't take the long hours the way he used to.

'It doesn't look like we're going to get any sleep tonight.'

'In a world like this, only the young can afford to sleep,' said Bryant, winding his scarf around his neck. 'Let's go and wake the coroner. Nobody rests while I'm up. Tell me about Peggy Harmsworth.'

'She's been taken to the Royal Free Hospital, sedated and placed under observation. She assaulted the ambulancemen and bit one of the nurses. Screaming and laughing, clearly suffering from hallucinations.'

'At least *someone's* having a merry Christmas.'

'That's an extremely tasteless remark, Arthur. The admitting doctor thought she'd probably been forced to ingest something, some kind of poison. They're pumping her stomach, but without knowing what she's taken there's a chance she'll still die. They'll let us know more once they've got blood and urine samples.'

'Wait just a minute ...'

'What?'

'Of course! *"Mad, I? Yes, very? But why? Mystery!"'* cried Bryant suddenly.

'What on earth are you on about?'

'Peggy's another name for Margaret, isn't it?'

'I suppose it is. Why?'

'She's become Mad Margaret. An insane figure in tatters, creeping through a darkened graveyard. A character from *Ruddigore*. Don't you see? It's Gilbert and Sullivan again.'

As she walked back along the corridor, Jerry peered through the window of the next office and spotted Joseph. He lay curled up on a seating unit, wrapped in a heavy grey blanket with his huge boots sticking out of the end. His eyes were closed, his face framed by a corona of dirty blond hair. He looked like Burne-Jones's painting of Perseus, except he was covered in scratches and bruises, and had a bloody nose.

She wanted to place her arms around him and kiss the curve of his bandaged neck, wrapped in his sleeping warmth. She wanted to tell him things she had never told any man. He would probably never want to speak to her again. After all, she had done nothing but cause him trouble. That seemed to be all she was good for. It felt as if she had never given anyone reason to admire or even like her. Perhaps it was too late.

If she fell asleep now she might never wake up. Jerry stayed beyond the smeared glass for a moment more, then went out into the freezing gloom.

# CHAPTER

*The Sun, 23 December*

## LITTLE DAISY AUTOPSY HORROR

The body of little Daisy Whitstable will today be sliced open in a desperate attempt to find clues to her killer. Despite horrified protests from her parents, the autopsy is still scheduled to go ahead.

At noon today she will be placed naked on a steel slab and:

**SLICED** open with razor-sharp knives.

**GOUGED** apart for her stomach to be studied.

**SEWN** together with huge darning needles.

Detective Superintendent Stanley Marsden said this is normal procedure in such cases.

**The Sun says:**
Her parents have suffered enough. Shouldn't they be spared the gruesome details?

David Balbir Denjhi, aged twenty-nine, was survived by a wife and three children, Christina Crosse noted as she pulled back a corner of her hastily compiled background file. He and his young bride met in London, although they had both emigrated here at an early age with their respective parents. David had clashed with the legal system several times, first with tax inspectors and a filed claim for company bankruptcy, then with an unfounded accusation of handling stolen goods. This had attracted the unwelcome attentions of the immigration authorities, but he'd come through the ordeal and had satisfactorily proven his right to remain in the country.

The woman who now sat before Christina seemed calm and sensible. If she had been crying earlier, she gave no sign of it. Mrs Denjhi poured coffee and sat back in her chair, waiting to be asked more questions. The sergeant knew that her life had become a nightmare, culminating in the identification of her husband's body. She had spent several hours making statements to the police, and now she faced another interview, this time on behalf of the separate task force handling the case. Matters would not improve for her; soon she would receive the less sympathetic attention of the press.

'My children are staying with a friend for a while,' she said quietly, 'until the worst of this has passed.'

'I understand,' said Christina, accepting her coffee. 'I know how difficult it is for you to answer questions in the face of this tragedy. We need to understand what happened as quickly as possible.'

Christina knew that ultimately Sirina Denjhi would gain peace of mind from knowing the truth, no matter how difficult it proved to be. It was a problem constantly raised by members enrolled in victim support groups, the pain of not knowing.

'I must appreciate what has happened,' said Sirina softly. 'It is impossible for me to believe that this has happened to my husband.'

Standard interview procedure dictated that the sergeant could not reveal details of the investigation in progress, even if she felt that doing so would facilitate the discussion. Instead she decided to concentrate on David Denjhi's background.

'Our families had known each other in Pakistan,' Sirina explained, 'and although our marriage was not arranged it was understood that one day we would wed. Our parents were business partners, you see.'

'What kind of business were they in?' asked Christina.

'Imports and exports. At first it was very successful, but David's father died, and the world recession took its toll. Our money was invested with BCCI. When it went bankrupt, we lost everything. David was a good father, a good provider. He worked hard to keep his company afloat, still dreaming that one day his children would run it. But it was not to be.' She folded her hands in her lap, looking away.

Better to stop her from remembering, thought Christina, and keep her mind occupied with providing answers. 'What happened after the company collapsed?' she asked.

'David was always looking for new opportunities. He set up the window-cleaning firm. He was about to expand it, to include office cleaning. His head was filled with ideas.'

'Did your husband have many friends?'

'We were his friends. His family. He had no others. People saw him in the street, at his job, but I don't suppose they really saw him. People don't, you understand? They don't notice us. We go about our work, we spend time with our families, but to most English people we're quite invisible. The hostile ones see us, of course. The others are neither angry nor happy that we're here — just disinterested. When we came to this country, we thought we had left the castes behind. But we hadn't. We simply became a new one.' Silence settled in the room. Christina forced herself to break into the young woman's thoughts.

'We need to talk about David's disappearance,' she said. 'I know you've already made a statement, but I must ask you to think harder still. You say he'd been troubled ...'

Sirina Denjhi withdrew a handkerchief from her sari and dabbed her nose. 'That's right. It was on Friday morning, Friday the seventeenth. The devil was in him. He would not go to work, and he would not tell me why. He was angry with the children. Our youngest daughter broke a saucer, and he slapped her face. He had never touched her before, never raised his hand in violence. His mood grew worse and worse. Finally, just after ten in the morning, he stormed out without a word.'

'You asked him where he was going?'

'Of course, but he gave me no reply. I watched from the window as he drove off in the van.'

'Had he ever done anything like this before?'

'No, never.'

'And the name Peggy Harmsworth, he'd never mentioned it to you?'

Sirina shook her head. She looked up at the sergeant, her dark eyes glittering like amber beads. 'You must find out why this terrible thing happened. Perhaps he was possessed. All I know is that we have been visited by a devil, and there will be no rest for us until we know the truth.'

By lunchtime the blustery day had swept the sky clean of cloud, and the two detectives sat in the operations room at Mornington Crescent bathed in late sunshine. Bryant was trying hard to stay awake, but the long hours were beginning to take their toll. They were anxiously awaiting the preliminary forensic report on David Denjhi's body. Finch had been working through the night. The initial documents would only offer broad indications of the findings. As such they constituted inadmissible evidence, but were useful in investigations where time was an essential factor.

'You haven't found any connection at all between Denjhi and the Whitstables?' asked Bryant.

'No, not on the surface at any rate. But both families were once in the same business. I'll have to go through his company records. And I'll see if he'd ever had window-cleaning appointments at any of the Whitstable houses. God, Arthur, a window cleaner. It doesn't feel right, any of it.' He shoved the folder away from him. 'Jerry saw him leave the crypt seconds after Mrs Harmsworth screamed, so there's no doubt about who attacked her.'

'It's in,' called Sergeant Crosse, walking briskly between the computer terminals with a pair of document pouches in her hand. Bryant had fallen in love with the new sergeant. Last night, without a word of complaint, she had stayed with them through the shift in order to help clear the backlog of interviews. 'Dr Land wasn't going to release it without speaking to you first, but I managed to persuade him.'

'You know what that means,' said Bryant, accepting the papers. 'He and Finch must have found some positive matches. No one else knows about this yet, do they?'

'I'm afraid he's already copied in Detective Superintendent Marsden, sir.'

'Blast, there goes our head start.' Bryant yanked open the first document pouch and studied its contents. 'Hang on, there's no paperwork here, just stupid damned floppy-whatsits.'

'Give them to me,' said May wearily, taking the discs from him as if dealing with a child, and inserting the top one in the nearest available terminal. He pulled down a file window and examined the group of access codes, selecting one of them.

'We've got multiple matches here,' he said, studying the screen. 'Fingerprints all over the crypt, and on the Stanley knife Denjhi threw into the grass. For some reason he decided not to use it on her. Peggy Harmsworth's blood on the crypt floor, and on Denjhi's shirt and trousers. It looks as if she banged her head in the struggle. Keys fitting the crypt found on his body. All conclusive stuff. What else have we got?'

He inserted a second disc into the machine, checked through the codes and keyed up the forensic profile which indicated initial print and blood comparisons with the murders.

'No positive matches with the other deaths, but it's early days yet. They need to check with the partials found on segments of the bomb that killed Peter Whitstable.' He scrolled down the screen and drew Bryant's attention to the column at the bottom. 'Definitely no match with the prints we found on the razor from the Savoy barbershop. So we're dealing with two different people. What's more alarming is this.' He ran the cursor to a highlighted paragraph. 'Denjhi's body shows all the right signs of decomposition, tissue breakdown, the presence of anaerobic bacteria, loss of contractility in musculature — at a lower level than normal — and yet his limbs show signs of constant recent use. How can that be?'

'You can tell a man is dead by sticking his finger in your ear,' said Bryant unhelpfully. 'If you put your own finger in your ear you hear a buzz from tiny muscle movements. When does Finch think he died?'

'That's just it. He places the death some time around last weekend. So what do we have here, a member of the living dead?'

'Some occult groups believe such things to be possible.'

'I suppose that would fit in with your Victorian conspiracy theory,' said May, pushing his chair back. 'Anything new to report on that front?'

'I've got some people working on it.'

'A couple of clairvoyants and a palmist, no doubt.'

'There's no reason why you should place more faith in this piece of electronic wizardry than in the supernatural.' He thumped the top of the terminal.

'There's every good reason. And who said anything about the supernatural?' asked May, alarmed. 'Each move this computer makes can be reliably predicted, which is more than you can say for your crystal ball merchants. I know you've been seeing them again, Arthur, don't pretend that you haven't.'

'It's just as well I have, if we're dealing with walking corpses.'

Just then the overhead lights momentarily dimmed, and the screen before them rolled into blankness. May had accessed a terminal that was unconnected to the main-frame, and without power backup.

'Damn.' May turned off the machine and withdrew his disc.

'So much for the reliability of science,' said Bryant with a mocking smile. 'It's not much good without electricity, is it? Suddenly we're back in the Dark Ages, telling ghost stories in front of the fire.' He turned to the sergeant who waited behind them. 'Christina, your interview with Mrs Denjhi was very thorough, but there's still one thing I need to know. Where did he get the money?'

'I'm sorry, sir?'

'Denjhi lost everything when his company collapsed. You can't start a new one without capital outlay. Find out where he got the cash from.'

The telephone rang, and Bryant answered it. The junior arts minister sounded extremely cheerful. 'I just wanted to be the first to offer my congratulations to you and your colleagues,' he bellowed. 'A job well done I'd say. I haven't received your full report yet, of course, so if you'd—'

'I have no idea what you're talking about,' snapped Bryant, although a terrible thought was forming in his mind.

'Catching our vandal,' Faraday explained. 'The news couldn't have come at a better time. Things were getting pretty sticky with the Aussies, I can tell you.'

Suddenly the realisation dawned on him. Marsden had read the report and had immediately contacted the Home Office. Faraday seemed to have assumed that with the death of a confirmed assassin all of the loose ends connected to the vandalism of the loaned Waterhouse painting were now tied up. It was essential for Marsden to prove that the new unit was getting results; it was only funded for an eight-week trial period.

Bryant knew that he would be expected to back up his superior. He also knew that he could not do so without compromising everything he believed in.

'I'm sorry to disappoint you, Mr Faraday,' he said finally. 'It's true that the identity of the person who assaulted Mrs Harmsworth last night is known to us, but the case is far from any possibility of closure.'

'How can that be? I don't understand,' said Faraday with an anguished squeak, his spirits audibly sinking.

'Put simply, there's a murderer very much at large.'

'You mean you still don't know who he is?'

'Worse than that,' said Bryant. 'We don't know *what* he is.'

# CHAPTER

32

Daisy Whitstable's funeral had been scheduled for Thursday afternoon. It would be the grimmest of Christmases for the family attending the closed service beneath the bare sycamore branches in Highgate Cemetery. Arthur Bryant did not need to be reminded that he and May had been asked to provide some kind of conclusion to the investigation within the next forty-eight hours.

After a night of bad dreams he arose unrefreshed and sat on the end of his bed, trying to order his thoughts. This pestilence attacking the Whitstable family would try to run its course before they could discover its root. The venerable detective hated to admit it, but they had failed. Failed the public, and failed themselves. He had not felt this depressed in years. Checking the page of notes he had left for himself on the bedside table, he rang Jerry Gates at her home. A frosty-voiced woman, presumably her mother, asked him to hold. A minute later, Jerry picked up the extension.

'Mr Bryant? I was just washing my hair. This is an unexpected pleasure.'

'It's been a long time since a woman said that to me,' admitted Bryant. 'Yesterday you mentioned something about your father working with the Whitstables.'

'That's right, he has contracts with several of their companies, importing mostly. He and my mother are avid followers of the whole scandal. You should see them hunched over the breakfast newspapers.'

'Then I want you to do something for me.'

'Anything. Just name it.'

'I'd like you to find out whatever you can about the people he deals with. I realise this involves a certain amount of − ah, disloyalty to your father. Specifically, look for documentation concerning deals with Indian manufacturers and exporters. Failing that, talk to your father and find out if he's seen or heard anything unusual. You know the investigation almost as well as we do. You should know what to ask, and what to look for.'

'Don't worry about that. I'll get on to it right away.'

'Good girl. Call me if you find anything, anything at all. Do you have the number of my beeper?'

'No.'

'Neither do I. It's written down somewhere−'

'I'll ring you at Mornington Crescent,' she promised.

The morning dawned cold and dull, weather Bryant loathed the most, when London seemed sealed away from the rest of the world. The sky formed a grey ceiling over his Battersea apartment, so that entering the street and stepping into the parkland opposite failed to relieve him of the sense that he was somehow still indoors.

He checked his watch and walked up toward the river. His appointment with Peregrine Summerfield was set for 10.00 a.m. He would walk as far as Vauxhall Bridge, then hail a cab. It was a pity the trams had stopped running in 1952; one used to pass right by the front door of his building. He missed the hiss and crackle of the gliding cars.

That was the difference between he and May. John had no attachment to the past, sentimental or otherwise. He was only interested in moving on. He saw life as a linear progression, a series of lessons to be learned, all extraneous information to be tossed away, a continual streamlining of ideas.

Arthur was the opposite. He collected the detritus of history as naturally as an anchor accumulated barnacles. He couldn't help it; the past was as fascinating as a classic beauty, infinitely fathomable and forever out of reach. But this was one secret he was determined to lay bare. He would stake his life on the answer existing in the family's burst of good fortune at the end of the last century. Could there really have been an event of such magnitude that it involved an entire dynasty? A moment of such far-reaching consequence that even now, a hundred years later, it was reaping a revenge of misery and destruction?

As he reached the eastern edge of the park, a phrase rebounded in his head. *The sons shall be visited with sins of the fathers.* James Whitstable and his kindred Olympian spirits, the Seven Stewards of Heaven. The Inner Circle. The Alliance of Eternal Light. They were one and the same. How the Victorians loved their secret societies, their gentlemen's clubs and hermetic orders, their table-rappings, recitals and rituals, gatherings primarily designed to *exclude*.

Was that it? Who had James Makepeace Whitstable and his friends wanted to exclude this time? Their little society was no mere parlour game for the menfolk, somewhere to escape from family responsibilities. No, their alliance was built *within the family itself.*

If its purpose was not to exclude, then it must be to protect. To protect the lives of the Whitstable clan? No, these men were well respected and powerful. They would have made dangerous enemies. What else might they have wanted to protect? He looked out at the Thames, a curving grey ribbon two hundred and fifteen miles long, flowing back and forth with the pulse of the moon.

Was it to protect their money? Wasn't that far more likely? An idea began to form in the back of his mind. He would call the lawyer, Leo Marks, as soon as he had concluded his business with Summerfield.

The art historian was late, as usual. He was sporting the traditional English Art History uniform, an ancient tweed jacket with leather elbow patches, a brown woolly tie, ill-matched corduroy trousers and battered loafers. Presumably this identified him to civilians in the event of an art emergency. Summerfield noisily hailed Arthur across the tarmac forecourt of the Academy in a shower of pipe ash, then clapped him on the back as they entered Burlington House together.

Although he had been a regular visitor in his youth, Arthur had not called at the Academy for quite a while, and was pleased to find it quite unchanged, Michelangelo's spectacular Carrara marble tondo of the *Madonna and Child with the Infant St John* occupying its traditional space. Every accepted member of the foundation submitted a piece of their work to the Academy as a gift, with the result that Reynolds, Gainsborough, Constable and Turner were all splendidly represented on the walls within. The Academy's summer exhibition, an event open to all artists irrespective of nationality or training, had been dismaying critics each year for more than two centuries.

'Glad you could make it,' boomed Summerfield, looking about them. 'I love this place. Some halfway-decent pictures are hung in around these walls. Y'know, this business of yours has got me hooked. The Waterhouse study is being examined and authenticated downstairs. I told them it's genuine but they insist on checking for themselves. Tossers.'

They made their way through the crowded entrance hall to a winding marble staircase which led to the workrooms where paintings and sculptures were unpacked and studied. Bryant sniffed the air, noting a cocktail of chemical smells that suggested restoration — or indeed, painting — was taking place somewhere nearby.

Summerfield pushed open a door marked PRIVATE and led the way across a large white studio, one wall of which consisted of opaque backlit glass, to a cluttered wooden bench, on which lay the study Arthur had discovered in Bella Whitstable's basement. Seeing it again reminded him of that unpleasant experience, and he shivered involuntarily.

'Tell me what relevance you imagine this picture having to our investigation,' he asked, watching as the historian lowered his bulk onto a corner of the bench. 'Beyond the obvious fact that one of the victims defaced it, I mean.'

'Ah, I think you understand why I've asked you here,' replied Summerfield. 'I wondered if you'd see it first.'

Arthur stood before the study and examined it once more. Although just two-thirds of the five-foot-long picture had been blocked with colour and all but two of the figures were only roughly delineated, the formal structure of Waterhouse's finished painting could easily be discerned.

'Perhaps I should explain my thinking,' said Arthur, picking up a paintbrush and running his thumb across the sable tip. 'At some early point in the investigation I decided — no, I *knew* — that the answers lay in the forgotten history of the Whitstable family. There was a madness of purpose that suggested a curious kind of Victorian sensibility at work. Each death has been achieved with grotesque flair, an eeriness beyond anything we find in our bright, modern world. Naturally my partner doesn't agree, so I've been forced to go it alone.'

He paused to think for a moment, scratching his nose with the end of the brush. 'I only had a vague date, sometime at the beginning of the 1880s, and a number, seven. Seven men in an alliance, six courtiers and an emperor gathered in a painting. I tried to imagine seven wealthy businessmen, heads of a successful trading family, forming themselves into a club of some kind. A club that would protect their self-made fortunes from harm, one with an acceptable public face and occult private pastimes. But how to commemorate the occasion without giving the game away? What would the traditional Victorian do?'

'Commission a painting,' said Summerfield.

'Exactly. But there is a problem with this theory. When the details of this club finally came to light — The Alliance of Eternal Light — I found that its foundation date was some time in 1881. And you say that Waterhouse produced his painting at the end of 1883. I have a two-year discrepancy in the dates ...'

'I can explain that easily,' said Summerfield, pointing back at the study. 'The first oil sketch for *Emperor Honorius* was knocked out on a manky old bit of board less than a foot square in 1882, and there was probably a gestation period predating that. So it could easily have been commissioned by your Alliance. You've got a bigger problem to think about.'

'What?'

'Well, look at it,' said Summerfield, waving at the study. 'If this really was commissioned to celebrate the founding of a new organisation, it doesn't do a very good job. Think of the subject matter. What the finished painting shows is a society out of control. Honorius's councillors can't get his attention because he's too busy sodding about with his birds. I told you before — as the supreme ruler of an empire, he was a plonker of the first order.' Summerfield sucked his whiskers, thinking. 'Suppose this bloke Whitstable chose Waterhouse for the painting, and then the artist discovered something unpleasant about his patron? Talk about having your cake and eating it! Waterhouse got to keep the commission by producing this wonderful, satisfying piece of work, and he got back at his patron through the classical allusion contained within the picture.'

'There's no way of proving that.'

'Perhaps not, until you remember what the finished painting looks like.' Summerfield scrabbled beneath the study and produced a crumpled colour photocopy, which he proceeded to flatten out on a cleared part of the bench.

'Here,' he said, pointing at the copy. 'Remember I told you that the key character changes? In the study, the central figure is the emperor's attendant. In the end result, he's been relegated to the background. The former picture shows a group of men in repose. The allusion is reduced in terms of offense. The latter shows a master surrounded by sycophants. It's as if Waterhouse was intending to have a gentle dig at his patron, then — some time between 1882 and 1883 — found out that the situation was far worse than he had imagined. So, he changed the finished picture.'

'James Whitstable was an educated man. Surely he would have understood the allusion and taken offence?'

'Let us imagine that's exactly what happened. The painting was sold to an Australian gallery soon after its completion. Waterhouse remained true to his ethical code. He produced a magnificent work of art. He simply went too far.'

'Which helps to explain why William Whitstable threw acid on the picture. The painting was an affront to his ancestor, and by extension to his entire family. It was the first time it had been exhibited in this country for a century.'

'Incidentally,' added Summerfield, 'I have another seven for you. John Waterhouse was a Royal Academy painter. The Pre-Raphaelite Brotherhood was begun by seven men. Rossetti, Millais, Holman Hunt and four others dedicated themselves to a "childlike submission to nature". The actress Ellen Terry once told Bernard Shaw that she always visited Burne-Jones at his studio when it was foggy, because he looked so angelic painting by candlelight. Subsequently the group was joined by many other artists, and Oscar Wilde started poncing around with his sacred lily, wetting himself over the Pre-Raff sensibility because it neatly fitted in with the fact that he was extremely camp. It didn't help having a fat screamer as a spokesperson, even a brilliant one, and pretty soon everyone started taking the piss out of the Pre-Raffs.'

'Including Gilbert and Sullivan . . .'

'That's right. One of their productions parodied the Brotherhood.'

'. . . at the Savoy Theatre.' Arthur reached for his cap and adjusted it on his head. 'Peregrine, I can't tell you what a help you've been.'

'Let me know how you get on,' shouted the historian, 'I want to see how this one turns out.'

But by then his friend had already left the gallery work-room.

# CHAPTER

## 33

Her eyes flicked wildly in the darkness, back and forth, bulging and clouding, sometimes rolling up into their sockets so that only the whites showed.

The glowing numerals of the wall clock read 4.55 a.m. A nurse would be in to check on her in five minutes. Perhaps she could find some way of communicating her pain, some way of telling her that although the muscles in her arms and legs felt like twisting bundles of red hot wires, her brain was on fire and her very soul was searing, she was now quite sane and lucid. The terror of delirium had passed, to be replaced by the fear of its return.

Five more minutes. It wasn't long to have to hold on.

'Mad Margaret' lay restrained by heavy rubber straps and clasps deep within the Royal Free hospital, not a stone's throw from the cemetery where Bryant and May would later be attending Daisy Whitstable's funeral. Her mouth had been gagged with a rubber stopper to prevent her from chewing through her tongue. Leather belts circled her wrists and ankles, crossed her chest and pelvis, locked into bolts that impaled her to the bed. She wanted to scream, to tell them that although the drugs still racked her body she was no longer mad. She knew that they would take her frantic signalling as further proof of insanity.

Three minutes to go. Only rational thoughts now. She tried to count to fifty, to remember the names of TV programmes, anything to stay awake and aware, at least until — until—

Moments before the nurse entered the room to check on her patient, Peggy Whitstable slipped into an ever-deepening coma, as chemicals ravaged her battered nervous system with renewed force and filled her sleep with unimaginable nightmares.

She wasn't supposed to know about the family's interest, of course. Gwen had made that absurdly obvious. Ever since the murders had been reported in the newspapers, her mother had gone out of her way to avoid any mention of them. This morning, Jerry had interrupted Jack's breakfast reading of his *Daily Telegraph* to draw attention to the subject, only to hear Gwen hurriedly change the conversation to something less controversial.

Her mother had always been an ambitious woman. Although she admired 'old money' like the Whitstables, she was probably glad not to be involved with them right now, seeing that they were being steadily killed off. Jerry looked around the lounge, at the cut crystal candlesticks set on the polished mahogany dining room table, at the cherub-encrusted mirror above the burgundy marble mantelpiece, at the sheer weight and solidity of the household, and she hated the presumption and perman-ence of what she saw.

Everything her parents owned was built to outlive them. Unable to have any more children after the birth of their disastrous daughter, they were determined to leave something of value behind.

She wondered what Gwen would say if she knew there was a spy in their midst. Right now, she was waiting for them to leave the house so that she could begin a search of her father's private study. Jack clipped the articles from the newspapers, but what did they do with them? She felt sure she would find something incriminating about the Whitstables in her father's desk.

Surely Bryant was wrong in his assumption that the Whitstables recognised the cause of their destruction? If they did, wouldn't they have taken steps to prevent further deaths from occurring? What could the family have done that was so terrible they were being persecuted for it a century later?

The slamming of the front door as Jack and Gwen left was the only signal she needed to begin burrowing from within. She walked into the hall and stood at the foot of the stairs. Jack's study was his private domain. Jerry had only ever entered the room when bidden by her father. The door was never locked, but it was understood that no one other than Jack should enter uninvited. She was about to violate the trust she had been granted.

Slowly she made her way up the stairs to the corridor above, pausing before the study door. She turned the heavy brass doorknob and pushed inward.

The book-lined room was dark and richly textured with inlaid wooden panels. A large Victorian escritoire stood on a heavy Chinese rug near the far window. Along one wall stood a pair of Georgian side tables, one of them supporting a nondescript marble bust. A blue crystal ashtray was filled with sepia butts. It was the one room in the house where Jack was permitted to smoke his cigars.

Jerry made her way over to the desk and tried the drawers. None of them was locked. She carefully removed the contents from each in turn and studied them, but found nothing of interest.

When she was younger she had often wondered what her father was doing locked in his study all afternoon. Now as she looked through the bills to be sifted and business correspondence to be answered, she saw that Jack merely used the place as a refuge from an overbearing wife. Suddenly the room seemed less exotic, diminished by mundane matters.

She pulled out the lowest drawer, expecting to see nothing more than further stacks of correspondence. Instead, she found herself staring at an early photograph of her mother, aged around twenty-three. She was standing in a garden with a small cluster of anemones in one hand, smiling tightly, shading her eyes from the sun. Jerry had never seen the picture before. It was hard to believe that her mother was ever this young.

As she studied the picture, she realised that another quality shone through it. Gwen looked happy to be alive. She radiated joy. Before the thwarted ambition, the bitterness and the recriminations, she had been an ordinary woman, attractive and carefree. Then had come a series of setbacks; the knowledge that she could have no more children. The gradual fading of Jack's interest in her. And the contemptuous, destructive anger of her only daughter.

Suddenly she was filled with remorse for the grief she had caused her family. And shame for the betrayal that she was even now attempting. Crumpling into the corner beside the desk, she began to cry.

*

'My God, it's cold in here,' complained Bryant, clapping his arms around his shoulders. 'If I'd known I was going to be standing in a crypt in December I'd have worn a thicker vest. The poor little mite. Did you see the crowds waiting outside the main gate?'

According with the wishes of her parents, Daisy's service had been conducted at a local church, and now the mourners were starting to arrive at Highgate Cemetery for the burial procedure. He and John May had come back to the vault where Peggy Harmsworth had been molested, ostensibly to attend the last rites but also to take another look at the scene of the attack.

The forensic team had finished their work, but the area was still closed off to the public, and would long remain so. The site was attracting a vast number of photographers, and ghoulish observers were pressed against the railings, pointing out the crypt to each other.

Although the outside of the family vault was overgrown with ferns and creepers, the white marble interior was clean and well tended. Eight members of the Whitstable family were buried here, including Peggy's husband. Each was sealed behind a small door marked with a plain brass plaque, and every door was fitted with a brass holder containing a single flower. Behind them the wedged-open portal flushed staleness from the tomb with loamy morning air.

'People are funny about drugs,' said Bryant, eyeing the chalked-up area of the vault wall. 'I must say it's not the kind of behaviour you expect from a respectable middle-aged woman.'

'Who can tell these days?' replied his partner, looking around. 'Especially with this family.'

A routine computer check had turned up a police file for Peggy Whitstable. Four years earlier she had been convicted for possession of cocaine. Yesterday, several grams of white powder had been found in one of the brass holders within the vault. Wary of keeping drugs at home, it seemed that Peggy had been in the habit of stashing her supply in the nearby family mausoleum.

'She'd arranged to meet a friend for drinks on Wednesday night,' said May, his smartly combed hair ruffling against the low ceiling. 'She stopped off to collect a livener on the way. There was an empty vial in her purse. But someone had doctored her supply, and was waiting for her to show up. Either he forced her to snort the new mixture, or she couldn't wait for a taste. Her nasal passage was seared raw.'

'Christina tells me that Forensics are getting conflicting results,' said Bryant, peering into each of the holders in turn.

'That's because she was poisoned by a complex amalgam of substances including atropine, meadow saffron, panther mushroom and betel nut seed,' explained May. 'There are other strains they haven't yet identified. The combined effect was to cause delirium, psychotic hallucinations and, perhaps unexpectedly, eventual coma as her brain became overloaded and shorted out.'

'Did the doctors say whether she'll pull through?'

'Despite the lethal sound of the mixture, it won't kill her. But they don't think she'll ever regain full use of her faculties.'

'I've been trying to fathom out the sequence of events,' said Bryant, reading the plaques as he passed them. 'See how this sounds. It all began with Max Jacob being summoned to London by his old friend and client, Peter Whitstable. Peter wanted him to oversee the removal of the Japanese from the Savoy deal. He had earmarked the theatre for CROWET. They'd placed their bid fair and square, but – to his fury – it wasn't accepted. Instead, the theatre was sold for a considerably higher sum to the Japanese.

'Peter was outraged. He was determined to own the Savoy. So he resorted to an illegal business strategy, arranging to have one of the heads of the Tasaka Corporation compromised. The number 216 was written in Jacob's diary, the number of the hotel room where the incriminating blackmail material was kept.

'I think we can presume that Jacob was to be employed as the legal go-between in the dispersal of the photographs. He arrived at the hotel, but there was a mix-up. He was given the wrong room. Before he could sort out the situation, he was killed — by a person or persons unknown.'

'But the photographs still found their target,' said May.

'Indeed.'

Arthur folded his scarf beneath his bottom and seated himself on the shadowed bench at the end of the crypt. 'Someone got into the room and removed the pictures in a hurry, leaving one behind. We have Jerry's evidence to support that. The compromised businessman was quietly exposed and the buyout collapsed.'

'Jacob was murdered *before* the Japanese were forced to pull out of the theatre deal, so we can dismiss any idea of a revenge killing.'

'Indeed. The bible found by Jerry in Max Jacob's room belonged to William Whitstable. Perhaps it was a gift, or the lawyer was returning it. Jacob was Jewish, so we must assume that the bible had symbolic value. The highlighting of all those passages to do with light and dark suggests some kind of deeper significance.'

'I'd forgotten about that,' May admitted. He glanced down at his watch. 'The service is due to start in five minutes.'

'You're right,' agreed John, heading toward the door.

Daisy Whitstable was to have a special child's memorial built, but for now she was to be interred inside the main family vault.

As they stepped outside into the deepening chill of the afternoon, the detectives knew how much hatred they were facing by attending. Below them, the pale city lay in gathering frosty fog. May turned to his partner and studied his face. Arthur was gazing off at the horizon, his thoughts unguessable.

'You know we're inches away from losing everything we've ever worked for,' he said. 'This is most likely the end of both our careers. They can forcibly retire us, John. Worst still, the Inspectorate can appoint a full-scale enquiry into our methods. Then we'll *really* be in trouble.'

'You've a point there,' agreed May. 'The case will go somewhere else, and it'll get a new team. They'll have our data access, but no physical experience of the investigation. In the time it takes for them to catch up, others will be dead.'

Bryant gave no reply.

'I know you have ideas you're not telling me about.'

Bryant slowly pulled his scarf free from his chin and observed his partner. 'I'll tell you what I really think,' he replied at last. He looked down at the straggling black-clad figures who had just entered through the private gate of the cemetery. 'In 1881 James Makepeace Whitstable set up a society called the Alliance of Eternal Light. On the surface, it was seen to carry out good works, building hostels, helping the poor, funding charities, restoring buildings. Privately, it was dedicated to something else, some secret occult cause. I think it was set up for the betterment of the Whitstable family — their fortunes prospered in the following years — but with that betterment came a price. The family is now paying that price.'

His eyes hardened to a bitter stare. 'Until we understand what was set in motion, nothing on earth can stop it.'

The service was brief and poignant. Few in the congregation were prepared to even look at the coffin, as if they were ashamed to be there at all. The detectives were leaving the cemetery when they were accosted by a seething Isobel Whitstable. Throughout the service she had held herself with quiet dignity, supported by her husband and her son. As she threw back the black veil of her hat, Bryant could see the debilitating effect of the last few days in her tortured eyes.

Having halted them in their tracks, she threw a molten glance from one to the other. At first, Bryant thought she was going to lash out at them with her fists.

'You two,' she spat furiously, 'I hold the pair of you responsible for this.' She threw out her arm at the gathering behind her. 'My daughter is dead, and you did nothing at all to prevent it. Ever since this whole fucking nightmare began you've done *nothing*. How many more of us have to die?' Tears spilled from her bulging eyes. 'What do we have to do to get protection from this – this—'

'Mrs Whitstable, every person here today has a police detail,' said May. 'Your houses are being watched around the clock. Until we find the information we need to make an arrest, there's nothing more we can do.'

'Well, there's something I can damned well do,' she hissed, thrusting her livid face forward at each of them in turn. 'I'm going to make sure your little play-unit is closed down and this investigation is turned over to someone with an ounce of fucking competence. You'll wish you'd taken the police pension, because believe me, both of you, this was your very last case.'

She turned on an elegant high heel and stalked from the cemetery entrance to the waiting Bentley parked beyond.

# CHAPTER

34

'Jesus, what happened to you?'

Joseph stood in the doorway before her. She knew she must look as if she'd been punched in the face; her eyes always grew puffy when she cried. Now that his cuts were starting to heal, Joseph had decided to wish her a merry Christmas in person. She hoped he wasn't going to act annoyed with her. She hadn't meant to involve him. On the contrary; he had invited himself along as her chaperone. Still, their last two dates had ended with him being locked up in the dark. It didn't auger well for a third try. Perhaps he had come here to say goodbye.

'How's your pelvis?'

'I have a bruise the size of Belgium.'

'Well.' He looked around. 'We could just stay here on the doorstep but your neighbours might think I'm selling the *Watchtower.*'

'I'm sorry,' she said quietly. 'Come in. I'm having a bad day.'

'Coming from you, that's one omen I'd take notice of.'

He entered the foyer and looked around, marvelling at the domed ceiling above the entrance hall. 'Nice place. What days do you open it to the public?'

'Around here, we are the public. In this neighbourhood the carolers sing in descant and get a tenner for their troubles.' She was making an attempt to hold together, smoothing back her hair and smiling too widely. *The effort might kill me,* she thought. Still, she was very pleased to see him. 'It doesn't feel like Christmas, does it? Can I pour you a seasonal toast?'

She led the way through to a large, light kitchen fitted with outsized gleaming utensils and an abundance of electronic gadgetry. 'My mother had all this installed, but she can barely cook an egg,' she said, removing a bottle of whisky and two tumblers from the cabinet.

'You never have a kind word for her.'

'Oh, you noticed. How are your war wounds?'

'I'll live.' He gingerly touched the plaster below his left eye. There were two more, one on his chin and another across his forehead. 'That night was like an incredibly bad dream.'

'She really had a go at you, didn't she?' Jerry passed him a glass and raised her own. 'Merry Christmas.'

'And a happy New Year. I understand you handled the bike pretty well.'

'So well that they may press charges,' she said, gently swilling the drink in her hand, 'Listen, I think I'm going to need your help again.'

'You must be out of your mind. Forget it, Jerry. You don't need me. I came by to tell you that I'm going back to Edinburgh.'

'You can't do that!' She turned on him angrily, betrayal on her face. 'I need you to help me, Joseph. You're the only friend I have, the only one I can trust.'

'You know, I felt sorry for you when I first met you. Poor kid, everyone's mean to her, I should make an effort to be friendly ...'

'I didn't realise it was that much of an effort,' she said, bridling. 'I was right though, wasn't I? About the murders and everything?'

'Okay, I admit it's been very weird since I met you, but you're just trying to make yourself part of it because you're confused about your future.'

'You sound like my parents. I thought you were on my side.'

'It's not a matter of sides, Jerry.' He held up a hand, suddenly losing his temper with her. 'I can see how you live. Life is so *tough* for you. You're bored and you're looking for the next game to play, and I'm not going to be part of it. Look at this place, for God's sake. You just want to get into a little gutter life to piss off your parents.' He pointed to the immaculate formal garden beyond the kitchen windows. 'It's hard to build up street attitude when you've been born with a silver spoon in your mouth, but you're certainly giving it a try.'

He turned in the kitchen doorway. 'From where I stand, your problems don't seem too big. You know—' He fought for the words. 'I've been living in a bug-infested room in Earl's Court. I've no money left. I can't find a job. I don't even have the fare to get home, and right now I don't have a future. I'm about to be kicked out on the street. I spoke to my parents. It's snowing and it's quiet up there. Now that sounds to me like a real Christmas.'

'Where's your girlfriend?' asked Jerry defensively. 'Why isn't she helping you out?'

'Marie — my *girlfriend*, if that's what she ever was, has decided to live in Australia for a year, and reached this momentous decision without consulting me as though it had nothing to do with my life. I've still got her books and her flea-ridden bloody cat.'

'I'm sorry,' said Jerry. 'How did you find out?'

'When I couldn't get through to her apartment I called her father.' He sounded annoyed with himself for having made the call. He came back into the kitchen and sat down at the breakfast bar with his drink. 'Fucking hell. Give me another whisky.' He held out his empty glass.

She refreshed the drinks, then opened the refrigerator. 'Do you want something to eat?' she asked, determined to be more convivial. 'There's cold pheasant, paté de foie gras, roast veal. Us rich people have got everything.'

He smiled without meaning to. 'Yeah, put everything in a white bread sandwich. Got any eggs?'

They made themselves cheese omelettes. He watched as she expertly turned them in the pan.

'How are you going to get home if you don't have any money?' she asked, handing him a plate.

'Listen,' he said through a mouthful of toast, 'I'm figuring this out as I go along. At six o'clock this morning I threw my clothes into a bag and slipped out of the hotel without paying the bill. Considering the amount of insect life in my room, I don't feel bad about it. The BBC could have done a documentary on the bedroom carpet. I'll manage; I always do.'

She thought for a moment, watching him. 'I wish you could stay here, but Gwen and Jack would never allow it. They'd think it was a sex thing, or that I had invited you to spite them. You don't look like the rest of my friends. I may have a place where you could stay, though. Just until you can get some money together.'

'No, I've made up my mind. I'm going home. I'm sorry, Jerry. It's been fun in a perverse, self-torturing way, but I have to figure out what *I* want now.'

She took a bite from her omelette, petulance masking her desperation to make him stay. 'But, Joseph, you could help me, and I could help you. I can't do it by myself.'

'And I can't do it for you.' He pushed back his plate and rose to leave. 'We have different working methods.'

'All right, but I really want to give you some money, just to tide you over. Take what you need.'

'I'm still not going to help you.'

'So you said.' She moved closer.

'It's disadvantageous to my health.'

'I know.' She ran her hand lightly over the hairs on his arm. Suddenly the fear was there, even without the darkness. If she was left alone now, she was unsure whether she would be able to control her panic.

'Please, Joseph,' she said, 'after you've finished your coffee, just give me ten minutes of your time. Then you're free to go if you still want to.'

He gave her a suspicious look. 'You're not going to explain another one of your crackpot theories, are you?'

'No,' she replied. 'I promise.'

He sat on the floor in her father's study while she sorted through the contents of the desk's lower drawers.

'Suppose Jack comes home early?'

'They're not due back until after lunch. I found this when I was looking for Jack's contracts with the Whitstable family.' She unfolded a sheet of white vellum and passed it across. 'It's three years old. It's from my doctor.' He studied the handwriting for a moment and began to read:

*Dear Gwen*
*You said not to use the phone. I barely know what to say to you about Geraldine. Naturally, I am completely horrified*

*by what has happened. If only there was some way to undo*
*the harm that has been caused. As her mother, you must*
*decide what is best for all of us.*

*Emil Wayland*

'Christ, what did you do, murder somebody?' he asked, handing back the letter. She unfolded another one and passed it to him. 'This is dated a few days after.'

*Dear Gwen*
*Everything has been arranged, just as you requested. She can*
*start on Monday. She'll be entering during mid-term, but*
*that can't be helped.*
  *No one will ask questions. It is unsafe to visit her. I am*
*only thinking of Geraldine's welfare. May God forgive us. I*
*can only pray that she remembers nothing of what has*
*transpired.*

*Emil Wayland*

Jerry sat back, carefully smoothing the envelope. She looked up at Joseph, waiting for him to comment.

'You don't remember any of this? What the hell happened when you were fourteen?'

'I told you, I had some kind of breakdown. I don't like to think about it. I was just angry all the time. I attacked a girl at school and she nearly lost her eye. Gwen had a Steinway that belonged to her mother. I took a chisel and carved my name in the top, then cut all the wires. They sent me to Dr Wayland, and then when I got too violent, they sent me to special school. I was tranked up for weeks at a time. I've blocked most of the things that happened then.'

'From the tone of these letters there's something else you've blocked. They're so incriminating, why would anyone save them? What made you hate your mother so much?'

Jerry sat on the floor with her legs crossed, hugging herself. That year had passed in a blur of pain, any recollection of which was to be avoided. She never spoke of it to anyone. Joseph was an outsider, though. Somehow it felt right to talk to him. Besides, who else was there? Wayland was in her mother's pay, and her father had avoided any kind of emotional commitment for the past three years.

'To begin with, Gwen was very concerned about my behaviour,' she explained. 'Never more so than when she had to cancel a lunch date because I'd thrown up all over the lounge. I can't remember the first time I did it, but I was surprised at how easy it was. She'd drop everything and come home. Make me soup, put me to bed. But she could never stay home for long. I suppose she thought she was missing out on something. Motherhood hadn't turned out to be as satisfying as she'd expected. Social climbing had always been her hobby.' She shook the memories from her head. 'So now she took it seriously. She had her nose pressed against the window and could see them all having a good time inside, families like the Whitstables, all except her, saddled with a wimp for a husband and a headcase of a daughter. She was eaten up with jealousy, always nagging Jack. He'd done nicely for himself but it wasn't enough.' She gestured around the room.

'And Gwen never quite got what she really wanted. The social standing. This isn't about money at all. It's about breeding. She's got the dosh but she still hasn't got the class, and it really fucks her off. It all looks perfect, like a show house with clockwork models that make all the right moves. But she's still outside, still out there with her nose pressed against the glass. She has me to thank for that. I took it from her, her rightful place in society. Just when it looked as if all the charity lunches were paying off, just when she was beginning to be introduced to the right names, I began to behave badly. And soon people began to stay away. They started turning down my mother's dinner invitations. They never knew what they might find when they got here. I made a showy attempt at cutting my wrists in the middle of one of her little soirées. That's why she sent me to a psychotherapist. Even then, she couldn't resist showing off. He was the most well-connected — and the most expensive — doctor in town. She could tell everyone I was being treated by Lady So-And-So's shrink.'

'You sound almost as bitter as you make your mother out to be.'

'Why not? That's where I get it from.' She hunched herself forward, black hair falling into her eyes. 'There's something else, though. The letters prove it. If only I could remember more.'

'Why don't you ask Wayland?'

'I can't. He's gone away for the holidays. I could ask Gwen, but if it's as bad as it sounds, I'm not sure I want to know.'

'What makes you think you can change anything, Jerry? The past is too screwed up to make any difference now.' Joseph climbed to his feet and slipped his bag onto his back. 'I hate to leave like this, but I can't stay any longer. I'm hitching, and I need to get on the road before dark.'

'Joseph, you can't just go.' She had really believed that he would stay with her. She had never been denied anything in the past.

'Jerry, how can I say this?' He smiled awkwardly at her.

'The Savoy suits you. It's not my style. There's too much of a gap between us.'

'No, there isn't,' she said, wanting to add, *Not when you're in love with someone.*

'Please, Joseph, I'm frightened of what might happen. I don't want to stay here alone.'

'You're not alone. Just leave the investigation to the police. You could have been killed the other night.'

'Why won't you help me anymore?' she asked him again, standing at the open front door.

'Because,' he said, embracing her, 'now you have a reason to help yourself.' He kissed her lightly on the cheek, then stepped out into the falling rain. 'I'll call you.'

'You won't,' she called back. 'People always say that but they never do.'

He raised his hand in salute, waving without turning. It was up to her now, she thought. No one else could help. It was where the real search for truth began. As she closed the door the sadness faded, to be replaced with a growing sense of purpose.

# III
# DARKNESS TRIUMPHANT

Death, attended with the most cruel train of
circumstances, I plainly perceived must prove our
inevitable destiny.

*John Holwell, survivor of the Black Hole of Calcutta,*
*20 June 1756*

# CHAPTER

35

The bitter frost that had begun to crust the windows of the Mornington Crescent Serious Crimes Division shortly after dusk that evening was felt inside the building as well as out. In the streets below, gangs of homegoing secretaries swayed together and sang drunken Christmas carols. The light traffic had dissipated further as commuters returned home to be with their families. Tomorrow was Christmas Eve, but inside the division there would be no Christmas. All leave had been cancelled, and the regular duty roster had been posted. A few miserable paper chains had been strung across the operations room. Bryant's desk displayed two Christmas cards. May hadn't had time to open his.

The detectives returned from another round of interviews to find spines of ice gathering at the windows like skeletal hands, and Marsden seated in their office with a mortified look on his slack, tired face. One glance told them that their deadline had been reached.

'Be seated, gentlemen,' he said, waving expansively at their desks. He waited while Bryant laboriously unwound his scarf and draped it over the hatstand like a sleeping purple python.

'What can we do for you?' asked May casually. Bryant took the cue from his partner and offered his acting superior a careful smile.

'First things first. I'd like to know why you contradicted my report to Faraday,' Marsden measured his words with care.

Bryant raised a tentative hand. 'We didn't think you'd contact the arts minister before discussing the matter with us,' he explained. 'As it happens, we disagree with the inferences you seem to have drawn from the forensic reports.'

'Perhaps you'd like to tell me what conclusions you think I've reached?'

'All right,' said Bryant, steadily eyeing his partner. 'You told Faraday that this man Denjhi is responsible for the death of William Whitstable, whom you presume he killed in some squabble over the painting. You know as well as we do that there is as yet no forensic proof connecting Denjhi to any other member of the family besides Peggy Harmsworth. You must also be aware that Denjhi had been dead for several days.'

Marsden coloured. He couldn't have known that Christina Crosse had reported his first sighting of the forensic evidence to the detectives. 'But it's only a matter of time. We're tearing that man's house apart, and until—'

'You've ordered this?' asked May angrily. 'You had no right.' Denjhi's widow had been through enough without having the indelicate hands of the Special Branch ripping her sofa cushions open.

'Until you could present me with some solid evidence, I

had every right to supersede your orders,' said Marsden. 'You may have ruled the roost at Bow Street and West End Central. Here you take orders from me until I'm replaced by a permanent officer.' He released a sigh and rubbed a pudgy hand across his brow. 'You have to understand the kind of pressure that's been exerted on us. These are calculated assassinations, for God's sake. We've never had anything like this! Front page of *The Times*, page three of the *Telegraph*. The *Mirror* had four pages on us this morning. Maps. Diagrams. Baby pictures, for God's sake. If it wasn't for the situation in Eastern Europe we'd be splashed over the broadsheets. Isobel Whitstable is attempting to sue the unit for deliberate obstruction during the course of the investigation. She's also suing you both personally for incompetence in the wake of her daughter's death.'

'We don't know how she died. The medical examiners maintain that it's impossible to exactly reconstruct the events leading to her death. She was kept somewhere and killed. We have some ideas, but there weren't even any fibres on her clothes. We can't tell her mother theories that we cannot prove.'

'This morning our legal department received a fax detailing outlined lawsuits from several other members of the Whitstable family.'

'Charging us with what?'

'Failing to protect and uphold the law, among other things.'

'Can they do that? Is there anything else we should know about?'

'Oh, sure. For a start, I've been asked to close the division down. But I'm determined to avoid that course of action. Know why? I'm not an idiot. I can see that you're holding out on me.'

Marsden looked from one man to the other. 'There's not a chance in hell of wrapping this thing up before tomorrow, but I know you have something. Do you understand that you're about to lose everything you've ever worked for? The only possible way you can stay on is by giving me complete information. Even then, I'm not sure I can keep this within our jurisdiction any longer.'

'Stanley, the only reason we're holding out on you is because you'd find it impossible to believe what we're uncovering.'

'Try me,' said Marsden, squaring up. 'I'm pretty gullible.'

Bryant shot his partner a look, then proceeded to explain their findings. Forty minutes later, after he had watched the incredulous expression growing on Marsden's face, he sat back in his chair and waited for a reaction.

'You're saying some kind of century-old satanic ring is killing off the family? And that they're using *fucking zombies*?'

'Perhaps the terminology's a little contentious, but I don't know what else you call a man who drives a truck a week after he dies.'

'Don't get smart with me. I saw *Night of the Living Dead*, it was just a stupid horror film. Even with sophisticated microsurgery techniques you can't reanimate a fucking corpse.'

'Perhaps there's another way. I'll tell you something else,' added Bryant. 'I think Denjhi was the one who kidnapped Daisy Whitstable and couldn't bring himself to murder her.'

'She was killed, though.'

'Because he was finally forced to obey his orders.'

'This is madness, Bryant. This satanic circle, do you think the family know about it?'

'Somebody must, certainly.'

Marsden slapped his hands onto the desk. 'How can I tell the H.O. about any of this?'

'Now you understand our predicament,' said May. 'We need you to keep the pressure away for just a little longer. That means planned leaks to the press and keeping all the case files here in the building. Nothing to go on the mainframe. We can't risk hackers.'

'But what about the Whitstables?' asked Marsden worriedly.

'You can leave them to us,' replied Bryant with a reassuring smile.

The family's first reaction when they heard the detectives' demands was one of total outrage.

It was May who had thought of moving them all into William Whitstable's house. The property was enormous and standing empty. It would be easy to secure from both outside and within. Also, considering the elaborate security operation that was currently in force, it would stop resources being stretched over the yuletide season and save the taxpayer a considerable amount of money.

Twenty-four members of the family had remained in Britain for Christmas. Of those, two were in nursing homes and one was bedridden. That left twenty-one Whitstables to be rehoused and settled without fuss or publicity. The detectives informed the family that anyone wishing to opt out of the arrangement was perfectly free to do so, but they would find police protection no longer afforded to them at any residence other than the Hampstead house.

Four of the younger family members, Christian and Deborah Whitstable and their children Justin and Flora, took this option, and chose to remain at their home in Chiswick. The rest reluctantly accepted the deal, but not without letting their annoyance be heard and noted by anyone who came within earshot.

By 10.00 p.m., several unmarked police vans had succeeded in discreetly moving clothes, bedding, personal effects, security equipment and food supplies into the house. By midnight, the remaining seventeen Whitstables were driven to the rear entrance of the house and installed within its gloomy rooms. Shortly after this, Bryant and May risked a visit to make sure that their reluctant charges had settled in.

'No matter what they say, I don't want you to lose your temper,' said May as they passed the undercover surveillance car parked in front of the main entrance. 'Try to remember that we're public servants.'

'That shouldn't be difficult,' muttered Bryant. 'They treat everyone as if they're hired help.'

May approached the brightly lit porch and rang the doorbell according to the prearranged signal. 'This attitude of yours isn't easing the situation, you know.' He glanced at his watch. 00.43 a.m. 'It's Christmas Eve now. Try to be nice.'

'What am I supposed to say?' asked Bryant. 'It's demoralising, trying to save the lives of a bunch of arrogant ingrates who wouldn't normally be prepared to give us the time of day. What have they got to feel so superior about? If we weren't doing our duty and providing a service we'd be invisible to them. Our kind always is. That's the class system for you. It's always been there and it always will be. We should have got rid of it over two hundred years ago, when the Frogs had their spring clean. *Let them eat cake.* Try saying that with your head in a wicker basket.'

'Anarchist,' said May. 'You're just as guilty as the rest of us. Look at the way you've been treating the workmen repainting the office.'

'That's different,' sniffed Bryant. 'They're common.'

'So what would you do? Machine-gun the royal family?'

'Now that you mention it, that's not a—'

'So you've finally arrived to gloat.'

Berta Whitstable, a heavy, overdressed woman in her fifties, was holding the door open before them. She had elected to wear all of her most valuable neck-chains rather than leave them behind. She looked like a lady mayoress receiving unwelcome guests. 'We're freezing to death in here,' she complained. 'The least you can do is show us how to start the boiler.'

The detectives entered. In the hall, a group of noisy children chased each other to the foot of the stairs, thrilled to be staying up so late. Several adults sat morosely in the lounge as if waiting to be told what to do. Bryant recognised most of them from their interviews at the station.

'Is there going to be any turkey?' asked one pimply young man with a half-broken voice.

'I don't know,' replied Bryant truthfully. 'Did you remember to bring one?'

'Cook takes care of those things.' The boy scratched his adam's apple, thinking. 'There *are* people coming in to cook and clean, presumably?'

'Surely there are enough of you here to handle the household chores.'

'We never cook at home. Annie does everything, but they wouldn't let us bring her because she's just a domestic.'

'Well, this will be an exciting experience for you, won't it?' said Bryant, starting to lose patience. 'You'll be able to write a book about it. *How I Survived Without Someone To Make The Beds.*'

'Arthur ...' warned May angrily.

'You mean we have to make our own beds?' said someone else. Bryant turned to address the speaker, a young woman in a blue Chanel suit with elaborately knotted blonde hair.

'I'm afraid so – Pippa, isn't it? You'll be roughing it for a while, putting on your own pillowcases, emptying the hoover bag, that sort of thing. It'll be grim, but I'm sure you'll pull through. We'll bring supplies into you, and you'll be allowed out in pairs, accompanied by a guard, but only for short periods. Like being in prison, really.'

Everyone groaned. They wanted more protection, thought Bryant. That's what we're going to give them.

'Of course, I *will* be allowed to attend my exercise class, won't I?' asked Pippa. 'And I have to look after Gawain. He's my horse.' She turned to the others and smiled. 'A present from Daddy.'

'That shouldn't be a problem, providing of course that it's your turn on the roster to leave the house,' said Bryant viciously. 'Unfortunately you won't be able to telephone out, because of the risk that one of you may accidentally mention your whereabouts.'

Luckily the Christmas holidays meant that those with businesses to run would not be adversely affected by the new security arrangements. Any urgent company problems would be dealt with by telephone and fax, through prior arrangement with the police unit.

'Just how long do you propose to keep us here?' asked Berta Whitstable, her voice overriding questions from the others.

'Nobody's keeping you here,' replied May. 'Remember that. This is for your own protection. Until we find out why this is happening, and who is causing it.'

'And just how long will that be?'

Bryant looked at his partner. 'I hope it'll be for no more than two or three days,' he said. 'There will be a roll call every night and every morning. And, I'm afraid, a curfew.' More groans. It was harder to protect the outside of the house at night. There were too many trees around the building. Once all the questions had been answered, the detectives ran through the name-list checking everyone off.

Bryant looked at his notepad in puzzlement. There was one name down here he didn't recognise. 'Who is C.H. Whitstable?' he asked. 'Can anyone here explain?' There was an uneasy silence.

Several of the men awkwardly turned their attention to their children. Berta Whitstable was standing behind Bryant. She looked like the only member of the assembly who might know how to fold a sheet. She also looked as though she might tell the truth. He turned to her. 'Do you know?'

'That would — probably — be Charles,' she replied.

Bryant frowned. There had been no Charles Whitstable marked on the geneological table. 'I don't understand. I thought everyone was accounted for.'

'Your family tree only shows the Whitstables living in this country. Charles is based overseas.'

'Where?'

'In India. Calcutta.'

'Are you absolutely sure about this?' asked May.

'Of course I am,' said Berta huffily. 'I should know. He is my son.'

'Do you have a number where he can be reached?'

'Of course—'

'Berta!' called one of the men, reaching toward her. 'You have no right to bring Charles into this. It's better to leave him where he is.'

Bryant's interest was piqued.

'I think perhaps we should discuss this in more detail,' he said, placing a hand on Berta Whitstable's broad back and guiding her out of the room.

# CHAPTER

As Jerry walked toward the entrance of the restaurant, she felt her stomach involuntarily lift. She was no longer just helping the police with their enquiries. She was taking matters into her own hands. She checked her watch. 1.05 p.m. Gwen would already be at the table waiting. For a moment she wished Joseph was here with her, but he was already on his way back to Edinburgh. Besides, this was family business.

The Imperial was an elegant eaterie overlooking the Thames, newly furnished to look old. Its floor-to-ceiling windows ensured that the rooms were airier and lighter than anything on the menu, and its waiters had been especially chosen for their arrogance. As such the place had instant appeal for the kind of inherited-wealth forty-somethings who salted their meals before tasting them, and who referred to dessert as pudding. Gwen had begun to eat here all the time. But never before with her daughter.

Jerry was surprised to find the restaurant so busy on Christmas Eve. Did no one stay home with their families anymore? She had donned a dark suit and blouse for the occasion. It made her look older, it made her sick, but it was Gwen's favourite outfit, purchased for an engagement party that she had ended up not attending.

She spotted her mother sitting at the crimson-clothed table, morosely studying the centrepiece. She looked thinner in the face, as if some private burden had begun to take its toll. The severe lines of her blue suit emphasised her weight loss. She smiled wanly at Jerry's approach, unsure of the reaction she would get.

'Mother.' Gwen accepted a light kiss on each cool cheek. She liked to be called that.

'So.' She studied her daughter as she unfolded a napkin into her lap. 'I thought we should at least spend part of the holiday season together. Your father sends his apologies. He's having one of his migraines.' They both knew this meant he had drunk too much at his company dinner the previous evening. He always spent Christmas Eve sleeping it off in preparation for a major onslaught on his liver.

Well, she thought, now's as good a time as any. 'Mother, there's something I want to discuss with you.'

Gwen raised the flat of her palm. 'Please, let's just try to enjoy one another's company tonight. It's Christmas Eve. I'm too weary for another declaration of independence. Before you insist on telling me why you want to leave home, perhaps this nice waiter could get you something to drink.'

She ordered an unseasonal dry martini for herself. Usually her mother's brisk attitude exceeded the fashionable limit of rudeness, but tonight she could sense that Gwen was toning down the act. They hadn't seen much of each other lately. Perhaps Gwen had genuinely missed her.

Jerry picked up a fork and pretended to study it. For a while they sat in silence. She wasn't going to tell Gwen what she had discovered in her father's study. There was nothing to be gained by that. She had decided to head the conversation in a different direction.

'I'm fed up with working in the hotel,' she said finally. 'I want a proper job with some responsibility. I've proved to myself that I can do it, and I really think I have some ability.' She decided not to mention that she hadn't turned up for work in days. 'I want to join Dad's company.'

Gwen was in mid-swig of her martini and looked as if she'd swallowed the olive. Obviously this wasn't at all what she had been anticipating.

She decided to push on. 'I don't expect to be paid much at first. I know I'd have a lot to learn, but I'm willing to try, at least.'

'Well — I don't know what to say,' said her mother, happily nonplussed. 'You've always been so set against the idea. All those lectures you gave Jack about capitalism. This is the last thing I expected to hear from you.'

'If you don't think it's a good idea ...'

'No, it's not that,' she said hastily. 'If this is a genuine change of heart then I don't see why we can't organise something. Are you sure about this? You know what it would involve.' Sure she knew. They had told her often enough. It would mean being apprenticed in one of her father's boring businesses, courses in bookkeeping, accountancy or brokerage if she preferred. It would mean being controlled.

She had to allay any remaining suspicions her mother harboured. During the course of the meal she attempted to explain her change of heart, describing her hopes for the future. By the time she had finished, Gwen was finding it so difficult to contain her delight that it looked as though she might spontaneously combust at the table.

'Well, I think this is something to celebrate,' she said, ordering a very decent bottle of Bollinger. 'Would you like to tell your father, or do you want to leave it to me?'

'Why don't we both tell him?' said Jerry, raising her glass with an evil smile.

'This really is excellent news,' said Jack, making a miraculous recovery from his headache. 'You don't know how much this means to us, Jerry; to see you taking your future into your own hands. You've grown up overnight. I think you'll soon discover that you've made the right choice.' Her father broke off to blow his nose, then lurched from the room and returned with another bottle of champagne.

'We always wanted the best for you,' he insisted, filling the glasses, 'but the final decision of what to do with your life was always in your hands. This can only bring us closer together as a family.'

Jerry secretly congratulated herself for coming up with such a brilliant idea. In the space of a single evening she had revealed her mother's true nature. By volunteering for the family business, she had exposed Gwen's eagerness to employ her as a re-entry point into decent social circles. No longer would she be the bad mother, the woman who had failed to raise her daughter properly. Now she'd be able to say that it had all turned out for the best. She was like some horrible stage mother, using her offspring to wedge herself into the life she never had. Jerry felt no malice toward her father, only sadness. Jack had always done as he was told. She tasted a raw bitterness, and felt her hatred for Gwen deepening.

Most of all, though, she felt the freedom of control.

As she accepted the champagne flute, she wondered how much longer the old man was going to gush on.

Gwen was sitting in the centre of the sofa delicately sipping, looking like a cat who'd just managed to fish the family goldfish out of its bowl.

'So, what's the next move?' she asked, looking from one pleased parent to the other.

'I think I can arrange some kind of apprenticeship for you,' said her father. 'You'll get a chance to see what opportunities are available, and which company you're best suited for. There are all sorts of positions we might look at. You don't suppose—?' he looked over at Gwen as if requesting permission. 'Perhaps we should tell someone.'

Jerry had wondered how long they'd be able to contain themselves. Jack mumbled an apology and left the room to make a phone call, despite the fact that there was a telephone beside his armchair in the lounge. Gwen sat there patting her hands and smiling at her, stumped for further conversation.

No one had thought to probe the reason for her change of heart. She hoped they wouldn't decide to do so.

After a few minutes, Jack returned to the room. 'It's all fixed,' he said cheerfully. 'There's no point in wasting any time. You've some catching up to do. I've arranged drinks for you tomorrow morning.'

'But it's Christmas Day tomorrow.'

'That's all right. Just a seasonal snifter with someone before lunch.'

'With who?'

'Someone I've been working with quite closely lately. He's an absolutely charming man. I'm told he has powerful connections. He's on one of our boards, and I happen to know he's on the lookout for new blood. He's the chairman of the Watchmakers Company,' explained Jack. 'His name is Charles Whitstable.'

\*

John May's Muswell Hill apartment could not have been less like his partner's. After the sudden death of his wife in 1982, May had sold the house in Bethnal Green where they had planned to spend their lives together, and moved to an area which held no memories for him.

Now there was nothing in his surroundings to remind him of the past. The walls of the flat were bare and bright. Various pieces of electronic gadgetry stood around the room in nests of wiring: a portable multi-system Panasonic video—TV, a fax—ansaphone, a CD player and minispeakers, an IBM PC2 home computer, unkempt stacks of books and discs, cassettes, computer magazines and an alarming pile of washing up, despite the presence of a dishwasher.

He had returned home a little after seven in the evening, depressed by Marsden's attitude but thankful that they had managed to buy a little more time for themselves. He was coming down with a cold. He'd probably caught it from Bryant, who managed to pass on the usual winter diseases without undue suffering himself, like Typhoid Mary. At noon his throat had grown sore and his head had begun to throb. By the end of the afternoon he could tell that he had contracted this year's mutant flu germ, and Christina Crosse had sent him home, assuring him that she could easily finish handling the Whitstables' security demands.

It annoyed him that, far from feeling tired, he was nervy and irritable and wide awake. He had specifically blocked the family's more petulant requests in order to reduce distractions during the investigation, but now that they had been assembled en masse he knew that they would be far harder to ignore. Several of them possessed pocket cellphones, and were still using them to vigorously protest, complain and demand items from the Mornington Crescent unit, despite the fact that they had specifically been requested not to tie up the division's phone lines.

The fact that they were under voluntary containment had escaped them; one of the Whitstable children had demanded that his Nintendo game system be brought to the house, otherwise he would tell Daddy to have a word with the Home Office. It had been that kind of day.

May stirred himself a hot lemon drink and poured a shot of brandy into it, looking out from the kitchen window across the misty panorama of London. Nearly ten o'clock. The fourth-floor apartment was situated at the top of a hill, and commanded spectacular views of the city by day.

Now the streets below were silent and deserted. Cars were garaged. Home lights blazed. It was the one night of the year families could be relied upon to spend time together. The city death toll would be up tomorrow; it always rose on Christmas Day. Surprising how many heart attacks occurred after lunch and the Queen's speech.

He had not heard from Bryant for several hours. The case was taking its toll on both of them. An astonishing amount of paperwork had built up in the office, and had yet to be cleared. The Mornington Crescent SCD differed radically from other experimental units previously tested by the Met, in that routine procedural elements were farmed out to auxiliary teams, leaving the senior investigating officers free to concentrate on other aspects of the investigation.

Hundreds of hours of interviews, forensic tests, fibre separations, evidence collections, blood and tissue typing, witness documentation and many other daily activities were handled by groups attached to West End Central.

This kind of specialisation had only been possible since the development of mainframe computers with powerful memory capacity. For all his complaining, Arthur Bryant was working with the new technology whether he knew it or not.

The sudden buzz of the telephone made him wonder if his colleague was calling to check on his health. Instead, he found himself speaking to Alison Hatfield at the Goldsmiths Hall.

'I'm sorry to disturb you at such a late hour, Mr May, but your sergeant told me it would be all right to call,' she explained. 'It's nearly Christmas Day.'

'So it is,' he said, 'Merry Christmas. I'm afraid I've rather lost track of the time. Shouldn't you be tucked up somewhere warm waiting for Santa to call?'

'I'm not a big fan of Christmas, to be honest. All that eating. My flatmate's a nurse and she's working around the clock, so I'm enjoying the peace and quiet at home. Other than that, I like to work. I've turned up some information I think you'll be very interested in. I mean, it looks important. Would it be possible for you to visit the hall?'

'I'll come now if you like,' said May, brightening. At least it would take his mind from his cold. 'I can be there in half an hour. Could you wait for me in the main entrance?'

'No problem. I'll bring a thermos of tea and brandy. At least we can toast the compliments of the season.'

'What a very sensible woman you are, Miss Hatfield.' Sensible, he thought, and rather attractive. After he had replaced the receiver, he called the unit, but Bryant had still not returned from Whitstable Central, as he called it. He knew he shouldn't be venturing out into the chill night, but he was sure that when the case broke wide it would be through the findings of someone like Miss

Hatfield, and not because of a spectographic fibre match.

At 10.37 p.m. he reached the main entrance to the Goldsmiths Hall. Alison was waiting for him. Once again she was dressed in heavy warm clothes that seemed too old for her, as if the sombre surroundings were trying to drain away her youthfulness.

'I hope I haven't dragged you away from anything,' she apologised, shaking his hand.

'Not at all,' assured May, 'I'm glad you called.'

'The place is empty. Everyone's gone for the holidays. The chambers are all locked up. I have the run of the building.'

They walked across to the Watchmakers Company through a deserted avenue of mirrored glass and ancient stone. 'Yesterday I received a call from a Mr Leo Marks,' said Alison, holding open the door for him. 'He wanted to know the whereabouts of certain documents pertaining to the guild.'

May remembered asking the lawyer to check out the financial history of the Watchmakers. It sounded as if he was finally following up on the advice.

'I've been with the guild for six years,' said Alison, 'and I still have no way of locating the older files which have accumulated here. A lot of stuff was moved out during the war. This area suffered terribly during the Blitz. There must have been hundreds of stored cardboard file boxes filled with paperwork. They were moved out for safety, but everything was done in such a hurry that no alphabetizing system was used. When they were returned after the war, there was no one left who remembered how the temporary storage system worked.'

They passed through the building to the basement goods lift, and May pulled back the heavy trellis, mindful of catching his coat between the oil-smeared bars.

'I told Mr Marks that it would be difficult to locate what he was looking for, as my records are incomplete to say the least.' Alison closed the trellis and pressed the brass wall stud behind her. With a shudder, the lift began its descent.

'What exactly was he after?'

'Oh, details of overseas payments made to religious charities, all sorts of things. I thought I'd come down here and have a look around for them. At least that way I'd be able to say I tried. I didn't have much luck, but I found something else I thought you should see.'

The musty dampness filled their nostrils as the lift juddered to a halt. Alison passed the detective a torch, and they entered the faintly lit corridor ahead. On either side of them, furry black watermarks stained the walls.

'Didn't you say there's another floor beneath this?' asked May. He could feel the distant rumbling of the underground river through the soles of his shoes.

'Yes, and there are probably a load of files still down there, but it's not safe. There are things beneath these old buildings that no one will ever find. You remember the old Billingsgate Fish Market in Lower Thames Street?'

'The City Corporation closed it down in 1982, didn't they? It's on the Isle of Dogs now.'

'That's right. When they came to tear up the floor, you know what they found? Two hundred years' worth of permafrost that the strongest steel couldn't cut through. The river had helped to maintain a natural ice age in the basement. So heaven only knows what's beneath us here.' She stopped before a brown-painted door at the far end of the corridor. May could see another dark hall stretching off in both directions.

'What's down there?' he asked.

'I have no idea, and I'm not sure anyone else has.' She

shivered and opened the door, her breath dispelling in the torchlight. 'It's always freezing, because of the river.' She tried a brass light switch on the wall, and a filthy low-voltage bulb went on above them. The room was filled with mildewed cardboard boxes. As Alison disturbed one, hundreds of small brown spiders scattered around and over their shoes.

'I had the caretaker locate the emergency lighting circuit for me before he went off duty,' she said. 'God knows what it runs from. Over here.'

She pulled open a box and shone her torch over its contents. The beam picked up the familiar circled flame symbol of the Alliance. She pulled out part of a heavy leather-bound file and handed it to him, wiping off a filmy nest of spiders. 'I didn't think I should remove these without you being here, in case it counted as disturbing the evidence or something.' Gingerly reaching into the carton, she removed a second file and passed it across.

'What are these?' he asked, puzzled.

'I think one of them's part of the original trading contract for the Alliance. It looks like there are some pages missing, but I'll try and find them for you. The other is someone's notes, but the handwriting's illegible. It's of the same era, so I thought it might be useful.'

'How much more is there?' asked May, pointing to the boxes.

'I don't think there's anything else quite as old down here. The files underneath that one were printed in the mid-1950s. It must have come from another box. To be honest, I don't much fancy digging any deeper, in case I disturb the rats.'

'Don't worry, I think you've found plenty to be going on with.' He flipped to the back of the document. The last page read: *This Agreement Witnessed and Signed on*

*December 28th in the Year of Our Lord 1881, at the Savoy Hotel, London, England.*

There followed seven signatures, the top one of which belonged to James Makepeace Whitstable.

'Can we go up now?' asked Alison. Her arms were wrapped tightly around her narrow shoulders. She was shaking with cold.

May stopped reading. 'Of course, how thoughtless of me. You must be freezing.'

When they reached the comparative warmth of the entrance hall, he gripped her hand fondly. 'This is the second time you've been a great help to me,' he said. 'When this is over I would most enjoy taking you to the restaurant of your choice.'

Alison laughed. 'I'd like that. But I warn you, I'm a healthy eater.'

He felt suddenly sorry for her, spending Christmas Day alone. 'Do you need a lift anywhere?'

'Thanks, I have my little car.'

'If you feel fed up at all, you're welcome to come over to the station,' he offered. 'We won't be celebrating much, but we'll always give you a welcome. We could spend some time together.'

'That's very kind of you.' She smiled shyly. 'I'd like that very much.' Reaching forward, she kissed him lightly on the mouth. The warmth of her lips took him by surprise, and he found himself returning the kiss with more passion than he had intended.

'I'll call you very shortly, John, I promise.' She turned up her collar and took her leave, walking briskly off into the rain.

On his way back to the car, May sneezed so hard that the document beneath his arm nearly disappeared into the gutter. His head felt terrible, but he was elated about the prospect of seeing Alison again. As soon as he reached home, he rang Bryant at his flat in Battersea.

'Do you know what time it is, calling here?' said Alma Sorrowbridge. She sounded tipsy. 'He still hasn't come back yet. He promised to spend Christmas Eve with me. I cooked him a casserole. I opened a bottle of sherry.' It sounded as if she'd done more than just open it. 'He never even rang to apologise.'

'You know his work has to take precedence, Alma.'

'I know, married to the job and all that. He's told me a hundred times.'

'Do you have any idea what he has planned for Christmas Day?' he asked.

'Yes, I do,' said the landlady, disapprovingly. 'He's going over to see that barmy woman, the one with the bright clothes and the funny earrings.'

Only one acquaintance of Bryant's fitted that description; the leader of the Camden Town Coven. 'You mean Maggie Armitage?' he said.

'That's the one. The nutcase.'

'Perhaps you could have him call me before he goes there. I'm sorry about your Christmas, Alma,' he added. 'None of us are having much of a festive season.'

As the rain rolled against the lounge windows, May blew into a handkerchief, opened the first of the files on his desk and began to read.

# CHAPTER

I've had enough of this, thought Pippa Whitstable, angrily eyeing the telephone at the side of the bed. She was supposed to be spending Christmas Eve with Nigel at the club in Beak Street. Instead, she had been forced to play nursemaid to a bunch of appalling, brattish children. She barely knew any of them. The only time the family met was at weddings and funerals. Now they were being forced to live under the same roof, and the police saw the whole thing as a big joke.

She reset the grip in her blonde ponytail and sat on the edge of the makeshift bed. If the dresser alarm clock was correct, it was just past midnight. It was too late to call him now; he would already have left for the club.

She could go there and meet him. Just turn up. It would be the perfect Christmas surprise. She'd heard he was buying her something very special. God, she'd dropped enough hints about the new Mazda convertible. Would he be cheap and pretend he hadn't noticed, palm her off with some pretty Lambert and Butler bauble? Thank God she'd brought her basic black with her. The problem was, how to get out of the house without any of the family seeing her? At least she had her own room here, even if it hadn't been aired in centuries and was the size of a rabbit hutch. Not everyone had gone to bed yet. She wondered how many were still in the lounge. She could manage the stairs without them seeing her provided the lounge door was shut, but the police guard would be waiting on the porch. Even if they could be persuaded to let her pass, they'd insist on telling her mother, who was always prepared to close off any promising avenues of pleasure a young lady might wish to explore.

The bedroom window looked more promising. She slipped off the casement catch and pushed the frame up as quietly as possible. A blast of chill damp air enveloped her. At least the rain had eased to a light drizzle. She was on the first floor, a drop of about fifteen feet. Too far to jump. It was then that she noticed the drainpipe. It had handles, for Christ's sake, ornate little grips for climbing. Thank God for the Victorians! She quickly changed into her black frock and pumps, placed her purse and makeup in a tiny black bag, and wound the strap to her collapsible umbrella. Very carefully, she stepped out of the window and onto the first rung, testing its weight. Solid as a rock. She smiled to herself in the darkness, pulling the window down as far as she dared. Moments later she stepped down on to the lawn.

Wiping her dirty hands on the wet leaves of a bush, she looked around for the best way out of the garden. The far end led off into woods. Not a good idea in these shoes, she thought. But the left hand fence backed against an alleyway, which was accessible via a bolted wooden side-gate. She wrenched open the latch and slipped through, careful to leave it slightly ajar so that she could re-enter later.

This was perfect. It didn't matter how long they were stuck in the house now; she had found herself an escape route. It would be easy to get a cab from Hampstead High Street, but which direction was that? The alley stretched off in pools of rain-sparkling light.

He must have seen her open the bedroom window from a hiding place in the garden, because she had only just turned from the door when he grabbed her, pressing an icy hand across her mouth and dragging her backwards from the cone of light thrown by the overhead streetlamp. The first sweeping fit of panic that assailed her senses quickly passed as she realised how small her attacker was. He had caught her by surprise and managed to knock her off balance, but now she uprighted herself and dug her heels hard against the ground. *You've really picked the wrong victim this time, you fucker*, she thought, preparing to take him. It would teach him to mess with a green belt.

She could feel his ribs against her spine and threw her elbows back as hard as she could. Bone cracked and shifted; the arm around her shoulder was released. Opening her mouth to admit the fingers pressing against her lips, she bit down hard and was shocked to feel her teeth meeting through parting flesh and crumbling bone. The fingers of his right hand had come away, the knuckles opening with a series of audible pops, the exposed veins splitting to leak hot stinking fluid over her chin.

Wrenching herself free with a sob, she began to run as her assailant threw himself at her legs and crashlanded on the flagstoned walkway with her.

She tried to shove him from her back, but his remaining fingers snaked through her hair, pulling her head up and slamming it against the wet stone. A blinding pain cut across her right frontal lobe, spurring her to twist him away. When she finally managed to catch sight of him, she was surprised to see the face of a sick old man. He was bald and grey-skinned, with lank clumps of hair above his ears — or ear; one was missing. His eyes were sunken deep into his head, and were opaque with cataracts. He reeked of bad meat and rancid body fluids. His blood was still bitter in her mouth. But most striking of all was his clenched expression, a look of agony and pitiful confusion, as of one departing the corporeal world for a realm of unimaginable pain.

As he raised himself on one leg she brought up her fist and punched out at the tortured face before her.

She felt a madness tearing at her senses as her hand ripped through the skin of his cheek, shucking the rotten teeth from his buckling jawbone and descending into the putrid liquefaction that had once been his oesophagus.

*Christ almighty, this thing is dead,* she thought, bile rising to her throat as she attempted to pull her hand free, *someone's playing a sick joke. I could pull him apart with my bare hands.* Shuddering with revulsion she battered at the corpse with her fists and knees as the jawless lolling head tipped to one side, its neck dislocated. It opened easily beneath her touch, spilling and separating like an over-boiled chicken. Her screams turned to light-headed laughter. *It can't hurt me, it isn't even alive.* As her stomach convulsed and she began to vomit, hacking and bubbling, she knew that the ludicrous creature had already achieved its aim. It had hurt her, and terribly so, for whatever lay putrefying within the rotten sac of its body was so viciously toxic that already an excruciating void was appropriating her senses. Red pinpoints of light seared and stung her widening eyes, and a rasping tintinnabulation echoed in her head. She dropped back to the ground as the corpse collapsed over her, smothering the knotted musculature of her torso in its embrace, riding the furious, poisoned paroxysm of her death.

# CHAPTER

Christmas Day. 11.55 a.m. As the British Midlands aircraft approached Penzance, Jerry looked down at the scrabble-board of frosted white fields surrounding the tiny airport and speculated about her coming meeting with Charles Whitstable. Why had he agreed to see her at such short notice? What was the rush?

She was about to be introduced to a leading member of the Whitstable clan. According to Jack, as soon as news had reached him of the assassinations, Charles had left unfinished business overseas to return to England. Perhaps he alone knew the reason behind his family's decimation.

Jack's keenness to set her working in the family business obviated any guilt she felt about deceiving her parents. She possessed a new clarity of mind that came from being alone. She was determined to be present at the conclusion of the investigation, just as she would uncover the meaning of Wayland's letters to her mother. If the cost was the loss of her own peace of mind, so be it.

Charles had sent a car to collect them. The polished black Mercedes 500 was waiting beside the tiny baggage reclamation area, its exhaust purling clouds into the chill morning air. The driver, a young Indian boy who spoke to them in absurdly perfect public school English, gave an eager smile and showed every sign of recognising them.

Charles Whitstable's residence was waiting behind a veil of wind-blasted trees which parted for them as they turned the corner of the drive and revealed the magnificent Georgian simplicity of a country estate. His father turned to her and smiled reassuringly. 'Quite a place, isn't it?'

'It's beautiful. Have you been here before?'

'No, but Charles has often mentioned it.'

'How do you know him?'

'He has many business interests, several of which coincide with mine. We met at a lodge dinner two years ago, and since then we've occasionally negotiated deals together. Lately, though, Charles has been operating overseas. He's very rarely here, and wouldn't be now if it weren't for this appalling problem with his family. It's adversely affecting his stock. He's having to daily reassure his shareholders.'

'It sounds like he's got his hands full. Why would he want to see me?'

'Because he's looking for someone he can train to bridge the gap between his export business and my own trading agency, and he's not prepared to trust the job to an outsider.'

'You mean it has to be a member of the family?'

'His or mine. And with the press the Whitstables have been getting lately, mine is preferable. That's why your change of heart has come at such a fortuitous time.'

This is the lion's den, she thought, and they're happily

placing me in it. The chauffeur brought the Mercedes to a halt in the curve of the pale gravelled drive and turned off the engine. Her father fidgeted with his tie, and coughed lightly into his fist. He looked nervous, but of course he had every reason to be. This was the moment his wife had been waiting for. Too bad she wasn't here to enjoy it. Apparently, Charles had only extended his invitation to the two of them.

The front door was opened by an attractive young Indian maid. She showed them into the large breakfast room where Mr Whitstable would presently join them, bade them be seated, and silently withdrew.

Jerry took stock of their surroundings. They were sitting within a cluttered treasure trove of Victoriana. The wallpaper featured rose sprigs tied with satin ribbon. Ebonised cane chairs were set about an oak gateleg table. Decorative knick-knacks of every kind lined the low breakfast bench. On a green velvet runner stood several bronze animals, some small penwork chests in black and gold, elaborate rosewood boxes and sentimental figurines of children and dogs. The atmosphere was smothering, the room unaired.

Neither of them spoke. A slow-ticking grandfather clock provided the only sound. After two or three minutes the main doors reopened, and Charles Whitstable entered.

He was tall, six feet three inches at least, imposingly broad chested, in his mid-to-late thirties. His conservative black suit and slicked dark hair provided an image somewhere between city stockbroker and lord of the manor. He bore a natural air of authority, a sense of ownership. Jerry sensed at once that she was being introduced to the head of the Whitstable clan.

'Geraldine. I'm very pleased to meet you.' His handshake was firm and cool. Jerry smiled back and met his eye. He was evenly and deeply tanned, almost as if he was wearing stage makeup. Although his features were handsomely set, there was an absolute stillness in his face that quickly became unnerving. Charles approached the older man and welcomed him. 'Jack, I'm sorry we've seen so little of each other lately. I've been meeting with investors, trying to calm their nerves. Liverpool is not to be recommended in the winter. How are you?'

Before her father could answer, Charles turned and seated himself in one of the cane chairs.

'Well, young lady, you've blazed quite a trail, haven't you?' For a moment, Jerry thought her real motive in coming here had been discovered. 'Although business frequently removes me from the country, I try to keep myself apprised of potential talent. After Jack called, I ran a quick check on you. Let's see now — you dropped out of school and embarrassed your parents. You made yourself ill, took a spell in care, indulged yourself at the expense of those who clothed and fed you. You've been acting like a child for long enough.' Charles reached over and pressed a brass buzzer on his desk. 'You'll soon be eighteen, but why should I assume you're ready to start behaving like a responsible adult?'

The maid appeared in the doorway, and Charles gestured to her. Jerry shifted uncomfortably on her chair, straightening the lines of her suit in an attempt to hide her nervousness.

'I appreciate your honesty, Mr Whitstable, and I hope you don't mind if I'm as equally frank with you. I know only what I read about your family in the papers, so you have the advantage of me. My parents have frequently expressed a desire to see me employed in family business.' She could not resist a glance at Jack. 'They've always suggested that it is my duty to do so, but I've never felt that way. I'm old enough to form my own ideas, and to make certain judgements for myself. Now I'm ready to capitulate to my father. Not because he told me to, but because I want to. It's my decision, and mine alone. He thinks that I can be of use to you, and I'm willing to learn.'

'You have no plans for university, Geraldine. You haven't had a guild apprenticeship. What makes you assume you could handle my kind of managerial training?'

'I'm strong-willed but not pig-headed. I know that enterprise is served by individuality, not conformity. That rather makes me a Whitstable in body and spirit, if not in name.' She could sense that Charles was surprised but not displeased by her effrontery. The maid re-entered and served refreshments in silence. Once the doors had been closed, he rose and walked to the floor-length windows on the far side of the room that overlooked the estate's misty olivine gardens.

'I won't pretend that we have no need for you,' he said. 'I'm always looking to recruit future managerial material from within my own household. Lately, I've no longer been able to afford that luxury. There aren't many younger members of the Whitstable family left. Too few children. Besides, we need people with new ideas.'

'I belong to a different generation,' said Jerry. 'I don't automatically share my parents' beliefs, because I don't need the things they need.'

'That's encouraging to hear.' Charles turned from the window. 'Jack, I think you could leave the two of us to chat further.'

'I should stay with Jerry,' said her father, half rising in his seat. In that fleeting moment, she saw the abject misery in his eyes. He was afraid of Charles. But why?

'That really won't be necessary. I've only been home for a short while and few of the rooms are properly aired. I'll have them book you into one of the better Penzance hotels. Get a good night's sleep and you can collect Jerry in the morning.'

'We weren't expecting to stay overnight. I'm not sure—'

'That's settled, then. Your daughter and I need to talk business.'

Even though they had yet to discuss her terms of employment, Jerry knew that she had been accepted into the poisoned embrace of the Whitstable family.

Maggie Armitage lit a joss stick and set it in the nosehole of an African spirit head. 'That's better,' she said. 'Get rid of the smell of damp in here.' They were standing in the cluttered room above the World's End pub opposite Camden Town tube station. The streets outside were bright and empty, like an abandoned film set. The windows of the flat were misted with condensation and water was steadily dripping through a black patch on the ceiling. A few faded postwar paper chains had been strung between the corners in a desultory attempt to usher in some Christmas cheer. Maggie was only a little over five feet tall, but what the white witch lacked in height she made up for in vivacity. All problems, national, local or personal, were dealt with in the same brisk, friendly manner. For all the complexity of her personal belief system she was a practical woman, and it was this streak of sound sense that had kept the Coven of St James the Elder thriving in Camden at a time when so many other branches were shutting up shop.

With their ranks now swollen to include a number of part-time honorary members (each of whom monthly contributed a few pounds toward the rent plus fifty pence for tea money), meetings took place in the lounge of the flat every Monday evening promptly at 8.00 p.m., and continued rather more raucously in the pub downstairs. Much of the coven's weekly work was of a mundane nature; intercoven correspondence was dealt with, and a desktop newsletter was produced. Public queries had to be answered, a forum for the discussion of world events was chaired, and new excuses were invented for avoiding eviction notices.

'You've managed to hang on to this place, then,' said Bryant, warily eyeing the saturated ceiling.

'The landlord's been trying to sling us out for years, but his heart isn't in it anymore,' said Maggie. 'Especially since Doris put an evil enchantment on his car.'

'I thought you didn't do that sort of thing.'

'Well,' she confided, 'we don't as a rule but he was being a real pain in the arse.'

'Did it work?'

'I think so. Whenever he comes around to collect the rent he's always half an hour late and his hands are covered in oil. Would you like one of my special Christmas cups of tea?'

'I don't know,' said Bryant, narrowing his eyes at her. 'Is it full of strange herbs and aromatic spices?'

'No, PG Tips with a shot of brandy.'

'Oh, that's all right then.' He shifted a stack of magazines and seated himself. 'Where's everyone else?'

'We finished early with just a few madrigals because Maureen's cooking her family Christmas dinner, and now the others have gone downstairs to the pub. We won't join them. They're busy arguing about the origins of Yggdrasil, you know, the cosmic axis. Things can get quite heated.'

'I'm afraid I'm not familiar—' Bryant began.

'Well, you should be!' said Maggie, pouring a generous measure of Hine into his cup. 'That's why we put presents under the Christmas tree. Yggdrasil is the eternal tree of Northern belief, the axis of the world that links the earth to heaven and hell. Decking the tree is an act which symbolically brings us the gifts of wisdom. And strangely enough, it has something to do with your investigation.'

Bryant couldn't wait to hear this one. Still, she had been right a number of times before, although she had always dismissed the offer of public recognition.

Maggie crossed the room, skirting a pair of buckets collecting rainwater, and removed a large volume from one of the overflowing bookcases. 'I've been delving into your dilemma, and I believe I've come up with something that may help you.'

She set the book down on the table before her. 'This is an album of Christmas beliefs, printed in Scandinavia at the end of the nineteenth century. After our last meeting I started thinking about James Whitstable and the Stewards of Heaven. I couldn't see what had inspired him to form this kind of society, although it didn't surprise me one bit that he had.'

'It didn't?'

'Oh, no. You have to imagine the Victorian empire builders as they were. Champions of industry, taming the savages, spreading the word. How grandly they must have thought of themselves! How godlike! No wonder they formed so many societies like this. People like James Whitstable saw themselves as superior human beings, educated, enlightened and powerful. They wanted to separate themselves from the rabble, to have their worth acknowledged by their peers. And they sought methods of spiritual improvement. Sometimes, however, they got sidetracked into bad habits.' Maggie took a sip of her brandy tea and paused for a breath.

'These days one tends, rather naively, to automatically

dismiss the Victorian age as a time of mindless imperialism. It comes as rather a shock to find that the youthful Queen Victoria envisaged a new era of democracy, tolerance and freedom for all. Things turned out differently in practice due to the rigours of the class system, and because men like Whitstable put themselves above the common herd.'

She opened the book at its mark and revealed a pair of beautiful watercolour drawings. One showed a traditional evocation of St Nicholas with his reindeer. The other was a representation of the god Odin, astride an eight-legged creature with horns. They looked very similar. The distance between these two mythical icons was far less than he had realised.

'I felt it was significant that Whitstable saw himself as *Och*, the Bringer of Light. The photograph of the group reminded me of something, but I couldn't think what it was. Then I remembered. The room in which the seven men were standing was decorated for Christmas. You could see holly lining the mantelpiece. Now, Christmas is a unique festival originally celebrating not the birth of Christ, but the rebirth of light following winter's shortest, darkest day. Do you want a mince pie?' She shook a tin at Bryant that sounded as if it contained rocks.

'Midwinter has always been regarded as a time of terrible danger,' she continued. 'To primitive man, it must have seemed that the nights would continue to lengthen until darkness reigned continuously. The people of Britain sought to ward off this all-consuming darkness with rites and ceremonies, and have continued to do so for over five thousand years. What a relief it must have been for them to find the days lengthening again! What an excuse for a party! You probably know that the festival of Christmas celebrates this turning point; the triumph of light over darkness, and thus the victory of good over evil. Satan was held at bay for another year. People whinge about Christmas becoming too commercial, but before heavenly choirs of angels made it so bland and solemn it was a marvellously rowdy pagan celebration, a time of great excess.'

'And this has something to do with James Makepeace Whitstable.'

'Sorry, I thought I'd made myself clear. Let's assume that the photograph of the Alliance of Eternal Light was taken at the end of December. The Winter Solstice is 21 or 22 December. You see?'

'Not at all,' admitted Bryant.

'Look at the pictures,' said Maggie patiently. 'St Nicholas is a cleaned-up Christian version of the fearsome one-eyed Pagan god Odin, the original 'Old Nick'. Odin's horse, Sleipnir, becomes Rudolph the reindeer. When was the first murder committed?'

'The sixth of December.'

'The Feast Day of St Nicholas. The first day of the battle between light and darkness. A battle that can't end until the light starts to lengthen once more, after 22 December.' She closed the book and handed it to him. 'I'm afraid your murders aren't over yet.'

'But it's 25 December. The days have already started to lengthen again.'

'Have they?' asked Maggie. 'With the terrible weather we've been having in the past few weeks, we're well below the seasonal average for hours of daylight. Instead, we've had more and more darkness. Perhaps the sacrifices aren't working.'

'Dear God, I can't afford to believe that the world is descending into darkness because a secret organisation has failed to restore the daylight. Next you'll be trying to make me believe that there's a chamber full of cloaked figures somewhere clutching knives at a sacrificial altar. And there's something else that makes no sense.' Bryant scratched at his chin, confused. 'You're assuming that Whitstable's alliance is still active, but we've found no evidence of that. Why would they act now, after waiting for so long?'

'I'm not sure. Perhaps it's some kind of anniversary.'

'No, the big one would have been one hundred years, which means the murders would have occurred in 1981. And you're suggesting the alliance wages some kind of occult war by actually murdering people; if that were the case, they would surely be going after their true foes, the enemies of day and light. These deaths are occurring *within* their guild, not outside it. That means they're attacking their own people, their own blood. Why would they deliberately hurt themselves?'

'I agree with you,' said Maggie reluctantly, 'it doesn't make sense. But a lot can happen in a century. Perhaps the system inverted itself somehow. Perhaps it's not stoppable.'

'It's killing them one by one, Maggie. If they really did know about such an organisation, don't you think the Whitstables would try to expose it?'

'Perhaps they daren't confide in the police. Perhaps they're too scared of what may happen.'

Bryant thought of the uneasy silence that surrounded the mention of Charles Whitstable's name. 'And perhaps they know they can do nothing to halt it,' he said uneasily.

# CHAPTER

'I suppose I should offer you a sherry.'

Doctor Wayland rose from the leather armchair by his desk and moved to the mahogany drinks cabinet that dominated the far wall of the consulting room. Although his office was officially closed, he still sported the striped shirt and Etonian tie that he wore for his patients' sessions. He was so used to creating an impression of confident control that he no longer remembered how to relax.

'I'm not here to wish you the compliments of the season, Emil,' Gwen said sharply, 'but I'll have a drink all the same. Scotch.' She had piled her hair up and fixed it with an onyx slide, formal and severe. She looked for somewhere to hang her silver fox jacket and finally elected to drape it across the back of the couch. Wayland's illustrious clients expected there to be a couch, and they always got what they expected. Their gushing yuletide cards lined his bookshelves.

'My daughter told me you were spending Christmas in

France.' She accepted the heavy crystal tumbler from him. 'What are you still doing here?'

'You've always prided yourself on coming straight to the point, haven't you? Why is that, do you think?' He raised his glass. She ignored the toast.

'I didn't come to talk about me.' She walked over to the bay window and looked down into Harley Street. No traffic, no people. Christmas Day in London was to her mind one of the few days of the year when the city appeared in a civilised light. 'Well? Why *are* you still here, Emil?'

'To be honest, I can't really afford the time off. There's too much work to be done. And I wanted to see you.'

'You'll forgive me if I find that hard to believe. I understand that Geraldine had an extra session with you recently.'

Wayland set down his drink. 'A couple of them, actually. She's had something on her mind, and wanted to talk about it. I've been meaning to ask. How do you find her behaviour towards you at the moment?'

'The usual thinly veiled insolence. At least, until yesterday. She's gone away with her father. Why? What's been going on? She's told you something, hasn't she? You must have a good reason for calling me.'

'Did you know that she was seeing someone? A young man?'

'No, I didn't. Who is he?'

Wayland was leaning against the head of the couch watching her. The grey streaks above his ears lent him an air of sagacity. She wondered if they were real, or whether he had dyed them to achieve this precise effect.

'You realise how unethical it is for me to be breaking your daughter's confidence?' he asked quietly.

'It's a little late to start discussing ethics, don't you

think? I mean, given the somewhat unusual doctor–patient relationship you've had with our family. How long has she been seeing this person?'

'I don't know. Not long, but I can sense the seriousness of it. He's the first one she's ever mentioned.'

'My God. Do you know if they've done anything yet?'

'I gather they tried to make love, but things didn't work out. She became panicked and ran away.'

'Well, that's hardly surprising, is it? Obviously their relationship must be brought to an end, or at the very least, slowed down.'

'Or you have to talk to her.'

'I can't do that, Emil. You know I can't.'

'And I can't change the past, Gwen. If you had been there for her, perhaps the whole damned mess would never have …'

'Don't you dare, don't *you dare* blame me!' she shouted suddenly, her face draining of colour. 'I loved her like any mother with her only child. She rejected me first, remember.'

'Haven't you ever asked yourself why?' He patted his pockets for cigarettes, a sign that he was under stress. 'She sensed that you were play-acting a role.'

'What are you talking about? All I ever wanted was a child of my own, a daughter. You know that.'

'Come on, Gwen, you were busy staging performances of the Perfect Mother to your friends, and she saw through you. All those showy kisses. You used a little too much technique, darling.'

She slapped his face so hard that it stung her hand and surprised them both. Wayland always pushed her to the limit, just to see how much he could get away with. 'I loved her,' she said hoarsely. 'I always will, even if she never returns it.'

'Perhaps you do feel something,' said Emil, gingerly touching his reddening cheek, 'but so does someone else now. And we have to work out what to do.'

She turned back to the window, her arms folded as if she was cold. 'It was bound to happen sooner or later,' she said finally. 'What's the point of trying to stop it? Perhaps we should just let nature take its course.' There was a hint of pride in her voice. 'My daughter may turn out to be stronger than either of us realised.'

'I hope for all our sakes you're right,' the doctor replied, lighting his cigarette and exhaling nervously.

Laden with the volumes on pagan winter rituals that Maggie Armitage had lent him, Bryant drove back from Camden Town to his Battersea apartment. He arrived to find his partner furiously pacing the floor.

'Where the bloody hell have you been?' he snapped. 'We've been trying to page you for hours, but there's been no response.'

'That's odd,' said Bryant, pushing past him to remove a bottle of wine from the refrigerator. 'My pager's in the tie-drawer of my wardrobe. You should have been able to hear it from in here.' He searched for a corkscrew. 'I promise I'll try to get used to the new technology before one of us dies.'

'Arthur, we've lost another member of the family.'

'What are you talking about? I rang in first thing this morning and everything was fine.'

'That's because they didn't discover Pippa Whitstable was missing until they searched her bedroom.'

'Pippa ...' His cheerful demeanour evaporated. Not another young one.

'It looks as if she sneaked out last night and was jumped in the alley beside the house. Her assailant was dead,

Arthur. That is, he was dead when he attacked her. Just like Denjhi.' May ran a hand through his white mane, exasperated. 'It's insane. I've seen a bodybag full of rotting evidence lying in Finch's morgue and I still don't believe it. The implications are unthinkable. Finch says that unusual compound chemicals in the corpse have broken down into some kind of highly toxic waste-fluid, and that it was contact with this stuff that killed her. They're trying to analyse the components now.'

'You're sure no one's misread the times of death?'

'Finch swears his figures are accurate. That's what makes it so odd.'

'We need to think. I don't feel well.' Bryant looked around, momentarily confused. 'What's happening, John? Nothing makes sense any more. I've never frightened easily, you know that. I'm not scared of dying. But there's madness at work here. It's like an epidemic, the more you seek to contain it, the more virulent each outbreak becomes.'

May was studying him, concern in his eyes. 'Have you eaten anything today?'

He shook his head. 'It's been the last thing on my mind.'

'Then let's break bread together.'

They located the casserole Bryant's landlady had so thoughtfully prepared the night before. 'Where is Alma?' he asked, suspiciously eyeing the steaming bowl as he unwound his scarf.

'She gave up waiting for you and went to stay with her sister in Tooting.' He ladled chunks of stewed beef into bowls. 'Tell me what happened with the spiritualist.'

'She's not a spiritualist, John. The fields are only vaguely related. It's like calling your dentist an optician. She's managed to establish the source of our occult connection.'

'Whitstable's secret alliance?'

'Yes, and you won't like it. Someone in the family has failed to carry out the ritual that should ensure the renewal of light to the world.'

'*What?*' May carried a laden tray into the dining room, where Alma had grudgingly laid out a full Christmas table before departing. 'This is the end of the twentieth century, not the nineteenth. Are you telling me these are sacrificial murders?'

'I'm not sure about that,' replied Bryant, peering into his bowl and sniffing. 'It seems unlikely that James Whitstable would deliberately sacrifice his family, even a century later. I'm still missing something.'

'Part of your brain, by the sound of it,' muttered May, seating himself at the table. 'I hate to disappoint you, but the Whitstable alliance was formed for a more mundane purpose.'

'Which is?'

'Come back to the unit as soon as we've eaten. I locked the trading contract in my desk. It's safe there until I can arrange to have it properly analysed.' The forensic department operated beyond the official jurisdiction of the SCD, and was running shifts with a skeleton staff through the Christmas break.

'I suppose we'll miss the Queen's speech,' said Bryant gloomily, filling their glasses.

'I don't understand you,' said May. 'You moan about families like the Whitstables, and yet you're still a royalist.'

'In every constitutional monarchy there are pretenders to the throne,' said Bryant. 'The Whitstables survive by trading on the respect of an earlier generation, and that respect was gained through fear. There's nothing noble about power won in that fashion. And apart from that, they're horrible people. Thank you for my Christmas present, by the way.'

'I didn't have time to buy you anything.'

'Exactly.'

It was traditional for May to treat his partner to a box of Havana cigars at this time of the year, but the investigation had forced such civilised customs aside. 'I'll tell you what,' he offered. 'If we manage to keep our jobs, I'll take you to the restaurant of your choice.' He dragged an indeterminate piece of vegetable matter on to the side of his bowl and prodded it with his fork. 'If your landlady cooks like this when she's lovesick,' he said with a grimace, 'I dread to think what she'd prepare if she hated you.'

They arrived at the Mornington Crescent unit to find their office door wide open. The workmen had finished tearing away the paintwork and had downed tools for the Christmas holiday. Water was pouring in through the unsealed frames. The office reeked of turpentine. Although all leave had been suspended in the division, the rest of the staff had been granted lunch breaks so that they could at least share a quick Christmas dinner with their families.

May unlocked his desk and removed the sealed plastic bag containing the signatory contract.

'This document was drawn up to protect and further the family's business interests,' he said, spreading the damp pages carefully across his blotter. 'James Whitstable and his pals had powerful connections. I've been trying to understand the kind of businessmen they were. Not industrialists. The family was too old, too finely bred. They had little in common with their hardworking Northern brothers, who were running the mills and forging communication links across the country. No, the Whitstables were entrepreneurs, opening markets, creating new outlets. They had powerful Foreign Office connections; they made regular party payments to ensure favourable trade conditions; they provided a blueprint for some unhealthily symbiotic modern trading practices.' He tapped the pages with his forefinger. 'It's all here, couched in suitably euphemistic English. James Makepeace Whitstable set up an Alliance to protect his family by preventing their assets from falling into the wrong hands.

'These seven men declared their financial goals in writing. They had already made considerable investments in iron and steel, the railways, goldsmiths' and jewellers' concerns, and of course, the watchmakers. Remember you said that the Whitstables were the Victorian empire in microcosm? The terms of the contract they drew up between them suggests that they were something more; I get the picture of a politically far-right organisation aimed at the furtherance of the British financial dynasty. Look at this.' He singled out one of the handwritten clauses in the contract. '*In a Situation of Unfair Competitive Practice, the Alliance is Fully Prepared to Disaffect Said Competitor with the Utmost Vigour.* I wonder if they were prepared to kill in order to safeguard the supremacy of the company.'

Bryant sat and examined the document page by page. Finally he looked up at May. 'Have you been able to verify any of this?'

'I called Leo Marks. I thought he'd be bound to have a copy of the contract on file somewhere, but he says he's never heard of such a document. Legally binding contracts more than fifty years old are stored in a shared vault, and take a considerable amount of time to locate. He says he'll do his best — after his office returns to work on 2 January.'

'What about Jerry?'

'I was going to have her check through the Savoy's files for me, but she's an awkward little sod; said she had an idea of her own that would help. As she wouldn't tell me what it was, all I could do was warn her to be careful. I had Christina check with the Savoy Hotel to find out where they keep their guests' registration records, and how far they go back. As you can see, the exact date on the contract has been water-damaged, and I couldn't afford to wait for the page to return from Infrareds.'

The extreme age of the document would delay the forensic findings, because the chemical treatment of the pages would have to be modified. The lab technicians were used to pumping powerful compounds through modern pulp and cotton-based paper.

'I asked them to run through the last two weeks of December 1881. Fortunately, the Savoy's ledgers are well protected and stored in immaculate condition. They were able to verify that Mr James Whitstable and friends – he paid for the rooms of the other six – stayed there for just one night. But it wasn't on 21 December 1881. It was on the twenty-eighth.'

Bryant's face fell. 'You mean they missed the winter solstice by a whole week?'

'I'm afraid so. Your theory is wrong, Arthur. What's more, I've found no connection with occultism in the contract. These dates you came up with have to be pure coincidence.'

Bryant sighed, wearily rubbing his hand across his forehead. 'I don't know, John. According to Maggie's books the day of each death matches points in the supposed battle between day and eternal night. The culmination of the fight occurs at the end of December. I'd have written it off as coincidence myself if I hadn't seen the photograph of the Stewards of Heaven signing their contract at the Savoy. The whole business is filled with uncomfortable associations. Have you noticed how the lights flicker and grow dim just before there's a murder?'

'Oh, that's ridiculous!' May exploded. 'I'm willing to accept that Whitstable and his partners believed they were dabbling in some kind of black magic, but you can't tell me they've put a spell on their descendants.'

'I'm just saying that this contract of theirs was meant to bind them spiritually as well as legally. The others *had* to sign. They didn't dare not to.'

'You're sure all the dates match up?'

'So far.'

'You'd better see if there are any further events in the mystical calendar that we should be aware of.'

Bryant sat back behind his desk and stared at the pages of the contract, his thoughts far away. May knew the look. It meant there was something on his partner's mind that he had failed to mention.

Bryant opened his mouth to speak, then closed it again. It was like waiting for the other boot to drop.

'All right,' he said finally. 'What is it?'

'I've been thinking,' said Bryant, slowly looking up. 'Why did he pick the Savoy? The hotel had only been built two years before. Why sign the document there? Why not have it certified in legal chambers?'

'Well, no doubt the Savoy was the smart new place to be seen taking one's business partners.'

'I suppose if they were clandestinely signing the document, privacy would have been desirable. But I can't help wondering if there was something, some social function, associated with the hotel that gave James Whitstable a reason for signing up his Alliance partners there.'

'I suppose we could go through the Savoy records, but I feel like we're heading off track.'

'Look at the contract,' said Bryant. 'It's handwritten, filled with grammatical mistakes and anomalies, as if it were put together on the spur of the moment.' He fanned the pages wide before him. 'There are three different hands at work here. This was too much for one person to write by himself in an evening. No, Whitstable coerced his partners into writing out a blueprint for their financial future. Was the contract just one part of a broader ritual?'

'Arthur, I think we've spent long enough rooting about in the past. We're looking for someone who's alive today.'

'I agree,' rejoined his partner. 'But until the foot teams or forensics come up with a single shred of incriminating evidence, our only chance of finding a motive lies in understanding the family's ancestry. Find the motive and we find the culprit.'

'And your motive is human sacrifice for the return of the daylight?' May shook his head. 'We're not in the Dark Ages anymore. Human greed, jealousy, revenge, those are the only enduring reasons for murder. Some things don't change much in a hundred years. Oh, there are technological leaps, but human nature stays the same. This agreement was signed in late Victorian Britain, an age of supposed enlightenment. Advocating the murder of the family it was designed to protect a hundred years later is just a melodramatic notion. It makes no sense, can't you see that?'

'All I can see,' said Bryant stubbornly, 'is your refusal to acknowledge the debt we all owe to the past.'

'You're being unreasonable, Arthur. You can't bend the facts to fit your theories. Whitstable did not form his alliance on the day of the solstice. How much more proof do you need?'

'I could have sworn I was right about that. Everything pointed to a supernatural ceremony.'

'Are you absolutely sure? Look at your own interests. You love all this mumbo-jumbo about pagan worship. Does it honestly belong in the investigation? I have a theory of my own, but I'm not trying to force it into place.'

'And what is it, might I ask?'

'I don't think we're looking for a single murderer. I think there's a team of hired assassins, two or even three, carrying out instructions from another source, possibly from someone in the family who bears a grudge. They're leaving dead bodies at the crime scenes. Perhaps they somehow come to life — I don't know. But the way everything's so meticulously planned, it's as if someone's sitting down and working it out on a computer.'

He withdrew a disc from his drawer and held it up. 'I'm pulling together a programme of my own based on all of the existing data, to see if I can project where it will head next. The theory's just as valid as yours.'

'Now whose personal interests are coming through?' Bryant exclaimed angrily. 'I knew you'd have to get a computer into this somehow. You're clutching at straws. This is beyond the experience of either of us. You're telling me there are reanimated corpses out there, for God's sake, yet when I suggest the Stewards are occultists, you dismiss the idea.'

'You have no proof.'

'And neither do you! Look out there.' He pointed to the window. 'The days are *still dark*.'

'Stan Marsden's been telling people you're going senile,' said May, 'that you're intractable, bloody-minded. I told him not to be so damned rude. But unless you start working with me instead of developing these crazy notions by yourself, I'm going to start thinking he's right.' He stalked from the office and slammed the door behind him.

Hurt by his partner's uncharacteristic outburst, Bryant sat back and pressed his eyes shut, losing himself in thought. What was happening to the Whitstables was also happening to them. The investigation was losing its way in internecine fighting. The only solution to the problem would be to agree to May's theories and help him develop a practical appliance for them.

After a few minutes his spirits rose a little, and he began to compile a date-list of events in the pagan winter battle of light and dark. The articles in Maggie's books had been assembled in turn from extremely diverse sources, not all of them reliable. Eventually, however, he was able to create a list of the most important dates by cross-checking from more than two volumes. For once he had to admit that a computer could have handled the task more speedily.

Outside, the lights of Camden shone brightly on to empty wet streets. Bryant checked his watch. He needed to find a way of verifying his theories. If they held any truth at all, then there was not a minute left to lose. If only he could step back in time to that winter's night long ago, if only he could have seen what *they* saw ...

He needed some fresh air. Slipping back into his overcoat, his attention was drawn by the ragged patch beneath the window. Lost in thought, he examined the striated section of wall where the workmen had peeled away layers of paint, revealing their own inchoate glimpses of the past.

# CHAPTER

May knew he shouldn't have asked if there were any problems. Every single person in the room had their hand raised. The Whitstable family had been gathered together en masse now for forty-eight hours, and the strain of so many difficult people having to share with each other was beginning to manifest itself in a form of upmarket cabin fever. Pippa's mother had collapsed upon hearing that her daughter was dead, and now remained under medical supervision in one of the bedrooms.

As everyone was talking at once, May called for quiet by blowing the silver sports whistle he had strung around his neck, and pointed at Isobel Whitstable. 'You have a question?'

'Being cooped up like this is making me sick. How much longer will we have to stay here?' There was an immediate hubbub of assent.

'Until the danger to all of you has passed,' replied May, 'and at the moment we're unable to say when that will be. You saw what happened when Pippa ventured outside.'

The noise level rose sharply, and he was forced to shout. 'It's come to my attention that some of you have been trying to speak to the press about your treatment here.' Several abortive phone calls had been logged by the attendant security team. 'I'm afraid we're going to have to stop that.'

This was followed by a barrage of angry demands.

'It sounds as if you're frightened of the papers putting their own investigators on the case,' said a member of the most senior Whitstable generation. 'We want whoever's doing this run to earth. It's irrelevant who catches him, just so long as someone does before there's another death.' Everyone seemed to agree on that point.

'I feel the same way as you,' said May, 'but some of the journalists are showing a marked lack of responsibility in their hunt for a new angle. I'm afraid they might inadvertently reveal your whereabouts to your enemies, even though they would be committing a criminal offence by doing so.'

They hadn't been making his job any easier by giving bitter, sarcastic interviews with the press about their treatment at the hands of the incompetent police. God knows what they would say given half a chance now that he and Bryant had them trapped under one roof together.

Before May could field any further questions, Christina Crosse called to him with the telephone receiver in her hand. 'Alison Hatfield for you. Do you want to take it?' He looked over at the unruly assembly of mothers, fathers, sons, grandmothers, daughters and babies, all of them arguing and talking across each other. 'Tell her I'll call her back. No, on second thoughts, let me take it.'

The hallway outside was relatively quiet. He lifted the extension and waited for the sergeant to lower the receiver.

'Alison, how are you?'

'I'm fine. I hope I haven't disturbed you, but you did say to call if anything—'

'You did the right thing. Anyway, it's nice to hear your voice. What's on your mind?'

'I was going through the stack of basement papers I brought home with me, hoping to turn up the rest of your document. I didn't find it, but I did manage to uncover some correspondence between James Makepeace Whitstable and one of the other members of the alliance. It's mostly shipping arrangements, but he makes reference to the night of the signing, and states that a full account of the event was subsequently written up. He doesn't say what in, unfortunately.'

'Surely not a newspaper. You think he kept a diary?'

'That's what I wondered. All papers and personal effects pertaining to the guild eventually revert to the hall, many of them through bequests and donations. I was thinking of going in to the office later. Do you want me to look for it while I'm there?'

'Yes, if you don't mind. I mean, it is a public holiday. You should be enjoying yourself.'

'Oh, this *is* my way of enjoying myself. I can hardly hear you—' By the sound of it, tempers were flaring in the lounge.

'I have to go,' said May. 'Please, feel free to call me if you find anything. Hell, call me if you don't. It'll be good to talk to you, Alison.'

One of the Whitstable children was tugging at his trouser leg. 'Come on Mister Pleeceman,' he said with a grin. 'The mummies are trying to hit each other.' Clenching his teeth and his fists, May strode back into the tantrum therapy centre formerly known as the front parlour.

\*

Alison had fidgeted about in her apartment, unable to settle before deciding to return to the tiny elevator at the rear of the foyer in the Watchmakers Company. It was exciting to know that the police were relying on her assistance. She was looking forward to seeing John May again. True, he was considerably older than her, but there was something rather wonderful about them.

It would be even better if she had a good reason for calling him back. She had every hope of finding more information pertaining to the alliance; the basement filerooms had been closed for so many years that those in charge of maintaining their order had since retired. It was close to midnight by the time she pulled the trellis door shut and pressed the lower ground level button. As the lift descended, she thought about the boxes stored beneath her.

The Victorians were great notetakers, letter-writers and diarists. It was likely that their documents were kept here, within the guild, and had simply been forgotten. Although the guilds prided themselves on their noble history, they rarely had cause to re-examine old files, and such mundane artefacts as balance sheets fell beyond the scope of interested historians.

The corridor which came into view as the lift lurched to a halt was darkened. She had not asked for the emergency lighting to be turned on again, for fear of arousing suspicion. Her breath clouded across the beam of her pocket torch as she opened the trellis door.

Any further documentary proof of the alliance had to lie in the room she had already begun to explore with May. All of the rooms beyond that were used by the Goldsmiths to store their accounts. As she reached the door, she was surprised to find it partially open. She distinctly remembered locking it earlier. She pushed it wide and shone her torch into the room.

There was no noticeable disturbance, but someone else had definitely been down here; two chairs had been set aside so that access could be gained to the boxes stacked against the far wall. Frowning, she crossed the floor and shone her torch down into the first carton. This morning it had contained three tied packets of correspondence, now there were only two.

She had intended to move the bundles upstairs this evening. Technically speaking, she had no right to be down here, but as the responsibility for the upkeep of the files had been lost in a blur of changing regulations, she thought that no one would really mind. As she moved, her shoes slipped on sheets of paper. She looked down to find that a number of letters had been dropped or tossed aside. Gingerly brushing off a bristling cluster of wet black spiders, she lifted the sheets and held them in the light. Apart from the caretaker, no one else knew she had been sifting through the documents.

Who else had been here?

Her thoughts were interrupted by a light scuffling sound in the corridor outside. She scanned the torchbeam across to the door, but there was nothing to see. She knew about the rats that came up from the river; she didn't want to consider how many might have bred here in the damp of the ancient cellars. She was about to resume her search when a feeling of unease prickled at the back of her neck.

Alison was a practical woman, not given to easy fears, but it was suddenly clear to her that she was no longer alone. She lowered the light beam to the floor and quietly made her way back across the room. As she did so, she instinctively knew that she was nearing another human body. The darkness in the corridor was palpable. A slight breeze brushed her face. She began to slowly walk toward the goods lift, keeping the torchlight trained at her shoes.

There was someone within feet of her, of that she was sure. She looked at the beam. A chill cloud was dissipating in the cone of light, the remnants of someone's shallow breath. She took another step toward the lift, and another. The metal door stood less than three yards from her.

Far below, the river faintly pounded, rushing through darkness. She took another step.

A scrape behind her as someone or something divorced itself from the wall. Unable to contain her panic for another moment, she ran toward the lift with her arm outstretched, grabbing the brass handle and twisting it back, slamming the trellis open and forcing herself inside.

As she pulled it shut she saw the bulky shape of a man running directly at her. A hand thrust itself through the diamond-shaped gap in the bars, grabbing at her sweater. She screamed as she jabbed at it with the torch, but the fingers, groping for a purchase, seized on her flesh and pulled. The torchcase was lightweight and plastic, and cracked as she thrashed at the invading limb.

She slammed the flat of her hand against the floor buttons, and the elevator jerked into life, slowly rising. The fist remained locked around her arm, gripping tightly. Her attacker was being lifted from the floor, and had now braced himself against the lowering ceiling. Far above, the lift mechanism began to whine as it strained to raise the cage.

It was a stalemate; the lift could ascend no further, but her attacker could not recall it. After her initial fright she became silent, desperately trying to think of an escape. Bending her knees suddenly, she lifted her legs from the floor. The move caught her assailant by surprise as the deadweight hit his arm. With a sickly crack his hand lost purchase on the sweater and the lift suddenly shot up as he fell back to the floor.

She slammed to the rear wall of the lift, staying there until the door opened at the ground floor.

The corridor ahead was deserted. If he knew where the basement staircase was, he could be here in less than a minute. She ran toward the foyer, knowing that it would be empty. The porter wasn't due back until tomorrow. Until then, the main door keys were in her purse, inside her desk. She had planned to double-lock the entrance upon leaving.

Her heels clicked rapidly across the marble floor and echoed in the dark stairways above. She was scared to look back. She could feel her heart pounding against her ribs, blood heating her face. She looked around the dimly lit entrance hall. There was a muffled slam as the staircase door opened. She knew better than to waste another moment staying in the building. Without detouring to collect her coat or purse she ran to the main door and yanked it open.

Outside, the bitter evening air forced the breath from her body, causing her to gasp. The city streets were utterly deserted. After 6.30 p.m. on a workday it was usually quiet, but this was Christmas Night, and there was not a soul to be seen.

Her car was parked in the darkened alley behind the guild. She dared not head back there. Her best bet was to make for the nearest tube station. Perhaps some misanthropic employee would be working a lonely Christmas shift. There had to be someone still around. She ran along the empty pavement in the direction of St Paul's Cathedral.

Behind her, a dark, feral figure dressed in an almost ground-length raincoat emerged from the guild hall. She increased her speed, searching for traffic as she crossed the road. A new one-way system was being installed, and several of the streets around her were closed to vehicles. Behind, the figure gained speed, his unbuttoned coat beating about him, his broken wrist causing his hand to flop uselessly back and forth as he closed the gap between them with long loping strides.

The station was shut. Barred and bolted.

A noticeboard leaned against the entrance. Normal tube services would resume on 26 December. Boots hammered behind her as she lurched from the station and across the road ahead. The churchyard of St Paul's was always kept open. She ran through the gates in the direction of the main entrance. If the Christmas service was in progress, there was bound to be someone at the door.

As she fled up the steps of the cathedral he lunged out at her and almost snared her skirt. She only just managed to tear herself free as she ran through the doorway.

Inside, one of the clergymen was closing off the lights. She halted, trying to catch her breath.

'Father ... there's a man ...'

A young, bespectacled pastor with thinning hair looked at her quizzically, unsure of the problem facing him. She tried again, aware of the figure looming behind her.

'Someone is following me ...'

The pastor looked beyond her to the waiting figure. 'The service has finished. We're closing for the night—' he began.

'But this is a church,' Alison screamed suddenly, 'you're not supposed to close!'

'I'm sorry, but you two will have to sort out your differences outside.' My God, he thought they were having a lovers' tiff! She looked around to see the rain-coated figure striding quickly toward her.

The pastor stepped forward, shaking his head and raising his hands in front of him, refusing her entry. Ducking beneath his arm, she shoved through the glass exit doors and ran into the nave, expecting to find other clergymen ready to help her. There was no one in sight. Surely they didn't entrust the safety of an entire building to one man?

Scuffling footsteps made Alison turn in fright. Her pursuer had been apprehended by the priest, who was ineffectually attempting to hold him outside. Suddenly the raincoated figure struck him hard in the face with the flat of his good hand, knocking him back against the vitreous wall of the foyer and down on to the tiled floor. The glass doors reverberated through the cathedral in a series of dull booms.

Then he was through the doors and moving fast toward her.

A narrow opening in the right transept appeared in her vision. She took it without thinking, found herself in the steep stairway that led to the Whispering Gallery, and turned her head back, only to find him right behind her.

There was nowhere to go but up.

Up she ran, her heart hammering painfully, the hot blade of a stitch forming in her side. As he reached out for her she kicked back with her spiked heel, connecting hard with his chest.

She had reached the Gallery entrance. The icy stone balustrade curved away on either side. She intended to follow the path around, knowing that she would be able to see if he changed direction.

The vast dome rose above them to create a giddying sense of space, its monochromatic paintings fearful and austere. He was panting hard as he came through the door. Seeing that there was no time to put any distance between them, she stopped and looked back, but the dim exit sign above his head cast the light away from his face. His head seemed to be dented on one side, like a poorly inflated football.

'What do you want from me?' she managed to call out.

No reply came from the figure before her. He was breathing heavily from the exertion of running up the stairs, balancing lightly on the balls of his feet. His hand flapped and rotated, as though connected to his body by skin alone. He looked sick.

'I didn't find out anything.' She took a step back as he slowly approached. 'I swear I was only trying to help. I can't do you any harm — please, I don't want to end up like the others.'

The longer she talked, the more she felt she had a chance of being saved. But how? It was obvious that they were alone in the eerie vastness of the cathedral. There was no holy sanctuary for her here, only harsh judgement. He was beside her now, his arm reaching out around her shoulder. The touch of his withered, superfluous hand was soft and almost reassuring.

'Sorree, Ladee.'

His voice was little more than an exhalation of air, but suggested an Eastern accent. Alison was so surprised that he had actually spoken that she failed to move as his other hand suddenly reached out to seize her, his thick fingers snaking across her opening mouth. He was a powerful man, and effortlessly lifted her off the floor. She saw the bitter irony of dying surrounded by the very history she had spent her life loving and trying to understand.

She looked up at his face and saw that he had no eyes, just dry, empty brown sockets.

'So very sorry,' he whispered again in a tone of genuine regret. With a grunt, he hoisted her twisting body over the balcony and released it. With thrashing limbs and a throat stretched taut by the power of her screams, she fell a full hundred feet to the floor below.

Her last sight was that of the unforgiving cathedral spinning above her, as the sound of her death refracted back and forth between the tombs of sleeping saints.

# CHAPTER

The white traverse arches and tie beams of the greenhouse bore every kind of exotic hanging plant imaginable. Beneath these clusters grew profusions of crimson and scarlet flowers, bougainvillaea and beloperone, calliste-mon and strelitzea, surrounded by fan and sago palms, many of them over eight feet tall.

'This was my great-grandfather James Makepeace Whitstable's house, and these are the plants that he himself tended. Until recently they were like our family, deeply rooted, tough, surviving. Now it looks as if they might outlive us all.'

Charles had brought her here after dinner, and now they sat in facing armchairs beneath the glass roof on Christmas Night, cradling their brandies. His curiosity in her had grown throughout the day, as if he had somehow been expecting this moment to come. During the course of the afternoon there had been endless questions about her upbringing and complex explanations of how the

420

guild ran its businesses. He was a decisive man, a mason, a figure of restless intensity, and had chosen to admit Jerry into his world. From the way in which he had spoken about the supervision of Anglo—Indian exports, it seemed likely that this was where he was thinking of placing her. It was the area he had discussed more than any other, and it sounded incredibly, horribly, unbearably dull.

Understandably, Charles had led the conversation throughout. Although Jerry imagined that his main reasons for returning to England were connected with his cousins' deaths, at no point was the subject allowed to surface. She had a feeling that her new-found friend would raise the matter in his own time.

Beyond the greenhouse a lurid sunset flooded the sky in a vermilion wash, mirrored in shimmering fields of frost. Charles had humanised his appearance a little by changing into blue jeans and a heavy green cotton sweater. During the course of the afternoon he had not smiled once. A number of times he had started at noises in the endless dark woods beyond the house. Obviously he was under an unusual amount of strain. Now, as he sat warming the brandy in his hands, he seemed on the verge of imparting a confidence.

'I imagine it's been pretty boring for you today,' he began, studying his glass. 'Christmas and all that, you'd probably rather be with your friends, people of your own age. I'm not used to having youngsters around. Our family was always old and big and quite inescapable.'

'No, it's fine. I thought there would be other people here, that's all.'

'Normally there would be, but this year my visit is under extraordinary circumstances.' He looked back at the main structure of the building. 'You know, my childhood memories are filled with decrepit relatives tottering about these rooms. As a kid I was always being scolded for disturbing my sleeping elders.' He lay back against the headrest, recalling his upbringing in the vast dusty house above them. 'Our family. Until recently we were only fighting to stay alive in business. Now look at us. What a sorry state we're in. I suppose you've been following it all in the papers.'

He looked across at her, his pale blue eyes remaining still and eerily luminescent in the setting sun. He tasted his brandy and set it down. 'You have a very strong-willed mother, Jerry. I assume you're aware of her ambitions.'

His remark took her by surprise. How did Gwen always manage to enter her conversations with other people? 'What makes you say that?'

Charles studied his glass. 'Come on, I've had dealings with your father long enough to see what — or rather, who — drives him. Gwen would like to see you working with us. Jack has mentioned it to me more than once.'

'She had nothing to do with me coming here,' she hastily assured him.

'I wondered if perhaps you had her interests at heart.' He gave a rare smile. 'But you're different. I can sense a certain antipathy toward your parents. I know you're acting under your own volition.' That part was certainly true, she thought.

'You must understand something about us, Geraldine.' Christ, she hated that name. He gave a sharp smile, no lips, no teeth. 'The only way to effect an entry into the Whitstable family is to operate in its interests. Because the family always protects itself, no matter what. Always. Even if it means curtailing its own freedom.'

He drained his glass. 'No doubt it's hard for you to understand our behaviour. Try to remember that we're an ancient industry as well as an ancient family. We owe our success to century upon century of commerce and growth. And now it's dying fast. Our glorious business world has shrunk. Once we were the giants, the whip-wielders. Now we're nothing compared to the mighty modern conglomerates — Sony, Time—Warner, Exxon, ICI. They are the new imperialists, not us. Philip Morris is hooking the Third World on tobacco. Coca-Cola's buying real estate.' He pulled open a drawer in the small oak chest at his side and withdrew an engraved gold pocket-watch, passing it over for inspection.

'This is the sort of thing our guild used to make. Who wants it now? Who can afford it? Once, craftsmanship was as necessary as breathing. Now it's a curiosity, quaint and redundant. In order to stay alive, we were forced to diversify.' He poured brandies for both of them as she studied the watch. 'It was James Whitstable who put the family and the guild back on the right track.'

'How did he do that?' asked Jerry, carefully sipping her liqueur. She wanted to remember everything clearly.

'James Makepeace Whitstable was a great man. A visionary. An exceptionally gifted businessman, a man of great charity and honesty, a practising Christian, but a man who also believed in sciences not of this realm. For he was also an occultist, a pagan, a clairvoyant. How he reconciled this to his Christian beliefs we'll never know.

'When he rose to assume his position at the head of the family, he knew it would take more than sheer financial expertise to clear our debts and spread our business. He was convinced that a spiritual force was needed as well. There were those in the guild who had faith in him, and others who didn't. Over a century and a decade ago, on 28 December 1881, he gathered together the most trusted men in his guild. That night, seven brave believers formed an alliance designed to protect their craftsmen.

'James wanted to devise a formula that would keep the company in the right hands, not just then but for generations to come. After all, the future held great promise. The empire was at its zenith. The chances for expansion were limitless. New worlds beckoned.

'But James was a far-sighted man. He saw that, just as quickly as it had grown, the British empire could wane in the light of another rising nation. The Americans were establishing trade routes at an extraordinary pace. The Japanese had begun to conduct commerce with outsiders. Consumerism had begun. Importing and exporting reached new heights as it began to create *trends*. Gilbert and Sullivan wrote *The Mikado* to cash in on the fact that London had a fancy for anything from Japan. Liberty's in Regent Street was decorated like a Japanese pagoda. Ethnic purchasing trends were already in place. People were looking for the next big thing. What hope was there for an ancient London guild with so many keen rivals on the horizon? Rivals who didn't care about craftsmanship or tradition.'

'James Whitstable didn't think he could use the occult to control market forces, did he?'

'Better than that. He strode between two worlds,' murmured Charles. 'His innovation was to couple occultism to science. Some while after that night at the Savoy, our business returned to its former level of success and continued to prosper well into the next century. And our rivals, well, they always disappeared just as they grew strong enough to challenge us. Their trade figures would get this close to ours,' he held his thumb and forefinger half an inch apart, 'and they'd go out of business.'

'Didn't James tell anyone else in the family what they were doing or how it worked? Didn't people wonder?'

'I suppose they must have, but nobody minded so long as the sales figures continued to rise. The Watchmakers Company was happy to let its inner circle — the Alliance Of Eternal Light — take care of the problem. I don't suppose James Whitstable and his partners explained their actions to anyone.'

'What happened to the Alliance when the original seven members died?'

'It slowly disappeared. Eventually everyone forgot about it. I took over as guild chairman in 1981, exactly one hundred years to the day that my great-grandfather formed the alliance, and it was long gone by then. The guild's administration was in a shambles. Nobody knew what they were supposed to be doing. The old skills had been lost. I was forced to start the administration virtually afresh. I fired many of the old overseas staff, regrouped the companies, formed new business strategies for each territory. That's why I'm so rarely in the country. In England, the Whitstables still own all of the controlling stock. You'd be surprised how many staff members are direct descendants of the seven men who signed the guild Alliance.'

Jerry wondered if they were the same people who had eventually become murder victims. She knew so much more about the Whitstables now, but still the answers remained tantalisingly out of reach. She wanted to call the Mornington Crescent SCD and tell someone what she'd discovered. More than that, she needed to know how one man's recipe for economic recovery could result in a massacre over a century later.

Charles Whitstable raised his glass in a toast. 'You're entering an extraordinary family, Jerry,' he said. 'It'll take great bravery to be one of us.'

'Why do you say that?'

He gazed steadily at her. In the indigo gloom, only his eyes retained the light. 'Because what James Makepeace Whitstable used to make us extraordinary is fast destroying us,' he said, clearly amused by the paradox.

'Then can I ask you something?' she ventured. 'You don't have to answer.'

He allowed a half-minute of silence to pass between them. 'I guess I owe you one clear answer tonight,' he said finally.

She took a breath. 'You say James Whitstable coupled the forces of occultism and science. Do you know how his system worked?'

It was only now that she realised how oppressively dark it had become. 'I'm a direct descendant,' came the reply. 'Of course I know.'


'But you saw him. You even spoke to him,' said Bryant, exasperated. 'You must have some idea of what he looked like.'

The young curate grimaced apologetically. He had just been summoned back from the hospital. His head was bandaged where his nose had been broken, and his nostrils were packed with cotton wool, so that it was hard to understand what he was saying. He looked from the detective to the young female sergeant walking at his side, hoping to find some sympathy. The dawn would soon be rising on Boxing Day, and the nave of St Paul's was bitterly cold. Because of the murder, today's services had been suspended for the first time in decades.

'As you can see, this part of the cathedral's entrance hall is poorly illuminated,' the battered curate explained. 'Most of the main overhead lights were shut down last night. They're normally lowered after the tills have been emptied.'

'What tills?' asked Sergeant Crosse.

'There's an entrance fee, so there's a cash register in the foyer and another one inside for the gift shop.'

'So you have to pay to get into heaven now?' asked Bryant. 'I wasn't aware that they'd privatised it.' He was blasphemous, bad-tempered and cold, and furious with the curate for failing to help prevent Alison Hatfield's miserable death. The thought of having to tell John what had happened appalled him.

'The man was standing beneath an arch, and he was wearing a hat,' explained the bruised vicar of Christ. 'It fell off when he hit me, but his face was in shadow. At first I thought she was having an argument with her boyfriend. Couples often sit in the courtyard.'

'In the dead of winter? On Christmas Night? She didn't have a boyfriend. Did this man speak to her at all?'

'I don't think so. It all happened so quickly. I told them they couldn't come in, and he ran at me.'

Bryant rubbed his hands on his trousers, trying to improve his circulation. 'Is there any detail at all you remember about him? It doesn't matter how insignificant you think it might be. Anything at all.'

The curate knotted his fingers together. For a moment, Bryant thought he was going to pray for divine help. Finally, he looked at Christina. 'There was something wrong with his left hand. It just hung at his side. But all I could think of was his callousness. He must have followed her in here knowing that he was going to kill her. As if he was just doing his job.'

'If everyone had been doing that, Alison Hatfield might still be alive,' said Bryant. 'She came here expecting to find sanctuary.' He turned on his heel and angrily strode from the cathedral.

\*

He leaned on the Embankment railing, the scarf pulled tightly about his neck and shoulders, watching the low mist eddying across the whorled, shining surface of the Thames. A police launch chugged past, struggling against the ebb tide. That's what we're doing, he thought, fighting the flow. Trying to hold off a caul of darkness that grows thicker by the minute. Poor, lonely Alison. He had heard the report come over in the operations room, and could scarcely believe his ears.

Now no one was safe. Alison Hatfield had died for a specific, identifiable reason. She'd been searching for a diary, unaware that perhaps someone else was also looking for it. Her death had come as the cruellest blow of all. She had wanted to help them, and they had allowed her to venture into the darkness alone. He would never rest until he had found her killer. He owed John that much.

Right now, a hastily assembled forensic crew was removing every single one of the boxes from the store-room below the guild hall. He was already convinced that they would find no diary. Somebody had to have beaten Alison to the discovery. Could a colleague in the guild hall have overheard her on the telephone? The building had been closed for the holiday season. She had made a special trip in to open it up, so it was unlikely that anyone else would have been there. Tomlins probably had his own set of keys, but he didn't fit the physical description of her killer, and besides, he had gone to spend Christmas in the country with his family.

Seagulls circled above, dropping sharply from the still-dark sky like snapped-shut parasols. Bryant slipped his hands into his overcoat sleeves and waited, and watched, and thought.

Fancy killing her in a cathedral. Murder most foul

within a holy shrine. What did he know about the place? He tried to remember what he had read.

In the eighteenth century, St Paul's had been unpopular and unfashionable. Whores had paraded in the grounds. People used the nave as a short cut. Many had thought the place as pagan as it was Christian. And how the hell did Ivor Novello ever get to be buried in the crypt along with Nelson? This was no good; just when he needed it most his mind was cluttered with nonsense, pieces of game show trivia.

He stood at the railing as slivers of light grew between the clouds. The chill air was biting hard at his brittle bones. Stamping his feet on the slick pavement, he forced himself to clear his mind of ephemeral detail and think clearly.

Everything now hinged on the lack of motive, of that he was convinced. So many ideas had been put forward, and all of them wrong. So many dead ends. The Commonwealth conference. The Nazi symbol. The sacred flame. Cut through them. Look beyond.

Was it occult vengeance or simple monetary gain? How could their only suspects be corpses? May had suggested that a number of assassins were involved, that each murder had been logged and planned from the start. Could it be that he was right after all, and that Alison's death was their first panicky mistake?

There was something else that bothered him.

It was the business with the dates. The winter solstice had passed on 22 December. The document forming the Alliance of Eternal Light had been signed at the Savoy on the twenty-eighth. If James Makepeace Whitstable was genuinely concerned with the symbolism of bringing light to the world, he would have gathered his men a full week earlier.

It was almost dawn. Suddenly the Embankment lights began to flick off. Pearls of luminescence, familiar and friendly, strung in hazy necklaces along the riverline, were disappearing one after the other.

Bryant watched as row after row vanished into the night, all the way down the South Bank promenade, past Coin Street and Gabriel Wharf, past the OXO building and the Anchor pub and St Katharine's Dock and the *Point De La Tour* to Hay's Galleria and the distant lights of Greenwich.

'Oh my God.'

His mouth slowly opened as he realised the answer. 'How incredibly, irredeemably stupid of me,' he said aloud. 'How could I ever have been so blind?'

He jumped back from the railing, tucked his scarf across his midriff and set off as quickly as his frozen limbs would allow.

# CHAPTER

42

Jerry was awoken by fresh rain squalls brushing her bedroom window. Her tongue felt thick and dry from the brandy she had consumed. It was the first time she had not slept with a night light glowing in years. Slowly she raised her head and examined the room. She saw dark walls of densely woven brocade, a ceramic washstand and jug, a matching mahogany dressing table and wardrobe. A portable TV set was incongruously perched on a bench near her head. She rose from the high brass bed and drew back the curtains.

Grey sheets of rain obscured the fields below. A flock of miserable sheep stood huddled beneath a line of dripping beeches. Her watch read 9.15 a.m. She wondered if her host had risen yet.

She had spent the day with Charles, but was no closer to understanding him or his family. He seemed oddly unconcerned about the tragedy that was befalling them. She had the feeling that his sudden return to England had been precipitated mainly by the fear of losing his investors. Last night he had refused to elaborate on his closing remark about James Makepeace Whitstable. Perhaps he had no intention of confiding in his new-found apprentice.

After she had washed and dressed, Jerry began an exploration of the house. The sound of rain could be heard throughout the upper floors, which smelled powerfully of wood burnished with lavender polish, and more faintly of damp and time and emptiness. The rooms were kept in such immaculate condition that they reminded her of Joseph Herrick's stage sets. They needed the occupation of a boisterous family to bring them to life.

A broad central staircase led downstairs to the south-facing breakfast room where Charles Whitstable, casually attired in a cream sweater and chinos, was already seated with the morning's papers. The look of disturbance on his face when he rose to greet his guest suggested that further bad news was imminent.

'Please,' said Charles, gesturing at the heated tureens on the table, 'help yourself to breakfast. I've just had a call from my mother. There's been another attack on the family.'

'What's happened now?' she asked.

'Pippa Whitstable is dead. A very pretty girl. She was only a little older than you.'

'I'm so sorry,' she said, not sure what to make of his casual reaction. 'Were you closely related?'

'Distant cousins. We'd met once or twice. I thought they were all supposed to be under police protection. They're not saying what caused her death.'

'Have you tried calling the police for information?'

'The line is permanently engaged. I don't suppose there's anything I can do to help. The family already resent my interference. They think my great-grandfather caused this, and they know that I help to administer the Alliance's business system. What they fail to realise is that I am as much in the dark as they are. Of course I want to find a way to help them.'

'Do you think you'll have to return to England permanently?' she asked, seating herself before eggs and coffee.

'I hope so. Whether they like it or not, the family needs me. Aside from that, I need to think about taking a wife. With so many of us dying, it's time we produced a few new heirs. When I took over the family's affairs I didn't realise how much of my time I'd be forced to give up. For a hundred years they'd been relying on James Whitstable's system to bail them out whenever there was a financial crisis, but now it seems to have stopped working in their favour. Somebody had to do something before it was too late. I undertook the task of structurally reorganising each company. I began to clear away their lumbering, dated ideas. It's a task that's far from completion even now, and all I've succeeded in doing is earning their emnity.' He refilled his coffee cup.

'They're all getting old and cranky, and they think I'm cheating them. They won't see that the so-called Whitstable "empire" is no more. Much of the land they owned has been auctioned off, slowly pared away so that there's hardly anything left but the houses they live in. I'm streamlining the group, investing in technology they can't understand, and this way we may just survive into the next century. But to listen to them, Jerry, you'd think I was diverting their dwindling capital into a drug-running operation.' He drained the cup and checked his watch. 'That's why it's important to bring people with new ideas on board. I called your father and asked him to join us for lunch. I'd like you to stay on here until tomorrow. There are other areas I'd like to discuss, and I don't know when I'll have the chance to do so again. Besides, you're charming company, and you brighten this old house no end.'

She sat back and studied him carefully. He moved with an intensity of purpose that fascinated her. He was speaking and thinking in different directions, watching and listening as if he could divide his attention neatly between his senses. She had never met anyone like him before. Joseph had been creative, boyish and unsure of himself. Wasn't it a known fact that females matured more quickly than males? She had simply outstripped the young designer. His innate passivity had prevented him from handling her correctly. No wonder they'd proven sexually incompatible that night in his hotel room.

Charles, on the other hand, was mature and urbane. He treated her like a woman and seemed prepared to give her responsibilities. Her mission of subversion was taking on an interesting new aspect. It was all part of the learning curve.

'Do you think the police will catch anyone?'

'No. The deaths will end just as suddenly as they began, and no one will ever be able to say why.'

'How can you be so sure?'

'Because the same thing has been happening to our overseas rivals throughout the century. Of course, the attacks were never this densely concentrated before, and they took place on another continent, so the proper connections have never been made. It's harder for British justice to concern itself with the deaths of a few Indian businessmen. But now that the tables are turned on the British, there's hell to pay.'

'What's India like?' she asked, watching as he finished his breakfast.

'Vibrant. Shocking. A sink pit and a paradise.' He slowly looked up at her as he spoke, his eyes maintaining their serene quiescence. 'In India, the cycle of life is fast and full of fury. The rites of birth and death are closer together. We English seal away our emotions. Our grief, and much of our joy, remains private. Their feelings are more exposed, and it makes them strong. I admire their survival in the midst of so much damage and confusion. My relatives could learn a thing or two from them.'

If she performed well in her new career, he would probably take her away with him. But wasn't her request for a job just a ploy? She had to remember that she had no real intention of taking him up on the offer, even if it represented an escape from the house in Chelsea. The thought of returning there now depressed her. It was a pity she couldn't stay on in Cornwall for a few days. She was alarmed to discover how much she liked Charles.

'I have to make a lot of long-distance calls this morning,' he said, rising from the table. 'Why don't you take a walk around the estate? We'll reconvene just before lunch.'

'I'll be just as happy sitting in the library. Do you have any documentation on the group of companies that I can read?'

'Now that's the kind of initiative I like,' he said, smiling for the first time this morning. 'I'll see what I can find for you.' As he passed, he squeezed her shoulder affection- ately, and she found herself sharing his pleasure.

To be left alone in the library was a mark of how far she had gained his trust. The room couldn't have exuded more masculinity if it had been lined with dead stags. There were so many pipe-racks and gun-racks and lewd Indian carvings that it reminded her of Peggy Whitstable's house in Highgate. She was happy to leave huntsmanship to the gentry. Still, the library's stock was surprisingly varied, and contained many first editions. For the rest of the morning she read everything she could find about the Whitstables, but judging from the curious gaps in the bookshelves, any incriminating material had been carefully removed.

It wasn't until she had worked out how to operate the rolling stepladder that she discovered a top shelf filled with obscure Victorian volumes of occultist law. While several editions proved individually interesting, they sadly provided her with no collective insight to the mysteries of James Makepeace Whitstable and his Stewards of Heaven. Seating herself in one of the deep leather armchairs within a bay window overlooking the frozen fields, she began to read.

Just before one, a bell sounded in the hall. 'No doubt that will be your father,' said Charles, who had come to look in on her. 'Don't get up — finish what you're reading. I'll have him wait in the lounge until you're ready.'

The shift in authority was clearly meant to be noted. Now that she had been accepted into the family business, she was under the protection of Charles. Her father would meekly wait outside while she finished reading her book. The thought gave her little satisfaction. Poor Gwen and Jack. They had offered her up as a sacrifice to their ambition, only to find themselves excluded again.

Lunchtime with Charles and her father was uncomfortable, and punctuated throughout with awkward pauses. Clearly Jack was not happy to find his sphere of influence eclipsed by his daughter's. After the meal he was virtually dismissed and told to return to London. Charles would see to it that Jerry was returned safe and sound first thing on Monday morning.

For the rest of the day she and the entrepreneur worked side by side in the grand study, as he explained the long-term plans he intended to initiate for the guild. Now she saw that the work was not as dull as it had first appeared to be. Indeed Jerry could envisage certain circumstances under which it would be a pleasure to remain beside him all day.

Their meal together that evening had the intimate quality of a candlelit dinner, even if it took place beneath electric light.

Below him, a thousand people gyrated through shimmering spheres of luminescence, blood red, turquoise and vitreous green. John May carefully picked his way through the knots of teenagers who filled the rear of the upstairs bar. The music was so loud that it had lost any sense of form or content. All that was left was a heavy bass throb which vibrated the material of his jacket as he walked. As he searched each face, May hoped that the boy would remember the favour he had promised to repay.

The detective had not expected to find himself in an Elephant and Castle dance club at midnight, but there was no other way of locating Rufus. The eleven-year-old computer genius spent his life underground, and could only be lured to the surface with a bait of cutting-edge software. May was confident that the package in his pocket would not appear on the hackers' black market for weeks yet, and would be enough to gain an offer of help.

He was fighting to keep the horror of Alison's death from his mind. For now the matter would have to be set aside; there would be time enough later for grief. Sergeant Crosse had suggested taking his place tonight, being nearer to the ravers' age group, but the young black boy was wary of strangers. Nobody seemed to know where he came from, where he lived or who his parents were, if indeed he had any. He spoke with a slight New York accent, but was also smart enough to assume this as a disguise.

Rufus had been known to help the police on several occasions in the past, but only if the case suited his sense of the bizarre, and only under conditions of strict anonymity. He had an IQ in excess of 170, but what he saw as attempts at exploitation by adults had led him to a life beyond the law. These days his whereabouts could only be ascertained by following the E-Mail rumours and checking recent hacker outrages. His exploits left a trail through the electronic ether, faintly glowing blips in the technodarkness.

As if identification wasn't hard enough in the club, ducting pipes now jetted clouds of dry ice across the dance floor, filling the air with a dazzling pink haze. The dancers were moving in a grey concrete cave the size of an aircraft hangar which remained nightly filled until the sun rose over the river beyond. This morning — it was now one minute into the morning of 27 December — was no exception. The club sold no alcohol. It didn't need to, judging by the Ecstasy-glaze on many of the dancers' faces. May narrowed his eyes and peered into the stifling mist, but could see nothing. This was the third place he had tried tonight and definitely the last, although he had to admit he was starting to enjoy the music. He was about to leave when he felt a tugging at his sleeve.

'Whoa there. Incoming Blues, is this a raid?' shouted Rufus, glaring up. He turned to a tall blonde girl who stood beside him in a tight black rubber dress, and pressed a stack of notes into her hand. 'Take the bus, sugarlips, I got business to attend to.'

Rufus held out his hand and buzzed the detective with a complex handshake. He was four feet, eight inches tall, and in his baggy sweatshirt and baseball cap appeared even younger than his eleven years. May wondered how they ever let him in the club. Behind them the bouncers were frisking incoming clubbers for weapons and drugs.

'I assume you wanna talk a deal.' The boy jerked his thumb at the door, and they left the main auditorium. Rufus blew on his fingers as a long-legged Chinese girl was being frisked at the door. 'Babe-O-Rama, check it out.' He turned to May. 'I think my libido is developing at the same pace as my brain. Yikes, who wants to date a smart dwarf? Hey, how's your partner, Bryant? You two still a perfect match?'

'He's fine, and that's a terrible joke, Rufus. If you want to go somewhere quieter, I have a car outside.'

'*Ekk*cellent. There's a coffee bar a few blocks from here. How come you always look for me after the good restaurants are closed?'

'I was looking for you hours ago. You're a hard man to track down.'

Rufus hated being referred to as a child. He argued that he had the mind of an adult, although May knew that he found his accelerated brainpower as much of a handicap as a blessing.

They parked and walked to the cheerless all-night snack bar, set back from the main road that led to Waterloo. A few of the other tables were occupied by long-haul truck drivers. Rufus settled them away from the window, bringing a tray of coffee and sugary doughnuts.

'How are you getting along these days?' asked May.

'Same old story,' said Rufus. 'As bored as a person can be when he recognises that his band-width for development is infinite, but his access to resources remains limited.'

'You haven't been in touch for a while. We were

beginning to worry about you.' May knew that the boy could look after himself in spite of his size and age. He had a very wide-ranging set of friends. Hardcore contacts, Rufus called them.

'I've had the damned welfare people breathin' down my neck again,' the boy explained, tearing off a chunk of doughnut and sinking it into his mug. 'They're tryin' to put me back in care, and you know what happens when they do that.'

'You disappear.'

'I'm gone, outta here. High Beta, non-linear. I can lose social workers faster than you can scream Satanic Child Abuse. It's the old problem. The system doesn't recognise that anyone livin' outside what they regard to be the normal statistic majority could possibly be happy. They're talkin' about therapy and special schools again. I may even have to get out of London. The case against has *that much* granularity.'

'You're not thinking of leaving before you help us, I hope.'

'You're talking about the Whitstable case. Well, I been wonderin' about that too. What can you tell me beyond the usual random output?' He meant, what hasn't made it into the newspapers.

'This,' said May.

He handed over the chart of deaths they had logged to date, together with a highly classified set of internal reports. If the new division was to function according to its original intentions, it would have to bend the rules regarding access of information. 'They're following a sequence that conforms to no known pattern.'

'You say they. There's more than one murderer?'

'I'm pretty certain, but it's impossible to be sure,' May admitted.

'Yeah,' agreed Rufus, 'I figured there had to be a few of 'em. That's without loading this zombie deal on board.'

'The latest death has thrown us. It wasn't taken into consideration on Arthur's chart, and it's a different modus operandi. Once again the murderer was seen but not apprehended.'

He explained the circumstances surrounding Alison Hatfield's death. 'We have most of the family under lock and key, and those remaining outside are under around-the-clock surveillance, not that it's made much difference so far. If someone was working out a sequence for the murders, how would he choose his dates? That's one of the things we need to know if we're to prevent any more deaths occurring. Also, I think we're working to a dead-line. December the twenty-eighth.' He checked his watch. 'As we are now an hour into the twenty-seventh, that doesn't give us much time.'

Rufus examined the chart. 'There's no particular numer-ological significance here. What makes you think the dates aren't chosen at random?'

'The extreme premeditation of the murders suggests to me that someone is collating data and processing it. I've tried duplicating the method by gathering statistical evidence and adding it to the available data on each victim, without any luck. The spacing of the deaths feels mathematically arranged somehow, don't you think?'

'I suppose they could be scientifically random, kind of a Turing Code.' May assumed he was referring to Alan Turing's celebrated solution to the wartime Enigma Code. The logician had successfully cracked cryptographic messages created on a typewriter attached to a random print-wheel, and had suggested that computers would only be capable of human thought if a random element, such as a roulette wheel, was introduced.

'Why would anyone go to the trouble of doing that?'

'You say this guy was an occultist. Suppose his heirs are carryin' on his work? Maybe they're charting their victims according to occult significance. Bet that's what Bryant thinks.' He dunked the rest of his doughnut and dropped it, dripping, into his mouth. 'I agree with you about the methodology, though. There's logic at work. The deaths are irregularly spaced, but there's a kind of pattern. It's like those marketing companies who use computers to send out mailers, like the victims have breen demographically targeted. By what co-ordinates, though?' May could see ideas spinning through the boy's brain, each examined and discarded in rapid turn.

'December the sixth to the twenty-eighth. Why not the first of the month to the last? That would be more logical. Why not a correspondence to the lunar cycle? This new random element is easier to explain. You're getting too close. Panic's set in, an' that's dangerous for everyone. Can I keep this?' Rufus folded up the chart.

'Just as long as you don't show it around.'

'I'm only asking outta politeness. I already memorised it.' He looked over at the bulge in May's jacket pocket. 'You got a little something in there for me?'

'Just some prototype programs I'm taking home with me when I leave,' said May casually. 'You haven't given me any new ideas yet.'

Rufus thought for a moment. 'Okay, here's something. I noticed one corresponder, but it ain't a computer anomaly.' He tapped the chart with his finger. 'And you ain't gonna like it because it don't make any sense at all.'

'At this time of the morning it doesn't matter if things don't make sense,' said May with a sigh. 'Hit me.'

'Don't ask me how I know this, 'cause it's the kind of shit I just carry around in my head the whole time, okay?'

'Okay.' May moved forward, listening carefully. The boy had given him strong leads in the past and deserved a hearing, no matter how strange his ideas seemed.

'The murder dates correspond exactly to the December rainfall pattern so far.'

'Rufus, this is no laughing matter.'

'I ain't fooling you, man. You may not have looked outta your window, but we've had several days of ex-*cept*ional rainfall this month. Days when individual records have been broken for the most precipitation in a twenty-four-hour period. The murders kind of match up.'

'What do you mean, kind of?'

'Look.' He withdrew a chewed pencil stub from beneath his shirt and drew two lines on a napkin. Along both lines he marked days 6 to 28. On the first line he added a mark whenever a death had occurred. On the second line, he marked the record rainfall highs. 'Now, I say *kind of* because it's really the spacing that's the same. The rain-highs are precisely ten hours *to the hour* behind each of the deaths, except in the last case, which you yourself said is the odd one out.'

He tore one diagram free of the other and superimposed them. The troughs and highs were identical.

'Assuming that your memory is correct, what are the chances of this happening coincidentally?' asked May, exasperated.

'It'd take me a few minutes to work that out, but taking all the variables into account we're talkin' about several hundred thousand to one.'

'Rufus, this has to be an insane coincidence,' said May, dropping his head into his hands. 'What on earth am I supposed to do with information like this?'

'I don't know,' replied the boy. 'But you'd better start thinking fast; it just started raining like a son-of-a-bitch.'

# CHAPTER

'For God's sake, Arthur, you've been missing all day. Can't you come back in the morning?' said May, who had returned home at 2.45 a.m. to find his partner standing on his doorstep, sheltering from the rain and looking like a battered scarecrow.

'Don't ever complain about me not wearing my bleeper again,' he called, 'because I've been trying yours for the past four hours.' Only Bryant's eyes and ears were poking out above his scarf. The top of his head was an odd shade of greyish blue. 'A car pulled up a few minutes ago and some kindly Samaritan asked me if I needed a bed for the night. I had to see him off with a stick. Where on earth have you been?'

'At a disco,' said May, finding his keys and opening the main door.

'Aren't you a little old for that sort of thing? You didn't take ecstasy, did you? What's it like?'

'I was looking for Rufus.'

'Oh, the computer boy. I can never understand a word he's saying. Any help at all?' He trudged wetly behind May up to his apartment, his shoes squelching on the stairs.

'I'm not sure. He reckons the deaths are tied in with the monthly rainfall figures.'

'Excuse me, I'm going deaf,' said Bryant, unwinding his scarf and chafing his ears as he entered the room. 'For a minute I thought you said the deaths were tied in with the rain. They always used to say the butler did it. Now you're telling me it's the weatherman?'

'I'll explain after you tell me what you're here for.' He was used to working through the night with Bryant, but Arthur had never waited on the doorstep for him before.

'I know why James Makepeace Whitstable formed his alliance on 28 December. I know what he formed it for, and I know why people are dying. You'd better put the kettle on. This is going to take some time.'

While May made tea, Bryant turned up the central heating thermostat, then located a bottle of brandy and poured two generous measures. 'It's funny how things just hit you. I was standing at the railings on the Embankment this morning ...'

'God, where have you *been* all day?'

'Working it out. You know how I am.'

'You must have been freezing,' said May, setting down a tray.

'Got my thermals on.' Bryant tapped his leg. 'I needed the wind coming in off the river to clear my thoughts. Suddenly the lights went out, all the way along the Embankment. That was it. I made the connection. It was Gilbert and Sullivan, you see.'

'No, I don't see.'

'James Whitstable had called his men to town to discuss an idea he'd had. Think of his position. These were trusted friends, guildsmen born and bred, people he'd known all his life. Colleagues with whom he'd shared secrets, and shared a lifelong love of the occult. He wanted to justify their loyalty, to protect and strengthen the Watchmakers. He thought he could do it by providing the guild with a group of like-minded individuals dedicated to keeping the bright light of private enterprise burning, no matter what. His Alliance was to consist of businessmen who would see that British craftsmanship remained unchallenged by foreign rivals as it went out into the world. The Victorians were building for immortality. James Whitstable wanted to ensure that the Watchmakers lasted forever.'

'Arthur, I fail to see where this is leading—'

'The aims of the Alliance are stated in the signatory contract. We know that James Whitstable summoned his men and booked them into the Savoy at noon on 28 December 1881. The group took a light lunch in the hotel restaurant, and Whitstable arranged another reservation later that evening at 10.30 p.m. This is also clearly documented. What had Whitstable planned for the rest of the day? Well, we know they spent the main part of the evening in his suite, drawing up the charter and signing it. But what of the afternoon? There were plenty of red-blooded pursuits to take their fancy. Remember, this was a time of great licentiousness in the West End.'

'Whitstable ran reform charities. Surely he would have frowned on anything too risqué.'

'The Victorians weren't quite so naive as we like to think. They were well aware of what went on. Prostitution was rampant, despite the efforts of the various associations and societies trying to clean up the streets. During the day, society whores promenaded through Rotten Row. At night, Leicester Square was host to all kinds of delights. Three years after the Alliance was formed, the Empire Variety

Theatre was built there and became such a traffic-stopping spot for prostitutes that a plasterboard barrier was erected to shield them from the non-paying public.

'No, on this occasion James Whitstable had something else in mind. I was sure I knew what it was, and my theory was backed up when I re-examined the documents Alison Hatfield had obtained for you. For there amongst all those loose sheets of paper was part of a ticket.' He raised an oblong section of cardboard in his hand.

'This was James Whitstable's ticket for a trip next door to the Savoy Theatre, which had just been completed. Whitstable was a keen patron of the arts, remember. Gilbert and Sullivan were presenting their production of *Patience*. It had been running at the Opera Comique since 23 April and transferred to the Savoy on — let me see—' He flicked through his dog-eared black notebook. 'October 10. The Prince of Wales attended, and Oscar Wilde. Of course, it would have been hard to keep him away. *Patience* parodied him and the whole of the Aesthetic movement, as well as the Pre-Raphaelites.'

'And this was where James Whitstable took his partners.' May shrugged. 'So what?'

'Don't you think it strange? This particular opera was a topical joke. Its references weren't entirely understood by cosmopolitan audiences even then. We know from the Savoy records that most of Whitstable's colleagues had journeyed up from the country. Such esoteric entertainment would hardly have suited their tastes. No, he didn't want them to attend just so they could enjoy the show.'

'This had better have some point to it, Arthur. I'd really like to go to bed soon.'

Bryant savoured his brandied tea and smiled. 'There are moments in history that change our way of looking at the world, don't you think?' He always enjoyed himself when he knew more about a case than his partner. He paused for another sip, relishing the moment. 'Some are obvious events that we all agree on. Kings fall, battles are lost or won. Sarajevo, 28 June 1914. Dallas, 22 November 1963. Other changes are of a subtler degree, and some go quite unnoticed.

'On the night of 28 December 1881, James Whitstable and his partners witnessed an extraordinary symbolic moment. For the first time ever, a public building was completely lit with the new electric light. Darkness was thrown from the corners of the night. In this case, by over twelve hundred electric lamps. They'd tried to do it once before, on 10 October of the same year. On that occasion, the entire company came on stage and sang three choruses of "God Save The Queen" in a dramatic new arrangement by Sullivan, but then — fiasco. The steam engine driving the generator in a vacant lot near the theatre couldn't provide enough electricity, and the stage remained gaslit.

'But at the matinee on 28 December, they finally got it right. Richard D'Oyly Carte, ever the grand showman, walked on to the stage and ordered the gas lighting to be turned off. He followed with a lecture on the safety of electricity. This was news to the audience; many of them had thought it was fatal. Then he took a piece of muslin and wrapped it around a lit lamp, which he proceeded to smash with a hammer. When he held up the unburnt muslin, proving that there was no danger to the public, the audience went wild.

'Gaslight was unclear, yellowish, smelly and hot. The new electric illumination was here to stay. Imagine, John! To these men — businessmen, craftsmen — it must have seemed that the myths and mysteries of the shadowy past had truly been swept away by the cold, bright light of scientific reason. There couldn't have been a more appropriate symbol for them to adopt.'

'You think it was coincidence, or did James Whitstable know about this?'

'Oh, he knew all right. He used the performance as a display to show them they were doing the right thing by signing with him. What an extraordinary start for a grand new era! No wonder James had spoken of the winter solstice, the championing of light over darkness. Why, Victoria herself became a queen on Midsummer's Day! It was the beginning of a bright new Britain. The end of myth and magic, and I suppose, the end of a certain kind of gloomy warmth. The end of a humanity that could only exist and survive in an England of shadows ...' He trailed off, pursuing the thought.

'After they'd signed this pact, how much control d'you think the others had over Whitstable?' asked May.

'Not much, I don't suppose. He was free to expand his dubious business practices into new territories. The Alliance flourished, the original members passed away and their fortunes were handed down to their eldest sons. The money and the power stayed within the inner circle of the family. I'm not sure what happened after that.'

'This is where I can help,' said May, pleased that he could finally contribute something. 'Whoever obstructed the expansion of the guild's network of companies always ended up withdrawing their objections under threat or vanishing. One by one all their rivals disappeared. I'd say they were most likely beaten or killed for getting in the way of progress. It's all there in the company's overseas records, if you know what to look for. Not so many cases in this country, where investigation might have led back to the Alliance, but a lot of skullduggery overseas. Desperate for a British contract to pump revenue into your country's economy? Overlook a couple of complaining local merchants who quietly evaporate.

'In this new bright world I suppose you could say that Whitstable and his gang were the first yuppies. They took, and they didn't give much back. And they made sure that they retained control beyond their own deaths. I think the fortune they made was passed down to each generation on one condition. That at some future time, the heirs might be asked to secure the continuing good fortune of the company by performing a simple, unspecified task, something they would be notified about when the time arose.'

'You mean the fathers made their sons killers?'

'Oh, nobody high ranking got blood on their hands but yes, I think the winning formula — a formula that was way ahead of its time, I might add — was granted with a burden of responsibility.'

'It's a strong motive.'

'A series of murders that would ensure the continued survival of the guild's financial empire, carried out by the descendants of the Alliance's staff. Death by proxy. I just spoke to Christina. An hour ago she received a fax from the Bombay police confirming something about the window cleaner, David Denjhi. His father and grandfather had both worked for a company owned by the Whitstable family. Specifically, they were in the employ of Charles Whitstable.'

'But how would the Alliance know when someone was dangerous enough to require removal? And if they're still picking victims, why are they killing members of their own family?'

'The Watchmakers were — and still are — craftsmen. I think Whitstable got his inner circle to come up with some kind of system for fingering their enemies. But somewhere along the line the system has screwed up. And now, over a century later, nobody knows how to stop it.'

'Marsden is never going to believe this.'

'At least it beats your supernatural explanation.'

'That depends who you find more objectionable, capitalists or satanists. Besides, I haven't ruled out the influence of the occult, and nor should you. Where do we go from here?'

'To James Whitstable's most direct descendant, Charles Whitstable,' said May. 'We overlooked him because he was out of the country. Right from the start hardly any of the family have been telling us the truth, but Berta Whitstable is a very unconvincing liar. The more she insisted that her son knew nothing, the more I was sure he could help us. I've a feeling that if anyone knows about the Alliance's device, he will.'

'Charles Whitstable could have been in London when Alison fell to her death. Suppose he was at the guild when she called me about the diary? He could have reached the basement before her. She surprised him — he attacked her. It's possible. It's only a short distance from the guild hall to St Paul's Cathedral.' Bryant's brow furrowed. 'You mentioned the Alliance's *device*. I presume you mean that they came up with some kind of formula for removing rivals that they've stuck to ever since.'

'No, Arthur, I mean a device. They were craftsmen, remember? Rufus agreed with me that these deaths feel as if they were computed. I think we're looking for some kind of mechanical object.'

# CHAPTER

At 5.27 a.m. on the morning of Monday 27 December, the elegant Chiswick home of Christian and Deborah Whitstable lay in darkness, and would remain so until an alarm rang in one hour and three minutes. Only a small porch light, operating on a time switch, remained burning. The two officers May had insisted on appointing to secure the house were about to come off duty, and waited together in the front garden for the day shift to replace them.

Christian Whitstable had been badly disturbed by his sister Isobel's loss. For any member of the family to die so cruelly was a tragedy, but little Daisy had been the least deserving of such a fate. Her mother's health had declined so alarmingly over the Christmas break that she had been admitted to a private hospital in Fulham. And he'd heard that Pippa's mother was not doing much better either.

Despite the danger, Christian had opted out of the police protection scheme, preferring to spend Christmas at home as he had always done. He was determined to be the defender of his own family. There had been too much reliance on the authorities, and what had they done but consistently let them down?

He and Deborah had argued bitterly over the decision. Having seen what had happened to her sister-in-law's child, Deborah was keen to place her own children in the safekeeping of the police, but her husband had refused to join the rest of the clan huddled together in William Whitstable's house. He believed in being the master of his fate, and extended that belief to his children even if they were not yet old enough to appreciate the concept.

Deborah had complained that her husband's misplaced sense of machismo was putting their children in harm's way.

'Nonsense,' Christian had retorted over their cold turkey supper the previous evening. 'We have the police guarding us day and night. There are always two of them outside, in plain view where the children can see them. And even if, God forbid, someone managed to slip inside the house, we'd be able to summon help before anything untoward happened. There's only one door at the front and one at the back. They'd never be able to escape without capture.'

'I suppose you're right,' Deborah had sighed, knowing that she could never win an argument with a Whitstable, and had taken to sleeping with a carving knife beneath the bed. If she had no faith in her husband, she certainly had little more in their guards. Bored and cold, the two of them took turns to run for coffees from the burger bar in the high street. One of the night officers, PC Graham Watson, looked around seventeen years old, and was as thin as a stick. He spent his time sitting on the porch disconsolately picking his nose and playing Super Mario on his Nintendo Game Boy until the shift was over.

Now he was standing by the garden gate, looking up into the black sky, adjusting the strap of his helmet and hoping that the shift change would arrive before the rain began again. He looked around for his partner, who had gone to carry out a final check at the rear of the house, and had not yet returned.

Behind him, somewhere on the right hand side of the overgrown front garden, the bushes rustled heavily, water shaking from the leaves.

'Dez?' His partner for the night shift, PC Derek Brownlow, was not the most zealous of officers, and was in the habit of sneaking into the potting shed at the rear of the garden for a quiet smoke. Now it sounded as if he had lost his way.

'Dez, what are you doing in there?' Watson pulled the pocket torch free of his rainmac. The porch light had just snapped off, throwing the garden into darkness. He had been meaning to tell Mr Whitstable that he should reset his timer.

He shone the torch into the bushes and walked slowly along the path, watching the fractured pool of light as raindrops began to glitter in it. Ahead, the shrubbery shook violently once more.

'Dez?' he called softly. 'If that's you I'll bloody kill you. Come on out, you're making me nervous.'

Deborah Whitstable turned on to her stomach, trying to get comfortable. She hadn't been able to sleep properly since Daisy had been found dead. No such trouble afflicted her husband. He was lying on his back, snoring lightly. The bedroom door was ajar, and a cool draught was blowing into the room. She hadn't noticed it when she went to bed. It was always colder at this time, before the thermostat kicked in to heat the boiler and warm the children as they sleepily descended to the breakfast room.

She slipped silently from the bed and padded across to the window, moving aside the curtain. No sign of the policeman who was supposed to be guarding them, she noted, but the porch light had turned itself off, so she wouldn't be able to see him standing there anyway.

There was a definite draught coming into the room, as if someone had left a door open. She stopped to pull on her dressing gown, then walked out into the hall. Immediately she noted the smell, musty and brackish. Had she remembered to empty the kitchen bin? She switched on a light and peered over the balustrade, down into the hall. It looked as if something had been thrown across the grey slate floortiles. Then she realised that a batch of newspapers had been torn and scattered over the floor. It looked as if mud had been trodden in. The papers had been neatly piled when they had gone to bed. Who had knocked over the stack and rummaged through it so carelessly?

She was still trying to puzzle out the mystery when she heard the breathing, the terrible breathing. Deep and rasping, asthmatic and obscene. And she saw the door to the children's room moving back, widening slowly.

Her first thought was to run back to her bedroom and wake her husband. She considered calling to him, but knowing what a heavy sleeper he was, Christian would not hear her. It was when she saw what stood in the doorway that she attempted to scream.

Eight feet away from her, in the entrance to the room where Justin and Flora were fast asleep, was a fully grown male Bengal tiger.

It was insanity to think of such a creature standing in a suburban London house. But there it was, watching her with ancient yellow eyes, its tail restlessly swinging, rhythmically thumping against the door jamb.

The beast was over six feet long, and its shoulders rose higher than the door knob behind it. It was old and distraught, confused by its unfamiliar surroundings. Long white hair hung from its sunken cheeks. Its fur was a deep orange-brown, beautifully marked with dark ochre transverse stripes. Its underparts were a dirty cream, its large splayed paws covered in mud and hooked with vicious black claws.

As the creature raised its enormous head and dilated its nostrils, picking up her scent, it began to pad toward her, and she saw its ribs sticking painfully out beneath its hide. She had read somewhere that old or disabled tigers would eat human flesh if they were hungry, and considered their prey to be weaker than themselves. The animal moving in her direction looked half-mad from its starvation.

As Deborah found her voice, and her shrill scream filled the air, the tiger loped forward and threw up its forepaws in a half-hearted leap, smashing her to the floor. Within seconds she heard shouts from her son and daughter, and even the sound of Christian attempting to rouse himself, but the body of the beast was crushing the life from her, its fetid breath blasting over her as it batted her head from side to side with its claws.

The creature opened its jaws to reveal rows of tall brown teeth, and stinking saliva poured on to her face as it reached down to clamp its mouth around her head and bite down hard, cracking bone and flesh, tearing sinew and skin from its thrashing, defenceless prey.

As Christian stepped into the hall in his pyjamas, his eyes widening in disbelief, the tiger dropped the victim it was lifting by the head. Attracted by the sound of the children screaming behind him, it turned its attention toward an easier meal.

# CHAPTER

Arthur Bryant stood beneath the indigo stained-glass saints in the hallway, furling a dripping umbrella and slowly unravelling his wet brown scarf. What the hell was he doing here, she wondered? If the detective made a display of recognising her, her cover would be wrecked. Worse, he might decide to explain how they knew each other. She quickly slipped back against the wall, free from his line of vision.

Luckily, when Jerry next looked she saw that Bryant had shifted position and was now standing with his back to the lounge door. She watched him speaking softly to Charles Whitstable, but was too far away to catch their conversation. Moving closer to the doorway, she strained to hear what they were saying.

'... understood that you were summoned back to England by your mother just last week, is that right?'

'No, not exactly,' Charles admitted. 'I'd spoken to Berta before that. Naturally she was alarmed by what was happening, but she said there was little to be gained by my returning home, particularly as some members of the family have grievances about how I run the international group.'

'Then what made you come back?'

'Two things. Firstly, I was concerned that the current adverse publicity should not affect the status of the group or the faith of our investors. Second, I received a summons from a business colleague who wanted me to help him with a problem.'

'What kind of problem?'

'He was trying to locate a document that belonged to my great-grandfather.'

'Mr Whitstable, I need to know what you were asked to find for him.'

'It's no secret,' Charles shrugged, unfazed by the demand. 'Apparently James Makepeace Whitstable kept a personal chronicle covering certain key events of his life. It's possible it may help to shed some light on recent events. I was concerned about my mother's safety in London, so I decided to make the trip and check on her at the same time.'

'Did you have any luck finding this "chronicle"?'

'I'm afraid I was no help whatsoever. I barely had time to look. There were too many other problems weighing on my mind. Late on Christmas Day I received a call to say that I needn't worry about finding it anymore. By that time, though, I had decided to stay until this whole nightmare was sorted out. He didn't sound very pleased, I must say. Lawyers never are when you interfere with their plans.'

'It was Leo Marks who summoned you?'

'That's right.'

'I need to make a call to London,' said the detective,

pointing to the hall telephone. 'May I?'

'Of course.'

Arthur Bryant was furious with himself for being so easily misdirected. Of course the law firm would be privy to the secrets of their oldest and most valued clients. If Max Jacob had known about the Alliance's century-old philosophy, it explained why he had been carrying William Whitstable's annotated bible with him. The pages of the volume were marked up according to William's doctrine of light and darkness. He was a continuing part of the alliance.

May had foolishly dismissed Leo Marks from his mind after noting the youth and inexperience of the junior partner, ignoring the fact that he was acting on behalf of his ailing father. Marks had probably searched the guild for the diary, but it seemed unlikely that he would have murdered Alison Hatfield. He may, however, have un-wittingly caused her death.

But once the diary was in the possession of Leo and his father, what had they intended to do with it? If it revealed the cause of the Whitstable family's gradual destruction, surely they'd have wanted to protect the lives of their clients by turning it over to the police?

Bryant wished he understood the thought processes of lawyers. He had to make sure that Leo Marks was brought quickly and safely into custody. At least that part would be easier now that he had a pilot and a police helicopter at his disposal. Tomorrow was 28 December, and who knew what the anniversary would signify this time?

After the detective had departed, Charles came looking for her.

'Who was that?' she asked casually, rearranging a stack of books on the table before her.

'A policeman to whom I'm afraid I was no help,' he

replied, sounding almost pleased about the fact. 'He made
a phone call to London and left in a hurry. Judging by the
look on his face, I'd say he'd received bad news.' She
wondered what Arthur had discovered now. She'd been
right to go her own way. It was obvious that the police
were still miles from discovering the truth. If she could
only get Charles to confide in her. Last night he had
seemed upon the point of opening his heart and unburden-
ing himself. She just needed more time with him.

'I promised to get you back to London this morning,'
he was saying, 'so that's what we should do. I have to
attend to some financial matters in the City later, and then
I must look in on my mother.'

*Make another date*, she thought. *Make him want you and
he'll tell you everything. Don't let him slip away.* 'I'm supposed
to be back at work tomorrow, but I'm free tonight.'

He came around to her side of the table and stood a
little too close, looking down, smiling lightly. 'Then let's
meet later. I have an apartment in Mayfair. My cooking's
no great shakes, but there's an excellent Indian restaurant
nearby and they'll let us order out if we want. I promise we
won't talk about business. You can tell me all about
yourself.'

'Fine,' she replied, accepting his offer. 'And you can tell
me all about your family.'

John May had not been able to sleep. Rufus's prediction
about the rain was haunting him. The weather was
becoming ever more inclement. As rest was no longer an
option, he decided to rise and head for the SCD. He
arrived in Mornington Crescent at 6.45 a.m., just in time
to intercept a second report call from the Chiswick
residence of Christian and Deborah Whitstable.

Thumbing back through the incoming night reports he

found that the first radio call, timed at 6.05 a.m., had only mentioned that two of the family were dead, cause unknown, and two were alive. Stan Marsden had been the only senior official still on night duty, and had responded to the alert.

By the time May reached the crime scene, the entire house was surrounded with vehicles. He noted three ambulances, a fire engine, dozens of press photographers, an armoured truck, several squad cars and a mob of onlookers. So much for keeping a low profile, he thought as he approached the overcrowded garden.

'We managed to get him cornered, sir,' said one of the security officers. 'It took three tranquilliser darts to bring him down.' At first May assumed that they were talking about a human murderer, but before he could ask any further questions the unconscious orange-furred beast was carried out by guards on a long tarpaulin stretcher.

As the white-coated attendants reached the garden gate they were caught in a firestorm of flashbulbs.

'May, in here,' cried Marsden, shoving his way through a sea of blue uniforms. He looked as if he was about to be sick.

'For God's sake don't let the press see in through these windows, man,' shouted May as they reached the stairs. 'If they can get into the trees opposite with a long-distance lens they'll be able to shoot all of this.'

The officer he was addressing pulled the tall curtains closed, and turned on a battery of freestanding spotlights. An animal smell of rancid offal filled the building, mixed with the pungent odour that rose from the droppings left in the hall. May stepped over the forensic markers and walked on to the landing where Deborah Whitstable had met her death.

Broad arcs of blood had smeared and splattered the

walls, and lay coagulating in black pools on the stair
carpet. There were further splashes and bloody handprints
on the white-painted banisters. Chunks of meat and hair
still lay squashed against the skirting board where the tiger
had shaken the flesh from its victim. Mercifully, the bodies
had already been photographed and removed.

'How on earth did such an animal ever get in here?' he
asked, amazed.

'We've been trying to piece together the sequence of
events,' said Marsden. 'As far as we can tell, something
first went amiss shortly before 5.30., while the guards were
waiting to be relieved of their shift. One of them was at the
rear of the house. The other was beaten unconscious. The
front door was opened with his pass key, and the tiger was
admitted. A bloody *tiger*, John. What kind of people are
we dealing with here?'

'There had to be a large van or truck parked in the area,
and it must have been brought close to the house. We'd
better start checking with the neighbours.'

'That shouldn't be difficult. They're all standing at the
front fence in their dressing gowns.'

'What happened once the tiger was shut inside?'

'It would seem that the family were all still asleep. The
vetinary surgeon we called in from London Zoo reckons
the creature had been systematically starved. Apparently
you can train a tiger to eat human flesh.'

'Have there been any reports of such an animal going
missing?'

'It'll take a while to find out that information. It scented
the humans in the house and came up the stairs to here.'
Marsden pointed the claw marks on the surrounding
woodwork. 'It must have woken Deborah first, because
she came out on to the landing in her dressing gown.
That's where it attacked her.' He indicated a blackened

corner of the passage. Deborah Whitstable's body had contained around twelve pints of blood, and most of it had been spilled there.

'Then it turned its attention to the little boy. When the police arrived, they found the husband barricaded into the children's bedroom with his daughter. He'd been whacked in the shoulder and chest by its paws, and was haemorraging badly. Meanwhile the creature was finishing off Deborah, and had dragged the boy down the hall by his head. That was what most likely killed him. Maybe it was saving him for later.'

Marsden lowered his voice further. 'This is completely insane, John. Can you imagine the headlines we'll be seeing in a few hours?' May noted that his superior's first pang of regret was caused by the intervention of the press and not the plight of the butchered family.

'It's not insane,' he said. 'It's clever. They knew that whoever went in to kill the family would have trouble getting out again, so they chose a murderer whom nobody in their right mind would get in the way of. Someone — some*thing* — unable to confess when he was inevitably captured.'

He looked out of the window at the crowds gathering below. 'Everything's building to a peak, Stan. It feels as if the whole investigation is accelerating, cause and effect, faster and faster. Don't you sense that?'

'You need a good night's rest, May,' said Marsden, angrily heading for the stairs.

Just before noon, John May arrived by police helicopter in Norwich, descending through the rain squalls to the offices of Jacob & Marks. There he found the building sealed off and a team of officers ransacking each of the suites in turn, searching stacks of briefboxes for incriminating evidence. Meanwhile, Leo Marks had been detained at the local station before being moved to the Mornington Crescent SCD for questioning.

'What exactly are we looking for, sir?' asked one of the officers.

'According to Bryant it'll be in an old book,' replied May, seating himself on the nearest chair, 'a handwritten document, or just several sheets of loose paper. It's over a hundred years old, so it may have been sealed in something like a plastic folder.'

'You mean like this?' PC Colin Bimsley was holding up a clear plastic bag filled with loose cream-coloured pages of hammered vellum.

'Bimsley, I can't believe it. For the second time in your dismal career you've actually done something useful.' May took the bag and opened it, carefully unrolling the top page of the manuscript. It was marked *The Alliance of Eternal Light: A Proposal for Inducing the Financial Longevity of the Watchmakers' Company of Great Britain.* 'Where did you find this?'

'It was in the safe behind his desk, sir.'

May removed the plastic folder and dropped it into an evidence bag so that it could be checked for fingerprints. As he studied the handwritten text, he hoped to God it had the answer they were looking for.

'Do you think it'll help the investigation, sir?' asked Bimsley.

'I'm hoping it'll end it,' replied May.

# CHAPTER

At 3.20 p.m. Arthur Bryant arrived back in the interview room at Mornington Crescent, where he found John May arguing with a cornered, sweating Leo Marks.

'I keep telling you — I was acting on my father's orders,' he was saying. 'I rang Miss Hatfield at the guild and asked her to help me locate specific documents pertaining to the family's financial accounting system. It was simply what my father had asked me to do.'

'Then you went there yourself to look for them?' asked May.

'Yes — she was having no luck. I think she was too busy trying to help you.'

'What time was this, exactly?'

'I've already told you twice.' He pointed angrily at the wall-mounted cassette machine that was recording the interview.

'So you did,' said May. 'Tell me again.'

'It was just after noon on Christmas Day. My girlfriend

465

waited in the car while I went in. She was furious with me for having to come into work. You can check with her.' That placed the lawyer's visit before the trip Alison made. She had gone there in the evening. 'What I don't understand is how you managed to locate the very thing that Miss Hatfield was unable to find.'

'That's the point, I couldn't have found it without her help. She'd cleared away half of the cartons in the basement. And I had a better idea of where to look. My father had suggested trying certain file boxes. He was too ill to go to London himself.'

'I understand he's in hospital now. I'm sorry to hear that. Don't you think it odd that Miss Hatfield should be murdered immediately following your visit to the guild?'

'No – I mean, yes – I don't know.' He dropped his head into his hands and massaged his temples. 'I know how it looks but I didn't touch her. I didn't even see her.'

'Let me get this right.' May rose from his position on the far side of the desk and approached the young lawyer. 'Miss Hatfield tried to locate a long-forgotten document for you, and was killed for her troubles. You, on the other hand, actually found what you were looking for, and managed to stroll out of the building with it. Doesn't that strike you as odd?'

'No, it's just—'

'Why the hell not?' shouted May. 'Why should she be murdered and you be allowed to walk away?'

'Because she had more reason to be killed,' said the lawyer, looking around at the detectives. 'She was an outsider, interfering in other people's business.'

'Why didn't you bring the document to us? You must have realised that it was connected with Miss Hatfield's death.'

'Because,' Marks answered softly, 'my father was under

strict instruction never to reveal its contents to anyone outside the family, whatever the circumstances.'

'Who gave him such instructions?'

'*His* father. And he got them from James Makepeace Whitstable,' he replied, 'in 1883.'

May placed an arm around his partner's shoulder. 'Come on,' he said, 'I need some air. Let's get out of here.'

They could see their breath in the corridor. 'Why is it so cold in this building?' asked Bryant as they reached their outer office. 'My blood's stopped moving.'

'The workmen are still trying to clear the airlocks from the heating system,' Sergeant Crosse explained. 'We've had to let most of the staff go home. It should be fixed by next weekend.'

'I may be dead by then. Has there been any change in Peggy Harmsworth's condition?'

'I'm afraid not, sir. The doctor told me that if her present status doesn't change soon, she'll suffer permanent brain damage. They can only administer limited medication bcause of the impairment caused by the drugs in her system.' The sergeant hadn't slept for two days. There were pencils in her hair, and five half-drunk cups of coffee lining her desk. She was typing with gloves on.

'Where's Detective Superintendent Marsden?'

'He's over at the safe house. The family were demanding to see someone immediately, otherwise they're going to leave the building and report their grievances to the Home Office and then the press. Neither of you were available.'

'Thank God for that,' said Bryant. 'Even taking Pippa Whitstable's death into account, don't they realise how much safer they are staying together? Didn't they ever watch old horror films? It's the ones that go off to the cellar with a torch that get a sabre through the windpipe.'

'Get your stuff and let's go,' said May.

Bryant could hear people shouting beyond their office window. The noise level was extraordinary. He crossed the room and looked out.

'Just look at this lot, howling for blood.' He snapped the blinds shut and collected his bag from his desk.

Mornington Crescent SCD was under siege. By 11.00 a.m. that morning, journalists had surrounded the building and had begun calling up to the first-floor windows. They were furious that Marsden had failed to set a press conference following the deaths of Deborah Whitstable and her son, and had remained outside all day, demanding that the superintendent appear before them with an explanation. He had, however, managed to slip from the rear of the building without doing so. It was now 5.35 p.m., and there was no sign of the mob dispersing.

'You'd better use the rear stairs,' said Christina, who had arranged for the alley behind the building to have restricted access. 'Don't worry, I'll page you if things get worse.'

'How could they get any worse?' asked May. 'We've nothing to hold Marks here on. He has a watertight alibi for the night of Alison's murder. We can't even hold him for removing the diary without permission, because it was supposed to be in his father's custody in the first place. Has Jerry come in?'

'I haven't seen her for days,' admitted Christina. 'Mr Bryant, are you all right?' The old detective looked sickly, and was steadying himself against the wall. He looked as if he was about to pass out. Thunder rumbled ominously overhead.

'I will be when I get something to eat,' he replied. 'I need carbohydrates. Potatoes. Gravy.'

They caught a cab to the north side of Fitzroy Square, where Gog And Magog was just opening its doors for the evening. Named after the statues of two warriors that had once adorned the Guild Hall until it was bombed during the Second World War, and after the giants that still strike the hour on the clock of St Dunstan, Fleet Street, the restaurant offered a selection of Victorian and Edwardian delicacies that the uninitiated found highly bewildering.

Bryant only brought his partner here on birthdays and in times of great upheaval. As a consequence, they rarely saw the menu more than once a year. May knew that they should be feeling guilty, taking time to eat in such lavish style while mayhem was occurring around them, but sometimes more could be achieved across a meal table than in an interview room.

'"Nature has burst the bonds of art"' said Bryant, removing his wet coat. 'You remember who said that, John?'

'It was the night we confronted William Whitstable outside his house. You reckoned you'd heard the phrase somewhere before.'

'That's right, I had. And this morning I remembered where.'

Although they ate here infrequently, their host greeted them like old friends and showed them to a faux-Sheraton table beneath a pair of stained lead-light windows, opposite the moulting head of a wall-mounted elk.

'It's Gilbert and Sullivan, of course,' said Bryant. 'But I couldn't recall from which opera. Then I recalled that the poet Bunthorne sings the line in *Patience*. Taken with the marked bible, it confirms ...'

'... that William Whitstable knew about the Alliance as well.'

'Precisely. Perhaps all of the victims did. I think the whole of the Whitstable family is divided into those who know, and those who don't know about the survival of the Alliance. God, how they like to keep their secrets. Now we begin to see the real reason why William damaged the painting on that rainy Monday afternoon at the National Gallery.' Bryant slipped a napkin from its ring and draped it in his lap. He raised his hands, framing an image. 'Imagine this, John. After a severe fire the Savoy Theatre is put up for sale, and to everyone's horror an offer from the Japanese is accepted over the British bid. Government help remains unforthcoming. Peter Whitstable, appalled, concocts a strategy with the family lawyer; they will take charge of the Savoy by arranging to have the Japanese compromised and then removed. The Whitstables want the theatre very badly indeed — think of its symbolic place in their family history!

'The Alliance's celebrated system can no longer be trusted to take care of business rivals — for some mysterious reason it isn't working properly any more, and hasn't been for some years. The family is in disarray, having to fight its own business battles. Peter and his lawyer must take control of the situation. They discuss their plan with William, but he disapproves of their illegal tactics. The Japanese have shown nothing but good intentions. The Whitstables, on the other hand, are about to behave like common crooks, swindling them out of the deal.

'Does William tell Peter and Max that he'll have nothing to do with it, that family ideals are being betrayed? No, in typically excessive Whitstable fashion he makes a public statement by destroying the painting that commemorates everything that the Alliance once stood for.'

'Then William couldn't have known that his brother was simply planning to continue the practices of his ancestor.'

'There's the irony.' Bryant accepted a menu. 'Peter and the lawyer knew exactly what James Makepeace Whitstable had been up to, but it seems that William genuinely had no idea. If only we could talk to them now.'

'We don't need to. We have a first-hand account of the event from the old man himself.' May tapped the side of his briefcase.

'You have the diary with you.'

'It's not a diary, just a short chronicle of the Alliance and its aims, something he must have read out to his future partners. But he's added his own notes at the end.'

'Let me see it,' pleaded Bryant.

'In a minute. Food first.'

Their waiter listed the specials without explanation of their contents, it being assumed that if you ate here, you knew what you were in for. 'We have spring, crècy or julienne soup,' he offered, 'nice chaud-froid pigeons with asparagus, forequarter of lamb with stewed celery, thimbles and ...'

'What have you got for dessert?' asked Bryant, rudely interrupting him in mid-flow.

'Anchovy cheese, Aldershot pudding with raspberry water, rice meringue, cabinet pudding, and gooseberry jelly.'

Bryant sat back, delighted. Like the Victorians they emulated, the restaurant prided itself on keeping an ostentatious table. This was the first time he'd thought about something other than the Whitstable family in weeks.

May opened his briefcase and withdrew the folded yellow pages of the account. 'To be honest, I was having trouble reading it,' he admitted. 'It's written in such convoluted gobbledygook I thought it would be better to let you translate.'

Bryant wasn't sure whether to take this as a compliment or an insult. He accepted the document and carefully opened it, attempting to read the title as he searched for his spectacles. 'A proposal for inducing financial longevity, eh? Sounds dodgy.' There were pages of the kind one would find in a business diary, each covered in finely wrought black ink. After this followed a separate document, also handwritten. The heavy italicisation of the letters made deciphering difficult. While May tasted the wine, his partner read quietly on. After a while, he banged his fist on the table so hard that a pair of waiters resting at the rear of the restaurant jumped to attention.

'So that's it!' he cried, 'I knew it had to be something of the sort.'

'What is it?' asked May, not unreasonably.

'As much as I hate to say so, you were right. Why else would James Whitstable have invited craftsmen to be the founding members of the Alliance, and not financial experts? He did indeed suggest the building of a mechanical device. Listen to this: *For if our lawyers can create such a scheme for life annuity such that the overall dividend augments upon the demise of each subscriber, why not a form of mechanical tontine? These are modern times, and such an automated auguring device could be created wherein the subscribers and beneficiaries of the Worshipful Company of Watchmakers might be provided for long after their deaths, by the simple expedient of the creation of a device to inhibit the encroachment of our rivals.* I wish he'd used plain English.'

Bryant took a sip of wine and leaned forward, laying the pages before him. 'Let me fill you in on what's happened so far. James Whitstable sees the finances of the guild failing. Foreign rivals are producing cheaper wares in direct competition with the guild's own exports. He decides that he must act quickly, or their empire will be undermined and nothing will be left for their heirs. He is taken with the germ of an idea, and accordingly invites to London the men who may be persuaded to help him carry out his plan.

'On the afternoon of 28 December 1881, he lunches with his group, filling the craftsmen's susceptible heads with talk of light and dark and preserving the strength and sanctity of the guild, and God-knows-what-else. No doubt these loyal, hardworking men are easy to entice. They're probably amazed to be in London at all — and to be taking lunch at the Savoy!

'After the meal, he trots them next door — *to witness a display which he has already been informed will take place.* Suddenly they see that everything he says is true; James Makepeace Whitstable has predicted the future, when light will triumph over darkness for all time. They've been given proof that a bright new age is about to begin. Well, who could fail to be impressed?

'Whitstable leads them, awe-filled, back to his suite, and draws up a charter which they sign. He wraps their new society up in supernatural mumbo-jumbo, invokes the sacred curse of the Stewards of Heaven. Wait, something else happens here — see appendix, I'll read that in a minute. Then he swears them to secrecy, and looks to them for a solution to his problems.

'And his work pays off. The craftsmen put their heads together, planning far into the night, and they come up with a tracking device that will calculate the guild's accumulation of profit and share interest according to the information fed into it. The machine will also identify the owners of those shares.'

'You mean to tell me that they invented a primitive form of computer?'

'No, because their system isn't binary. Unfortunately,

they were still craftsmen before they were mathematicians. But you were on the right track. I'm only halfway through. Let me read the rest.'

'Your pigeon's getting cold, or hot, or something,' May pointed out.

But he had lost Bryant to the pages. Once in a while the detective would release a 'Hmmm' or an 'Aha!' Finally he looked up, realised that his meal was still sitting before him, and began to eat voraciously. Neither spoke until the plates were cleared.

'Well,' said Bryant, wiping his mouth with a napkin, 'it's made of brass.'

'Is that it?' cried May. 'Isn't there anything else?'

Bryant set down his napkin and checked the pages again. 'It took them two years to build and calibrate the device.'

'My God, how big is this thing?'

'I don't know, it doesn't say. But it's mechanical, and it runs on electricity. Is it possible that it could still be running? I mean, there's no such thing as a perpetual motion engine.'

'Does it mention how it works?'

'Only that it relays information to an outside source, where "the necessary steps" are taken.'

'Some help. What about its location?'

'Again no clue, presumably for the sake of security. There is one man who might know. We must talk to Leo Marks's father. I'll find out which hospital he's in. If the old man was supposed to be the keeper of this account,' Bryant wondered, 'why did he have to send his son looking for it?'

'Alison Hatfield told me all of the valuable guild papers were shifted to the vaults during the war for safekeeping. No doubt Marks assumed that it was the safest place for them. Later, when the attacks on the Whitstables started occurring, the family closed ranks, and Marks Senior realised that he was failing to honour his promise by leaving the document with the back-files at the guild. I wonder how many of the Whitstables knew what was in that document?'

'Even if they had heard tales of such a mechanical tontine, I doubt any of them believed it was real. And they'd never admit it if they did.'

'The older generation certainly must have noticed their unfailing good fortune and wondered. The guild even made money in the year of the General Strike. God, I bet the family did some paper-burning when they heard that William Whitstable had been murdered.'

May rose from the table. 'If they'd been less worried about their dwindling finances and a bit more concerned about each other, perhaps we'd have been able to halt the bloodshed right at the start. Don't go anywhere. I have to make a phone call.'

Bryant sat back with a sigh. He knew that they would end up visiting the hospital tonight, and saw his chances of enjoying a leisurely dessert retreating along with the possibility of a decent night's sleep.

# CHAPTER

In the taxi on the way to the Wentworth Clinic in Gloucester Terrace, Bryant read the remaining section of the chronicle, which bore the personal imprimatur of the family patriarch. It had been singled out as a relevant fragment from James Makepeace Whitstable's journal.

*28 December 1881, evening*
*Shortly after the performance, we returned to our rooms. One look into the eyes of my colleagues told me that our sojourn to the newly illuminated theatre had convinced them of the veracity of my design. These honest artisans would construct a mechanical tontine. They had each been granted Heavenly Stewardship, though doubtless they knew little of what that meant. They had each been granted the Grand Order. But would they still be willing to participate in the building of the device when they realised it was to end the lives of others?*

*In order to ensure their loyalty, it was now necessary to arrange a small show of strength. I had often spoken to them of the bridge from Science to the Occult. Now, in my rooms, they would bear witness to the existence of such a bridge.*

*They began to assemble a little after eight. Radford was the first, creeping into the room apologetically, his club foot sounding hard against the floor. He was closely followed by Lamb, then Chambers, then Suffling. As I had requested, each bore the satin sash of his Stewardship, and now I requested that they don their colours. Radford — Hagith — timidly asked something which had clearly been pressing on him. If, tonight, we would agree the terms under which our mechanical tontine could be constructed, what need was there for our collective presence as the Stewards of Heaven?*

*— I'm rather glad you asked that, I said, directing him to be seated opposite me, for you may recall our discussions on the role of occultism in the coming scientific age. Their attention held, my Stewards took their places around the octagonal baize table. Earlier I had given notice to the chambermaids that under no circumstances were we to be disturbed tonight. I had drawn the heavy green curtains shut and had lowered the lights, removing both of the copper lamps from the table and setting them aside, the better to impress upon the assembly the utter seriousness of our venture.*

*— The system that will preserve our fortunes and remove our enemies forever will succeed because it is both Occult and Scientific, I explained, studying each face in turn. So far you have been presented with little more than an engineering proposal, namely the construction of a device that will tabulate our expenditure and calculate the damage inflicted by the enemies of the Company. You agree, Lamb, that such a device is within the realms of possibility?*

*— Most certainly, Mr Whitstable, he agreed, although certain problems arise.*

*— Namely? I enquired.*

*His sausage-shaped fingers tugged at his cravat as he attempted to frame his reply.*

— *Keeping it hidden,* he said finally. *How shall we protect such a piece of equipment and maintain it finely tuned?*

— *You shall have no need to worry on that account,* I assured him. *Indeed, that is the least of my concerns at present. Instead, allow me to expound my theory of the Scientific Occult. We agree, do we not, that the solution to the Company's growing ill fortune is grounded in simple Scientific theory? The tontine is a mechanism that will provide us with advice. But how can we carry out its instructions? Will Science remove our adversaries? No. For this, we must cross the bridge we have built for ourselves, and arrive at the Occult. We are an organisation ahead of our time, gentlemen. One day all business will no doubt be conducted in such a manner. But let us be the first.*

It was Radford again, fear furrowing his brow as he cautiously raised his hand.

— *But in this gathering* — he stammered, pointing at each of us — *surely our Occultism is just the pose that we adopt to mask our real intentions?*

— *No, my friend,* I replied, *it most certainly is not. Even now, our Occultist Guild colleagues in India are working to solve the problem of removing our enemies. For without their help, the seeds of destruction are built into our system. Suppose one of our Guildsmen is apprehended in the process of vanquishing a hated rival? Should he attempt to explain his actions, why, we are done for. How then, to prevent him from doing so?*

I rose from my place at the head of the table with six pairs of eyes following my every move, and warmed myself against the blazing hearth. Tonight the loyalty of my most trusted men was being put to the test, and I was sure that they would follow me. I had not counted on Radford, of course.

— *And if any one of you were to carry out the deed, how might you feel after? Even the most righteous cause carries a burden of guilt when the death of another is required. The solution,* I explained, *lies in India, where there is a method for recruiting assassins which involves the revival of the newly dead. The placing of an enchantment, followed by the administration of a potion just as the soul of a man leaves our earthly sphere, traps his spirit and places him in our power until his task is performed.*

*— Are you seriously suggesting that we enslave the freshly dead to carry out our demands? cried Radford suddenly, leaping up. I'll be d—mned before I have a part of this, for it is against the will of God.*

*— As it is against my will that you leave our circle now, I replied.*

*— You have no power to stop me, he exclaimed, turning to the others for approval, but I could see that they were with me. It was time to provide Radford with a demonstration of my ability. As my foolish employee tugged at the door (from which I had removed the key) I donned the scarlet robe of Och and began to recite the profane commands that have been bequeathed for my voice alone. It was a strange sight; Radford tearing at the panelling of the door in desperate panic as the others sat on either flank, mute and immobile, siding with their mentor.*

*As I raised my hands and completed the summoning gestures of Bethor and Ophiel, the air in the room grew stifling, and the lamp-wicks lowered as though the atmosphere could no longer support their flames. The light grew dim and hazy, the air heavy and warm as we heard the sickly buzzing, faint at first, then growing louder as it coagulated in a thousand shining bodies.*

*To start with they were faint, and I could barely discern their forms in the black mist that had enveloped the top of the room. In seconds, the blackflies had massed as though it were Midsummer Eve.*

*Radford turned and saw them, and slammed his back against the door in shock. He tried to call out but they were on him, covering his face and chest as though they were bees and he was smeared with honey. The shiny black mass lay writhing on his face, in his eyes and ears and nostrils, filling his mouth and lungs, sealing his windpipe.*

*As he fell to the floor they followed him, clinging tight no matter how briskly he tried to brush them from his head. For a minute he thrashed silently at the winged insects, until the strength drained from his limbs. When he could no longer draw breath and lay still on the rug, his arms at his sides, they lifted from his swollen skin and departed into the slowly clearing air. Lamb drew back the curtains and opened a window. The draught raised the lamps to normal.*

*Radford was left with no sign of misadventure upon his lifeless body. His death that night was marked by the doctors as respiratory asphyxiation, and diminished by the hotel for the sake of their reputation.*

*Still shaking, the others turned back from witnessing Radford's alarming demise and concentrated their minds upon the formulation of the Alliance's founding document.*

*We had no further trouble that night.*

'The supernatural connection you dreaded finding,' said Bryant, slipping the yellowed pages back into their folder. 'It's all here, laid out by James Whitstable himself.'

'You'll have to fill me in later.' May wiped the window and peered out. 'We're here.' The clinic had ended its visiting hours for the night. The Grecian portico of the magnolia-coloured building would have looked more appropriate facing Regent's Park than standing back from the road which led to the environs of Notting Hill. The Wentworth was an expensive private recuperation home for heart patients, and enjoyed the patronage of financially upholstered clients from across the country.

May had been pleased to find that Leo's father, Mr Howard Marks, had elected to stay here; it had saved both of them a journey back to Norwich. As the taxi pulled up before the entrance, Bryant glanced at his ancient Timex. It was a few minutes after eight, give or take a few minutes.

He had purchased it after seeing a commercial in the sixties in which the timepiece was tied around the leg of a galloping horse. Unfortunately, his operated as if the horse had sat on it.

'If he doesn't want to tell us, we can't force the information out of him,' he said, checking the meter and digging around for change to pay the driver. 'Seven pounds forty?' he complained. 'Are you descended from highwaymen, by any chance?'

'If we have to, we can tell him that we have his son in custody,' replied May. 'Come on.'

'You're not getting a tip,' warned Bryant.

'Don't worry, mate,' said the driver, snatching his money from the detective's proffered hand. 'I've read about you in the papers. You haven't got any to offer.'

In the marble foyer of the clinic, a smart black-suited receptionist sat reading beneath a low light. On a corner sofa, a pair of Arabic women were thumbing through back issues of *Hare and Hound*.

'Look at this place,' marvelled Bryant. 'We should have been lawyers. Everyone hates you while you're alive, but at least you have a great time when you're sick.'

'I called earlier,' said May, a trifle too loudly. 'We're here to see Mr Marks.'

The receptionist raised her telephone receiver and whispered discreetly into the mouthpiece, as if she was ashamed to be seen using it. A few moments later a young woman in a discreet designer uniform appeared at the bottom of the stairway.

'Mr Marks is out of danger now, and quite awake,' she said, walking with them to the first floor. 'He was asking for a whisky an hour ago, so he's obviously on the mend.'

'I'm never going NHS again,' muttered Bryant, looking around. 'Has anyone else been to see him?'

'Yes,' said the nurse, 'you're his second visitors tonight.'

'Who else was here?' asked May.

'An Indian gentleman, I didn't catch his name. I think he's still with Mr Marks at the moment.' May's sense of unease caught alight. Grabbing his partner's arm, he broke into a run.

'Which way?' he called to the nurse.

'End of the corridor and right,' she replied, flustered. 'Third door on the left. There's no rush—'

They reached the end of the corridor, their shoes squealing on the freshly polished floor. The hallway ahead was in virtual darkness, but they could already see that the door to Howard Marks's room was wide open.

They ran the length of the hall and halted in the doorway. Their patient lay halfway out of bed, the drip feed severed from his arm, his mouth opening and closing like a fish out of its bowl, his left hand helplessly grasping the air.

His right wrist had been slit, and blood was blossoming across the starched white bedspread. As the nurse arrived and took stock of the situation, she immediately set about stemming the flow of blood on either side of the wound.

'Tell Charles,' the old man was saying to anyone who would listen. 'Tell Charles, the river. He must look in the river.'

'Of course,' whispered Bryant, 'Of course! Now we know where the machine is.'

# CHAPTER

On the flight back to London, Jerry had considered the new sense of melancholy in her father's attitude. She had given him exactly what he had wanted for so long, a daughter in whom he could now confide. Jack was not a gregarious man. He chose the monastic rigours of financial study to the flirtatious babble of his wife's cocktail rounds. Jerry was supposed to unite them, providing her father with a colleague and her mother with a higher social circle. Neither of them had imagined that she might prove desirable to Charles Whitstable in an entirely different way.

Upon arriving home, she saw that the dark mood had deepened and spread to her mother. Jack had obviously told Gwen the bad news: that Charles had decided to apprentice their daughter without including her parents in the social upgrade.

Unable to bear the long faces and awkward silences, Jerry had left the house. She had also reached another decision: to leave the Savoy. The job had been taken to spite her mother, and now that her parents had been reduced to a state of total confusion there was no point in staying on. Perhaps it would give them pause to think about what they wanted; from her, and from each other.

She had decided to stay away from Mornington Crescent, too. Normally she would have headed there hoping to find someone to talk to, only to end up helping Sergeant Crosse with the photocopying. So much for the glamour of police work. Everything had been set behind her now. From tonight there would be a new beginning.

Charles had given her the address of the flat, and had suggested meeting her there at nine. The intervening hours had passed in agonising inertia. Now she stood in the narrow road below Curzon Street ringing the polished brass bell marked C. WHITSTABLE ESQ.

She looked up at the darkened windows, but there seemed to be no one in. Perhaps his meetings had overrun. Surely he couldn't have forgotten their arrangement? Tugging the short black dress evenly around her thighs, she sat down on the step to wait.

Shortly before 9.00 p.m. the two detectives appeared in Mornington Crescent at a virtual sprint. Bryant looked done in, as if he was having trouble maintaining the pace. 'Christina,' he called, searching the offices as he passed, 'we need Charles Whitstable. What have you done with him?'

'He's still in the detention room on the second floor,' replied the sergeant. 'Detective Superintendent Marsden wanted to let him go, and he wanted to go—'

'I gave strict instructions not to let him out of the building,' said Bryant.

'I know, and I didn't allow him to leave.'

'You're worth your weight in diamonds, do you know

that?' shouted May, and they were gone. Sergeant Crosse smiled to herself and touched her hair into place. Like most policewomen, she wasn't used to being complimented in her job.

Charles Whitstable was seated with one of Bryant's nasty scarves tied over his shirt collar and his jacket pulled tight around him. The detention room was freezing. 'Get me out of here, Bryant,' he said angrily as they admitted themselves to the room. 'I have an engagement to attend. Your uniformed clowns interrupted a very important meeting. Those gentlemen at the guild were attempting to remove their investment from the group. I was trying to show them that business is back to normal. It didn't help having the police strongarm their way in to demand an interview.'

'I'm afraid they were acting on Detective Superintendent Marsden's orders, sir,' explained May.

'Your boss is a very frightened man. He seems to think that our family have set out to deliberately destroy his career.'

'Leo Marks's father was attacked in his hospital bed a little over an hour ago,' said May. 'He's lost blood but he'll live.'

'Congratulations,' replied Charles, unperturbed by the news, 'you finally managed to save someone's life. Do you have any idea who did it? At least you have proof that it wasn't me.'

'I think you have a pretty good idea who it was.' Bryant circled behind Charles and leaned on his chair. 'I should have asked myself exactly what you were doing in India.'

'What do you mean by that? Look, I know my rights. You can't detain me here without good reason. Do I have to call my lawyer?'

'No,' replied Bryant. 'What you have to do is remain in

town for the next twenty-four hours while I wait to hear back from the Calcutta police. Then we'll have this interview again.' Bryant tapped his partner on the shoulder, beckoning him from the interview room.

'Christina, we'll be out for a while.'

'Where are you going?'

'I can't risk giving you details. We'll radio in later. What time do you come off duty?'

'Tonight I don't,' she replied with a sigh. 'We haven't any back-up at the moment. Do you want me to come with you?'

Bryant looked her up and down. 'Make a muscle,' he said.

Christina crooked her arm.

'Huh,' grunted the detective. 'Sparrows' kneecaps. You're safer here. Where can I find a pickaxe?'

'Will a sledgehammer do?' She remembered seeing the toolbag that the workmen had left in Bryant's office.

'I suppose so.'

Overhead, the neon striplights fuzzed and momentarily dimmed. Bryant gave his partner a meaningful look.

'For God's sake stop doing that,' said May. 'You're starting to give me the willies.'

They climbed into Bryant's battered Mini Minor and headed into the rain-shrouded city. May was driving so that his partner could continue their conversation. Bryant usually managed to talk and drive simultaneously, but had a tendency to hit the disposable illuminated bollards that stood in the centre of the road.

'When Alison was showing me around the basement of the guild,' said May, 'I asked her about the strange rushing noise beneath our feet. She explained that there was an underground river there, and that part of the floor below had been cemented up at the beginning of the century because of problems with flooding. I'm willing to bet that James Makepeace Whitstable had the rooms partitioned off down there for a very good reason. He diverted the river around them so that no one would attempt to break through the wall, no matter how curious they became. I think if we open up that wall, we'll find our doomsday machine.'

'And if you're wrong?'

'With the heavy rainfall we've been having recently I wouldn't be surprised if we drown,' answered May.

It had just turned ten when they drew alongside the darkened entrance to the Worshipful Watchmakers. As they unfolded themselves from the miniature car, May looked up at the cheerless edifice. He was convinced that Charles had full knowledge of the guild's inner circle. The difficulty lay in forcing him to tip his hand.

'How are we going to get in at this time of night?' he asked Bryant, who was removing the toolkit from the rear seat and attempting to untangle his scarf from the safety belt.

'One good thing about having Charles Whitstable brought in when we had nothing to hold him on; I lifted the guild's master keys from his jacket. I didn't want to ask him for them in case he tried to warn someone. Alison showed me how to use them.'

Two locks had to be unfastened before the door could be opened, following which Bryant had to key off an alarm system in a cupboard at the foot of the main staircase. May located a battery of light switches and brightened the hall, but they would have to rely on torches, brought along to cope with the unreliable illumination afforded by the basement's emergency system.

'What do you know about London's underground rivers?' May asked as they headed for the lift.

'Well they're tributaries from the Thames, and most of them have been incorporated into the sewer system,' said Bryant. 'The problem is, there's no single map showing what's underneath London. There are so many tubes, pipes, tunnels and rivers that their existence is only marked on individual local documents. There are boarded-up tube stations that no one remembers, like Down Street, Dover Street, Wood Lane, Post Office, and British Museum. There's the Post Office underground railway that has driverless trains, and there are hundreds of crypts and vaults that ...'

'Rivers, Arthur, underground rivers,' reminded May, pulling open the trellis door of the lift and ushering him in.

'I suppose the Walbrook was one of the first,' replied the elderly detective, tugging his scarf clear of the door. 'That was covered over at the end of the fifteenth century. The Fleet was covered in 1760 and turned into a sewer in 1855, which it more or less had been for years. The Westbourne was covered as well, and passes through an aqueduct above Sloane Square tube station. You can still actually see it from there. The Princes Theatre in Blooms-bury — now the Shaftesbury — hosted many Gilbert and Sullivan productions, and had to be structurally renovated after an underground river ate away the foundations. The worrying thing is that the bricks of our once-magnificent sewer system are starting to crumble. Tunnels block and the water stagnates, breeding rats.'

The lift jarred to a halt. 'We're still on the first level below ground,' said May, puzzled. 'Alison said there was another floor below this.'

'Perhaps you have to take the stairs.'

'I remember now.' He pulled open the trellis. 'The electrics operate on a separate system. We'll have to walk.'

Overhead, dim red bulbs gave a glimmer of illumination. At the end of the hall was a firedoor which had obviously not been opened for years. May was unable to budge it, and finally it took several blows from the sledgehammer to release the locking bar. As they pushed open the door, their torch beams sent hordes of plump brown rats scurrying back into darkness. The air was filled with dust and condensation.

'Be careful on these steps,' called May. 'The cement's softened up in places.' From all around them came the rustling of disturbed rodents.

'It smells like something died down here.' Bryant placed his hand on the stair rail and quickly withdrew it. The bannister was covered with hundreds of glistening black spiders. They scattered across his trouser bottoms as he shone the piercing light on them.

Ahead, the stairway twisted around to the left. Bryant stepped gingerly downwards, and nearly fell when his heel pressed down on the bulky body of a dead rat. Turning the torch to his shoe, he saw tiny bleached maggots swarming about the rat's head in a diseased halo. The sound of dull rushing could be plainly heard now. They reached the foot of the stairway and shone their torches into the dark hole of the corridor ahead.

'Who's going first, then?'

'I suppose I will,' offered May.

'Thank God for that,' said Bryant, much relieved.

Their shoes splashed in shallow puddles of water as they walked slowly through the passageway. The surrounding walls were bare and grey, marked only with furred spears of damp. Two sets of irregular markings showed where doorways had been sealed up with cinderblocks and cement. 'It can't be either of those,' said May. 'The brickwork's too modern.'

'Nineteen thirties, at least,' agreed Bryant. 'What about

this one at the end?' They had reached another, larger sealed doorway. The entrance was almost twice as high as the previous ones they had passed, and had been closed off with standard-sized housebricks. The paintwork covering them matched the walls.

'This has to be the one,' said May, crouching to study the cementwork. 'I hope we can handle whatever's down here—'

'The best way to find out is by dismantling the wall,' said Bryant, running his fingers over the mildewed surface. 'It shouldn't take much. The bricks are almost soft to the touch. Too much water vapour in the air. Give them a bash with your hammer.'

May removed the toolkit from his shoulder and unzipped it, taking out the sledgehammer and giving a practice swing. A renewed rumble of water rolled past them.

'I hope to God you're right about this.' The first blow gouged a shallow path through the rotten bricks. The second actually depressed one from the centre of the doorway. May kept the hammer swinging, concentrating on one part of the wall. His partner stood off to one side, listening as the roar of water continued to grow. The next blow dislodged a pair of bricks. May lowered the hammer and shone his torch inside.

'My God. You won't believe this.' Before his partner could see, he continued to swing the hammer until the hole was large enough to climb through. Then he stepped back and made way for Bryant. 'You figured out where it was,' he said. 'You should be the first to go inside.'

'Er, thank you,' said Bryant uncertainly, stepping over the low brick wall and ducking his head. The floor of the room was filled with icy water to a depth of almost six inches. Something in the dark ahead was slowly ticking with a heavy steel ring, like a giant grandfather clock. Bryant pressed his back against the inner wall and slowly raised his torch.

'Good Lord. We've found it.'

The light from the torchbeam reflected a dull gleam of curved brass. The device was between twenty and twenty-five feet high, circular in construction, resting on a base of four cylindrical brass pipes. In appearance it reminded Bryant of an astrologer's instrument, an astrolabe, consisting of skeletal globes laced within one another, so that each could move independently of the rest.

At the centre was the most mechanically complex part of the instrument, a partially enclosed steel dome housing a series of cogs and ratchets that allowed the movement of the various metal bands comprising each globe. As they watched, one of the inner bands shifted fractionally, providing a subtle alteration in the composition of the whole.

Immediately there was a buzz and a tiny blue flicker of electrical light at the centre of the device, as if a new connection had been made.

As Bryant approached, he could see that each of the brass strips on the outer globe was calibrated with finely engraved measurements. Then he saw that all of the curving bands were marked, one with the minutes and hours of the day, another with the days of the year, and another with the years of the century. Others were inscribed with monetary equations for accruing interest, and financial configurations covering every possible eventuality. Bryant knew that they were looking at the cold, damaged heart of the Whitstable empire, a manufactured embodiment of everything that had grown flawed and failed in imperialist England.

The pair stood mesmerised by the vast, imperceptibly

turning machine, their torchbeams bouncing from one section to another. The room was silent but for the steady steel tick and the distant booming of the river in the walls beyond.

'It's like an orrery,' said Bryant, awed. 'You know, one of those mechanical models of the solar system.'

'It's beautiful,' agreed his partner, slowly stepping back against the wall. As he did so, he brushed against the warm flesh of another living creature. His shout of fear filled the room, echoing as the metal bands of the astrolabe acted like tuning forks, reinforcing his cry to an unbearable din.

# CHAPTER

49

'You already apologised for being late,' she laughed. 'You don't have to make any rash promises about the future.'

'They aren't rash promises, I assure you,' said Charles, refilling her wineglass. True to his promise, he had arranged for the delivery of an Indian meal. The choice of nationality was fitting, for the apartment was fitted throughout with Indian carvings and tapestries. Ancient terracotta figures of Harappan women, laden with jewellery, stood beside finely carved friezes of tigers and unicorns. She wondered if the museums were aware of such pieces being displayed so casually in a London flat.

'I really would love to show you India. My work there has only just begun. For a major industrial country, they export very little. It's a situation we're trying to help remedy. When I have time, I travel to the great plains beyond the cities, where the night skies are the deepest blue-black, so vast and dark that you think you'll never see the dawn again.'

'It sounds beautiful,' she said, suppressing a shiver.

'Not as beautiful as you.' He reached forward and kissed her lightly. She tasted wine and spice on his lips, something aromatic from the meal. He shifted his weight, holding her closer. This was the moment she had been expecting, even if she had refused to consciously acknowledge the fact. Everything in her life had taken on a contradictory quality, as though only part of it was now real, and part hallucination. She wanted to understand the Whitstables, to see their ordeal through to the end. She was convinced that by doing so she would somehow be provided with an insight into her own nature. More disturbing were her confused feelings for a much older man she barely knew. She was scared of becoming intimate with Charles knowing that she might well be forced to betray him. As she closed her eyes and he kissed her again she tried to touch him, but her arms would not leave her sides.

'What's the matter?' His face was still close to hers but he was looking at her oddly, and she realised how tense her body had grown. When she failed to reply, he detached himself from her.

'Jerry, it's okay. Nothing will happen that you don't want, I promise.'

'Scared. I'm so scared.' Finally the words emerged. She had not been able to speak them to Joseph, but was determined to say it now. 'I haven't done this before.'

'My God, I'm sorry. I didn't realise.' He gently took her hand in his. 'I thought — well—'

'You thought I must have had some experience by now. Believe me I've wanted to, but something—' she rubbed her hand across her forehead, trying to clear her thoughts. 'It's like the dark. I can't — I panic.'

'That's right; the dark scares you, doesn't it? But that's just a psychosomatic problem. It can be easily cured.'

'No.' Jerry shook her head. She had spent too many sessions discussing the problem with Wayland. The last thing she wanted to do now was revive the old arguments. 'My fear of darkness is a medical thing, pure and simple.'

'Nonsense,' he replied, releasing her hand. 'A phobia is a learned emotional response, didn't he tell you that? I should know. Hypnotherapy is one of my sidelines, as it were.' He seemed determined to discuss her problem whether she wanted him to or not. He sat forward, motionlessly studying her eyes. 'A phobia is just an extension of the fear that's produced in a frightening childhood situation, or at a time of emotional development. I can get rid of it quite easily for you.'

'How?' she asked, intrigued.

'Before I took over the custodial duties of the family business, I graduated from medical college. I became a qualified hypnotherapist. It's one of the reasons why I continue to work in Calcutta. My skills are more appreciated there. Behavioural therapy is the normal route to ridding yourself of anxieties, but I have a faster method. Here, I can show you if you like.' His role had suddenly switched from lover to family doctor. Confused, she laid her head back on the couch. She felt tired and close to tears.

'I know how you're feeling, but it's okay. I want you to rest.' She looked up and saw his pale still eyes fixed on her, never moving.

'I don't want to be hypnotised or anything,' she insisted. 'I've heard about the weird things people do under hypnosis.'

'Jerry, those are fallacies. I couldn't make you do anything against your will. The trick to hypnotherapy is that there is no trick. Anyway, you don't even lose consciousness. It's not like you're asleep. You hear everything around you, the traffic in the street, the rain against the windows. All you'll be doing, when I ask you, is thinking more clearly and deeply. It can't do any harm to at least try, can it?'

She looked across at the lamplight glinting on wet windowpanes, at the softly lit carvings beside the fireplace. He was showing his faith in her. It was time she showed some faith in him.

'All right,' she murmured, resting back. 'We'll try.'

He pressed his fingers gently against her eyelids and lowered them. 'Just relax. Think of a place where you've been happy. Somewhere by the sea, or in a sunny meadow ...'

He talked her down on to a pleasant, comfortable plateau. In her mind's eye winter dissolved into summer. She saw emerald grass and sapphire sky, and her own bright body stretched out below her. She was lying in a bikini, soaking up the heat, her skin warming through to her bones. She could hear Charles's voice softly seesawing in the distance, like the droning of bees in June. She looked back at her body and noticed that she was younger. He was regressing her.

'Jerry, you are now fifteen years old,' the voice was saying. 'Without experiencing the fear that you associate with the dark, are you aware of it being there, somewhere inside you?'

'Yes,' she replied slowly. 'It's here.'

'Then we'll go younger. You are now a young girl aged fourteen years. Don't worry, you are in the light. How do you feel about the dark, on the landing, in your room?'

'Bad. Frightened.'

'Tell me about this year, Jerry, your fourteenth year.'

'Trouble.'

'Why trouble?'

'I hate my mother's guts.'

'Why do you hate your mother?'

'She's a slut.'

'That's a strong word for a fourteen-year-old girl. Let's go to when you were thirteen, please. You are leaving the age of fourteen, going further back. Back to thirteen. Jerry, you are now thirteen years old. How do you feel?'

'Good.'

'Do you feel good about the dark?'

'Yes.'

'Then we must go to a time when you don't feel good about the dark anymore. Do you remember the day when you stopped feeling good about the dark?'

'No.'

'Why don't you remember?'

'Not the day. Days. Weeks.'

'I don't understand.'

Suddenly she was seeing glimpses of a past she had long expelled from her mind. Bad behaviour at school. A teacher's face, close, shouting. Fighting off a slap. Tears. Standing in a corridor beyond the classroom, counting the red waxed tiles. Gwen, furious, screaming at her. Something broken, blue china, water on a yellow rug. More tears, her mother crying. Guests around a dinner table, staring at her. A penknife stolen from another girl. A bloody hand. Wigmore Street in the rain. Alighting from a cab. Waiting in Dr Wayland's surgery. A chromium lamp on a springy steel arm. An old crimson couch of dimpled leather. Wayland talking and talking and talking, until his soft, reasonable voice merged with Charles's.

The blindfold.

Awake, sitting up, moving her shoeless feet from the couch.

The room was shifting beneath her. Disoriented, she put out a hand to steady herself.

'Jerry, what is it?' Charles was asking. 'Are you all right?'

'I'll be fine.' She rose and slipped on her shoes. Gwen would be at home.

'Wait, you can't leave like this. You're in no—'

'You wanted me to face up to my fears,' she replied, slipping her arm into her coat sleeve. 'Well, that's just what I'm doing.'

'Believe me, you startled me far more than I startled you.'

The face illuminated in the torchlight was old and Asian, thin and worn from a life of hard toil. Sparse grey hair straggled across a scarred bald dome. The man who stood before them was wearing a blue boiler suit, and looked like a maintenance engineer.

'If you would care to step through to my office—' He gestured to a small recessed door in the rear of the wall. Startled beyond speech, Bryant silently complied with the old man's request.

The antechamber beyond the room housing the astrolabe was fitted with a small overhead light, and at first glance was furnished in standard backroom style. A cheap desk and chair, filing cabinets, a stack of untended paperwork, a pair of static-dirty computer screens, a litterbin, a wall calendar with views of Norway.

Then Bryant noticed that the calendar was over forty years out of date, and that the paperwork was bound together with thick mildew. The little Indian man anxiously showed his visitors in, trying to find them places to sit. He reminded Bryant of a railway stationmaster still tending a long-closed branch line.

'You must excuse me,' he said, clearing the paperwork to the back of his desk. 'I have had no visitors here before.' He held out his hand to each in turn. 'My name is Mr Malcolm Rand, and it is my duty to tend to the equipment you saw in the next room.'

'How long have you been here?' asked May.

'At the guild, most of my life, sir, since I graduated from my apprenticeship. I took over the tending of the machinery in 1967, from my father's brother, God rest his soul.'

'How the hell do you get in here? You do go outside, don't you?'

'Of course, sir, I have seen you several times before, for I am also the head of the maintenance staff here at the guild hall. This office is connected to a passageway at the rear of the first lower level. I visit the equipment twice a day, once in the morning and once before I leave at night, to ensure that it is well oiled and able to continue functioning correctly.'

Now May remembered seeing Rand beside the staircase on his first visit to the Watchmakers. 'Does anyone else know about this?' he asked.

'No, sir, and nobody must know. It is written into the rules of my employment. You are not supposed to be down here. I could lose my job.'

'I'll see to it that you don't lose your job,' promised May. 'Have there been other custodians here before you?'

'Most certainly. It is our duty to ensure that the equipment is never damaged.'

'But it is already, man. Do you know what it does?'

'Of course, sir,' Rand quietly replied. 'It is the great Financial Machine. When it calculates that the profits and shares from the Company have been spread unwisely, or are falling into the wrong hands, it pinpoints the guilty party. When the financial loss reaches a certain level, the machine ascertains the culprit and transmits that person's fiscal details to the appropriate authority in the outside world.'

'Where to, though?' asked Bryant. 'How does it do it?'

'The machine is electrically connected to the telegraph, and now, just lately, to the Company's computer network. I do not know where the messages go.' Mr Rand was puzzled by the air of tension in the room. 'Beyond the fact, of course, that they go to Calcutta. Is there something wrong?'

'Do you know what happens after the machine transmits each message?' asked May.

The custodian shook his head uncertainly.

'It arranges the murders of the people it has named.'

'No, no. How is that possible?' answered the shocked custodian. 'It cannot be true.'

'I'm afraid it is, old chap,' said Bryant, perching on the end of Rand's desk. 'And I think Mr Charles Whitstable will be able to tell us all about it.'

The detectives looked back toward the ticking astrolabe.

# CHAPTER

Rand had turned on a dim overhead bulb, and the brass globe shone darkly beneath it, a monstrously beautiful engine of death, the shadow of its metal limbs revolving eliptically below the swinging light.

The mechanism rotated imperceptibly, marking off the calibrations as it moved. 'The marks correspond to the members of the family and their business associates,' explained Rand. 'Details of new companies entering the field are given to me by the lawyers, and I adjust and update the telegraph — and now the computer system — accordingly. This way, the Whitstable fortunes remain within the controlling heart of the guild.'

He indicated several taped pieces of paper on the brass arms of the interior globes. 'I would like to bring someone down here to etch the new names properly into the brass, as the original names have been, but it's against the rules of my employment.' He pressed one of the peeling labels back in place with his thumb. Rand took great pride in his work, even if he failed to understand the lethal nature of it.

'If it's targeting the wrong people, something must have changed the settings,' said Bryant, wading around the astrolabe. 'Have there been any roadworks carried out near the building recently?'

'Oh, yes,' said Rand, 'very many. The city is changing fast.'

'Do you ever feel the vibrations all the way down here?'

'Not normally, no. But last month developers demolished the old bank next door, and everything shook.'

'Then that's it.' Bryant ducked beneath the outer globe and carefully stood up inside the revolving mechanism. 'What setting is this inner circle supposed to be on?' he asked Rand. 'Do you know offhand?'

'Let me get my chart.' He returned with a clipboard and pages of computer paper, running his finger along a timetable line. '162337.918 at the inner core. The number is located beside the bar nearest your left hand, right at the end.'

Bryant dug out his reading glasses and checked the number. '162338.984. It's out by just one notch, but the gears have magnified the error. The whole thing's turned in on itself. A bad case of Chandler's Wobble.'

'What's that?' asked May.

'It's the movement in the earth's axis of rotation,' Bryant told his partner. 'It causes the latitude to vary. That's what's happened here. The vibrations from the demolition have made the calibrations incorrect by a single notch. The effect has been augmented through the device, so that it's selecting the wrong people.'

'I knew the river was a problem,' said Rand. 'Every time it rains, the room gets a foot of water at least, and it takes hours to go down again. I wondered if it could cause a mechanical malfunction. This is an electrical device. It could be dangerous.'

'So Rufus was right after all,' murmured May. 'Come on out from there, Arthur. We have to find a way to turn this thing off.'

'How on earth do we do that? Where does the electricity supply run from?'

'We are not on the main circuit,' said Rand. 'The supply here comes from an independent generator. The running costs are billed to a separate account.'

Bryant was still inside the device when one of the outer rings clicked another notch, causing an electric spark to crackle in the central housing of the machine. 'The wiring duct goes straight down into the floor,' he said. 'We need to get this shut down before the twenty-eighth.'

'What's the time now?'

'Somewhere approaching midnight.'

'Can't you be more accurate, Arthur?'

'Not really, no.'

May checked Rand's wristwatch. 'According to this one, we have about twelve minutes left in which to do something.'

'Obviously the damned thing needs to be unplugged.'

'It is not that simple.' Rand sloshed through the water toward them. 'There are a great many wires.'

'Then we'll have to jam it,' said May, picking up the sledgehammer he had leaned against the wall. 'Arthur, you've finally got your chance to do some damage to the British aristocracy. Have a bash about with this.'

He passed the hammer through to Bryant, who hefted it like a cricket bat, gauging its weight. 'Not bad,' he said, swinging it against one of the inner brass rings with a reverberating thump. 'God, the Victorians really built this thing to last.' It took six healthy strokes to dislodge a single section of one of the globes. As the metal band buckled and dropped, it jammed against the outer arms, seizing the rotational segments of the sphere firmly in place. One of the outer sections tried to move, but was prevented from doing so. The ticking suddenly stopped.

'I'd get out of there, Arthur. There's no telling what it might do when the pressure builds up,' said May, holding out his hand. There was an agonised rasp of metal and the structure shuddered, attempting to shift once more, like tectonic plates pushing toward an earthquake. This time, however, the globe succeeded in moving a single notch. As Bryant clambered between the jammed sections, propping the sledgehammer between the rings, there was a loud click and the central mechanism emitted a series of cracking electrical sparks.

'It's sending out orders,' cried Rand. 'That sound was the electrical connection being made.'

'How many orders?' asked Bryant, trying to untangle his scarf from the machine.

'I don't know, two, ten, twenty, it's hard to say.'

'Isn't there any way of checking, anything that we could — could somebody help me out of this damned contraption?' Bryant was wrenching at his scarf, which had become threaded between the inner and outer globes. May ran over and tried to pull him free.

'I know, wait a moment.' Rand splashed back to his room, peered around the corner and returned. 'This transmission didn't go overseas.'

'How can you be sure?' asked May.

'The computer registers the signal and annotates the destination country. But this one has a London code.'

'John, it's sending out another blasted death command.' Bryant gave up wrestling with the scarf, looped it free of his neck and abandoned it to the astrolabe. A horizontal arm of the inner globe attempted to move forward, but was restrained by the scarf. There was a sulphurous pop and sizzle as something shorted out in the central housing.

Bryant was just stepping free of the sphere when the cable-filled central core blew its ancient ceramic fuses and burst into flame. A second explosion followed as the electrical cables touched water.

Everyone started as a low voltage shot around their shins.

'The river will put out the fire,' said Rand, pushing them back in the direction of his office. 'I have never seen it this high before. You must hurry, you have no time to waste if you wish to stop the command from being fulfilled.'

'We have to find out where the signals went,' said Bryant.

'Sometimes they go all around the world,' said Rand. 'Not just to India, or to people who presently work for the guild, but to those who have gained from it in the past.'

'It's too late to stop the weapon being primed, but we can get to the targets first,' said May as they climbed the stairs. 'Luckily the whole family is still under one roof.'

'No, it's not. Christian Whitstable and his daughter are recuperating in the Royal Free Hospital,' Bryant pointed out. 'And Peggy Harmsworth's still being cared for on the floor above them. I'll go there; you take the house. I can drop you off on the way.' The time was now 12.17 a.m.

'Arthur, do you have your pager?'

Bryant patted his pockets. 'Er, no, I must have dropped it.'

'What do you do, sell them? We have to call out every unit we can rouse. I have no intention of going into this without all the available backup we can muster.'

Weary and wet, covered in spiderwebs and brickdust, the pair returned to the main hall. At the reception desk, May placed a call to Christina Crosse, who was about to end her shift for the night.

'We need everyone you can get hold of,' he explained, 'including Marsden. Tell him what I've just told you. You'll have to explain that there's no way of knowing how many assassinations we're dealing with. I'm sure he'll be thrilled to hear that. And I need you to bring in Charles Whitstable.'

'But we already let him go—'

'This time you can arrest him.' He replaced the receiver. 'Let's get out of here.'

'I've been trying to puzzle something out,' said Bryant as he turned the car back towards King's Cross.

'I'd rather you concentrated on your driving,' said May.

'You must agree that Rand is only guilty of crime by association. He's merely carrying out the duties he was employed to undertake.'

'I suppose so,' agreed May.

'Then who on earth killed Alison Hatfield? She's the only victim who couldn't possibly have been targeted by the astrolabe. As Leo Marks so kindly pointed out, she was an outsider.'

'I think you'll find that there are other custodians who know about the system, apart from Mr Rand,' said May. 'And I don't suppose they're all so agreeably disposed. Maybe they realised she was interfering in the guild's business, and arranged to have her punished.'

'You're right,' agreed Bryant. 'There has to be at least one other overseer. Whoever was appointed the task of eliminating Christian and Deborah Whitstable must have had help getting a damned tiger into their house. No, there are others around all right. Their ancestor seems like a man who would have covered every option. I'm willing to bet we've had spies following us since the day this began. I woke one in the cellar of Bella Whitstable's house.

Young Jerry was warned off by another at the Savoy theatre. They were probably just drones, paid help. But the machine telegraphed smarter assassins, special men for the harder jobs. Replacing the Savoy barber in order to kill the major took careful planning. And getting close enough to William Whitstable to slip him the bomb took great skill. If their deaths hadn't been filled with such baroque flourishes we may never have come to pin the blame on James Whitstable.'

'You think he planned the details of his rivals' deaths?'

'Certainly,' agreed Bryant, stamping experimentally on his accelerator. 'Why else were no modern methods of execution employed? The murders were deliberately exotic in approach, probably so that they would strike fear into other potential competitors.'

'It makes you wonder how James Whitstable's conscience could have allowed him to set this up.' May looked through the windscreen and blanched. 'Mind that bus, Arthur.'

'I suppose he thought he was more Christian than the rest,' replied his partner. 'Think of the times in which he lived. James honestly believed that his family was more worthy of preservation than others.

'Er, do you want me to drive?'

The little car swerved across into the next lane to avoid a pair of cyclists riding abreast, then accelerated through the lights.

'He behaved no differently from our missionaries,' said Bryant, 'smashing up the religious artefacts of one civilisation to replace them with statues of our own. I'm sure half of England still thinks that their religion is better than anyone else's. It's the same principle at work.'

'Dear God, I hope we can avoid the mass slaughter they caused,' said May. 'I hate to ask, but can't you go any faster?'

'We're doing over fifty and running the reds, which isn't bad for Gray's Inn Road in the pouring rain, considering I've only got one windscreen wiper and bald tyres and I can't see out of the rear-view mirror.' The little Mini cut across the five-way intersection at King's Cross, causing a builder's truck to slew sideways across the road, shedding its load as it ploughed into the safety barrier with a clang.

They had just reached Chalk Farm tube station when they noticed the rain-haloed street lights flickering further up Haverstock Hill. A moment later they went out, and the entire roadway ahead was plunged into darkness.

'They warned that this would happen if the rain kept up,' said May. 'The Electricity Board substations get flooded out.'

'Oh, that's wonderful,' snapped Bryant. 'We've gone full circle. They've got night on their side at last.'

# CHAPTER

## 51

'You knew, you bitch. You knew all along.'

'Geraldine, whatever else you may think I am still your mother, and you have no right — *no right at all* — to talk to me that way.'

They were facing each other across the lounge like a pair of evenly-matched actresses in a stage melodrama. Gwen was even poised in true West End fashion with a scotch in one hand. God only knew where Jack was, presumably sulking in his study, still smarting from his daughter's success with the Whitstables.

Jerry was operating on pure adrenalin now. With the past made clear to her, it seemed that her life had been building to this moment. 'You knew,' she seethed, forcing herself to remain on the far side of the room, 'because you were sleeping with him.'

'Geraldine, this is uncalled for.' She threw back the scotch and reached for the decanter with an unsteady hand. 'I don't know why you're behaving like this.'

'Because someone has just undone what he did to cover it up,' she explained. 'I was convinced I was ill, abnormal, incurable, and all the time it wasn't me at all.' She took a step forward. She feared she might rush at her mother if she moved any closer. 'Christ, you were having an affair with him, that's why I was sent to Wayland.'

'No, you're wrong, it wasn't until after — you'd been seeing Emil for a while — but I broke it off—'

'You broke it off when you discovered the truth about him. I remember it all now, so you don't have to pretend anymore. I used to arrive for his sessions so pumped up with tranquillisers it was hard to even speak. That's when he started the hynotherapy, gently putting me to sleep. What else did he use? Did he inject me? Did he ever tell you?'

'Geraldine, you have to believe me, I was horrified when I found out what—'

'I remember his hands crawling all over me, trying to get inside me. He used a blindfold, did he tell you that part?' She was hysterical now, shouting at the top of her voice.

'He never — had intercourse — with you.'

'He would have if you hadn't found out when you did.'

'I arrived early one afternoon to collect you and there was no one in the outer office, so I opened the door to the consulting room. He had — his hands were inside your skirt. You were asleep, you couldn't have felt anything or known what was going on. I started hitting him, screaming at him. I think he'd given you Valium, just a little pill. He said he'd done it several times before. He blindfolded you because he was ashamed of his actions. He couldn't look at you, but he couldn't stop himself. He said you wouldn't remember anything.'

'All I remembered was being touched in the dark. All the bullshit he fed me about my nyctophobia! It's not just fear of darkness any more.' Now she understood Wayland's legacy. Puberty had exposed the true complexity of her phobia. No wonder she had barricaded herself from Nicholas, and fled from Joseph's room. No wonder she had frozen at Charles's touch.

'I just wanted what was best for you,' said her mother. She touched her face and neck as if anxious to reassure herself of her existence. 'We had your welfare to consider. If I had gone to the police, the scandal would have made all our lives hell.'

'So you helped him cover it up. You had me shipped off in case I remembered anything, kept me out of the way. But then — *then* — you still let him treat me. Jesus, how could you do that? Knowing what he'd wanted to do?'

'You have no idea what he was like.' The tremor in her voice was a declaration of damage. '*No idea.* He knew my position with Jack and he used it.' She refilled her glass with unsteady hands. 'At first I really thought I loved him. I had no one else to turn to. He twisted me around to the point where I would do anything, say anything to remain near him.

'Afterwards, I refused to let Emil see you until you returned from St Gregory's. By that time he'd made a promise never to touch you again. I swear to you, Geraldine, our relationship ended the day I walked in on him. He said he couldn't help himself. What could I do? He was highly thought of, he'd treated royalty. He would have lost everything if the scandal had come out. I was about to leave Jack, did you know that?'

She wiped her eye with the back of her hand, pacing back to the drinks cabinet. 'When your father and I met, he was a different man. Full of energy, exciting to be with. Then Jack lost interest in me. He lost his drive, his ambition.'

'You knocked it out of him.'

'He said he no longer saw the point of wanting to improve our social standing. He was offered a directorship with one of the finest guild companies in Britain and he turned it down! I turned to Emil, and then his foolish, weak mistake cost us everything. After the horror of finding him with you, I thought I had the upper hand. I didn't, of course. He just carried on, talking his way around me, and then I found myself doing anything I could just to keep him quiet, to keep him from harming us.'

'Jack must really despise you,' she said viciously. 'No wonder he keeps your letters in his desk drawer.'

'What letters?' She threw her glass back on the cabinet counter with a crack. Whisky splashed on the floor.

'The notes you and Wayland sent each other. When he couldn't call the house. Jack found them, and he saved them. It's his proof, you see. It's how he keeps his hatred of you alive.'

'Geraldine.' She was crying now, smearing her lipstick with the heel of her hand. 'I just wanted the best for us all. I let myself be — I should have made you my priority. But it was my life too.'

'And now you have nothing.'

Jerry turned from the room and closed the door as her mother sank into her corner chair with her face in her hands.


The Royal Free Hospital was a modern concrete building constructed on the side of a hill approaching Hampstead. Tonight it was one of the few in North London with any electricity, and shone like a beacon as they approached it. The hospital's emergency generators had taken over, and the patients and nurses could be seen at the windows moving through a sickly half-light.

Two squad cars had already arrived in the visitor's car park before them. Both were empty. May slipped into the Mini's driving seat as Bryant alighted.

'If everything's all right here,' he called, walking backwards toward the main entrance to the hospital, 'I'll join you up at the house.'

'Good luck.' May started to reverse the Mini out of the forecourt. Bryant was about to enter the main foyer of the hospital when Jerry pulled him back.

'Where did you come from?' he asked, startled.

'The division told me where you were.' She couldn't stay at home tonight. It seemed a better idea to dispel her anger with action. Catching a cab to the hospital, her stomach had knotted at first sight of the darkened streets. Then, wonderfully, the feeling had lightened and faded to a fraction of its normal strength. Now she was ready for anything the night held. 'Can you hear something funny?' she said, her head tilted, straining to listen. She was sure she had heard a muffled thud, someone calling.

'Don't let your imagination run away with you, young lady.' Bryant grabbed her arm and was about to frogmarch her inside when he heard the noise himself. Someone was banging on the glass above them. As they looked up there was a loud crack, like the shot from a gun. May had stopped the Mini in the car park exit and was half out of the vehicle, pointing upward.

Spears of glass showered down as the body fell, its scream mingling with shouts of horror from the room behind the burst window six floors up.

The figure in white hospital garb hit the ground head first as Bryant pulled Jerry aside and shielded her eyes. The sound of flesh and bone impacting on concrete was like no other on earth. The victim lay dead before them, the body arched and twisted into a position that was only possible if its spine had been severed in two.

May jumped from the car as the police began to arrive at ground level. One junior constable turned white and began to vomit against the wall of the building. Christina Crosse came running across the foyer and stopped before Bryant.

'He bluffed his way into the room, sir,' she said, trying to catch her breath. 'He was wearing a doctor's coat and walked right past the night nurse. We arrived just after, and that constable there,' she pointed to the one being sick, 'walked into the room to find him strangling the life out of the patient. We were just in time.'

'What do you mean?' asked Bryant, looking over at the corpse.

'Peggy Harmsworth's upstairs, sir. She started to come out of the coma a couple of hours ago. She's going to be all right. That's the man who tried to kill her.' Bryant looked back at the body and saw that what he had taken for a hospital gown was in fact the white of a doctor's coat.

'My God,' said Bryant. 'If the first thing she saw when she awoke was someone's hands around her neck, it's surprising she didn't go right back into a coma. What happened then?'

'He ran at the window before anyone could stop him, went through head first. Why would he do that?'

'Just obeying orders, Sergeant Crosse,' said Bryant, patting her on the shoulder. 'Let's get to Christian Whitstable and his daughter.' He made for the hospital entrance, pulling Jerry in his wake.

'This one's like the others, sir,' called Christina, pointing to the body in the forecourt. 'He's been dead for quite a while. But he can't hurt anyone now. His spine is broken.'

'I can see he won't be doing the polka for a while,' snapped Bryant. 'I told you, there are more like him on the way. We have no idea how many.'

The sergeant hastily caught them up.

In the corridors of the fifth floor, dim emergency lights dragged at their shadows. The hall ahead was deserted and silent. Sergeant Crosse slowed to a walk. 'I don't understand,' she began, alarmed. 'I left a detail of men to guard the room. They were here just a few minutes ago.'

'Which is Christian Whitstable's ward?'

'He and his daughter are in a separate room, the last door on the left.' When he had first regained consciousness, Christian Whitstable had demanded to be taken to a private hospital, but Bryant had refused permission to have him moved, explaining that he was residing in the same building as Peggy Harmsworth, and that it was safer if the family was grouped together.

The three of them approached as swiftly and as quietly as they could manage. The linoleum floor had been polished so that every contact with it caused a squeak. Bryant was the first to arrive. The door was wide open. In the half-light he saw Christian, up and out of bed, warning him back. As he walked further into the room he saw the reason why.

'He has my daughter,' said Christian, never moving his eyes from the white-coated figure in a paper face-mask, standing against the far wall of the room. Two other officers stood impotently nearby, their hands at their sides. Flora Whitstable was held close against his leg, a rubber-gloved hand fastened across her mouth, a glittering scalpel at her pale throat.

'All right, nobody move an inch,' said Bryant quietly, holding up his hands. 'He has nothing to lose. He's not alive.'

That didn't sound too good. Bryant had been placed in similar situations before tonight, but never facing a dead man. The killer had no interest in his victim, and probably no vestigial consciousness to speak of. Like his accomplice he was simply an automaton programmed with one task; paying off a debt of honour that demanded the ultimate payment of a taken life.

Was there anything more than the smallest spark of human life left inside these assassins? If there was, it explained why Daisy Whitstable had been spared for a while before she died. What a crisis of conscience her killer must have faced. Perhaps he had tried to find a way of sparing her, realising that if he did so it would prove some trace of his former self was still alive. Finally he had carried out her execution, unable to comprehend why such a young life had been targeted for termination.

This pitiful thing standing before him was one of the tattered men for whom they had been searching so desperately. Poverty stricken in life, he had been prepared for burial in ragged clothes; a new suit was too expensive an item to waste on a corpse. Did he have any idea of the complex occult and scientific forces that had brought him to this spot tonight? Was his soul in torment or at peace? Was he prepared to fulfil his allocated task with a clear conscience, like Bella Whitstable's murderer, or was he suffering the uncomprehending agony of being here at all?

'I know you don't want to harm the girl,' he said gently. 'We know all about the job you've been instructed to do. If you let her go, I promise I will see to it that you are put to rest.'

He took a step toward them. The hand tightened, the blade nearing Flora's neck. He could hear the assassin moaning softly behind his face-mask. Bryant stayed where he was. Christina and Jerry were motionless in the doorway. Did they realise he was trying to talk down a reanimated corpse?

'Listen to me,' he said. 'You were supposed to finish the job after the tiger failed to do so. Neither of these two must be allowed to live. Am I right? Nod your head. Just nod once if I'm right. I won't come any closer.' He raised his hands in a gesture of peace. 'Please, just nod your head. Show us that you can still understand.'

Slowly, the assassin gave a slight nod. Judging by the confused, rheumy eyes that showed above the mask, he was confused by another's awareness of his undead state. 'Put down the knife,' said Bryant. His voice was monotonous, drained of opinion. 'Your orders are no longer valid. You don't have to do this now. Nothing more can happen to you. It's over. I know the burden you're under, the terrible pain you're in, and I want to relieve you of it. I know how your body hurts, how you were once a man of honour. Terrible things are happening around us. You don't have to do this anymore; I beg you, let us help you find peace at last.'

As they watched, the eyes above the mask glossed and spilled, and the dead man began to shake, the pressure of the moment racking his body, tearing at his soul. Flora ran forward as the knife fell and stuck in the floor. Christina stepped in with the other officers and took control.

'Now let's give the black bastard what's coming to him,' said Christian Whitstable.

Before anyone could move, the tormented creature fell to the floor with a terrible guttural wail, his soul wrenching from the dry, dead shell to leave its host inert, and finally free.

'I have to get up to the safe-house before we lose any more,' said Bryant, hitching his raincoat about him. They had returned to the hospital forecourt, which had now been sectioned off with makeshift barriers. The lights were still out in the streets ahead of them, and the rain was continuing to fall in soaking waves. Bryant felt as if his body was fast falling asleep on him. His arms and legs seemed to have been carved from blocks of wood. Still, there was no time to think of himself now. Without knowing how many assassins were on their way to the Hampstead house, everyone was in danger.

'Jerry, if you want to risk your life for this worthless family, you might as well get in the car.'

The girl was still standing looking back at the hospital, trying to work out what had happened. Bryant turned her back in the direction of the Mini. 'You're not having any trouble with the blackout?' he asked, surprised.

'I'm over that problem,' she replied casually, climbing into the car.

'Well. Score one for the daylight,' he said with a smile.

# CHAPTER

52

As the headlights of the rusty blue Mini caught the reversed-out lettering on the street sign in Mulberry Avenue, they found that the route to the house had been cordoned off with miles of yellow plastic tape. Police cars blocked the road ahead, several with their lights still flashing.

'I asked them to be discreet about this,' grunted Bryant. 'Pull over here. We won't get any closer.' As they walked toward the house, Stanley Marsden came running toward them.

'What the bloody hell is going on?' he demanded. The rain was falling in a thick soaking drizzle. Marsden looked as if he'd recently fallen in a pond. 'You *cannot* place the whole division on alert without my authority. Your damned sergeant should have known better than to take such an order.' May appeared beside them, trying to head Marsden away from his partner. 'What if there's another emergency tonight?'

Thank God for the courageous and wonderful Christina, thought Bryant. 'Then we'll pull someone out of here,' he suggested, hailing May. 'Hello, John, what's wrong with your nose? It looks like your cold is getting worse.'

'Considering I spent part of this evening standing in filthy, freezing water, wonderful.'

'I'm sorry to break up the pleasantries,' said Marsden sarcastically, 'but could someone give me an update on the situation?'

'We're reaching the end of a long, bizarre journey ...'

'Then what the hell are we all doing here? Your sergeant gave me some cockeyed story ...'

'There are still a few loose ends to clear up.'

'Like what, might I ask?'

'Some reanimated assassins are on their way here to wipe out the Whitstables. And we can't kill them, because they're already dead.'

'What are you talking about? How many "assassins"?'

'I couldn't tell you. I don't know how many members of the family they've been instructed to finish off either, but if they can arrange to slip a starving Bengal tiger into a suburban house I think we should be ready to expect the worst, don't you?'

Jerry followed the detectives as they stepped past their astonished superior and walked toward the house. At the main gate, two of the duty constables attempted to stop her, but Bryant waved them aside.

'She's earned her right to be here,' the detective explained. He placed a hand on her shoulder. 'Let's go inside.'

'Well, I'm surprised you have the nerve to show your faces in here again,' said a sour-faced Berta Whitstable, examining them by the light of her raised hurricane lamp. Even at this time of night she was dressed in expensive, garish clothes. She looked like Imelda Marcos playing Rochester's first wife. 'I wouldn't be surprised if you were somehow responsible for killing us off.'

'I can assure you it's nothing to do with me,' said Bryant, removing his wet trilby and placing it on the hatstand. Candles had been placed in saucers and ashtrays throughout the hall. The flickering yellow gloom had reversed the century, returning the building to its true status as a Victorian mansion. 'Gather the family together please, if you would.'

'Who the hell do you think you are, Mr Bryant?' Berta's eyes narrowed in fury. 'You can't just keep ordering us about. This is still William Whitstable's house, and you are trespassing on—'

'Just fuck off and get the family, will you?' said Bryant wearily. He turned to the others and shook his head. 'I'm sorry. It's late, and the night is far from over.' Berta stormed off up the stairs, calling for the others in an injured, tremulous voice.

'How many officers do we have altogether?' May asked Marsden, who had appeared behind them in the hall.

'Eight,' he replied. 'Nine counting me.'

'Is that all?' He couldn't believe it. At any one time there should have been sixteen men and women available.

'Four are at the hospital with your sergeant,' the detective superintendent explained. 'I think you'll find that the rest are making a protest at the way you two have been conducting this case.'

'God, why did they have to pick tonight, of all nights?' cried May. He had been expecting something of the kind ever since Marsden had warned him of the bad feeling that existed amongst some of the staff passed over for the new division. 'Have we got all of the windows covered?'

'As much as it's possible to cover them,' said Marsden.

'At least we've managed to get the men well-armed. There are dense woods behind the property. No way of stopping a sniper in there, I'm afraid.'

'You see?' Bryant told his partner. 'If William Whitstable had lived in a council house this wouldn't be a problem.'

He looked up to see a crowd of arguing, angry-faced relatives heading down the stairs toward him bearing torches and lanterns. 'My God, it looks like they're getting ready to go and set fire to Frankenstein's Castle. Right, let's get everyone into the dining room. Jerry, give me a hand.'

As usual everyone was talking at once, but this time fear showed beneath the anger and confusion. The dining room was illuminated by a large crystal chandelier filled with fresh candles. Shadows bounced crazily about the ceiling. It looked as if the Whitstables were assembling to tell each other ghost stories.

Bryant turned to the gathered family as Jerry and his partner seated the last of the older children.

'You might not realise it, but this house is under siege,' he began. 'We have good reason to believe that assassins will try to attack one or more of you during the night.' Better to frighten them into behaving themselves, he thought. 'No one is safe until dawn. I want you to keep away from the doors and windows, and stay as near to the centre of the house as possible. We'll protect the outside of the building as best as we can, but we can't guarantee you one hundred per cent safety. After this, however, we can promise that you will have nothing more to fear.'

'You mean you've finally pulled your finger out and managed to catch someone,' snorted one of the older men. 'Perhaps you'd like to tell us who the culprit is.'

'Now is not the time,' said May, pulling his old friend to

one side. 'We're duty-bound to protect them.' He led Bryant away as the others began hurling insults after him. One of the children threw a plastic beaker at his head. 'You're a pair of hopeless old failures,' he called.

'I can't believe they're so rude to you,' said Jerry, following the detectives to the door.

'I suppose they're going through a nightmare,' said Bryant. 'They don't know if they'll even be alive in the morning.' He turned to one of the officers standing inside the front porch. 'Have you seen anyone around? Any sign of disturbance at all?'

'Nothing yet, sir.'

'The sight of you lot has probably put them off.' He scratched his chin thoughtfully. 'On the other hand, the people we're after are more loyal and diligent than the men who employed them. They'll find a way to carry out their instructions in any way they can. It's the only way they can earn their peace.'

'You sound as if you know more of what we're dealing with than you're prepared to tell us,' complained May.

'John, I've done some reading from Maggie Armitage's books about Indian death cults, and what's been going on here shows just a fraction of their power. These bodies have been kept alive until they complete a final task. They remain in a sort of purgatory until then. If you can't believe in the supernatural, think of it as an intense hypnotic state. Look, there's no point in you getting any wetter. Why don't you oversee operations inside the house? I can take the perimeter with Madam here.'

'I suppose it's better than leaving you to get into a fight with them,' sighed May. 'Just be careful.'

Outside, the drizzle had grown heavier, and rain drummed through the trees in the woodlands beyond, crackling like a forest fire. Marsden was seated in the front patrol car making a call. Around the house, disconsolate soaked policemen stood in pairs, unsure what they were watching for.

'Go and get yourself a sou'wester,' said Bryant, aiming Jerry at the nearest police car. 'It's going to be a long night.'

Inside the house, things were just as bad. May was having great difficulty holding the family together in one room. The children had a habit of ducking out the moment his back was turned, the men's moods ranged from threatening to abusive, and the women were all complaining.

'I have to use the bathroom,' said Berta Whitstable, rising from her armchair and pushing her way through the door in a jangle of jewellery. 'I really can't believe we're prisoners in our own property.'

As she reached the foot of the stairs, she thought twice about going up. Several of the candles on the landing had blown out, and the first floor was virtually in darkness. As she climbed, she found herself listening for sounds from above. The detective had shut the lounge door behind her, and she could no longer hear the familiar sound of the family arguing.

Somewhere overhead, rain was falling on a skylight. What a relief it was to be away from her relatives for a moment. She had forgotten how appallingly self-interested they were when gathered all together. She wondered where Charles was. His place was with family. He had promised to come. Why wasn't he here?

At the top of the stairs she leaned forward and peered down the darkened hall. The bathroom was right at the end, and only one candle had remained alight. No wonder — there was a chill draught coming in, and now she felt several tiny spots of rain on the back of her neck. Someone had stupidly left a skylight open. She walked on down the hallway, the wet air wafting eerily around her shoulders.

She reached the bathroom and saw that the door was half open. The candles on the sink had blown out, but she thought she could see a box of matches beside them. She was reaching out for it when a cold hand grabbed hers and she found herself facing a wide-eyed man in tattered rags who slipped his hand across her mouth and pulled her to him as he slammed the door shut and locked it.

'They can't come down the street because they'll see the police cars,' said Jerry. 'If I had to assassinate someone, I'd climb up one of the beech trees in the wood and shoot them through the windows. With a bow and arrow, so it would make no noise.'

'That wouldn't work,' said Bryant. 'These things are given specific targets. You can't tell one person from the next through the drawn curtains.'

They were standing by the dustbins at the end of the garden, shining their torches into the woods. Rain filled their beams like glittering steel needles. Jerry checked her watch. 2.45 a.m. Her shoes were full of icy water.

'How long have you been in the police, Mr Bryant?' she asked.

'Next year will be my forty-sixth year,' said the detective with unconcealed pride.

'That must make you the oldest man on the force.'

'Not if I keep lying about my age.'

'I bet you've worked on some really exciting cases in your time.'

The detective's eyes caught hers. 'There's been the odd trunk murder I wouldn't have missed for the world.'

'Bryant, if you were a criminal, how would you go about getting inside the house?'

'Me?' He thought for a moment. 'First of all I'd wait until the initial activity had died down, say around about now. This is the danger time. Everyone's getting tired, and the family are starting to feel a little safer again. They're lowering their guard. Some of them have probably left the room, because they won't be told what to do by a stupid policeman. Security's a bit looser now. The other officers are thinking we've got it wrong, that nothing's going to happen after all. That's when I'd make my move. I'd come in disguise, as someone in a position of trust. Say, a policeman.'

'One of the policemen guarding the house?'

With one thought between them, they started to run back through the flooded garden just as the first shot was fired.

# CHAPTER

One of the constables was holding him down on the grass when they arrived. The young Asian man was wearing a standard police-issue navy blue raincoat and cap, and had been stationed alone at the side of the house.

P.C. Colin 'Mad Dog' Bimsley, clearly elated by his new-found respect as a useful member of the force, had spotted the bogus officer reaching into his jacket as he crouched beside the lounge window studying the family through the curtains.

'It was his shoes, sir,' said Bimsley, panting. 'Black plimsolls.'

'Well done, Bimsley,' said Marsden. 'You can take your foot off his throat now.' Together they helped the silent figure to his feet, and the detective superintendent pulled him close to get a good look.

'Look at his eyes, Stan.'

'My God.' Marsden took a sharp step back. Their captive's eyes had an opaque, filmy appearance, as if they had been boiled dry. He was quite obviously sightless. Even Bimsley reacted as though a spider had just run across him.

'There's no point in questioning him,' explained Bryant. 'He's been dead for a week.'

'You know that's impossible,' shouted Marsden suddenly, furious with his own inability to comprehend what was plainly the truth.

'I know what I see,' replied Bryant. 'When you take him to the van, be careful with him. He's in great pain, and may try something.'

The constable tried to move his prisoner, but he refused to budge. Suddenly it was as if a plug had been disconnected, for the assassin dropped silently to his knees and fell forward on to his face in the grass.

'They're learning,' said Bryant. 'That's the second one to release itself upon capture.'

'What do you mean?' asked Marsden, '*release itself*?'

'Their souls — their life-forces, if you like — are being prevented from leaving their bodies, even though their corporeal state has reached an end. It's a complex Eastern ritual developed at the end of the last century, based on a combination of scientific and occult principles involving hypnosis, fringe medicine and profane invocations. I've read a lot about it, but never actually seen it in action.'

'Christ Almighty, Bryant, this isn't Open University,' complained Marsden. 'If it's possible, I'll have to take your word for it. I'm a pragmatic man. I like my explanations clear cut. *This*—' He pressed the toe of his boot against the prostrate prisoner's shoulder, disgusted. 'This doesn't fit in anywhere. There are no rules in this kind of situation. How the hell are we supposed to know when we've caught them all? Take it away, Bimsley, for God's sake.'

'Sir, there's a call for you in the car,' said Christina

Crosse, who had just arrived from the hospital. Bryant walked briskly around to the front garden and across to the vehicle parked with its doors open, nearest to the gate. He slid into the passenger seat and pulled the handset free. 'Bryant.'

'Sir, this is Mr Rand at the guild.'

'Has the machine burned itself out?'

'Yes, sir. The damage is shameful. After all these years ...' He sounded disappointed that the astrolabe had been shut down. Even though he was merely a maintenance man, Rand had the true spirit of the guild craftsmen. 'I have been working on the computer, trying to decode the final set of transmissions. The calls went to North London, seven of them in all. I think I can get the addresses of the recipients.'

'You can give those to an officer after you've finished talking to me,' said Bryant. 'What about the targets?'

'That's why I called you, sir. It's all of them.'

'What do you mean? The whole Whitstable family?'

'That's right, sir, every single one.'

Bryant thought fast. The machine's final command had fallen on the anniversary of the founding of the Alliance. In its attempt to clear away its enemies in one broad sweep, the misaligned device had targeted the wrong group.

'Thanks for the warning, Mr Rand. There's something I wanted to ask you earlier.' It had bothered him when he'd first seen Rand's office, but the question had been pushed from his mind by more urgent matters. 'When you need supplies for the maintenance room, who approves the orders?'

'Mr Tomlins, sir. I'm to report only to him.'

Bryant had been convinced of the guild secretary's involvement at some level. Tomlins had tried to obstruct the investigation right from the start.

'Do you have a way of contacting him at home?'

As Rand was giving him the address, Bryant kept the front of the house in view through the rain-smeared windscreen of the car. There was a sudden flash of movement as someone darted between the bushes. Leaving Rand holding on the line, he ducked out of the vehicle and began to run back to the house. The officer at the porch had his back turned away from the figure, who was speeding up behind him with his arm raised.

'You there, look out!'

The constable turned in time to deflect the blow but could not avoid it altogether. He slipped backwards and fell into the grass with his attacker landing squarely on top of him. Before Bryant could reach the fighting pair, Christina Crosse ran forward and swiped the assassin a hefty blow across the back of the head with her torch.

'Duracells,' she said, rolling the newly inert body off the squashed constable. 'Very dependable. Oh, gross!' The figure in the grass was older than any they had previously seen. Christina's blow had staved in the back of its head, and as it thrashed, powder and bone scattered from its opened cranium. The skin of its neck was as withered and leathery as chamois. 'Seven assassins,' said Bryant, fighting to regain his breath. 'Of course, it would have to be seven. The Stewards.'

Bryant wanted to check that May was all right inside the house, but he was worried about Jerry. He hadn't seen the girl since he had gone to take the call, and there were still five more assassins to be located.

'Don't put this thing anywhere near the other one,' he told the sergeant. 'You'd better call for another secure van. We're going to need it.' He left them and walked off along the side of the house, shining his torch into the bushes. The rain was growing heavier once more, and the beam's visibility was reducing to a tunnel of grey mist.

As he turned the corner, he first assumed that the figure walking briskly toward him across the lawn was Jerry. Then his torch picked up a streak of steel in the figure's left hand, and he realised that he had located the third assassin. This one was younger, tougher. Fresher.

He looked back at the side of the house, but the remaining officers had moved to the front where they were presumably helping Sergeant Crosse with her prisoner. He had no weapon on him of any kind. He was alone.

Bryant felt a cold prickling behind his knees and at the back of his neck as he realised the recklessness of the situation he had placed himself in. He had done the exact thing he had warned the girl against. The assassin was almost upon him as he backed up against the brickwork and shone the torch at his eyes. For a moment the corpse faltered, blinded, as Bryant rolled away from the wall and ran up on to the lawn.

The wetness of the grass had greased the slope; his foot slipped beneath him and over he went, painfully on to his knees and then his back, helplessly spread before his attacker. The cadaver stood over him, swaying slightly in the rain. Then it fell forward on to him with the knife raised at its waist. Bryant felt the cold hand of death seize his heart.

Suddenly there were two of them, one clinging to the back of the other. Jerry had seized her chance and was attempting to haul the assassin over on the garden steps. 'Run, Bryant!' she shouted as their protagonist's left arm flew up and his blade slashed the air, striking at Jerry's chest. The girl cried out as Bryant staggered to his feet shouting for help. Officers were pouring into the garden, and two of them pulled her free, grabbing the assailant by his wrists and forcing him to release the knife, which spiralled harmlessly into the turf. Bryant caught Jerry as she slipped back, the front of her sou'wester slashed apart. He tore open the raincoat and examined the wound. The flesh of her chest had been cut, but not deeply. The heavy material had absorbed the brunt of the attack.

'You're going to have a small, intriguing scar,' he said, tousling the shocked girl's hair. 'Aren't you glad I made you wrap up warm?'

Jerry looked back at the anguished young Asian twisting his captors' arms. 'This one looks almost alive. I mean, really alive.'

'The poor devil hasn't been dead long,' explained Bryant. 'There's still a fair amount of strength left in his muscles. There are four more on the loose. I think one's already inside. Look at the roof.'

As Bryant loped off in the direction of the front door, Jerry looked up and saw the smashed glass of the skylight lying on the tiles.

Marsden was returning to the patrol car when he rounded the end of the garden wall and walked directly into an elderly, ambulatory cadaver. His shout of surprise alerted the men in the car, who ran to his help just as the dead man lashed out at the soft flesh of his throat. Shocked to the core, the superintendent stumbled against the wall, gasping for breath as his men faced the snarling, snapping old corpse. As it bit and lashed at the officers, the rotten stubs of its teeth came loose and fell from the puckered, crusted hole of its mouth. It was already undergoing a change, visibly ageing. As one of the officers drew it back, it lolled its head forward and spat, voiding its putrid system of any remaining liquid. Marsden glanced once more at the creature and vomited.

As Bryant pushed open the front door of the house, Susan Whitstable hit him on the head with an omelette pan. 'I'm sorry,' she said, not sounding sorry at all. 'I thought you were one of them. Why are you making so much noise outside? The children are trying to sleep.'

'Where's my partner?' asked Bryant, rubbing his skull and shoving past her to the foot of the stairs.

'We have enough trouble keeping track of our own people without having to find your staff for you,' she said archly, walking back to the lounge still clutching the pan. As Bryant began to climb the stairs, his torch beam faltered.

'Oh no, not again.' He felt sure that somewhere up above, the spirit of James Makepeace Whitstable was watching over the house, enjoying their continuing fight to hold back the darkness. Upon reaching the landing he found himself without any light. From somewhere further along the hallway came the sound of scuffling. Then a hand shot out and pushed him back against the wall.

'He's got Berta Whitstable tied up in there,' whispered May. 'I think he's arming some kind of explosive device. I saw him removing a large metal object from a bag. There are wires hanging from it. I suppose it could be some kind of mortar bomb.'

'I wondered if they would resort to something like that,' hissed Bryant. 'Nothing short of an explosion would get rid of this lot. They have orders to remove all of the remaining Whitstables tonight. What can we do?'

'Go back downstairs and start getting everyone out of the house as quietly as possible. Send one of the armed officers up. No more than one, though. I need the element of surprise, but I daren't tackle him alone. Berta's still in there, and he could trigger off the device.'

Bryant ran lightly down the stairs and opened the lounge door. Everyone was watching television. One of the younger set had rigged up a battery-operated Panasonic

TV-Video on the dining room table. He quickly gathered a pair of officers, sent one upstairs to May, and had the other assist him.

'I want your attention,' said Bryant, stepping in front of the screen. '*Everybody*, please.' Several people craned their heads to one side, gesturing for him to move.

'We're watching a video, *Thelma and Louise*,' said one of the girls. 'It's nearly the end and you're spoiling it.'

'They drive over a cliff and die,' said Bryant maliciously. 'Now, I want you all to move outside as quickly and as quietly as possible.'

There was a chorus of protest. 'But it's *pouring*!'

'Have the girls got time to go and change?' asked Susan, indicating her offspring with the omelette pan.

'Everyone must go right now, in the clothes you're wearing.'

'I'm wearing a two hundred pound sweater,' complained Nigel Whitstable. 'If the colours run I'm sending you the bill.'

'If you're not all out of this room in twenty seconds, I'll have you dragged out,' Bryant warned, hoisting two of the smaller children to their feet. 'You shouldn't be watching this anyway, you're too young.'

'Daddy says we can do whatever we please because you're public servants,' said Berta's grand-daughter, Delilah Whitstable. The others started to file out, complaining as they went.

'He does, does he?' Bryant looked for her father as he hoisted the child into his arms. 'I must remember to see if his road tax has expired.'

Outside, in the dark, in sliding sheets of rain, Jerry stood alone, watching the trees for movement. She was no longer afraid, for she knew what the darkness hid from her eyes. The male of the species. Now she could learn how to deal with that particular creature. It was something to look forward to. She wiped her torch against her sodden jeans. When she raised the beam, she saw the assassin walking toward her from the end of the garden. It was the marked dissimilarity in their body language that had thrown her at first. Each one was totally different from the next. They didn't behave at all like undead beings were supposed to, shambling along with their arms outstretched. They refused to conform to their stereotype. No wonder she had been so confused about the manner and appearance of each assassin. Tall, short, old, young, capable of speech or not, they had presented the face of a single killer until it was no longer possible to do so. The creature was fifteen feet from her. She saw now that its brown tatters were burial garments. It had reached the end of its life several days earlier, at around fifty years of age. In its left hand it held a weeding fork, presumably all it could find in the gardener's shed near the wall.

She walked toward it, unafraid.

It came to an unsteady halt and peered at her. Both eyes were functioning. Something black was running from its nose. The rain had plastered its hair flat, giving it a more skeletal appearance. Now that she had a chance to study the shambling thing, she felt nothing but pathos for it. Lumbering at her half-heartedly, it raised the red metal fork, but long before it could connect she clouted it with the housebrick in her hand, stone cracking against bone. Knocked from its feet the carcass fell into the weeds and died a second time. The twitching of a stray nerve in its leg came to an abrupt stop as its power departed, leaving a sad earthbound husk behind.

Jerry tossed the brick aside and walked away. Finally, the night belonged to her.

Upstairs, May and the constable had been discovered.

The assassin was standing in the bathroom doorway, unsure of his next move. Behind him Berta had been pushed to the ground, and lay whimpering on the tiled floor with a towel knotting her ankles and a flannel stuffed in her mouth. In front of her was a heavy six-inch thick steel disc, joined to an electronic detonator. After appraising the situation and recognising the conditions of a stalemate, the assassin knelt and calmly continued setting the detonator.

'We have to get him to hand her over,' May whispered to the officer. 'He's going to set the thing off without worrying about himself.' In his life on the force, May had encountered the most dangerous kind of assassin; a fanatic unconcerned for his own survival. This time the situation was exacerbated by the perpetrator's prior departure from life. He turned to the officer, who was checking sight lines between himself and the target. 'Can you pick him off from here?'

'I can't be certain. He's too close to the woman.'

'Then hold your fire. We don't even know if bullets are likely to stop him. Wait here for a minute.' He slowly crept forward, fixing his eye on the detonator.

'Your orders were wrong,' he called suddenly, making the assassin start and Berta Whitstable flinch. 'You're not supposed to hurt these people. I know that's what you've been told to do, but there's been a terrible mistake. Please, don't move.' Knowing he could not dissuade, May spoke to divert. He directed the armed officer to edge toward the assassin, who briefly looked up before returning his attention to the bomb.

'Stay there and keep me covered,' he said, lowering himself slowly to the ground with a sigh. 'As if I wasn't already close enough to meeting my maker.'

He began to move forward, one foot shifting quietly in

front of the other. The assassin saw him approaching and finished twisting the wire caps of the detonator shut. He turned a switch, set the box down and took a step back, bracing his wasted body for the worst. Behind him, Berta spat out the flannel and began to scream.

Judging by the size of the casing, the bomb blast would be too big to contain by simply throwing himself on it. May looked at the tiled floor, judging the positions of assassin and captive. Towels had been dragged from the rail above the radiator; several of them had fallen on the floor against the wall. It was all he needed to see.

The assassin was still staring at him, waiting for the countdown to end when May threw his torso forward, dropping to the floor. Moving with a speed that surprised them all, he held his hands out flat and slid into the bathroom with as much force as he could muster, slapping the steel disc across the floor. It skittered across the polished bathroom tiles like a hockey puck and thudded into the towels which had fallen in rolls against the far wall.

Berta released a howl of fear and jumped back as the armed officer darted in, bringing his knee up hard into the assassin's stomach, punching the stale, dead breath from him. He fell to the floor, ruptured wide, as May ran to the bomb and switched the detonator off. The stench of rancid offal filled their nostrils.

'Some help up here please,' he shouted, jerking the sobbing Berta to her feet and pushing her from the room, out of harm's way. As officers thundered up the staircase and prepared to take their prisoner, May leant against the wall to regain his breath, and realised how very, very tired he had suddenly become.

Behind him, still connected, the bomb's countdown readout zeroed itself, jumped back to OVERRIDE:

MINS: 5:00 and began to flicker downwards once more.

'Take him downstairs, quickly,' he told his men as he passed them on the stairs. 'He's leaking everywhere and we don't know what's inside him. There's still one assassin loose, in or around the house. Nobody's safe until he can be found.'

# CHAPTER

'Can we go in yet?' complained Nigel Whitstable. It looked as if the colours were running in his sweater. Several of the younger ones had started to cry. 'This is an absolute bloody outrage.'

He looked around, as if noticing the police cars for the first time. 'It would help if you were to explain what you're hoping to achieve with all this ... fuss going on.'

Bryant and Sergeant Crosse were busy trying to settle as many of the children as possible in the cars. Most of them were treating the evening as an adventure, and had to be slapped away from the dashboard cellphones.

May led Charles Whitstable's sobbing mother out to join the group as the remaining police gathered around to help the family. She looked more human in the rain. As Bryant backed out of the last car he realised that everyone was staring at him, waiting to be told what to do next.

In this brief instant, he almost felt sorry for them. Huddled together in the downpour with no coats or

jackets, frozen, sopping wet, confused and utterly miserable, the Whitstables looked a pathetic lot. Whatever else
happened he would always remember them like this, the
bedraggled dynastic dregs, capable of complaint but little
else, waiting for someone stronger to direct them.

The moment was quickly broken by Nigel Whitstable,
who started shouting again. 'When the papers get hold of
this,' he cried, poking Marsden in the chest with a bony
forefinger, 'you'll be about as popular as the Gestapo.
You're finished, all of you. And especially those two
pathetic old has-beens you call detectives.'

Bryant had had enough. He stepped forward and called
for silence.

Behind him the neighbours were watching, standing in
doorways with their arms folded, or peering from around
their curtains. When everyone had finally stopped complaining, he began to speak.

'You asked me earlier to tell you who caused all of this
to happen. I'll tell you now, if you haven't already
realised.' He drew himself to his full height and studied
the faces in front of him. 'It's *you*. The Whitstables. The
Company. The Alliance. The family. You did this to yourselves.'

There was an immediate uproar. Finally, Berta made
herself heard above the furious chatter.

'What on earth are you talking about, you silly little
man?' she cried. 'We would *never* knowingly harm
ourselves. We know how to protect our own.'

'That, Madame, is precisely what caused the problem in
the first place,' said Bryant, growing heated. 'If you want
to blame anyone, blame James Makepeace Whitstable. If
your ancestor hadn't been so determined to keep your
money from the hands of lower-class upstarts by killing
them off, and if you hadn't been prepared to pass on his

secret from father to son, mother to daughter, then you wouldn't have accidentally turned this destruction upon yourselves.' He strode angrily before them. 'My God, instead of helping to cast out the dark and keep the fire of free enterprise alight — that precious symbol of the burning flame that none of you professed to have any knowledge of — you've all become party to a new darkness. It's been descending on you all this time, and not one of you noticed. All to preserve the values of your guild. Purity. Decency. The new bright light.' He pointed at each in turn, unable to control the fury he and May had fought to keep in check since hearing of Alison Hatfield's death.

'You people are supposed to be the apex of civilisation, but you're just the opposite. The only thing at which you all excel is lying; to us, yourselves, and each other. And now that we've managed to save your miserable lives, you'll undoubtedly show your gratitude by having us thrown out of the force. Well, go ahead, do your worst. Our job is ended here.'

He turned his back on them and walked away, leaving the bewildered group staring after him.

'Sir,' called Colin Bimsley, 'I just saw someone run in through the front door. He's going upstairs!'

'It can't be one of us,' said May. 'Everyone's outside now. Looks like you've found our last man — you'd better go after him.'

'Yes, *sir*,' said Bimsley, sprinting off toward the house, going for the hat-trick.

Just then, the entire upper floor of William Whitstable's house exploded with a deafening roar that set off every car alarm in a three-mile radius. The night sky billowed out in a boiling wave, causing their ears to sting. The surrounding trees were filled with the sound of scattering glass and brick. Small pieces of blazing timber fell on the gathered assembly. The air was filled with the acrid stink of burning as flames executed exuberant flourishes in the upper windows.

As the horrified family picked themselves up off the pavement and dusted themselves down, May climbed to his feet and ran back into the garden, searching for P.C. Bimsley. The constable was looking up at the roaring building with a dazed expression on his face.

'I wouldn't bother going in after him now, Bimsley,' May said consolingly. 'By the way, your jacket's on fire.'

Behind them, the top floor of the house burned brightly on, a pyrogenic beacon that ignited the stars and stole the sombre blackness from the night.

'Thank God we managed to get everyone out in time,' said May later, as they were heading back toward Mornington Crescent SCD in the Mini. At this hour of the morning it was safe for Bryant to drive, providing you weren't a cat or a pigeon. 'I thought you were a bit hard on them. Did it ever occur to you that it might be just as difficult for them to be who they are?'

'If they don't like it, they can opt out,' said Bryant. 'It doesn't work the other way around. The poor can't choose to be rich.' He stared thoughtfully out at the deserted streets of Camden Town.

'Jerry Gates has been accepted as one of them now. Charles offered her a job. Did you know about that?'

'No. It will be interesting to see what she decides to do after this.' May blew his nose. 'Do you think I could have caught pneumonia?'

'It's possible,' said Bryant, never one to look on the bright side. 'There's a distinct chance that I may die in my sleep tonight. I can't take the pace anymore. My valves feel bunged up.'

'I know what you mean. We haven't had this much excitement since that business with the Deptford Demon.'

'Wait a minute, we can't go home yet,' said Bryant, slapping the wheel. 'We have to pick up Tomlins and bring him in to the station.'

'It's ten past five, for heaven's sake. Let someone else do it.'

'We daren't do that, John. We can't risk losing him. Somebody on the inside has to relate the full story to Marsden. We can't leave it to Charles. He doesn't know about the astrolabe.'

He turned the Mini around and headed for the Maida Vale address that Rand had given them.

The city streets were still in darkness. The house they sought was pale and pebble-dashed, a bay-windowed thirties villa. Below the social standard of the Whitstables' homes. On the fifth buzz, a middle-aged woman in a quilted dressing-gown opened the door and attempted to stifle a yawn. Bryant and May identified themselves, and expressed a desire to see the lady's husband.

'I'm afraid you've missed him,' she said, waving a hand in the direction of the garage adjoining the house. 'He got a phone call, said he had to go out, that it was to do with work. I didn't understand what he meant. I mean he's not a doctor, he doesn't get housecalls.'

'How long ago was this?'

'About half an hour.'

'Did he say where he was going?' asked Bryant.

'To the guild, I think.' She rubbed her pale cheeks, trying to remember.' He said he was seeing someone called Rand.'

\*

The Mini slid to a halt outside the entrance hall to the Worshipful Watchmakers at 5.42 a.m. The first signs of life were stirring in the city, and the traffic was already starting to build. The front doors had remained closed since the night of Alison Hatfield's death.

'I don't want to alert him in case he does a runner,' said May. 'How are we going to get in?'

Bryant smiled and dug into his overcoat. 'I still have Charles Whitstable's keys,' he reminded May. 'We'll have to bring in poor old Rand as well, you know. I bet Tomlins will try to swing the blame on him.'

'You want me to call for backup?' asked May, looking about.

'Not much point. I imagine they'll both come quietly.'

They alighted from the car and walked to the door of the guild hall. Bryant unlocked it as quietly as possible and stepped inside. The hall was dark and empty, and answered their footsteps with muted echoes. Switching on their torches, they made directly for the staircase at the rear of the building. Using the lift would only draw attention to their approach.

'I'm getting used to finding my way around by torch-light,' said Bryant, gingerly descending to the lower landing. 'I'm starting to look like a mole. Can you hear something?'

From the darkness below them came the sound of an angry, ranting voice. They increased their pace, descending through the mire of the lower floor, then leaving the stairwell and running along the corridor. From here they passed through Rand's deserted office and into the room which housed the astrolabe. The emergency lighting circuit evidently ran from a generator, for the bulb above the huge brass globe was still lit.

They found Tomlins standing over the little Indian with

the sledgehammer raised in his hands. Rand's twisted, terrified figure on the floor indicated that he had already been struck.

Tomlins started at their arrival, his dismayed, disapproving face turned to them.

'Stay back,' he called. 'This has to be ended properly.' He turned back to the prostrate figure beneath him and swung the hammer once more, driving it hard into Rand's back. 'I should really crush his skull for what he's done,' he explained dispassionately.

'What has he done?' asked May, stepping closer.

'He's destroyed everything. Betrayed his sacred trust. To the Alliance, to the guild and to the family.'

'He didn't know what the machine was capable of doing.'

'Well, it can't do anything now, can it?' He raised the sledgehammer again. 'All the work, all the years of loyalty and hardship and *duty*, all for nothing.'

As the weapon began its descent May jumped forward and grabbed Tomlins's forearm, forcing the hammer back. With a terrified moan, the Indian scrambled painfully across the floor heading for the safety of his office. As the two men grappled with the hammer, Bryant tried to pull Tomlins down from behind.

The clerk was stronger than either of them had realised. He pushed Bryant away with one hand and threw himself backwards, slamming May hard against the wall once, then a second time. Bryant heard his partner's skull crack hard on the bricks and watched as he fell into the water. Tomlins turned on him, his teeth bared in fury, and swung the sledgehammer, the weight of its iron head carrying the momentum of the swing.

Bryant jumped back and realised that he was pressed against the edge of the astrolabe. With a stumbling fall he found himself inside its structure, the brass rings protecting him from his enraged attacker.

The hammer swung again and smashed against one of the globe's support poles. The machine clanged sonorously as the blow reverberated through the rings. Bryant's torch was shocked from his hand and he fell back against the defunct central housing. Another blow hit the poles and they buckled, the entire structure creaking and starting to twist. Bryant tried to raise himself up in the water, but found the brass arms of the inner 'planet' descending on him. In another moment the astrolabe had turned from its stand to seal him inside.

'You're not going to get away,' called Bryant, gasping for breath as one of the brass bars was brought to rest on his chest. 'It's over. Your rivals are still alive. The machine was faulty. It killed the family instead. It failed you.'

Tomlins walked away from the shattered globe to the far side of the room so that Bryant had to twist his head to see. He was saying nothing. Instead, he began to swing the hammer at a patch of the wall behind him. Bryant realised the deadliness of his predicament.

He had known that if Rand possessed no knowledge of the astrolabe's assassins, there had to be an overseer. Someone was needed to organise the details, to take care of the money, to help with the cover-ups. At first Bryant had considered Charles Whitstable most likely to be the remaining link in the chain of command, but he'd been handling business in India.

It had to be someone in daily contact with the guild. Tomlins had watched Alison Hatfield getting closer to the truth. Finally he'd been forced to remove her. There was more Bryant had to know.

'If you were aware of the astrolabe's existence, you must have realised that it was inaccurate,' he shouted, trying to slide his body from the grip of the brass arm as a white-eyed rat swam past, inches from his face. Tomlins lowered the sledgehammer for a moment and wiped the sweat from his forehead.

'Who's to say it was inaccurate?' he said. 'It was designed to protect the Watchmakers' investments. The Whitstable family does little more than leech from the guild. Let them die, and return the money to the system's true administrators.' He swung the hammer at the wall again, and this time the brickwork cracked, releasing a fine spray of filthy water.

'If anyone deserves to benefit, it's the craftsmen,' cried Bryant. 'Without them there would be no guild in the first place.'

'Three generations of my family have worked for the Watchmakers,' said Tomlins, grunting as the sledgehammer split another brick. 'All of them were paid a pittance for guarding someone else's fortune, and all were sworn to secrecy. Where did it get us?'

Now that the astrolabe had failed, Tomlins had finally discovered an advantage over his employers.

'So the money was coming in to you,' said Bryant weakly. He tried to free himself from the pressing weight of the metal exoskeleton, but was unable to budge any further. He could see May's legs from the corner of his eye. His partner had not moved since he was hurt. He prayed the old boy hadn't drowned while unconscious.

'It was until you interfered.'

His next blow smashed a hole clean through the wall. The rumble of the river beyond it grew louder as a black fountain rained across the chamber. Another blow weakened the wall further. Bryant knew that with the rainfall they'd had Tomlins would easily be able to flood the room, and it would be unlikely that anyone would ever find their bodies. He would be able to claim his share of the tontine after all.

Icy drainage water poured into the shallow depression within the area of the globe, raising the level around the trapped detective. The temperature was falling sharply as the vault became filled with the stench of the sewer. Tomlins was swinging at the wall like a man possessed, but it was refusing to give any further.

The bitter water disgorged itself around Bryant's trapped body as he strained against the imprisoning brass-work. May was lying face down against the wall. He had fallen with his head propped up against the fallen bricks, so that the rising river was still clear of his nose and mouth. In the next few minutes he would be drowned. Only Christina Crosse knew where they were, and she had no cause to be alarmed. On the contrary, she would be expecting both of them to take a few hours' rest before reporting in to Marsden.

Somewhere behind the sound of rushing water he could hear Tomlins hammering at the wall. To perish in such an ignominious fashion as this was terrible. To die below the streets of the city he loved, within its very heart. He wished he was at home, surrounded by his Gilbert and Sullivan records, his books and his memories. It seemed such a grotesque, undignified way for life to leave him.

He twisted his head to watch as the guild secretary swung insanely at the wall. Each blow carried in it the frustration of a blunted life. The wall was cracked in several places, and had begun to bow outwards.

Tomlins, blinded by his bitter zeal, driven by a lifetime wasted in subservience, once more charged the bricks with his sledgehammer. Suddenly the concrete membrane bulged further and split wide in an explosion of water and brick. Tomlins was lifted from his feet and hurled backwards as the deluge burst over him, slamming him against the fallen astrolabe.

As the unleashed river rocked his metal prison, Bryant seized the moment, shoving against the brass bar across his chest. He could summon little strength. The freezing water was rapidly dulling his senses. He hammered against the bars again, and was surprised to find the cage rising of its own accord.

'You're pleased to see me this time, are you?' asked Jerry, holding out her hand. Amazed, unable to catch enough breath to reply, Bryant reached out and allowed himself to be hauled to his feet. 'John,' he gasped, pointing to the figure floating face down in the rising water.

Jerry steadied him and set off to help his partner.

Bryant pushed himself free of the mechanical rings and began wading across the room to help her. Through the hole in the wall he watched as the black torrent rushed past, part of it swirling and diverting into the chamber. The stench rising from its foul waters was unbearable. The river of darkness thundered on beyond the shattered wall, denied access to the world above.

He had waded halfway across the room when a pair of wet arms seized him around the neck and pulled him back beneath the surface of the vile torrent.

Tomlins's hands sought purchase on his throat, but as Bryant tried to twist free, one of them pushed down on the top of his head. He forced his eyes to remain shut in the pulsing effluent, knowing that the poison content of the river would kill him if absorbed for too long. Now both hands were locked firmly over his skull, holding him under.

A dull booming sounded in his ears as the deluge hammered through the steel cage, twisting it back and forth. Red flares of light exploded against his eyelids. His distended lungs were filled with fire.

And then the hands went limp, and his head bobbed up above the surface of the river, suddenly released. Tomlins had rolled back in the water with his pupils turned up in their sockets. His upper arm had become trapped in the shifting blades of the astrolabe, pulling him beneath the waterline.

Bryant fought himself free of flesh and steel as the structure groaned and shifted once more. As soon as he was unsnagged, he allowed the current to carry him across the room. Jerry was wading over in his direction. He could not tell if his partner was alive or dead.

He looked back in time to see Tomlin's arm sever from its mooring as the secretary's body swirled toward the opening in the wall, where it was sucked back into the fast-flowing river, to be swept off into the pounding Stygian darkness.

The three of them sat beside one another in the back of the patrol car, soaked and shocked, wrapped in blankets, as one of the officers drove them to the nearest hospital clinic, where they would doubtless have to undergo a series of powerful innoculations.

'Do you mind if I open a window, sir?' asked the driver. 'I can't breathe.'

'Are you insinuating that we smell?' asked Bryant weakly.

'Well, you did get dipped in sh, er, the sewer, sir.'

'Oh, all right.'

May turned to Jerry. She looked as if she was having a wonderful time. 'How did you follow us back to the guild?' he asked.

'I got a lift with Sergeant Crosse. I was there when you

radioed in your destination. The main door to the building was open, and there was an incredible noise coming from the back of the hall. I just followed it down.'

'Yes, but what possessed you to come here?'

'I wanted to return Mr Bryant's bleeper,' she said, pulling the slim plastic box from her sodden coat. 'I found it lying in the garden. It must have fallen off when he was attacked.'

'Why on earth didn't you wait and give it to him another day?' asked May, amazed. 'He never uses the bloody thing.'

'I had to return it immediately,' said Jerry. 'His apartment keys are taped to the back.'

May's mouth fell open.

'That's the point,' said Bryant, taking the bleeper and turning it over to reveal a pair of labelled Yale keys sellotaped in place. 'I thought I wouldn't lose it if I needed it to get into my flat.'

'Do you mean to say that I owe my life to — to—'

'That's right,' said Jerry, pleased with herself. 'If it wasn't for your partner's annoying little habits, you'd have drowned.'

The patrol car sped on across the bridge, towards a lightening sky.

# IV
# THE GLIMPSING OF THE DAY

O'er the season vernal,
Time may cast a shade;
Sunshine, if eternal,
Makes the roses fade.
Time may do his duty;
Let the thief alone —
Winter hath a beauty,
That is all his own.

*W.S. Gilbert*

# CHAPTER

For once, Charles Whitstable was at a loss for words. He was still wearing the same clothes, and had not slept.

'We just want to know how you did it,' said May, hunching forward on his chair. The workmen were back in the office at Mornington Crescent, and there were tools all over the floor. There was also, inexplicably, a large hole in the ceiling.

'I'm not sure what you'll even be charged with,' said Bryant, 'but it'll certainly be as an accomplice to murder. Try to explain what happened. Then we'll decide what you need to put in your official statement.'

Charles lifted his head from his hands and attempted to smooth his hair back in place. 'All right, I'll do my best,' he said, resigning himself to the first in a series of trials. 'When I went to Calcutta, I found the guild's group of companies still operating under archaic conditions. The buildings looked just as they had in the early part of the century. There had been no technological advances, no updating of the infrastructure. The offices were staffed by the grandsons of the original owners. Bureaucracy was rampant, even by Calcutta's standards. Nothing had changed from James Whitstable's time, nothing.

'Back in London, Peter and Bella Whitstable were moaning about profits dropping. They were all complaining, even the damned lawyers, and no one had the balls to come and sort out the mess. Everything was left to me. I soon noticed that certain "obligations" transmitted from London were being honoured by staff members. Every once in a while, someone would disappear for a few days on "company business", financed by money-orders transferred through the lawyers' office in England. That staff member would then reappear and continue working without a word of what had transpired. Apparently, this had been going on for years.

'I noticed a pattern in the type of people chosen for this clandestine work. They were always the sons and grandsons of men who had been granted a great favour by the guild at some point in the past.'

'What sort of favour?'

'The usual sort of thing, a cash advance for a newlywed, an executive post for a son, a favour that demanded repayment at some unspecified point in the future,' explained Charles. 'Employees of even the most distant branches of the Watchmakers could, in extreme circumstances, be granted special deals in the form of large high-interest loans. In return, a brown-paper package was delivered to the home of the borrower, to be kept within the family and opened at a time specified by the company.

'When the call came, in the form of a telegram or a computer printout, instructions were to be carried through to the last letter. The favour was cancelled once the rival was out of action. There could be no defaulting

on repayment. At least, that was how the system had
worked in the past. I arrived to find dissent. People had
begun to refuse to honour these "obligations". They
couldn't see why they should perform favours for the
English any more. Victoria's reign might have gone, but it
was a damned long time dying.'

'You discovered that your staff were actually raising the
dead?'

'They weren't raising them, so much as maintaining the
semblance of life in the dead. And they weren't personally
doing so. They just followed the instructions left by James
Whitstable. Upon taking leave, they were supposed to
employ the services of the revivifiers.'

'Revivifiers.'

'Keepers of the arcane secrets, occult scientists. It's a
misnomer, really, because they just—'

'Maintain the semblance of life, you said. We'll get to
that later. Go on.'

'They'd been trained by their fathers, their grandfathers.
A family business, just like James's own. And when their
services were required in England, the revivifiers headed
here. What could I do? I couldn't completely abolish the
system. But the Calcutta police were becoming suspicious.
I had to take control. I had the family's best interests at
heart. The machine provided the names of those marked
for death. I heard about men who took the bodies from
London burial parlours. I learned how this miracle of
forced life could be made to come about. The irony is, I
had no idea that the system had begun to backfire, or that
I was allowing a system to continue which would kill my
own family. James Makepeace Whitstable used everyone,
his craftsmen, his lawyers, the heirs of his most loyal
members of staff. That was the simple beauty of his scheme.
All the dirty work was done overseas, thereby keeping

his own hands clean. He never dreamed that one day it would all come home.'

'What an apt Victorian process,' said Bryant. 'Butcher your rivals, dupe the wogs and improve your own fortune. If anyone gets caught it's only an invisible foreigner, a third-class citizen, and who'll believe them against the word of an Englishman?'

'Tell me something,' asked Bryant. 'When these "obligated" individuals went off to see the revivifiers about fulfilling their duties, why did the latter group suddenly turn to murder?'

'You figured out that part,' said Charles, surprised. 'They couldn't get hold of appropriate bodies so easily in London. Not just any dying man will do. Without my knowledge or consent, they picked suitable living candidates and began to murder them.'

'Like Denjhi,' said Bryant. 'But he was too fresh, wasn't he? He remembered too much from his life. His conscience delayed him from killing Daisy Whitstable. So, as a punishment, he was used again. But, once more, his old-life conscience took over. Instead of lethally poisoning Peggy Whitstable, he diluted the concoction hoping to spare her life without failing to honour his debt.'

'I guess that's what happened. I never thought that the branches of our empire outposts could murder my own family. I had sanctioned the damned system. There was no way of stopping it.'

'And now you have their deaths on your conscience.' Bryant rose and refastened his shapeless brown cardigan. 'We need to know where we can find these Revivifiers of yours.' He handed Charles a pencil and notepad. 'Now, if you don't mind.'

# CHAPTER

Gwendoline Gates inhaled hard and blew aside the smoke from her cigarette. She stared at the glowing end and smiled ruefully.

'Somehow I knew this would happen,' she said finally. 'You and Charles weren't cut from the same cloth.'

The lounge was flooded in cold sunshine as panels of light reflected on to the walls from the wet pavements outside. Her mother wore no makeup and was wrapped in a heavy white towelling robe. Jerry had rarely seen her like this, in what Gwen would regard as an unfinished state.

The hour was still early. Jack had gone to thrash a ball about at the Highgate Golf Club. Gwen had heard her moving about and had come down, almost as if she had sensed something was different about today. She looked up at her daughter now, and for a moment Jerry felt a miniscule flicker of sympathy. It had been a shock to discover that Gwen's desire to improve her social standing had outweighed her love for her only daughter, but it was as if something Jerry had always suspected had now proven to be true.

The knowledge produced little satisfaction, only the bitter taste of betrayal. It was as though her love had been weighed as a commodity, quantified and traded off for something more rewarding. And yet, there was still the faintest trace of a bond between them.

'I thought that perhaps you and he would get on together.'

'You wanted me to work for him and be accepted by the Whitstable family,' she replied, folding the flap of the nylon bag over and clipping it shut. 'Even if I'd taken up his offer, he'd never have given you the things you wanted. If and when he gets out of jail, that's assuming he even goes, he'll carry on with business quite happily without me or you. All of them will. The Whitstables will carry on long after all the press and television coverage, after all the scandals and investigations. They don't need anyone else. Poor Gwen, let down by yet another man. First Jack, then Wayland, and now Charles Whitstable.'

'You're a very cruel girl.'

'I'm not a girl any more, Mother. You must have been able to see that nothing would ever change for us. What were you hoping for, for God's sake? Did you think you would get Jack's respect back? That's long gone. What do you want any more privileges for anyway? It's not as if they would have made us different people.' She checked the spines of some paperbacks and added them to the bag. There were some books she had to take with her wherever she went.

'I wanted you to marry well.' Gwen's voice was soft and tired.

'Well, I wouldn't have married a bloody Whitstable. They'll pursue their ambitions in blissful ignorance of the real world, just as they've always done. They'll say anything to anyone so long as they think it will advance them in some way. If I really wanted what they have, I'd have to be as dishonest as them.'

'I never meant to be dishonest with you, Jerry.' She seemed to find the taste of the cigarette disagreeable, and ground it out. 'I simply wasn't honest with myself. You have no idea what it was like being so close to them, and so far away. To tiptoe around the edges of their lives, always within sight of something better. I wanted to have what they had, for you as well as me. It didn't seem fair.'

'Well, it's not what I want.' She picked up the bag and walked to the door. 'That's why I have to go. You can see that, can't you? I want to make my own changes. You're right, the Whitstables aren't fair. They keep what's theirs by building barriers. The whole country's founded on them. It's a nation of boxes and walls. Mostly walls.'

'You're being naive if you think you can change anything. Nothing changed for me.' Concern shadowed her face. For whom, Jerry couldn't tell. 'You have no idea of the things that went on.'

'Perhaps not,' said Jerry. 'You never talked about—'

'What could I have said? How could I have described the contemptuous looks on those damned faces?' She checked herself, trying to sound disinterested. 'Half the family hasn't talked to me for years. Oh, they'll give cold smiles when you're around, and cut me dead behind your back. All the clever little cruelties, the endless subtle indignities. Because of you, and the way you behaved. The trouble you caused.'

'I'm sorry, Gwen, I didn't know—'

'Well,' she said bitterly, 'there's a lot you don't know. People are monstrous. When you're protected by money, there are a thousand ways to hurt someone.' She clearly had no intention of allowing her daughter to feel sorry for her, and changed the subject. 'What are your plans? Where are you going to go now?'

'I'm not sure. Try to find some places where there aren't so many restrictions.'

'That'll be a lot harder than you think. God, you've some learning to do.'

'Then I'll learn.'

Her career at the Savoy had ended. She had been forced to give it up after realising that it was Nicholas who had collected the photographs for Peter Whitstable. May had uncovered that particular detail during his interviews. The management had caught her slapping Nicholas around the face. The satisfaction of her stinging palm still stayed.

Her mother was pacing in front of the lounge door, as if frightened to see it opened. 'You barely know this boy Jacob.'

'His name's Joseph. He wants to travel for a while, and so do I.'

'You're not planning on getting married, are you?' she asked cautiously.

'Of course not. We're just friends.'

'Well, I don't suppose there's anything I can say that will make you change your mind.' She searched for a fresh cigarette, something to do with her hands.

Jerry was proud of herself for calling him. It had felt like the right thing to do. Joseph had talked about touring Europe, and she had jumped at the chance. His Christmas, unlike hers, had been a quiet one.

She could see that her mother was no longer anxious to prevent her from leaving, and the thought made her happy. 'Say goodbye to Dad for me. Don't let him worry.'

'I think he'll be rather pleased for you. Especially if he sees it as a defeat for me.'

'Oh, Mother. What are you going to do?'

She glanced up at the clock. 'I'm supposed to be chairing one of my charities in an hour. I have a feeling its bulimia.'

'Then you'd better get ready,' she said, smiling.

Gwen lit her cigarette and looked out of the sun-smeared window. 'I don't know. I may go for a walk instead.'

'The park should be nice.'

'I was thinking more of Harrods.'

She turned back to Jerry, her eyes narrowing imperceptibly. 'Tell me,' she asked, 'what's the point of having children if they only leave?'

'Because of the love,' she replied.

'Yes.' Gwen agreed, taking a step toward her, then thinking better of it. 'It may surprise you, but there is love.'

'I'll let you know where I am,' she promised. As she looked back at her mother from the door, standing squarely in the centre of the hallway, her hands by her sides, her feet bare, she saw how fragile her life had been, and how much emptier it would be now.

'I'm going to come back,' she said.

'I'd like that very much, Jerry. I wish—'

'What?'

'I wish I could go away somewhere. Start learning again.' She gave a rueful half-smile.

'You can learn right here,' she said. 'You don't need to go anywhere.'

'That's simple for you to say. Everything's easy to the young.'

'At least you could try, Mother.'

'Mother.' Gwen turned the word over, as if hearing it for the first time and trying it for size. Finally, she raised the palm of her right hand in farewell, coolly watching as Jerry walked to the end of the road, her casual pose affecting disinterest. But even as Jerry turned the corner, she knew that Gwen would be standing at the door long after she had passed from sight.

# CHAPTER

Tower Bridge is the gateway to London; the first bridge a ship encounters upon its passage into the Thames. Its gothic turrets are merely stone clad over steel, and have guarded the river for barely a hundred years, yet it is as definitive a representation of the city as the Tower of London itself. Below the bridge, dace, roach, smelt and perch have been known to swim with flounders and elvers through the thick brackish water of the Thames. The river-bank here was once a thick slope of orange sand known as Tower Beach. From the 1930s to the 1950s, families swam and played on it as if daytripping to the Brighton seashore.

On a Friday evening at the end of January, as a sulphurous sunset jaundiced the roof of the Southern turret, two gentlemen surveyed the river scene. Above them, the tower's massive pressurised-water pistons rose on either side. The bridge had recently been repainted a rich blue, the colour of a summer sky. It was deserted as they crossed it on the west side, their hands thrust deep into their pockets.

John May paused to lean on the wooden handrail and peer over the edge. Arthur Bryant had summoned up another vile scarf from his infinite collection of knitwear and was even now peering over its folds like a perished frog. The top of May's head was still swathed in bandages, lending him an oriental air.

'I don't know what the bare-breasted woman on roller skates was supposed to be doing,' he said, puzzled. 'And why on earth was she wearing a centurion's helmet?'

'That was Britannia,' Bryant explained. 'I told you, it was a modern interpretation. Still, it was nice to see the Savoyards again.'

'Yes,' agreed May, 'they weren't bad for a group of people who are obviously deranged. I'm afraid it's not my cup of tea, all that theatrical stuff. It's just not real enough. Good tunes, though, I must say.'

The Savoy Theatre had finally reopened its doors to a brand-new production of *Patience*, staged at the end of January, a month after the anniversary of the founding of the Alliance. Bryant had dragged along his reluctant partner on this, the first night that they had been provided with a corresponding respite from their duties.

'Actually, I think I might have dozed off in the second half,' May admitted.

'I know. I heard you. So did everybody else. You should have your sinuses seen to. Look, John.' He stopped in the centre of the bridge and looked back at St Paul's. 'It's nice to see that the cathedral still stands high above the other buildings.'

'That's just because they haven't given planning permission to build offices around it,' said May unsportingly.

'I love this skyline. It's not as spectacular as those of other cities, but when I think of the men and women who firewatched for the domes and spires through the war, the mere fact that it still survives at all amazes me.'

'Sentimentality, Arthur. Look at the crumbling tower

blocks and the empty docklands buildings.'

'I know they're there, and I can't do anything to change them. Anyway, at my age sentimental goodbyes are allowed, and I don't know when I'll be saying farewell to all this, do I?'

'If you're going to be maudlin, I might as well give you a good reason,' said May.

'What do you mean?'

'Check your diary. Next week we'll have been working together for twenty years.'

'Good Lord, you're right,' exclaimed Bryant. 'The Shepherd's Market diamond robbery, our first case. Remember Sidney Dobson, the deaf explosives expert? The mastermind behind Mayfair's finest safecracking ring. His old dad ran the Smithfield black market sausage syndicate during the war. To think that Sidney would have got away with the diamonds if he'd taken London Bridge instead of this one.'

'That's right. I almost felt sorry for him, stuck in a lorry full of pigs on the north side while they opened the bridge for a tanker.'

'He was very decent about it. The last of the gentlemen crooks. Had a nasty three-legged cat called Wilfred. I visited him in Strangeways, you know.'

'That was nice of you.'

'Not really,' conceded Bryant. 'His sister-in-law sold me a Ford Zephyr with no brakes. I was trying to find out if he'd heard from her. Sidney told me she'd emigrated to New Zealand, but on the way back from the prison I passed her at a bus-stop.'

'What happened?'

'Nothing. I couldn't slow the car down. I suppose men like Sidney are into computer fraud now. That seems a rather sleazy, backdoor style of crime. The old ways felt more honest.'

'That's enough, Arthur,' said May, raising his hand. 'Looking back is morbid and unhealthy. I think I prefer you cantankerous.' He pressed his palms on the chill steelwork of the bridge. 'Anyway, there are all kinds of interesting computer crimes now.'

'Did I tell you? I got a postcard from Jerry Gates. She's on her way to India with some chap. She'd do well to stay away from the Calcutta Revivifiers. They must all be back there by now. There certainly weren't any still living at the addresses Charles Whitstable gave us. I'd love to catch one of them and find out how they do it, you know, see if it's some kind of incredible trick.'

'So would a lot of people. I heard the BMA is planning to publish a paper on the subject,' said May. 'Raymond Land says they're going to refute the possibility of such things with tested scientific evidence.'

'I saw it with my own eyes, and so did you. How can they refute that?'

'There's no physical proof, Arthur. That's all they're interested in. The bodies yielded nothing but necrotic tissue. Try convincing them that dead corpuscles can be revitalised through spiritual rituals. Even Marsden doesn't believe it anymore, and he was there.'

The 'walking dead' theories had allowed the tabloids to speculate in all kinds of colourful, alarming ways. Yet, despite this and other damning publicity resulting from the investigation, the fickle press had decided to champion the new division at Mornington Crescent. After all, it had provided them with gruesome entertainment through the dull winter days. Although the official hearing had yet to take place on the unit's future, there was now at least hope.

They had finished the last of the interviews with Charles Whitstable, whose future still languished in the hands of the British magistrates court. May had to admit that James

Makepeace Whitstable's system had been ingenious. It was impossible to estimate how many families on the continent and sub-continent had been bullied into accepting his sabotage orders. He had no doubt that many families would still be keeping their secret packages for years to come — just in case the cycle renewed itself and the system returned one day.

The most capricious casualty of the investigation had passed from her life barely mourned. May had been one of the few people to attend the funeral of Alison Hatfield. He had forced himself to stop thinking of an alternative future where she was still alive and perhaps by his side. He knew that her memory would be better served by destroying every branch of the organisation that had ultimately caused her death. Sadly, this would never be entirely possible. Too many companies within the system carried the seal of government investment and approval. They would continue to prosper, aided with financial protection provided from more powerful quarters.

His thoughts were broken by the ghastly sound of Bryant chuckling to himself. 'What's so funny?' he asked, leaning back against the painted balustrade.

'I was just thinking about the Whitstables,' said Bryant, his breath clouding the air. 'How W.S. Gilbert would have loved to write about them.'

'Oh? Why?'

'He adored paradoxes. He lampooned every institution in the land by putting lawyers and ministers in topsy-turvy situations. Without realising it, the Whitstables managed to create a paradox worthy of Gilbert himself. The astrolabe, you see.'

'Talk to me while we walk. My ears are getting brittle.'

'The astrolabe destroyed the children of the aristocrats who set it in motion. And its instruments of death were the poor, the very people the system was designed to keep out.' He sighed and continued walking. 'Of course, the paradox still exists. We're in a land of upper and lower orders. People are kept in place at the cost of their lives. For every man willing to help those less fortunate than himself, there are ten others ready to exploit him.' Bryant waved his moth-eaten gloves about. 'Thanks to families like the Whitstables, the circle may one day close again from light to darkness.'

They were standing at the far southern end of the bridge looking back along the river. Above the gleaming curved steel of Charing Cross station the clouds shone with a soft citrine light.

'I don't think London will ever be completely dark again,' said May. 'Look.'

'It's a shame, really,' replied Bryant. 'What must it have been like in the world that existed before 28 December 1881? There was such a thing then as absolute darkness. And there was something else perhaps, a collective warmth, a hidden strength. People were bound together by superstition and folklore. Families were made strong by myth-making and tale-telling. I think something was lost the day they turned the lights on. Something indefinable and very important.'

May slapped his old friend on the back and set him off in the direction of the restaurant once more. 'Did I tell you?' he said, 'You remember the landlord of the Nun and Broken Compass was trying to tell me how the pub got its name, but kept getting interrupted?'

Bryant's melancholy thoughts were pulled up short.

'He finally told you?' he asked, scratching his nose, curious to know. 'Go on then, what's the story?'

'It's incredibly disgusting,' replied May with a broad grin. 'You're never going to believe it.'